ACCLAIM FOR
ALICE BLANCHARD'S
THE BREATHTAKER

"Nothing could have prepared us for the howling horrors of this gale-force thriller . . . Blanchard's artistry whips up excitement . . . She writes so well that she rattles the rafters."

—*New York Times Book Review*

"Splendid . . . riveting and addictive . . . a heart-pounding, highly literary novel full of stunning art and science."

—*Chicago Tribune*

"Brilliant . . . a dark and stormy novel and a particularly thrilling one."

—*New York Daily News*

"A breathtaking vortex of a story . . . gripping . . . well-paced and beautifully written."

—*Library Journal* (starred review)

"What makes *The Breathtaker* so exceptional is that it works on so many levels . . . A real twister of a tale."

—*Denver Rocky Mountain News*

"Blanchard delivers a knockout blow . . . A complete treat for readers."

—*San Jose Mercury News*

more...

Life Sentences

Also by Alice Blanchard

The Breathtaker
Darkness Peering
The Stuntman's Daughter: Stories

Life Sentences

ALICE BLANCHARD

WARNER BOOKS

NEW YORK   BOSTON

Copyright © 2005 by Alice Blanchard
All rights reserved. No part of this book may be reproduced in any form or by any electronic or mechanical means, including information storage and retrieval systems, without permission in writing from the publisher, except by a reviewer who may quote brief passages in a review.

Cover design and cover art by Tom Tafuri

Warner Books

Time Warner Book Group
1271 Avenue of the Americas
New York, NY 10020
Visit our Web site at www.twbookmark.com

Printed in the United States of America

Originally published in hardcover by Warner Books
First Paperback Printing: April 2006

10 9 8 7 6 5 4 3 2 1

Once again,
for Doug

Remember me when I am gone away,
Gone far away into the silent land.

Christina Rossetti

THE GHOST IN THE HALLWAY

1.

Daisy Hubbard headed down the hallway past the equipment room with its centrifuges and spectrophotometers and listened to the light, fast click of her own heels. The echoing stillness inside Berhoffer Medical School late at night was unlike any other stillness in the world. Over a century old, the Wessels building was an enormous creaking labyrinth of twisting corridors and submarine sounds—hissing radiators, gurgling water pipes, the constant hum of machinery. This was Professor Marlon Truett's lab, the top neurogenetics department in the country, and Daisy was one of its rising stars. She had worked her entire life to get here. Blind ambition had fueled her. She wasn't afraid to admit it, her career came before everything else—a husband and children, family obligations, her crazy sister.

Daisy could hear dissonant sounds coming from somewhere inside the lab and paused for a moment to listen. The cleaning crew had come and gone. According to the sign-in sheet, she was supposed to be alone in the lab tonight. She glanced at her watch. Half past midnight. Her best friend, Fiona Wu, was convinced that the lab was haunted, but Daisy didn't believe in ghosts. She wasn't a superstitious person. Now she moved a little further down the hallway, where she could hear it distinctly— a tinkling, musical sound. "Sugar, Sugar" by the Archies. What a relief. Somebody had left the radio on in the X-ray room, that was all. No ghosts.

Her hands trembled slightly as she dug around in her pockets for her keys. She unlocked the door to the Mouse Facility, switched on the lights and was hit by a familiar mixture of animal and chemical odors. The Mouse Facility was composed of two rooms—a larger "outer" room containing a chemotherapeutic workstation, an operating table and a refrigerator for specimens, and a smaller "inner" room which housed the mice. Professor Truett's lab of forty graduate students, postdocs and technical assistants worked as a team, their mission to isolate the specific genes that caused certain rare inherited brain disorders, some of the rarest in the world. Truett's shining achievement stood right in front of her now, the old DNA model on its rickety metal stand, a four-foot plastic double helix resembling a spiral staircase. He'd won a Nobel Prize for his work, and just looking at the model strengthened Daisy's resolve to work harder, to push beyond the boundaries and unlock the secrets of these fatal diseases.

High above the model on a dusty shelf were a dozen empty champagne bottles, the celebratory symbols of past accomplishments. Truett had a special bottle waiting just for her, a rare vintage: *Cuvée Williams Duetz 1990*. He believed in Daisy. He had the utmost faith in her, and she didn't want to disappoint him. She wanted to be the first person in the world to cure a neurodegenerative disorder using gene replacement therapy.

Pocketing her keys, she went over to the aluminum sink and started to wash up, then thought she heard a scratching sound. She turned the water off and stood listening for a moment. All she could hear was the radio in the distance. Shrugging it off, she grabbed a paper towel and wiped her hands. Taped to the wall above the sink was a list of screw-ups that had occurred in the lab so far this year, and Daisy was relieved to see that her name wasn't on it. Fiona had dropped the agarose gel; Archie had forgotten to switch on the hot lid for the PCR cycler; Carlson had tried to filter water through the "hydrophobic" filters, talk about humiliating. To the sides of the screwup sheet were colorful signs that served as unnecessary reminders: HUMANE IS THE WAY WE TREAT OUR VALUABLE GUESTS! and MICE SAVE LIVES! Of course Daisy treated her mice humanely. She loved her mice and gave them the kind of overweening attention that had made her the butt of Carlson's jokes. *Daisy and her pwecious wittle babies . . . She wuvs her meeses to pieces . . .*

There was a loud noise down the hall now—a thump or a bump—and she spun around and peered into the darkness beyond the door's single pane of smoky glass. Scientists weren't supposed to be afraid of the unknown, were they? She stood poised on the brink of panic, goose bumps breaking out on her arms.

"Daisy, Daisy . . . give me your answer do . . ."

Her body began to relax. "Truett?"

"I'm half crazy . . ."

She ventured out into the hallway, where she could hear Professor Marlon Truett's mellifluous voice echoing throughout the corridor. She stepped into the X-ray room and turned off the radio, then checked the tissue culture room. "Truett?" She followed the sound of his voice all the way back to her workbench with its moody printer and terminally ill fax machine, black electrical cords slithering across the floor into multiple sockets. Three benches occupied this side of the lab, along with a shared sink. Daisy's workstation was wedged in between a large uninsulated window overlooking the parking lot and a broken autoclave. Truett stood in his rumpled gray suit and colorless tie in front of the autoclave, trying to lift it off its rusty platform. He was obviously drunk, just back from a scientific conference in New Mexico, and her heart fluttered delicately at the sight of him.

"What do you think you're doing?" she asked in a gently chiding tone.

"Oh, there you are." He dropped the autoclave back on its base and spun around with the grace of an aging Baryshnikov. "Why do we keep all this broken equipment around, Daisy? Seriously, what's the point?"

She listened with a vexed expression. Truett and his moods. There was a low hum in the air that never went away, and the night pressed black and starless against the windowpanes. From her second-story window, she could see down into the Boston cityscape below, where the streetlamps cast icy streaks of light across the patchwork asphalt. Earlier in the day, she'd discovered the stitchlike footprints of a mouse in a frail arc of snow on her windowsill. Field mice were distant kin to the genetically pure mice they bred inside the lab. "So how was the conference?" she asked him.

"Oh, terrific. Have you ever spent seventy-two hours with a bunch of mental midgets?" He waved his hand in disgust. "They keep asking the same old boring questions, Daisy. Everybody wants to talk about cloning, for God's sake. Nobody wants to discuss what's never been discussed before." In his mid-fifties, Marlon Truett had the silver hair and trademark glower of an academic legend. Whenever he walked into a room, there was no doubt in his mind who God was. He'd never been handsome in the classical sense, but now he was very distinguished-looking. He possessed both a monster ego and the kind of power that could be incredibly seductive. Truett could raise his students up to great intellectual heights, or else crush their hopes with a few carefully chosen words. He could ruin careers, but if you stood right next to him, some of the limelight might rub off on you.

"It was so damn hot down there," he complained, great furrows opening on his tall forehead. He moved a little too close, his powerful ego looming before her like a boulder about to tip over. "The air-conditioning wasn't working, we were all swimming in our own sweat, and Munson's giving one of his laborious speeches on science and God . . . when all of a sudden, there's this raging debate going on about genetics and morality. And I'm the bad guy, because I want to cure the world's most incurable diseases. I'm being vilified in my own time, Daisy."

"I doubt that very much," she said.

He snatched her hand and focused sharply on her

face. "God, you're drunk, Daisy." He giggled. "Shame on you."

Very gently, she reclaimed her hand. "Somebody needs a cup of coffee."

"Shh, keep your voice down! Mice are sleeping."

"C'mon," she said with her best schoolmistress air. "I'll make us a fresh pot and you can tell me all about it."

"Forget the damn coffee. Give me a kiss."

She held his gaze for a moment, then pretended this exchange hadn't happened. "Follow me, Professor."

"I'd follow you to the ends of the earth."

"There are no ends of the earth." She did her best to keep two paces ahead of him. Truett was married to another professor at the university, but it was an open secret that he cheated on his wife. Last year one of the department secretaries passed around a confidential letter from a woman whom the esteemed professor had met during one of his many scientific conferences. The woman had written, "I know I promised never to contact you, but I just had to let you know that last night will be with me forever. Your ideas are endlessly fascinating, and if we ever meet again . . ."

It was a startling revelation, but then again, nothing Truett did shocked people anymore. He had the attitude of an adolescent boy, the body of an aging college athlete, an intimidating intellect and a southern drawl so deceptively down-home his competitors had a tendency to underestimate him. The odd thing was, Daisy couldn't hate him for his infidelity. She understood that this was no ordinary mortal. Truett was bigger than life and could get away with these things. She wondered if his wife felt the same way.

Now he followed her obediently into the lunchroom, where she switched on the fluorescent lights. Recoiling in mock horror, he said, "Oh God, let's get out of here before I lose the will to live." The harsh light illuminated every dingy corner, every aging appliance.

"Take a seat," she said.

He swayed in the doorway. "Some drunk I am."

"Should I call your wife?"

He winced. "No, don't do that."

"I'll make us a fresh pot."

"Don't do that, either."

She walked over to the calcified coffee machine and dug around in the cupboards for the filters while he took a cautious step inside.

"Daisy?"

She looked up.

"I'm afraid I've got bad news." He sounded serious. "We have to abandon the Dahlberg trials."

"What?" She dropped the filters on the floor.

"Turns out a private company already owns the patent."

Stupefied, she bent to pick up the filters.

"What's happened to the scientific community?" he said with a dramatic groan. "We used to be so generous with our research. We used to share our findings, Daisy, but not anymore. I remember the days when science was a calling, an actual calling. Now you can't ask for start-up funds without consulting the patent lawyers first."

"We still have Stier-Zellar's and Rostislav, don't we?"

He nodded. "Thank God."

She pulled out a chair for him. "Sit, Truett."

He sat down and cradled his chin in his hands, then

watched her with solemn curiosity. "Do you know what I like the most about you, Daisy?" He paused before answering his own question. "You have no life."

She felt an angry flush crawl up her neck. "That's a rotten thing to say."

"Relax. It's what I *like* about you."

She poured them both a cup of coffee, then sat down next to him. The first time they ever met, five years ago, his angry eyes and wild gray hair had terrified her. Now he moved her in a deep, inexplicable way. He'd received a genius grant at the age of twenty-seven and, as the father of rare orphan brain disorders, was the medical school's most prominent prima donna. Daisy treated his words with the utmost respect. Still, she didn't like being alone in the lab with him late at night. He was complicated and demanding, and she wasn't sure where their working relationship ended and their personal relationship began.

"You haven't asked me about my trip yet," he said petulantly.

"I thought I did."

"Ah, but you didn't."

"So, Truett." She played along. "How was your trip?"

"Dismal. Met a colleague on the plane. Claude Bagget." He wrinkled his nose. "The thief."

"What did Claude do now?"

"Published that article on viral vector systems. Beat me to it, the bastard." He rolled his eyes. "He's got spies everywhere, you know."

Daisy laughed. "I doubt that very much, Truett."

"Oh, you do, do you?" He wagged a finger at her. "*Oh, to suffer the slings and arrows of outraged colleagues* . . . I'm just a poor South Carolina farm boy, you know. A simple man at heart."

"Simple," she repeated with a skeptical nod. "Right."

"You don't believe me?"

"I've never met anyone more complicated."

He scowled down at his cooling cup of coffee, then reached into his jacket pocket and produced a silver flask. He took several swallows before offering her a taste. "Want some?"

"What is it?"

"Arsenic. Bottoms up."

"Since when do you carry around a flask?"

"I was born with a silver flask in my mouth." He shook it in her face. "Come on. Be a man."

She smiled reluctantly, then took the flask and tipped her head back, wincing as she swallowed something bitter and strong.

"For God's sake," he said with a delighted smile. "You look like you're twelve years old."

She enjoyed this mindless flattery. She was pleased that he'd singled her out. They had a unique relationship in the lab, a close student-mentor bond. He hyped her efforts, and she worked five times harder than anybody else.

"Your wife must be worried," she said now.

"Julia? She doesn't worry."

"Never?"

"Nah. She sleeps like a baby." He eyed her curiously. "What about you, Daisy? Do you sleep like a baby?"

"Ha." She tilted her head to drink again, feeling a warmth in her belly. "I'll sleep when I'm dead."

"Would you sleep with me?"

"You're an outrageous flirt, you know."

"Are you shocked?"

"Nothing you do shocks me anymore, Truett."

"Liar. I think you're deeply shocked."

"Right. I'm such a prude. I have no life, remember?"

His look was stern. "Such a waste."

She gave an involuntary shiver. She handed back the flask, and their fingers touched briefly. There was something raw and dangerous about his gaze, and she wanted him to stop. He was making her feel vaguely threatened. She edged his coffee cup closer and said, "Drink up."

With a mischievous grin, he put the flask away and took a sip of black coffee. "Mm. Terrible."

She smiled.

"Go home, foolish girl," he said softly. "Before I devour you alive."

"You've got a pretty high opinion of yourself, don't you?"

"Go home before I say something I'll regret." He fished his car keys out and promptly dropped them on the floor. "Ugh." He leaned over and reached for them but kept drunkenly missing.

"Truett," she said, "you're in no condition to drive."

He looked up.

"I'm taking you home."

With a heavy sigh, he staggered to his feet. "Your wish is my command."

As they drove across town, Truett breathed deeply beside her, looking old. She could feel butterflies in her stomach as she thought about the line he had crossed. Still, she could forgive him. He was drunk. He would probably have no memory of it tomorrow. The tree boughs sagged with snow on this blustery March night, and the moon had disappeared behind the clouds. The parking spaces in Boston were so hard to come by that people dragged old armchairs or cardboard boxes over to the curb in an effort to save their places, and a dusting of snow gave these items a ghostly glow.

"Daisy," he said, sliding her a look, "what are you thinking about?"

"Nothing."

"Nothing? You look so damn sad."

"I'm not sad."

"Your eyes have that faraway look."

"I'm not sad, Truett."

"Daisy . . . you leave your unhappiness behind you like the wake of a canoe."

She didn't like where this was going. The streetlamps cast mutating shadows across the snowdrifts while the car's chains rattled over the slippery road. She swung into the circular driveway of Truett's expensive Colonial, her high beams illuminating the cat-poop-studded snow. Truett and Julia owned several cats, whereas Daisy didn't have any pets. She didn't own a goldfish or even a houseplant. It was true what he'd said about her—she had no life outside the lab.

While the car idled in the driveway, he turned to her and said, "Look at you. Now, there's a whole lot of lovely in one place."

"Truett . . ."

He raised her chin with his finger. "Pleasure and pain are this close right now. Do you understand what I'm saying?"

She shook her head.

He leaned forward and kissed her.

His kisses were sweet and sour. His lips were the lips of an older man, and for the first time in her life, Daisy felt sorry for him. He smelled of the lab, of his boring conference in New Mexico, of his hatred for Claude Bagget and his desperation for government money.

She drew back. "Good night, Truett."

He got out and slammed the door, then stumbled up the porch steps.

She didn't understand what had just happened. Her hands wouldn't stop shaking as she pulled out onto the road, where elusive shadows darted from her headlights' glare.

2.

Detective Jack Makowski stood in the hot sun in front of a nondescript Southern California bar with a shingled roof and desert-tan stucco facade and wondered what had happened to his latest missing person. Two days ago, forty-five-year-old computer programmer Colby Ostrow had left this defeated-looking establishment sometime before it'd closed for the night, never to be seen or heard from again. They'd found his 1998 Buick parked around back with the doors locked and no key in the ignition; Colby's car keys had apparently disappeared right along with him.

As lead investigator in charge of this dog detail, Jack's track record was beginning to worry him. Last year a grandmother of three had vanished from De Campo Beach under similar circumstances, and the case had gone cold on his desk. De Campo Beach was a little hole-in-the-wall beach town, its population hovering around 25,000. Thousands of people went missing in California every year, and even though De Campo Beach had been annexed to Los Angeles, the people who lived there didn't consider themselves part of a metropolis. It was a small oceanfront town, where neighbors took in each other's mail and chatted in the supermarket checkout lines. People didn't go missing here.

Now he caught a glimpse of his reflection in the window and didn't like his hair in this heat. It was collar-length and curly, like rigid surf. He brushed it back with his fingers, then stared deep into his hungover eyes. At thirty-eight, Jack Makowski was an average-size man with blue eyes and graying brown hair who reminded himself more and more every day of his middle-aged mother—he had her slightly sagging jowls, same violet circles under the eyes, her propensity for self-pity. Jesus, he felt like this building. Not yet falling into ruin, but beginning to. Just beginning to.

Back in her day, his mother had been beautiful, and Jack was just vain enough to be thankful that he took after her side of the family and not his trollish dad's. Dick Makowski had been a wealthy man, a TV producer of several successful cop shows who secretly yearned to direct Bergman-like films. Years ago, Jack had stood in front of a bar a lot like this one, on a day as hot as this one was, watching his father shoot *Freddie the Fuzz* on location. *Freddie* was a big hit back in the 1970s. It was blazing hot, and the actor playing Freddie carried around a pocket fan wherever he went, since his makeup was continually dripping down his face. On this particular day, the street looked like something out of a disaster movie, since a bomb was supposed to have gone off. The crew ran around lighting fires, littering the street with glass and debris and blowing smoke from a smoke machine. During one of the takes, Freddie's hair caught fire, and everybody panicked. Nobody knew what to do, except for the rent-a-cop who'd been assigned to direct traffic. He raced over, put out the fire before it could do any damage, then went back to directing traffic again. The odd thing was, everybody acted as if nothing unusual had happened. People barely acknowledged the cop or his heroic deed. Freddie was fine. Disaster averted. *Let's move on. Relight!* Only Jack thought it was a big deal, because that was the moment he decided to become a cop—not an actor playing a cop, or a producer making cop shows, but a real live cop. One of the good guys.

Now he opened the door of the Broken Spoke and paused to take in the bar's atmosphere. He liked the sense of anonymity you got from a bar when you first entered it—a nightclub wanted you to show off, but a bar wanted you to disappear. He took a moment to study the eclectic collection of tables and chairs, the rock-and-roll memorabilia collecting dust on the walls, the long-forgotten piñata hanging from the rafters. All it did was make him thirsty. Los Angeles was in the middle of a severe drought, and these high temperatures were unusual for March. Water had gotten so scarce the city fathers were considering building a desalination plant. Maybe they should take all that money and buy everyone a beer.

He spotted the bartender and, crossing the floor, flashed his badge. "LAPD. We spoke earlier."

The tall, ashen-faced man gave a curt nod of acknowledgment, then went back to his bartending duties.

"This guy." Jack showed him a photograph of Colby Ostrow.

"Comes in pretty regular, yeah," the bartender said. He had a receding chin and misaligned teeth, and he was chewing on a stick of gum. "Colby something."

"When did you see him last?"

"Two or three days ago."

"So Tuesday? Wednesday?"

"Wednesday. I remember thinking it was super-busy for a Wednesday night."

Jack nodded. "What time did he leave?"

The bartender shook his head as he poured another blended drink, his jaws working overtime. According to Ostrow's doting middle-aged sister, Colby was the quiet type, a lonely bachelor, practically invisible. She'd called it in yesterday when he failed to show up for work. A thorough search of his apartment had ruled out robbery as a motive.

"Give it a shot," Jack said. "Was it midnight? Closing time?"

"That I do not know."

"Did you see anybody with him?"

"It was super-busy, like I said."

Jack nodded. "You from the East Coast?"

"Yeah. How'd you guess?"

"Everybody from the East Coast chews gum."

"Look, I'd like to help you out, Detective. But that's all I've got."

"Relax. I'm passing out migraines today. So what else can you tell me about Colby Ostrow that night? Was he in a good mood? Bad mood? What?"

"You're talking about a guy with zero personality. He comes in pretty regular, like I said. Sidles up to the bar. Says things like 'Nice weather we're having.' One of those. Last Wednesday, he orders three, maybe four Bloody Marys. That's all I remember. Like I said . . ."

"It was super-busy, I know. You didn't see him leave? Alone or with another person?"

The bartender shook his head and started rinsing glasses. "Eve Garrett talked to him."

"Eve?"

"She's over there. Next to the jukebox."

"Thanks."

Eve Garrett had a head of brittle, overbleached hair. Her extra-wide hips were squeezed into a lime-green miniskirt, and her breasts strained against the fabric of her embroidered peasant blouse. Deep into middle age, she was one of those sad, unrepentant hookers who'd lost their assets a long time ago but who couldn't stop the habit of trolling the street for customers. "Excuse me, Ms. Garrett?"

"Call me Eve. Like in the garden." She kicked out a chair. "Take a load off."

"I'm investigating the disappearance of this man." He showed her the photograph of Colby Ostrow. "He look familiar?"

She squinted at the picture. "Yeah, I met him a few nights ago."

"He a regular customer of yours, Eve?"

"No." She laughed. She had a scary, asthmatic laugh. "I let him buy me a drink."

"Was he alone?"

"More alone than you."

Jack winced. "What's that supposed to mean?"

"Whatever you want it to, sweetie."

He shifted uncomfortably in his chair. The sense of

melancholy was strong in here. "The bartender saw you two talking. Did you leave together?"

She rested her hands on the table. "Look, okay. He might've suggested that we go someplace."

"Someplace like where?"

"Like his car. But I had to pee real bad, so I told him to wait for me by the exit."

"Front or back?"

"Wouldn't you like to know?"

"Eve . . ."

"Back exit." She drew on her cigarette.

"So you went to the ladies' room and then what?"

"I was in there five minutes maybe. It's so pleasant in there, you know? Graffiti all over the place. 'Crabs jump twelve inches.' 'A hard man is good to find.' Such terrific advice from the bathroom walls. Things to live your life by."

"Five minutes?"

"I took my time because . . . let's face it. I know who I am. I know what they call me. Eve Two Bags. I'm Spam, okay? But you work with what you've got. And so I put on some lipstick and combed my hair and whatever. I was five minutes tops, but when I get back outside, the little bastard's gone."

"What time was this?"

"Ten . . . ten-fifteen."

"He just disappeared?"

"So I sit back down." She took out a comb and parted her hair to one side, then pulled it back with a metal clip. Frank Sinatra was crooning from the jukebox. "It happens sometimes," she said.

He felt sorry for her. Her bland acceptance of her

awful life made him want to punch somebody's lights out. Exactly who was to blame for this train wreck? "Did you see him with anyone else?" he asked. "Did he talk—however briefly—to anybody in the bar that you remember?"

"No. He came right over and sat down next to me, far as I know. Seemed really awkward, like he wasn't used to picking up girls. I don't know. Maybe that's just an act."

Jack handed her his card. "If you think of anything else, gimme a call."

She took his hand, turned it over. "Where's your wedding ring, Detective?"

He looked at the pale band of flesh on his tanned hand where the ring had once been. "You know what they say about marriage, don't you, Eve?"

"Enlighten me."

"First comes the engagement ring, then comes the wedding ring . . . then there's the suffering."

She smiled. "That's what prostitution rings are for, baby."

Jack chuckled and headed out.

3.

Daisy was having a hard time getting motivated today. She'd spent the better part of the morning digging her car out from under a four-foot drift which the snowplows had thoughtfully left behind, and now her back was sore. Her arms ached. She'd shoveled and shoveled and shoveled, and she was sick of all this snow. *Melt already!*

Last night a bilious force had buried half the state under a moonscape of white, dumping a good six inches on the city of Boston and launching a fleet of snowplows and school cancellations. Her head was splitting. For once in her life, she didn't feel like working. Instead, she wanted to sit at her desk and watch the plump white flakes drift down from the sky and collect against the windowpanes. The snow piled up and caught in little patterns on the screens. It was beautiful. She felt about as distant from her work as if she were covered in gauze. Across the street from the medical school, a line of parked cars was buried under vast drifting vistas, and beyond the parking lot, the city trees were dark as wrought-iron bones.

Daisy propped her chin in her hands and wished that last night hadn't happened. Just her luck to have been there when Truett was drunk. Now she was going to have to deal with the fallout. She was going to have to explain to him that she didn't want to hurt their working relationship. She'd been avoiding him all morning long and was dreading the encounter. She checked her watch. Time to get back to work.

Inside the Mouse Facility, she washed up at the sink and put on a pair of latex gloves, shoe coverings and a disposable face mask, then entered the sterile holding room and flipped on the light. There were two light switches on the wall—the top one activated a red light-bulb, the bottom one activated a white lightbulb. Since mice weren't able to detect color, the red light registered as darkness and didn't disrupt their sleep patterns. "It's okay, guys," she whispered. "Keep on snoring."

Like most animal and plant species, mice had a circadian rhythm, and the lab used a standard light/dark cycle—twelve hours of light, twelve hours of darkness. Inside cage number 17A, four adult mice slept soundly while a fifth one shuffled around restlessly, trying to get comfortable. She recognized Louis XIV by his floppy left ear and little blue dye mark on his back. "Hey," she said, raising the wire lid of the cage and lifting him out by his tail. There were new scratches on his body she would have to monitor, since wounds were signs of aggression among cagemates. Louis' hind legs scrambled for a foothold as she checked his balance. "Looking good. This looks real good," she cooed as she cupped him in her palm.

Six months ago, she'd divided thirty mice into three groups of ten: one group of normal mice, and two groups of mice with the genetic defect that caused Stier-Zellar's disease. Of the twenty mice with the disease, ten had been randomly selected to receive the corrective gene. In order to administer gene therapy, Daisy had encoded DNA with the missing enzyme, then loaded it into a harmless virus that'd been stripped of its own genetic information. She injected this "viral vector" into the brains of the affected mice and now, six months later, the results were nothing short of astonishing. The latest MRI images showed marked improvements in myelin levels across the board. The brain cells were clear at the injection site and in the areas around them.

Children born with Stier-Zellar's disease had an enzyme deficiency that caused the erosion of myelin, an essential part of the nervous system. The sad result was the same in every case—gradual paralysis, mental retardation and early death. To date, there was no cure. Stier-Zellar's became apparent when an infant was around two years old. Symptoms included lack of head control and abnormal muscle tone, also known as floppiness. The disease slowly wiped out the ability to think and move, and most children born with Stier-Zellar's rarely lived beyond the age of eight.

Now Louis XIV paused to sniff at the air, his whiskers twitching delicately. He was very special. All the mice named Louis were special, since they'd been bred to have the mutated gene. The trial results looked promising, but Daisy was cautious in her assessment—there were still too many unanswered questions. Gene therapy worked, but for how long? A year? Two years? And how would her success with the mice translate to human subjects?

She carefully grasped the mouse by the scruff of his neck and, working quickly, collected a blood sample. "Easy, big guy," she said, smoothing the spot on the back of his head with her finger. "All done. Not so bad, huh?" Very gently, she lowered him back in his cage and released him onto the bedding, then watched for a moment as he settled down.

There was a sharp rap on the glass, and she panicked, knowing how much it would distress her mice. She pulled off her face mask and gloves and hurried out of the holding room, where she ran smack into Truett's arms.

"Hey, you," he said with a warm smile.

Daisy untangled herself and smiled nervously back. "You startled me, Truett."

"Have you been avoiding me?"

"What?" She frowned. "No. Why?"

"Because this morning you ignored me for a moment before you changed your mind and said hello. I can detect even the smallest slight, you see."

"Don't be ridiculous. I'm not avoiding you." It embarrassed her that she was lying to him. Why was she lying to him? She needed to be honest. "Truett," she said, "about last night . . ."

"I was drunk. I'm sorry I behaved badly."

She glanced at the open door and pulled him back inside the holding room with her, the red light washing across their faces. "Because I wouldn't want anything to hurt our relationship."

"I agree."

"You do?" She pinched the bridge of her nose. "I was really worried . . ."

"Relax. I'm the bearer of good tidings. The FDA has approved our proposal for human clinical trials for Stier-Zellar's."

"Are you serious?"

"As a preacher's wife."

She felt a warmth rushing through her. It was great news. The best.

"We'll start next month, ten kids, ages one through six. You did it, Daisy. Congratulations."

"*We* did it," she said excitedly.

"I think there's room on that shelf for another bottle of champagne, don't you?"

She glanced at the shelf with its dusty bottles and laughed, her mind reeling. There was so much work to be done. She wanted to get started right away.

"By the way," he told her, apropos of nothing, "Julia and I are getting a divorce."

She could feel herself suddenly spinning out of orbit. "What?"

"Julia and I . . ."

"A divorce?"

"Is there an echo in here?" He read the panic on her face. "Daisy," he said in that condescending tone he sometimes used with her. "You're hardwired to be miserable, aren't you?"

"This isn't because of last night, is it?"

"No."

She didn't believe him. Outside, the wind was blowing the trees around in gray swirls, and wet snow lashed down from the turbulent sky. She rubbed her forehead with vigorous fingers. "Because, listen . . . it would be really awkward."

"Oh really?" He crossed his arms. "Just what was so awful about it?"

"Not awful. Awkward. You know what I mean."

"Not really."

Her cell phone rang just then, rescuing her. The line was riddled with static. "Mom? I can't hear you." She cupped her hand over the mouthpiece and said, "I have to take this, Truett. Can we talk later?"

"Look, my marriage has been on life support for years," he told her. "Julia thumps her foot when she eats. She's got a mouth like a feeding fish. Things have gotten so bad between us she'll wave at me with one finger." He raised his middle finger in a mocking salute. "There. Feel better now?"

She walked out of the Mouse Facility and was halfway down the corridor by the time she realized Lily was crying. "Mom? What's wrong? What is it?"

"Anna's missing."

She grew instantly annoyed. "Again?"

"Yes, again," Lily said. "And this time I'm worried."

4.

The following morning, Daisy wore the bright red scarf her mother had given her last Christmas, a red wool muffler that made her neck itch. She drove her 1969 Mustang over the railroad tracks and across the covered bridge at McCallum Creek, then began the winding uphill ascent through the dense, familiar woods that gave off the aroma of pine sap and woodsmoke. She couldn't believe she'd been dragged back into the same old drama. *Anna's missing, Anna's sick, Anna's gone off her meds.* Wheeler's Pond was frozen solid today, covered with laughing kids and silent ice-fishers, old men hunched over their fishing poles and little girls in raggedy pink parkas like the kind she and Anna used to wear, their tiny figures making lacy zigzags across the ice. Edgewater was one of those quaint Vermont villages that relied mostly on tourism for its existence, although it had once been a booming mining town. Now it sprouted inns and antique barns like fast-food chains. "Step Back a Century" was the town motto. In the fall, the woods crawled with hunters, and when the girls were little, they used to put curses on the bad mens' heads and hope that the huge-eyed deer would spot their phosphorescent-orange vests and flee before the booming sound of their guns could thud against the distant hills.

Today was April Fools' Day, yet everything was white, the relentless snows of winter having bludgeoned last year's vegetation into the ground. They would probably skip spring this year and go directly to summer with its oppressive humidity and black flies. She drove through downtown Edgewater, past the redbrick eighteenth-century buildings and gleaming white church spires, then crossed the rusty bridge that spanned the ice-covered river. After a few more miles of breathtaking vistas, she climbed the short hill to Woodpecker Road, where stubborn cornstalks poked out of the drifts like dead fingers. Daisy's stomach cinched with a familiar worry. What if Anna was in trouble this time? How could they possibly help her? Los Angeles was three thousand miles away.

Lily Hubbard stood hatless and coatless on the front porch, batting her arms against the cold. She waved as she spotted her daughter's fiery red Mustang, and Daisy sighed, "Oh, Mom." Her mother never changed. Lily had just recently recovered from the flu, and now here she was, darting half dressed across the snowy front yard.

"Crazy lady," Daisy muttered as she pulled into the driveway and parked next to Lily's balloon-blue Toyota, feeling big and pushy in her American-built classic.

"You made it!" Lily said, galloping down the snowy incline into her daughter's arms. She gave Daisy a hug that didn't feel half as hearty as it used to; it felt fragile and careful, lacking in muscle tone. Lily held on a microsecond longer than Daisy wanted to be held, then they both pulled away at once. "You look pretty sharp," Lily said, flipping the red scarf playfully.

"Where's your coat, Mom?"

"Back inside. I'm just so happy to see you."

"Your lips are blue. How long have you been standing there?"

"You're very predictable, sweetheart. You said you'd be here at ten, and it's five minutes past." Her pale face was mottled and flushed from the cold, and her breath came out in cottony puffs. She wore a thin white blouse, a lilac sweater vest and a matching skirt that came to just below her knees. Her winter boots were unlaced and partially filled in with snow, and behind her, smoke puffed from the chimney and the icicled roof gleamed like something out of a storybook. Clutching her shivering frame with both arms, Lily said, "You're right. It is cold."

"Let's get you back inside before you turn into a Popsicle." Daisy looped her arm through her mother's and helped her up the incline and across the front yard. Lily's hair was stylishly cut and dyed its former blond, and her fingers were swollen with arthritis. In her early sixties, she took insulin for her diabetes, and Daisy was constantly worried about her. Lily worked as an accountant, certifying company books, and loved numbers more than people because, she said, numbers were less confusing. They either added up or they didn't.

Three enormous blue jays sprang from the bird feeder as they approached the house. The two-story Queen

Anne with its original windows and wraparound porch sat in majestic isolation on the western slope of a hillside overlooking the valley. From this vantage point, they could see down into the bare winter woods. The clapboard house was white with a green-shingled roof, and in the springtime, the red window boxes were filled with geraniums. In the front yard of this once-cheap-but-now-prime real estate, the elegant hickory trees clung to a few withered leaves.

"I really think we should file a missing-persons report," Lily said. "Five weeks is an awfully long time to be out of touch, even for Anna."

Daisy sighed. "What happened?"

"She sounded really happy last time we spoke. She was seeing Dr. Averill and taking her meds. Then about five weeks ago she stopped returning my phone calls."

"She's done that before, Mom. Cut us off without warning."

"I know, but it's never a good sign."

Daisy refused to worry prematurely. Her younger sister was always disappearing on them, always creating scenes. Diagnosed as bipolar or schizophrenic, depending on which doctor you talked to, Anna had been living with their mother for years now, but every once in a while, she would venture out into the real world and try to make it on her own. Sadly, these gambits never worked out, and before too long, twenty-eight-year-old Anna Hubbard would come running home with her tail tucked between her legs and swear she'd never leave Edgewater again. Then she'd call Daisy in the middle of the night to complain, "Guess what the Momster did today?"

This time Anna had stayed away from home for ten whole months, almost twice as long as her longest prior adventure.

"Oh, look, you've got burs on the back of your coat," Lily said, whacking at Daisy's shoulders with her hand. "Where'd you get these?"

"No idea, Ma." Daisy took off her coat and scarf and went rummaging around in the pantry for the coffee mugs while her mother stepped out of her wet boots and into a pair of house slippers. Daisy had a sinking feeling that things might be different this time as she poured them coffee from the pot on the stove. She'd lost touch with Anna months ago and was feeling a little guilty about it. Now she fished around in the refrigerator for the nonfat milk, added a splash and sat down at the kitchen table with her mother. Lily's place mat held the remains of that morning's breakfast—pulpy orange juice, a half-eaten pancake in a puddle of maple syrup.

"How are you doing?" Daisy asked her. "Are you eating okay?"

Lily seemed more distracted than usual. "Hm? Oh yes, fine."

"Are you following your diet, Ma?"

"Oh, honey, I'm sure even Mother Teresa cheated once in a while." Lily eyed her plate. "Would you like something to eat? There's plenty of pancake batter left. Or I could scramble you some eggs."

"No thanks."

"You look tired."

"I'm not tired."

"Your eyes are bloodshot."

"Yeah, Ma. I've been hanging out on street corners snorting Dristan."

Lily frowned. "Don't make fun of me."

"I can't help it. You always dance around what's on the tip of your tongue."

"Well, anyway. Thanks for coming."

"Of course I came. Why wouldn't I? I'm the dutiful one, remember?" She couldn't help sounding bitter. It was just that Anna was forever getting into trouble, and Daisy was always cleaning up after her.

The morning sunlight gave the kitchen a vintage glow. Lily took off her oversize, amber-tinted glasses, the skin around her eyes creasing like crepe paper. She paused for a moment to cough. She had a big cough for such a frail-looking person.

"Mom? Are you okay?"

She waved away the worry. "Right as rain." Her mother wasn't always dependable about injecting her insulin three times a day. Her diabetes was a self-managing condition that got worse with stress or illness, and death was always a risk. At Daisy's insistence, Lily now carried her insulin around with her wherever she went.

"Okay, so what instigated it this time?" Daisy asked. "Did you two have a fight?"

"No, that's what's so puzzling. She's been calling home for months now—once a week, like clockwork. Then poof, no more phone calls. I must've left a dozen messages on her machine."

"She'll show up eventually. She always does."

Lily shook her head. "It's different this time."

"How do you know?"

"It just feels different."

Daisy twisted her fingers together in her lap, more worried than she cared to admit. "Remember when she joined that stupid cult?"

"You're right." Lily patted her arm. "I'm getting all worked up over nothing."

Sometimes Anna would disappear for weeks at a time just to punish them. She'd camp out at a friend's house or else take the bus to Rutland and hole up in some battered-women's shelter, pretending to be somebody else. The two sisters were so different, and yet all their lives, Daisy and Anna had been told how similar they were. Daisy couldn't see it. The main facial feature they shared was a mouth whose thick, curvaceous lips wrapped articulately around big words. Daisy had her mother to thank for the rest of her—same aristocratic nose and light blond hair, same startling blue eyes and well-rounded figure that skinny Anna was so jealous of. The girls' father had died when Daisy was three, right before Anna was born, and as far as Daisy could tell, the only trait she'd inherited from Gregory Hubbard was a permanently worried look on her otherwise symmetrical face. Anna, on the other hand, had inherited their father's towering stature and all-American good looks, same coppery red hair and dark blue eyes and those wide-open features, which she accented to ghoulish effect with brushstrokes of Gothic eye shadow and black lipstick.

"Did you call Dr. Slinglander?" Daisy asked. "Maybe he's heard from her."

Lily shook her head. "They haven't spoken since August."

"That long?"

Dr. Slinglander was Anna's psychiatrist in Edgewater.

Pushing seventy, he resembled a white-haired Mr. Rogers with his comfy clothes and serene gaze. Over the years, he'd managed to keep Anna pretty well stabilized and medicated, but he kept encouraging her independence from Lily, often with disastrous consequences.

"What about Maranda?" Daisy asked.

"Maranda, Sylvia . . . nobody's heard from her."

She warmed her hands on the chipped brown mug they seemed to have had forever, purchased from some craft shop that no longer existed. "So nothing triggered it?"

"Back in January, I noticed . . . oh, I don't know, something strange about her speech. But she kept assuring me that everything was fine. Everything was 'cool.' She was seeing Dr. Averill and taking her meds. So I figured, well, if anything happens, Dr. Averill will catch it. But then one day she stopped returning my phone calls. I tried not to panic. So I waited. And now I've waited long enough. Maybe too long."

The house was homey rather than elegant and smelled pervasively of gingerbread. The windowpanes were frosted over with ice, each one its own crystallized continent. Since when had this become an old lady's house, Daisy wondered, full of delicate things artfully arranged? Hints of bargain hunting were everywhere, and cobwebs gathered in places high on the ceiling where Lily could no longer reach them.

"I mean, what's so great about Los Angeles?" Lily asked rhetorically. "The traffic is terrible. They have drive-by shootings. They have earthquakes."

"It's not your fault, Mom. It's nobody's fault."

Lily sagged in her seat. "I shouldn't have let her go off on her own like that. It was stupid of me."

"Mom. Please. She's a grown woman."

"She's been out there an awful long time, don't you think?"

"Ten months is a record," Daisy agreed.

"Ten months." She stood up. "I've almost forgotten what she looks like."

"Mom? Where are you going?"

"Upstairs. I need to see her face."

5.

Lily's bedroom was a shrine to her ordinariness, her sense of comfort and thrift. Nothing had been altered in years—same lumpy mahogany four-poster bed, same painted bureau with its mismatched knobs, same worn Persian rug that the girls used to pretend was a flying carpet. And making up for all the drabness was the view. Through the French slider doors, you could see the changing seasons and catch spectacular leaf transformations and outrageous neon sunsets. Today the fields were blanketed in a whiteness so bright you'd have thought you were in Death Valley.

Lily sat on the edge of the bed and patted the mattress. "Come sit," she said, then reached into the top drawer of her bedside table and took out an old photo album.

Daisy sat next to her mother and ran her hands over the nubby white bedspread. She liked the marbled mirror with its cherry frame, the old Windsor chair that Mr.

Barsum had painted apple green, the floor lamp with its fringed pink lampshade. It comforted her to know that everything would always remain the same. That everything inside this house was forever.

"Look," Lily said, opening the photo album and showing Daisy a succession of color snapshots—Daisy and Anna as babies, Daisy and Anna as little girls, Daisy and Anna as snotty teenagers. She could see the gradual transformation in her sister's demeanor over the years— that caged look in her eyes at thirteen, the growing pessimism of her high school years, the creeping mania of her early twenties. These pictures also captured the chronology of their little brother's illness—Louis in his stroller, Louis in his hospital bed, Louis in his wheelchair. In a typical shot, Louis's parenthetical sisters, Daisy and Anna, would be seated on either side of him, angling their heads sharply to fit inside the frame. It struck Daisy that in almost every picture, Louis had his head shaved. He'd died of Stier-Zellar's disease at the age of six, and the girls had no idea who his father was. To this day, Lily had kept it a deep, dark secret. In the final photograph they had of him, Louis's eyes were wide with awe and tension, as if he could see death hurtling toward him like a tidal wave.

Stier-Zellar's was inherited in an autosomal recessive pattern, which meant that two copies of the gene had to be altered in order for a child to be born with the disease. That meant that both of his parents had to be carriers. Lily was a carrier, and because of that, Anna and Daisy were potential carriers. Genetic testing was available, but Daisy had yet to determine whether or not she was at risk for passing the disease on to her children. She figured there was still plenty of time to get the bad news.

The girls had spent half their childhoods trying to figure out who Louis's biological father was. Whenever they asked their mother, Lily would put up barriers around herself, thick and impenetrable. Eventually, they stopped asking and instead resorted to hushed speculation and marathon conjecture sessions late at night in their shared bedroom. It couldn't be Mr. Barsum, since he'd come into the picture a whole year after Louis was born. They had a list of suspects, including the mailman and their mother's boss, Mr. Grady down at the CPA's office. The only certainty about Louis's father was that he carried the other recessive gene that had sealed their brother's fate at the moment of conception.

Now Lily turned the page, and Daisy smiled down at the faded images of her father, an aesthetically pleasing stranger. She couldn't remember anything about him, except for his hands. She remembered how strong and clean they were, the nails pared down to the quick. That was the main memory she had of her biological father—of a bright summer afternoon when he'd tossed her up in the air and then caught her in his strong, clean-smelling hands.

Gregory Hubbard and Lily Eggleston were childhood sweethearts who'd lived next door to one another since birth. They'd gotten "married" in the third grade, swearing allegiance over plastic Cracker Jack rings. Many years later, Gregory was drafted and did a tour of duty in Vietnam. When he came home from that contentious war, all he wanted was to settle down with Lily Eggleston, for real this time. A successful real estate agent with a bright future ahead of him, Gregory was killed in a car crash two months before Lily gave birth to their second daughter.

Their father had passed on more than just these faded images in a photo album—he'd passed on the internal programming that would determine everything from the girls' eye color to their susceptibility to heart disease. DNA was a four-letter language. A single strand of DNA was made up of endless combinations of just four letters— A, T, G, C. These letters made up words, and these words made up sentences. The sentences were called genes. The DNA alphabet produced various genes the way the English alphabet produced words. Each human being had a unique genetic "book"—a life story written in the genes. It was the study of these books that had absorbed 98 percent of Daisy's waking moments for the past fifteen years.

"So how's your job going?" Lily asked as she closed the album on the past.

"Fine."

"Tell me about the rats."

Daisy stared out the window at the falling snow and tried to single out one individual whirling snowflake to the exclusion of all others. "Mice, you mean," she said. "I work with mice, Mom. Not rats."

"How are your mice, darling?"

"Thriving."

"Good. That's good. How many Louis are you up to now?"

"Fourteen."

Lily turned to her. "What happens when you hit nineteen?"

"Nothing will happen. We'll keep on going."

"But there were only eighteen King Louis."

"I know, Ma."

"So there'll be a Louis XIX?"

"I named the mice after my brother, not the French king."

"Oh."

"I'm going to cure Stier-Zellar's in his honor."

Lily nodded, her eyes glazing over. "I think Anna's in real trouble this time," she said. "Did I ever tell you she thought there was electrical wiring in her chest once?"

Daisy felt a spike of alarm. "Recently?"

"No. When she was thirteen. Right after she came back from the hospital that time."

She relaxed a little, then became irritated.

"Anna skulked around the house with her hands over her heart and grew more and more secretive, but I kept after her. 'What's wrong? What is it?' Finally, she told me there was electrical wiring in her chest that connected her to heaven. Sort of like a telephone. She said it pulled questions out of her heart."

Daisy hadn't heard that one before. "What kind of questions?"

"The deep, painful kind." Lily glanced at her. "What do you remember? About Anna getting sick, I mean."

Daisy remembered chaos and heartbreak, her sister's hateful words and those interminable crying jags; she recalled the hospital visits and faceless doctors and the ongoing battles to get Anna to keep taking her meds. "I remember being trapped in the kitchen once," she said, "while Anna did these crazy martial arts exercises. She almost kicked you in the head. I was so angry." With this memory, something broke like the skin of a blister. How could her sister put their mother through this time and again?

"Poor Daisy. You're like your father, same worry wrinkle between the eyes." Lily reached for Daisy's forehead and tried to rub it out.

They both fell silent for a moment.

"So," Lily said, "what should we do now?"

Dr. Susan Averill was so soft-spoken Daisy had to strain to hear her. "How is Anna?" the doctor said.

Daisy clutched the receiver. "Excuse me?"

"Is everything okay?" Dr. Averill operated out of an office in Beverly Hills, and although they had never met, Daisy couldn't help picturing a petite, well-groomed woman sitting in a sunny designer office full of glass-and-teak furniture.

"I was just going to ask you the same thing."

"About Anna?"

"Yes," Daisy said. "We seem to have lost contact, and I was wondering if you could ask her to call us."

"But . . . I haven't seen your sister in months."

Daisy focused on the faded buttercups on the wallpaper. "When was the last time?"

"Hold on. Let me check."

"What is it?" Lily hissed, but Daisy shushed her.

"Let's see . . . yes, that's right." The doctor fumbled with the phone. "We decided to end her sessions last October."

"So . . . six months ago?"

"That's right."

"Six months ago what?" Lily whispered.

"She seemed to be adjusting very well to her new environment," Dr. Averill said, "so I let the decision rest with her."

"Okay. Thanks."

"Is something wrong?"

"No, it's okay. Please don't worry about it." Daisy hung up.

"Well?" Lily said anxiously.

"Anna stopped seeing Dr. Averill about six months ago."

"You're kidding me!"

"It wouldn't be the first time she's lied to us, Mom."

"So that's it, then," Lily said resignedly. "She's gone off her meds."

"Do you have any idea what could've triggered this?"

"I told you." Lily plucked at the embroidered sleeve of her blouse, her soft features folding in on themselves. "We were getting along fine."

"Did you notice any tension in your last phone call?"

"Daisy, honestly. If I had a clue, I'd tell you."

"So you really have no idea?"

Lily frowned. "You were such a quiet baby. Not a peep. I nursed you, but not Anna. Maybe that had something to do with it."

"Mom, stop it."

"Stop what?"

"Blaming yourself." She sat for a moment, then said, "I'm calling the police."

6.

The blistering heat was expected to last throughout the weekend, with temperatures hovering in the high nineties. Jack drove past tacky-looking restaurants and motels toward a cluster of gray apartment buildings on Godschalk Road. The car's A/C was cranked, but his hands burned on the hot steering wheel. He kept changing the radio station, since certain songs made him cry. He'd never told anyone about it before, but he couldn't listen to "Pretty Woman" by Roy Orbison without shedding a tear or two, and his reaction to "Stand Inside Your Love" by Smashing Pumpkins was downright embarrassing.

Jack took a left on Godschalk and found a parking space between two dusty construction trucks, then got out and was instantly overwhelmed by the oppressive heat. Even the flies were lethargic.

The Sea Breeze may have been appealing once, but

it'd long since fallen into disrepair. The peach-colored stucco was soot-stained and crumbling around the windows, the swimming pool filter was clogged with jacaranda leaves, and the swimming pool itself was a vivid, astonishing green due to some strange species of algae growing on the bottom. The three-story structure was surrounded by other multistory buildings of similar styles and differing sizes, and next door was a weed-choked vacant lot where drug deals took place late at night. Jack knew this, because he used to work vice. Not the greatest place in the world for an emotionally unstable young woman from Vermont to end up in.

Twenty-eight-year-old Anna Hubbard had been missing for five weeks now, according to her sister. Jack didn't hold out much hope as he climbed the front steps, then paused to inspect the cheap hardware. You could break into this building fairly easily. All you needed was a metal slot cover from a computer. Insert it into the doorjamb, jiggle it around a little and *presto*. Some security.

He rang the doorbell. "It's Detective Makowski."

"I'm in unit twelve. Take a right after the mailboxes," the building super said before buzzing him in.

The interior of the building was sweltering, and Jack felt himself melting faster than a pat of butter on a baked potato as he proceeded down the fake-oak-paneled hallway and took a right after the metal mailboxes. The door was open. He passed through an arched entryway into a dimly lit foyer that smelled of curry and chickpeas, then entered an L-shaped living room, where he confronted a long-dead Christmas tree. "What's with the tree?" he asked, circling around it, the rust-red needles littering the carpet.

Seated behind a wooden desk nicked and scratched from years of abuse was a man of possibly Eastern European descent, his soft cow eyes skittering back and forth as he struggled to open a potato chip bag. "Sorry, chief," he said. "Haven't gotten around to it yet."

"It's April already. It's almost Passover, my friend. Get rid of it or I'll cite you."

"Absolutely." He tossed Jack the keys. "It's a mess up there, just to warn you."

"When was the last time you saw her?"

"I haven't seen her in months," the super said. "Not since Christmas."

"What'd you two talk about?"

"Nothing much. She was a little strange."

"Strange how?"

"She kept to herself, mostly. Came and went at odd hours. Very unfriendly. Only said hello if you said it first, that sort of thing. But she paid her rent on time. Until last month, that is."

Jack could feel the sweat collecting underneath his arms and soaking into his pin-striped shirt. There was something embryonic about this apartment. Something womblike. He felt like an egg inside an incubator. "When she stopped paying the rent, you didn't try to contact her?"

"We have a procedure we're supposed to follow. First you give the tenant a written warning, then a notice. Then you start eviction proceedings. I left a bunch of messages on her machine, but she never called me back."

"Which apartment?"

"Two oh six. Stairs are faster."

The stairwell held a mingling of smells—exhaust fumes from the underground garage, cat piss, faint traces of booze from an impressive array of empty liquor bottles. The cement walls were painted nicotine yellow. He found the apartment down the second-story hallway, inserted the key in the lock and, bracing himself for the nightmare which would surely flare before his eyes, opened the door.

A terrible odor hit him, and he drew back. "Christ." The garbage hadn't been taken out in weeks. The shades were drawn, and the place was dark and stifling. Slipping on a pair of latex gloves, Jack entered the apartment, swept aside the living room drapes and cracked a few windows. He saw steel-blue carpeting, cream-colored walls and plenty of trash strewn about. A rancid odor pervaded everything. It would follow him home tonight, back to his apartment in Santa Monica, where he'd take a tepid shower, crack an ice-cold beer and watch the game on ESPN. His social life consisted of a wing chair and a Wega flatscreen, since very few women wanted to date a guy who'd just gone through the pockets of a dead man.

A faucet was dripping somewhere inside the cluttered apartment. Jack broke the filter tips off two cigarettes, shoved them up his nostrils and breathed through his open mouth. The dead plants on the windowsills resembled prehistoric lizards, their bony arms reaching for the sky. Several old movie posters (*Jaws, Alien, Rosemary's Baby*) had been ripped off the walls, and mysterious stains bloomed on the carpet—brown stuff that sort of made you wonder. The ceiling was leaking in places, swelling the wood and depositing lacy cloud formations with rusty borders. The haphazard sofas and armchairs were so saddle-backed you could probably suffocate in them. There was a stereo system in fairly poor condition and a working computer, a large glass ashtray overflowing with the same brand of cigarette, a bunch of candy wrappers and banana peels strewn about. He picked up a travel book from Idaho. Who went to Idaho for whatever reason? He upended a paper bag full of receipts and phone bills, and out spilled dozens of snapshots.

Fingerprint evidence was fragile; one touch could destroy it. Jack held each snapshot gingerly by its edges and examined various candids of the missing woman—inside her apartment, out on the balcony, down by the beach. Her poses were silly and provocative. She matched the description her sister had given him over the phone—dark blue eyes, long red hair, scattered freckles across the bridge of her upturned nose. He couldn't help falling in love with her. There was nothing unusual in that, since Jack fell in love with crime victims the way most people fell in love with babies. His heart went out to them. He wanted to protect them, to defend them, to speak for them when they could no longer speak for themselves. Somebody must've taken these pictures. If only he could find the camera, they just might be able to pull a print off the release button.

Next he turned his attention to the telephone, a robin's-egg-blue handset and base unit. There were twenty-five unanswered messages on the digital display. He picked up a pink phone pad that somebody had doodled all over. The handwriting was girlish and naive, little circles over the *i*'s and happy faces after each exclamation point.

"Try to have a positive self-image, even though this is hard for you!"

Jack found rolling papers and a razor blade on the coffee table, along with a white substance that looked like cocaine residue. He found a few marijuana seeds inside a fish-shaped ashtray.

Dead bodies didn't shock him anymore, but the dead rats did. Three dead rats laid out on the kitchen table, each one dissected down the middle and mounted on a piece of cardboard. Their hides had been pinned back, their body cavities exposed. Their innards had begun to rot. Flies buzzed listlessly overhead. Several different kinds of knives were lined up with precision on the table, like surgical tools. There was a box of straight pins and more flies—dead this time—sealed inside an empty mayonnaise jar.

The kitchenette emitted a fetid aroma due to the rotting groceries on the countertop and the dirty dishes in the sink. Cockroaches infested the garbage can, scrambling in and out of scummy soda cans. Jack rapped his knuckles on a hard-as-rock layer cake that'd been left out for a millennium or two, and more roaches skittered across the Formica. They'd have to dunk the whole place in boric acid. An old-fashioned clock ticked on the wall above the stove, and the refrigerator hummed noisily. He paused at the stoppered sink full of dirty dishes and noticed that one of the eight-ounce water glasses wasn't fully submerged in the milky water. He leaned forward, then bobbed back, trying to catch the light. Looking for lip prints. Fingerprints.

Some of the dishwater had flooded over the aluminum basin and trailed across the countertop, leaving a visible residue. The trail of water had spilled over the edge and dripped down onto the floor. Jack got on his hands and knees and examined the linoleum, where he discovered a sneaker impression—size 7 or 8, probably female, relatively worn down at the heel.

He tagged and photographed the shoe impression and the water glass, then swept through the rest of the apartment, looking for latents and tagging all points of entry and exit. When he first entered the premises, he'd noticed that the doors and windows were locked. He didn't see any signs of forced entry. Those scratch marks around the keyhole were old. The drapes were drawn shut. The air-conditioning unit was off, and the only light on was the kitchen overhead. Anna Hubbard had most likely left her apartment of her own volition one night, date to be determined. Now he called the tech team and headed for the bedroom.

The boxy bedroom was a virtual shrine to the Virgin Mary. The walls were covered floor-to-ceiling with pictures of the Blessed Mother torn from art books or magazines and photocopied over and over. A hundred pairs of beatific eyes gazed down at him from the walls. The sturdy mahogany bureautop held melted candles and plaster statuettes of biblical figures, along with a papier-mâché parrot with curling yellow wings. The morning sun illuminated the drifting dust. There was a Virgin Mary alarm clock, a Mother and Child pen, an Our Lady night-light, and dozens of Blessed Mary T-shirts inside the bureau drawers. The unmade bed had striped pillows and pastel-green-and-pink linens, and strewn across it were articles cut out of newspapers: *Mouse Helps Man, Gene Therapy Results Promising, Congress to Debate*

*Stem Cell Research, Boy Finds Father After Yearlong
Search.*

He glanced up at the popcorn ceiling. Spray-painted
in huge Day-Glo-orange letters was a cryptic message.
Each letter and numeral was at least three feet tall.

END 70

END 70. What was that supposed to mean? He found
the same thing written in pencil on the back of the bedroom door, over and over again. *End 70, End 70, End
70 . . .* from top to bottom in tiny, precise script.

In the adjoining bathroom, he found the toilet lid up, the
seat down. The scum in the porcelain tub was grotesque. A
kinetic little cactus struggled to grow on the painted windowsill. Jack found a purple tie-dyed scarf draped over
the medicine cabinet mirror and removed it. He fingered
the purple silk, then caught sight of his lined, unshaven
face in the mirror. Hell. Who was he to judge? He ate his
dinner in front of the TV with a paper plate balanced on
one knee. He staggered home at three in the morning and
threw up Chinese takeout. He got so drunk sometimes,
he fell off the stage on karaoke night. It wasn't like
everybody wanted his DNA. His first marriage had been
real, but the other two weren't. They were disasters, like
this apartment. When it came to his marriages, Jack had
gotten worse with practice.

Back in the bedroom, he found the victim's camera on
the bureautop hidden behind a two-foot-tall statuette of
the Virgin Mary. She wore a sky-blue gown and a serene
smile, and draped across her outstretched arms were
necklaces of beaded glass—mandarin orange, ruby red,

avocado green. The Blessed Virgin seemed to take great pity on him, her kind eyes forgiving him his many transgressions. Jack sealed the Instamatic inside an evidence bag and continued preserving and protecting the scene.

7.

Daisy sat on a soggy bale of hay in the old barn, shaking the snow off her soft knit cap and smoking the joint she'd found tucked away in Anna's favorite hiding place. The old cigar box was full of odds and ends—their father's high school ring, Anna's childhood ballet slippers, a handful of love letters from an eighth-grade boyfriend. Daisy had found the joint pressed between the pages of her sister's diary. She'd scooped up both the diary and its illicit contents and brought them into the barn to sample. Anna was inconsistent with her diaries. Sometimes she filled many pages in one sitting; other times she abandoned her diary for weeks at a stretch. The leather-bound journal in Daisy's coat pocket covered the months of January through June of last year, before Anna's departure for L.A.

The barn doors were open, and Daisy watched the whispering snow transform the world outside into a wonderland of white. She drew her coat snug around her neck and sighed. It was so peaceful in here, so quiet and beautiful, she never wanted to leave. Outside, leaden clouds hung in the sky and the ice crunched and crackled underfoot, and she remembered snowball fights and sleigh rides and experiments with maple-syrup-flavored ice. *Where are you, Anna? Why are you tormenting us?*

Daisy studied her hand in a detached manner, as if somebody else were causing the fingers to flex and spread apart. Her relationship with her sister felt like a thought inside her head rather than a feeling inside her heart. She dropped her hand in her lap, and her vision blurred, darkness and sparks, then gradually widened again. The world outside the barn doors sparkled like diamonds. A pair of cardinals flitted from tree to tree while huge kaleidoscopic flakes came sifting down.

Detective Makowski of the LAPD had promised to call her right back. That was yesterday. She dug her hands in her pockets, hunched forward and shuddered violently. She didn't want to think about Mr. Barsum, but it was practically unavoidable in here. Mr. Barsum had lived with the Hubbards a long time ago, when the girls were very young. He'd stayed with them for several years, until Lily finally discovered what he'd been up to and kicked him out. The memory was painful, but it reminded her of Anna's favorite joke. *How many parents does it take to screw in a lightbulb? Two. One to screw in the lightbulb, the other to screw up your entire life.*

Daisy shivered and sighed, making breath clouds. Over the course of her troubled lifetime, Anna must've consumed an entire pharmacy of drugs—Haldol, lithium, Depakote, Vistaril. And that didn't include all the illegal drugs she'd taken—speed, cocaine, ecstasy, pot. Anna went through periods of calm, periods of normalcy, periods of chaos; but always there was that underlying neediness, the sense that you owed her something. Daisy was tired of feeling guilty all the time.

"Did you know that no two snowflakes are alike?" Lily asked. She was standing in the doorway with her arms crossed. She wore an old parka with a fringed hood that looked ridiculous on her.

Daisy dropped the joint on the rough-hewn floorboards and stomped it out with her boot. "Um . . . yeah," she said.

"And that each flake has six sides? Did you know that?"

It was terribly quiet inside the barn.

"I'm sure she's fine, Mom."

"God isn't malicious, right? He won't take my baby girl away from me. Not after all the losses I've had to endure."

Daisy suddenly realized that she was stoned in front of her mother. It hit her with the force of a gigantic pillow. The world outside the barn doors glowed from within, like an enormous night-light. Lily looked like an Eskimo. Each flake seemed to leave a vaporous neon trail in its wake. The smell of pot was palpable inside the barn, but Lily didn't seem to notice. She probably thought it was the fermented hay.

"Anna and I used to cheat in Sunday school," Daisy confessed. "Did you know that, Mom?"

Lily frowned. "No."

"We never cheated in regular school or anywhere else.

At least I didn't. I can't speak for Anna. But we cheated in Sunday school."

"Whatever for?"

"Out of spite, I think. We couldn't stand our teacher, Mrs. Galina. She was so dementedly happy all the time, so sickeningly up-with-people, you know? My attitude was that she didn't deserve our respect."

"I don't pretend to understand you girls." Lily tipped her face skyward and blinked as eddying, dizzying snowflakes caught on her eyelashes. She looked like a child with her face held like that.

"I feel bad about it now," Daisy said.

"You don't sound like you feel bad."

"I bumped into her one day, shortly after Anna was hospitalized for the first time. I was feeling pretty glum, and when I saw Mrs. Galina coming . . . I gave her such a dirty look. I wanted her to know how much I hated her. And do you know what she did?"

Lily shook her head.

"She smiled at me. She said hello. She was genuinely friendly. It shocked me. It was as if she could see right through me. She could see how miserable I was, and she didn't care whether I hated her guts or not. She was going to like me anyway, in spite of myself."

They gazed in silence at the falling snow. A stone-colored bird landed on the cement ramp and plumped its feathers against the chill. "One of us has to fly out there, you know," Lily said, breaking an ice puddle with the toe of her boot.

Daisy greeted the thought as a threat.

"To Los Angeles." Her mother looked at her expectantly. The silence stretched.

"If it wasn't for this diabetes," Lily said, "I'd go there myself. In a second."

"Mom, I'm at the most critical stage of my research. I can't just drop everything."

"But you have to, sweetheart."

"Why?"

"Because. There is nobody else."

And she knew this to be the sad, horrible truth. She gazed beyond her mother at the falling snow, at the big drifts scalloped by the fluting wind. Anna was right. It took only one parent to screw up your entire life.

"You're the strong one," Lily reminded her. "You can handle it."

But before she could respond to this familial curse, Daisy's cell phone rang. It made a chirping sound, and the bird on the ramp flew away. She took out her phone and said, "Hello?"

"Daisy Hubbard?"

"Yes?"

"This is Detective Makowski from the LAPD. We spoke yesterday."

Her spine straightened.

"I have news about your sister. Hello?"

"I'm still here," Daisy told him, while little wisps of snow metastasized into the barn.

8.

"Is there anything I can do for you?" Truett asked Daisy the following morning. "Anything at all?"

"I don't think so. But thanks."

The lab was empty. Everybody else was downstairs in the lecture hall, listening to Claude Bagget's seminar on viral vectors. Last night another foot of snow had fallen over Boston, winter clinging to spring like a bad joke. The events of the past few days had left Daisy feeling hollow inside, and she desperately wanted to fill in the void. Maybe the truth could fill up this empty space. She buttoned her overcoat, put on her soft knit cap and drew on her gloves. "Truett," she said, "I care about you a lot . . ."

He put a finger to her lips. "I don't want you to feel in any way responsible for the end of my marriage, Daisy." He took her hand—his hands were surprisingly small for such a big personality—and stood there with a hangdog expression. Truett couldn't help himself; he had more culture than Yoplait. In his double-breasted blazers, silk ties and expensive Italian shoes, he exuded class and style. He'd transformed himself from a southern farm boy into an elite intellectual, whereas she still splashed around in the great sea of the American middle class. "We make a good team, Daisy. I wouldn't want to break that up."

She smiled at him gratefully. "It feels like I'm deserting you right when you need me the most."

"Fiona can handle it until you come back. You need to focus on your sister. Just be careful, okay?"

"Good-bye, Truett."

"And do me a favor," he said. "Stop calling me Truett. Gives me the creeps."

"What should I call you, then?"

"Marlon."

She shook her head. "I'm afraid that would make me giggle."

"All right, fine. I don't wish to quarrel with a respected scientist." He kissed her on the cheek and said, "Be safe."

CAPTURED ROTATION

1.

Daisy caught herself staring at the flight attendant's elegant French knot and wondered why she didn't have the flair some women had with their hair. As a scientist, she'd always been hopelessly pragmatic when it came to her looks, and she seldom wore jewelry, never used perfume or nail polish. Now she pressed her unpowdered forehead against the cold glass. They were hurtling through the atmosphere, cruising along at six hundred miles per hour under an illusion of stillness. The moon floated in the night sky as if it were tethered to the ground by an invisible line. Daisy gazed at the landmass below. They were flying over scattered American cities— cities she'd never been to, cities whose identities evaded her now, constellations of light blossoming out of the darkness. Clusters of wattage, billions of bulbs.

She caught sight of her troubled reflection in the window and tested her forehead for a fever. It felt like a migraine had moved in and unpacked its bags. She'd taken the night flight from Boston to Los Angeles and was on her third glass of sour-tasting Chablis, the Boeing 747's turbo engines droning steadily in the background. She tried to process what the detective had told her over the phone: *Your sister stopped paying the rent and disappeared from her apartment without a trace. Her current whereabouts are unknown.*

The plane began to shake with turbulence, and the FASTEN SEAT BELT sign blinked on. She hadn't reviewed the emergency instructions yet—a ritual she performed before each flight—so she picked up the laminated sheet and started reading. The printed instructions reminded her that the seat cushions doubled as flotation devices, the life rafts were stashed inside the overhead compartments and the nearest exit doors were pretty far away from row 23, seat A. As she studied the brightly colored diagrams, she became convinced that should the plane crash for whatever reason, she and the strange man seated next to her would plummet into some polluted, unknown city and become one with the asphalt.

Daisy shoved the laminated sheet back in its plastic sleeve and closed her eyes while the plane bucked and shuddered against the oncoming wind. They were thousands of feet above the cold, silent earth. She wanted an aspirin badly but had packed the bottle inside her checked luggage. The next jolt against the jet stream took her breath away. Fear was shortness of breath. Fear was rapid breathing.

Now the strange man seated next to her said, "Watch the flight attendants. If they're not scared, don't you be."

She smiled at him gratefully.

He offered her a peanut. "What's your name?" he asked.

"Daisy."

"Hi. I'm Bram."

"Hello, Bram." They shook hands.

"Are you from Boston, Daisy?"

"Yes." She wasn't very good at idle chatter. Most people didn't like to talk about the things she wanted to talk about—quantum physics, the earth's rotation around the sun, the fact that Einstein got his best ideas while shaving.

"Just visiting?"

"Sort of."

"Sort of? What brings you to L.A.?"

"My sister's missing," she blurted.

"Missing? Really?"

"She's schizophrenic. I'm a little concerned. The police have no idea where she is."

He was looking at her oddly now, as if she'd rattled off a list of fatal plane crashes.

"Wow, that's a conversation stopper, huh?" she said with an embarrassed laugh, trying to make light of it, but he'd already smelled the raw fear on her, and there was no turning back.

They exchanged a few more pleasantries before he fumbled for a magazine, then Daisy turned to stare out the window again. It was dark on Planet Earth tonight. After a while, the turbulence eased, and she could swallow normally again. She gazed at the pitch black below, at the seeming emptiness of the American West. The sun felt all of its 93 million miles away. She could hear Detective Makowski's voice inside her head, low-pitched and authoritative. *We checked the Jane Does. We've checked all the morgues. Nothing's come up.* She stopped breathing momentarily, unable to absorb the fact that the police were already thinking that her sister might be dead.

After they landed safely at LAX, the man named Bram followed her silently off the airplane. The terminal was a blur of activity. She trailed a huge crowd down a long green corridor toward the baggage pickup area. There were countless twists and turns, and they passed by two metal detectors. Daisy found an ATM, but it was broken. She looked around and realized she was lost. "Which way to baggage pickup?" she asked a passing stranger.

"Follow me." Bram took her by the elbow.

Daisy didn't trust men who steered you places, since there was no telling when the steering would end. It was only eleven o'clock (2:00 A.M. back in Boston), and she'd had too many bravery drinks. Most of the people inside the terminal were dressed for the beach, colorful logos splashed across their jeans and T-shirts, and Daisy was feeling seriously overdressed in her tailored blouse and knife-pleat skirt. These terminals were well air-conditioned. She felt a chill and wished she'd worn a sweater.

They found the baggage pickup area and waited for their luggage to rotate by. The baggage handlers kept hurling people's suitcases through a trapdoor in the ceiling. Bram got his right away, then stood around waiting for hers to arrive.

"It's okay," she said. "I'm fine."

"I'll wait."

"Thank you. Really."

He left looking mildly disappointed.

She didn't like the sickening fluorescent wavelengths and grew dizzy watching people's luggage rotate by. Several other night flights had arrived from the East Coast, and soon this corner of the terminal was noisy and overcrowded. As the suitcases with matching totes came flying through the trapdoor in the ceiling, Daisy instantly recognized her ugly yellow suitcase, the one she'd dragged around with her from college to graduate school to her internship at Berhoffer. She'd always been embarrassed by that cheap, cheese-colored vinyl, which had never failed to give away her lowly status as a scholarship student who knew nothing about cotillions or summers in East Hampton, and who'd never set foot inside a country club. She'd made the mistake of attending a liberal-arts school for spoiled rich girls whose doting dads bought them Thoroughbred horses to be stabled nearby, whereas Daisy had been brought up on her mother's accounting salary. It'd never occurred to her how poor the Hubbards were until she'd gone away to college.

Now the baggage handlers tossed Daisy's suitcases down the chute as if they were trying to see how far they could throw. The wheeled Pullman landed with a crack on the terminal, its lid popping open, her unmentionables spilling out.

"Idiots," she grumbled, snapping it shut. She couldn't help feeling small and insignificant as she wheeled her bags over to a plastic bench molded to fit the contours of something—not the human body, that was for sure. She sat in exhausted silence while people became pinpoints. The airport was so huge and impersonal she dissolved into apathy. Banks of fluorescent lights made a constant hum, like a dull chorus. So this was how Los Angeles swallowed you whole? Right away, before you'd even set foot outside the airport gates.

She leaned against the cement wall until the back of her head began to throb. She swore she could feel the earth's motion somewhere underneath her breathing. Conflicting noises washed over her like dust disturbed by a fan. *Anna's missing.* She didn't want to think about it. Fear was paralyzing. Fear was immobilizing. She stood up, determined to keep moving, and dragged her luggage across the lobby and through the sliding glass doors, where she was hit by a torrid blast of muggy air.

She swam through this soup down the gritty sidewalk toward the taxi stand. The cabdriver was tall and gaunt and reminded her of an aging character actor. He deposited her luggage into the roomy trunk of the cab while she slid into the backseat. All around them, concrete terminals stood in beams of washed-out light.

"Where y'all from?" the driver asked in a southern drawl that reminded her of Truett.

"Boston," she said, feeling suddenly nostalgic for everything she'd left behind.

"Beantown, huh? Miracle City?" He glanced at her through the rearview, tires squealing as they swerved away from the curb. He drove past monolithic buildings and dark alleyways—was the city always this desolate? "Remember Dukakis riding around in that tank, looking like an idiot?" he said. "And then his campaign tanked, remember? Miracle City, ha. That was some miracle."

She didn't know what he was talking about. She leaned against the sticky vinyl seat, the pain milling aimlessly around inside her head now. They drove past a series of squat, empty-looking buildings, then took an entrance ramp onto the freeway. The sky was filled with millions of stars struggling to penetrate through the smog layer. It was hard to believe that, thousands of years ago, there had actually been glaciers in Hollywood instead of palm trees.

"I'm from Alabama originally," the cabdriver said, turning around briefly to look at her. His nose began with a broad bridge and grew vigorously from his face before ending abruptly in a pair of deeply grooved nostrils. "Me and the missus moved here twenty-five years ago and never regretted it for a second. Nossir. There's plenty of advantages to living in the second-largest city in America, you know? Out here, you've got more of everything. Out here, everybody has their own set of wheels. Well, that's not exactly an advantage for me, heh."

And it was true, the driveways were crowded with vehicles of every kind—SUVs, motorcycles, trucks, minivans. They were cruising through a residential area now, the gridlike streets stretching for miles past identical-looking bungalows painted pink or persimmon or peppermint. Everything seemed so promising here, so full of hope and opportunity.

"Hey, do you like pie?" he asked out of the blue.

"Pie?" Daisy blinked. "Um . . . sure. I guess."

"Well, okay, then. You've got to try the Pied Piper down on La Brea. They make fifty different kinds of pies, I kid you not. You won't find anything like that back East, I'll bet."

He dropped her off at a small, ugly motel in the middle of West Los Angeles. A low-grade fear was making her ill. The sky was deep cobalt, and the closer you looked, the more stars you could see. She paid the driver, who tipped his hat and sped off. Then she dragged her luggage across the asphalt toward the manager's office.

The middle-aged manager had a face like a tight ball. His mouth was slightly open, and he stared at the color TV on his desk. A ball game was playing.

"Daisy Hubbard," she said. "I made a reservation."

The motel promised low rates, air-conditioning, free parking and a swimming pool. AAA members received a 10 percent discount.

Inside the privacy of her own cabin, Daisy stretched out on the double bed and tried to find her inner self. The air conditioner hummed noisily, and the room reeked of Lysol. She thought she understood what might have drawn her sister to the West Coast. Out here, you could reinvent yourself. You could slip on a whole new personality, and nobody would care or even notice.

She went to the bathroom and splashed cold water on her face, then tugged at her hair with wet fingers, all her motions anxious and hard. The paleness of her skin alarmed her. She had a bad hangover and pinched her cheeks, trying to feel something. Even pain was preferable to this present torpor. She smiled at her reflection, revealing a set of perfectly proportioned teeth. Back in the sixth grade, she'd forgotten to brush them on a regular basis, and when the orthodontist finally took her braces off, there were cavities in her front teeth as random as bullet holes. These days, her porcelain fillings were faintly stained because of all the coffee she drank. But she liked her smile. It was wide and friendly, unafraid to show off its defects.

Daisy collapsed on the motel bed and squeezed her eyes shut, trying to block out the luminous neon glow leaking in through the cracks in the miniblinds. She tossed and turned, while outside her window, fragments of light whizzed past. After a while, she fell into an exhausted sleep, her dreams shallow and disturbing as mild stomachaches. She had a dim memory of Anna back home in Vermont, shuffling downstairs like a zombie and squinting into the noontime sun as she entered the kitchen with a cigarette dangling between her lips. Her long red hair was caught up in an elastic band at the base of her neck, her eye makeup was smudged and her face was puffy from too much sleep. Or maybe it was the meds. "Hey, you," she said, trudging over for a lethargic hug and kiss on the cheek. "Finally made your way home, huh?" She smelled of sleep, of the desire for oblivion.

Daisy stirred and opened her eyes. The clock said 1:00 A.M. She sat up and turned on the TV, and some kind of plucky banjo music assaulted her ears. A man in a cheap suit was standing on his head. "You won't find a better deal, I guarantee!" he hollered at the camera. He reminded her of Truett, same lanky sex appeal and hard-sell sensibility. In the next shot, he was doing cartwheels.

She wondered how there could possibly be fifty different kinds of pie and tried adding them up in her head. *Apple, pumpkin, lemon meringue, Boston cream . . .* She counted all the way up to fourteen and figured there couldn't be any more than that. Then she remembered. *Pecan.* Of course. *And peach.*

"Sixteen," she said out loud, the unexpected smallness of her voice sending shivers cascading across her scalp. Great. Instead of curing fatal diseases, she was counting pies. How could Anna have been so careless with her life? Was she trying to ruin everything? *Because congratulations, Anna, you're succeeding.*

Sweating profusely, Daisy got out of bed and decided to take a shower. She peeled out of her damp clothes, balled them up and tossed them on the bed. Her back was knotted. The bathroom door didn't close all the way. She worked her hands over her tense neck muscles as she stepped into the shower. She unwrapped a bar of complimentary soap and let the cool spray hit her. The shower stall smelled of other people, and the tiled floor was spotted here and there with mold. How well did they clean these places, anyway? She avoided rubbing up against the milky glass doors when a sharp tepid spray hit her in the face. She lathered herself all over, hands circling her skin, and hoped that by the time she was done, things would have magically righted themselves again.

With a gathering sense of optimism, she stepped out of the shower and dried herself off with a terry-cloth bath towel, then put on the extra-large T-shirt she used as a nightgown. Constantly aware of Anna all along the edges of herself, Daisy collapsed back in bed, her heart racing, and had a hopeful image of her sister taking refuge in some local homeless shelter or halfway house. Once or twice a year back in Edgewater, after she and Lily had had a particularly nasty fight, Anna would freak out and disappear. But they always knew where to look for her— at her best friend Maranda's house, or else the Edgewater

Presbyterian Church or the local battered-women's shelter. Anna always showed up eventually, like a cat.

Soon Daisy was sound asleep, dreaming of the flight out to Los Angeles, of the dark earth below and the man seated next to her. *Bram. Short for Bramwell.* In her dream, he grew horns, and the peanuts he offered her looked like miniature penises.

She woke up in a clammy sweat. It was dark outside, still the middle of the night. She switched on her bedside lamp and stretched, contrasting the paleness of her skin with the dark blue of the motel wall. There was a pattern of miniature gold anchors on the blue background. She'd always envied her sister's close relationship with their mother. Lily and Anna had to have the biggest case of love-hate Daisy'd ever seen. She was always getting caught in the middle of their feuds and taking frantic phone calls from first one, then the other. *She's doing this, she did that, she said blah, blah, blah.* Still, Daisy envied their bond. Sometimes she felt as if her entire life had been swallowed up by Anna's problems. *How's Anna? What're we going to do about Anna? What's wrong with Anna?* From the time she was eight or nine years old, ad nauseam, ad infinitum, Daisy and Lily had rarely had a conversation that didn't somehow revolve around her.

Suddenly thirsty, she remembered the soda machine in the front office and got out of bed. Pulling on a pair of jeans, Daisy left the security of her cabin for the vastness of the hot, muggy night. She'd once heard that Los Angeles was seventy suburbs in search of a city, and she was somewhere in the middle of that lostness now, surrounded by concrete and glass. Out here, everything was called something-wood. *Brentwood, Hollywood, Inglewood.* And where were these so-called woods? All she saw were two rows of palm trees running along the spine of Santa Monica Boulevard, swaying in the balmy breeze. The palm trees, stamped against the night sky, reminded her of movie props. Back in Boston, it was probably snowing, the New England sky dropping more and more inches, as if it wanted to obliterate spring.

The front office behind the Moorish-style fence and plastic-webbed lawn chairs was brightly lit. "Hello?" Daisy said, but the place was empty. She found the soda machine, inserted a few quarters, and out clunked a can of ginger ale. On her way back to her cabin, the asphalt's warmth surprised her. She padded along in her bare feet while a Buick Regal drove past, casting a large shadow over the motel's facade. Her own shadow grew like a cornstalk, then slid sideways in the headlights' glare as the car sped up the boulevard. These shadows were reborn again as another car drove past, detritus stirring and skittering in its wake.

Back inside the false security of her cabin, Daisy took a seat in a moldy-feeling armchair and drank her soda, gripped by an undefined panic. There was nothing to do now but wait. She rubbed her shivering arms. It was too early to call Lily. She had to fix her eyes on something. Anything. Fear was a slippery incline. She turned on the TV and wrapped her arms around her knees. She had brought the smell of outside in, her molecules mingling with the heavy metals of this polluted city.

2.

The next morning, Daisy woke up in a strange place and stared at the nautical wallpaper a full minute before finally remembering where she was. She was in the cheesiest motel in America. She assessed the ugly plaid furniture, the novelty clamshell smoking a cigar on the dresser, the plastic sign on the wall that insisted: ENJOY OUR BEA-OO-TIFUL POOL! She struggled to sit up, all the muscles of her abdomen tightening as if to ward off a blow. *Anna's gone. Anna's missing.*

She checked her watch. Almost nine o'clock. Time to go.

She hopped out of bed, got dressed and called a cab.

Outside, she could feel a sweat breaking out on her skin while the sun shone in all the sleepy crevices of her face. A green and white taxi pulled up to the curb, and she gave the driver the address of the police station, then took out her cell phone and speed-dialed her mother's number. "Hi, Mom, it's me," she said.

"Daisy? Do the police know anything yet?"

"I'm on my way there right now." Fragments of light hit her eyes, the sun's reflection bouncing off the sleek hoods and tinted windows of too many BMWs, Mercedes and Porsches.

"What's the weather like?" Lily asked.

"Hot."

"Really? It snowed again last night."

"I figured," Daisy said.

"How was your flight?"

"Bumpy. We fought the jet stream the whole way. L.A.'s huge, Mom. So huge and impersonal. I don't know how she lasted a month, let alone ten."

"You know Anna . . ."

"I've gotta go." She squinted into the bright sunshine. "Call you later, okay?"

"Daisy?"

"Yes?"

"I want you to know how much I appreciate this."

"It's okay, Mom. Love you."

"Love you, too."

She put her cell phone away.

The closer they got to the beach, the cooler it became, and Daisy started to see an abundance of T-shirt shops, tattoo parlors and sidewalk cafés. There were people out jogging and sightseeing. As they turned left onto Ocean Avenue, the glimmering Pacific came into view, its rough surf kicking up sea spray beyond a strip of sand. She was tempted to press her nose against the dirty glass as they drove past bikini-clad Rollerbladers and shirtless boys showing off their abs. She enjoyed the circuslike atmosphere of the street musicians and fire-eaters competing with acrobats and jugglers for tourist dollars. There was entertainment on every corner, bold murals airbrushed onto the sides of buildings, boardwalk booths selling everything from caricatures to knockoff designer sunglasses. A pink-haired woman with a large snake draped over her shoulders rode her bike dangerously close to the cab, smiled at Daisy and veered away.

After another mile of on-again, off-again traffic, they drove further inland, away from the beach, then pulled into an ugly minimall. "Here you go," the cabdriver said, stopping the meter.

Daisy looked around. There was a Thai take-out place, a funky shoe repair shop and a used car lot festooned with lime-green plastic flags. Only the swaying palm trees broke the monotony of the gritty, prefab landscape. "Where's the police station?" she asked.

"That gray building over there."

She spotted the square gray stucco building anchoring the northeastern corner of the minimall. "If you say so."

"Nothing is what it seems in L.A.," he told her.

"Thanks." She paid the fare and got out, then entered the nondescript building through a gray metal door and gave her name at the front desk.

Inside the police station, the HVAC system was antiquated and Rorschach water marks dotted the sagging box-beam ceiling. The desk sergeant told her to take a seat in the cramped waiting area, and she realized how jet-lagged she was as she sank into a maroon sofa and instantly closed her eyes, her eyelids scraping together like sandpaper.

After a few minutes, footsteps echoed down the hallway's black-and-white-checkered linoleum, and a man wearing brown slacks, a brown sports coat and a sea-blue tie extended his hand. "Jack Makowski," he said. He had a confident grip and looked like an aging surfer with his graying, collar-length hair and sun-weathered skin. Daisy decided he was the kind of man who, once he threw that switch, could be radiant. "Let's go into my office where we can talk," he said.

She followed him down the hallway toward a cluttered office with an old-fashioned clock on the wall and a metal desk buried under a New York City skyline of paperwork. Tacked to the bulletin board were dozens of Wanted posters—brutal, heartless faces gazing down at her. Detective Makowski cleared a space for her on one of the cluttered chairs, then settled in behind his desk. "So," he said, "tell me about your sister."

"We think she went off her meds," Daisy said, her hands collapsed in her lap. "She might've run away and—"

His old-fashioned phone jangled. "Excuse me," he said, picking up. "Yeah? Okay. No, I'm with her now. Yup. Bye." He hung up, then stared at her absently. "Where was I?"

"My sister," she said, heart pounding in her ears. "I was telling you about my sister."

He gave a curt nod. "We have three unsolved missing-persons cases in De Campo Beach, Ms. Hubbard. The first victim disappeared over a year ago. The second was reported missing just last week, and your sister makes it number three."

She reacted with confusion. "You think they're related?"

"We found bloodstains in her apartment. Now, please don't jump to any conclusions just yet. We don't know whose ABO it is. Could be menstrual blood, could be somebody cut their hand, could be from a previous tenant. These are minor bloodstains I'm talking about."

She heard a whooshing sound inside her ears as the far corners of the room grew fuzzy.

"What's your sister's blood type?" he asked.

"O positive."

He glanced down at the file folder that lay open on his desk. "Same blood type we found inside her apartment. So you think she stopped taking her medication?"

"I don't know. She quit therapy six months ago. There was nobody monitoring her."

He nodded. "We found drug paraphernalia in her apartment, along with some pot and cocaine residue."

"Schizophrenics have a tendency to self-medicate," she explained. "Sometimes they'll stop taking their prescription drugs and compensate by doing illegal drugs."

He eyed her curiously. "You're a scientist?"

She nodded. She'd given him a brief autobiographical sketch over the phone. "I specialize in neurogenetics. I'm trying to cure inherited fatal brain disorders."

His eyes widened. "That's pretty admirable."

"Yeah, well . . . I've been told I have no life."

He nodded knowingly. "I lost three marriages to the job."

"We're a pathetic pair."

He gave her what she considered to be his first genuine smile.

She smiled back.

"Does your sister own a cell phone?" he asked.

Daisy shook her head. "She worries about the 'radiation' affecting her brain."

"Okay. No pager, then?"

"No."

"And you say she's run away before?"

"It happens once or twice a year."

"Uh-huh. What usually provokes it?"

"She and Lily . . . my mother . . . will have a fight, then she'll run away and hole up in some homeless shelter or church or something. Anna's very into the drama of it all."

"So you think she might've run away this time?"

She frowned. "The thing is, my mother says they were getting along just fine. No arguments. No triggering episode. Have you looked in any of those places yet? Local homeless shelters or halfway houses?"

"Our resources are stretched pretty thin." He folded his arms across his chest. "Listen, we have your sister's computer. Who's Louis?"

Daisy's scalp jumped. "That's my little brother. Why?"

"Some of the files contained detailed information about her search for Louis's biological father. We were able to trace her Internet activity as well. She's been looking at lots of genealogy Web sites, 'fathering' Web sites, ancestry message boards and the like. Louis died of a childhood illness?"

"Stier-Zellar's disease."

"A fatal brain disorder?"

She nodded.

"We found a bunch of articles downloaded onto her computer. Articles you had written for *Genetics* and *Journal of Gene Medicine*."

"I didn't know she was even aware of them."

His eyes were steady on her. He waited for her to continue.

"They're very technical," Daisy said. "I doubt she's read them all the way through."

"Why would she be interested in them?"

"I don't know. Anna's very competitive. When we were growing up, she had to have the same things I did. If I got the latest Cyndi Lauper album, then she had to have it, too. My mother bought us everything in duplicate, practically."

"Do you think she's competing with you now?"

"Maybe."

"Do you work with rats?"

"Mice. Why?"

"We found three dead rats laid out on the kitchen table, each one dissected."

Daisy shook her head, trying to make sense of it all. "I have no idea why she'd be doing that, but . . . once she goes off her meds, all bets are off."

"Why would she be looking for your brother's father? Don't you all have the same father?"

"No. Anna and I share the same biological father. His name was Gregory Hubbard. He died a couple months before Anna was born. I was three, and I barely remember him."

"But your brother had a different father? And you don't know his name?"

She nodded. "It's a big secret in our house."

"Your mother never told you?"

"No."

He squinted. "Why not?"

"I don't know. You'd have to ask her."

"Do you suppose Anna moved out to L.A. in order to search for Louis's biological father?"

"I don't know." Daisy groaned, her head beginning to hurt. It was a massive struggle just to think straight. "Look, can I be honest with you? All I want to do is go back to Boston and continue my research. I want to get back to work . . . I can't believe this is happening . . ." The air filled with insects, neon-winged insects flurrying into her face, and then everything went black.

Daisy woke up moments later on the detective's over-size pearl-gray sofa. On the wall above her head was a detailed map of De Campo Beach, with multicolored pushpins identifying various crime hot spots. "What happened?" she said.

"Shh. Just relax. You passed out."

She tried to sit up, but he stopped her.

"Here. Have some water." He handed her a glass, and she took a sip, her head banging like a gong. "I know this must be quite a shock . . ."

"I don't faint," she said angrily. "I'm not a fainter. Not even in medical school when we had to dissect corpses."

His eyes were kind. "Drink," he said. "You're probably dehydrated from the flight."

She sipped some water, then said, "How long have you been a detective?"

"Fourteen years of service. Five in uniform, two in vice, seven in homicide. I got my bachelor of science degree in law enforcement from USC and graduated from the FBI National Academy. Those are my diplomas."

She glanced at the framed diplomas on the wall. "FBI, huh?"

"Take a deep breath," he said. "Try and relax."

She did as she was told. She closed her eyes and took a deep breath, but it didn't make her feel any better. Her body remained on high alert. She opened her eyes and said, "You think she's dead, don't you? Her and those other missing people?"

"I haven't come to any conclusions yet."

She knew he was lying. Her fingers twitched.

"Look, I need your help, Ms. Hubbard."

"Please call me Daisy," she said. " 'Ms. Hubbard' sounds like a kindergarten teacher."

"Okay, Daisy. I need you to come down to the apartment with me and identify some of your sister's belongings. Do you think you can handle it?"

"No," she said. "But I'll go anyway."

3.

Detective Makowski touched his brakes at the bottom of Kester Street, then took a right onto Godschalk, where the brown lawns were dappled with sunlight. The Sea Breeze was flat-roofed and peach-colored with mostly pre-owned cars parked out front. Dead weeds hugged the building in those hard-to-reach places, and a dozen bouncy, smooth-skinned Hispanic kids shot hoops in the vacant lot next door. When their basketball rolled across the dead grass toward the walkway, Detective Makowski punted it back to them. *This is Anna's place,* Daisy thought numbly. *Anna spent the last ten months of her life on this street, living in this building.* Her apprehension grew incrementally as they climbed the cement steps and rang the superintendent's doorbell. After a moment, the whine of the buzzer broke the lock's hold, and Detective Makowski held the door open for her.

"After you," he said, as if they were on a date.

The blunt-faced superintendent greeted them in the lobby. He had patent-leather hair and spoke in loud letters, and Daisy hated him almost instantly for having failed to protect her sister. "She was a very nice person," he said. "Always polite and considerate. We had a tenant OD on drugs last year, but murder? Sheesh. That's never happened before."

"This isn't a homicide investigation." Detective Makowski snatched the keys away. "Thanks. I'll take it from here."

She followed him up a flight of stairs, then down a fake-plush hallway, where they stopped in front of a recessed door with yellow crime tape stretched across it. "The tech team's been through the place already," he said, ripping off the tape and fumbling for the keys. "So it's kind of a mess." He pushed the door open, then stepped aside.

Daisy paused on the threshold of a sunny one-bedroom and thought she could detect traces of Anna in the swirl of strange smells. The white walls were coated with blue fingerprint powder, and dozens of trash bags lined the front hallway, waiting to be taken out.

Detective Makowski located the thermostat and turned the air-conditioning on high. The blinds were rolled up, letting in broad patches of sunlight that heated the living room like a pizza oven. She couldn't bear the sight of the blue sky through the wide windows. Anna's blue sky. The popcorn ceiling was cracked and watermarked in places, chips of plaster dotting the slate-colored carpeting. It made her sad to think that her sister had been living under the illusion that she was creating a whole new life for herself.

"The contents of her mailbox were four and a half weeks old," Detective Makowski said. "The earliest postmark was February 21."

"So you think that's when she disappeared?"

"Could be. Was it her habit to check the mail every day?"

"Back home she'd practically ambush the mailman." Daisy drew numbly into herself. "Where are the bloodstains?"

"Right over here."

She followed him into the kitchen, where she bumped her head on a wrought-iron chandelier. It swung back and forth on its creaking chain until she steadied it with her hand. The detective switched on the light, and cockroaches scattered every which way. Blue fingerprint powder covered the backsplash, the windowsills and stove. In the aluminum sink was a pile of dirty dishes, all the water bled out.

"The place didn't look ransacked when I initially entered it," he said. "Just messy. No signs of disarray. No attempted staging of the area." He pointed at the floor. "We found the bloodstains on an area rug right here. It's down at the lab, being processed."

She felt an icy finger trailing up and down her spine. "Maybe she cut herself. It's so near the sink. Maybe she cut her finger while she was cooking."

"Could be," he said. "Does she have any boyfriends or lovers that you know of?"

"She's had plenty of short-term relationships. She was engaged for about ten seconds. Her problem is that she hooks up with all the wrong people. All these borderline sleazeballs."

"Could you make a list for me?"

"If I can remember them all." She followed him into the bedroom, where a double bed dominated the floor space. She looked around at the four walls and noticed a lot of small gray patches where many pieces of tape had once been, the white paint peeling in places. "Where's all the Virgin Mary stuff?" she asked.

He seemed surprised. "You know about that?"

"Anna has her obsessions. The Virgin Mary, angels, exorcism, spirit guides, documented 'miracles.' "

"Are you Catholic?"

She shook her head. "Protestant. We're not exceptionally religious, but Anna became obsessed with the Virgin Mary after one of her friends took her to Mass."

"When was this?"

"Years ago." She glanced at the ceiling and noticed the spray-painted message. "End 70? What does that mean?"

"I was hoping you could tell me."

She frowned. "A biblical reference?"

He shook his head. "I checked. There is no 'End 70' in the Bible. See over there?" He pointed at the back of the bedroom door where her sister had written *End 70* over and over again in pencil on the varnished wood. "Doesn't ring any bells?"

Daisy shook her head. "Her illness has a tendency to manifest itself in mysterious ways, Detective."

"Call me Jack."

She smiled, then stood moodily.

"Why don't you take a good look around and see if there's anything missing from the closet or the bureau drawers. Any clothing or jewelry or personal items she might've brought with her from Vermont."

The closet smelled remarkably like Anna—her smoky sweat, her intensely sweet perfume, that inexpensive fragrance that reminded Daisy of cotton candy. She found her sister's skirts and blouses and designer jeans folded neatly over their hangers. She touched Anna's motorcycle jacket, the soft black leather clinging to the shape of her. Anna's fuzzy bedroom slippers were grouped together at the bottom of the closet like the passenger list of Noah's ark—fuzzy ducks and lions and bears and monkeys, some so ancient and decrepit they had to be duct-taped together. Daisy slid the clothes from one side of the closet to the other, their various textures making it seem suddenly so real. People left their footprints behind them, their shadows, flakes of dead skin, strands of hair, acts of kindness, acts of cruelty. "What exactly am I looking for?" she asked him.

"The outfit she was wearing on the day she disappeared. I know it's a long shot, but maybe you'll recall some clothing that isn't here."

Daisy stood for an unsettled moment. There was an eerie silence inside the apartment. A lack. She felt as if she were floating between the real world and an imaginary one. With trembling hands, she slid the metal hangers from one side of the closet to the other and recognized Anna's silk tie-neck blouse, her gold cowl-neck sweater, the kiwi pin-tuck blouse and flax-colored chinos and those Nordic-blue corduroy jeans. She slid the hangers along the painted rail, back and forth, then said, "Her sundress is missing."

"Could you describe it for me?"

"It's yellow with a pattern of fuchsia flowers. The fabric is cotton with an Empire waist. I don't see it here."

"Okay." He jotted it down in a dog-eared notebook. "Anything else?"

She studied the haphazard collection of shoes—black leather pumps, baby-doll flats, banana-yellow flip-flops, orange Keds. "She had a beat-up pair of black Nikes she liked to kick around in. Five or six years old maybe. I don't see them anywhere."

"Good," he said. "What about jewelry?"

Daisy circled the room, her thoughts spiraling inward. Anna was a lot like the New England weather—wait a few minutes, and her current mood would change. She went through bouts of depression and periods of elation, and sometimes you couldn't tell the difference between her crying jags and the gales of inappropriate laughter. Without warning, she might smash everything in her room, but she never threw anything away, and consequently, almost everything she owned was cracked or chipped. Daisy had spent countless hours helping Anna glue together her ruined keepsakes.

Now she rummaged through her sister's bureau drawers, feeling like an intruder. Anna's bras and underpants came in all colors of the rainbow—mango, pale rose, salsa red, sunset orange, olive green. She opened the Hello Kitty jewelry box on the bureautop and said, "She loves big earrings. The bigger the better." She found the silver hourglass watch her mother had given Anna for her high school graduation; she found their dead father's insignia ring; she scooped up the cherry quartz bracelets Anna wore on her slender arms, the white bronze "believe in yourself" ring, the St. Jude pendant on its long gold chain.

"Hm." She frowned.

"What is it?"

"I gave her a pair of earrings for her Sweet Sixteen. They were these dangly silver feathers, inlaid with turquoise." She looked up. "They aren't here."

"Good." He jotted it down. "Anything else?"

A column of sunlight pushed in through the window behind him, and she could see the rooftops of De Campo Beach—a checkerboard of pastels shimmering in the sweltering heat. She was alone in her misery. She acknowledged this. The view outside the window was unearthly, a mirage of hot air rising in distant ripples. She could see the ocean from here, just a pale haze along the horizon.

"Her pocketbook," she suddenly said. "It's dark brown leather, a shoulder bag with a front flap and a magnetic clasp."

He shook his head. "We didn't find any wallets or pocketbooks inside the apartment."

"You didn't find a brown cowhide wallet?"

"No ID on the premises."

This gave her hope. "She must've run away, then. Right? She took her pocketbook and her wallet with her ID and some money and ran away."

He answered her question with a question. "Did she ever run away on foot before?"

Crestfallen, she shook her head. "Is her car still here?"

"Parked in the underground garage."

Back in Vermont, Anna's shitbox 1979 Ford Ranchero

used to pull to one side whenever you hit the brakes. The engine's timings were off, but she loved that car. She beat that thing to death. Last April, shortly before moving to L.A., Anna had sold it for a thousand dollars. The ad said simply, *Ford Ranchero. Runs. Best offer.* According to Lily, she'd purchased another rattrap in California—a 1989 Chevy Nova that needed new brake calipers and a front-end alignment. Different car, same problem.

"The vehicle's being processed for evidence," he told her, and Daisy's heart sank.

"You think she's dead, don't you?"

"Hey. I don't give up that easy."

She waved her hands in front of her face. "I can't breathe."

"What? Are you all right?"

She was staring at her feet, at the way her long pale toes dug into the sweaty soles of her sandals. She noticed the coffee stains on the dove-gray carpet. Suddenly, Jack was right next to her, one arm draped around her waist, his shoulder holster pressing into her side. The carpet looked as if it hadn't been cleaned in years.

"Let's get you some air," he said, guiding her toward an exit.

Jack and Daisy stood outside on the leaf-strewn balcony, inhaling the scorching ninety-seven-degree heat. She could see down into the street, where the detective's battered Ford Topaz was parked crookedly beneath a jacaranda tree. Funny, when they'd first pulled up to the building, Daisy had expected to see several police cars with their lights flashing, staccato dispatches emitting from their radios. Something to indicate that this was a big event. Her sister was missing. Anna Hubbard was missing! The world should stop spinning. People should pay attention.

"What type of meds was she on?" Jack asked as he leaned against the balcony railing and fingered his cheap sunglasses.

"A combination of antidepressants and antipsychotics."

"She was seeing a shrink, you said?"

"Until about six months ago, when she quit and didn't

tell anyone. My mother was still sending her checks to cover the cost."

"Is she in the habit of lying?"

"All the time." Daisy's knuckles grew white from gripping the rust-colored railing. "We haven't spoken in months. I've been busy at work, and frankly, her collect calls were beginning to hurt my budget. She always called in the middle of the night, and I have to get up pretty early."

He gave a resigned nod. "So you last spoke . . . how many months ago?"

Daisy shrugged. "Two or three." She remembered the last time Anna had called her collect from the West Coast to share the "important news."

"Can you talk?"

"What is it, Anna? What's wrong?"

"Nothing's wrong."

"You just told the operator it was urgent."

"I wanted to hear your voice, stupid."

"Jesus, Anna. It's two in the fucking morning," Daisy complained.

"So? I've got important news."

"Like what?"

"Like I'm going to have a baby."

"You're what?" She struggled to sit up. *"You're pregnant?"*

"Happy for me?"

"Who's the father?"

"You haven't answered my question yet."

Daisy didn't believe her crazy sister. As far as she knew, Anna had spent the past seven months moping around her L.A. apartment, eating ice cream and getting stoned. There were no men in her life. She couldn't hold down a job and had very few friends, and as far as Daisy could tell, she lived off her disability checks, Lily's generosity and a handful of credit cards.

"So when is the blessed event?" *Daisy asked with all the sarcasm she could muster at two in the morning.*

"Soon."

"Soon when?" *There was no response, and Daisy knew it was nonsense. Anna was lonely, that was all.* "I don't even know how to respond to this," *she said.*

"You don't have to, Daisy. It isn't up to you."

"Anna . . . are you taking your meds?"

"Pfft. That is so like you not to trust me."

"Well, what do you expect? You call at two in the morning to tell me you're pregnant . . ."

"In a dream, I said."

"What?"

"I was having a baby in a dream."

"You didn't say 'dream.' You said nothing about having a baby in a dream, Anna."

"What a grumpface. Why are you such a grumpface?"

Daisy rubbed the bridge of her nose with vigorous fingers. "So you aren't pregnant?"

Anna laughed. "No."

"It's not funny. I'll hang up."

"Go ahead."

"Are you taking your meds, Anna? Because if you aren't . . ."

"You know what? This is pointless." *She hung up.*

That was the way it always was with Anna—exhausting, confusing, pointless.

"I'll need a list of all the medications she was on," Jack said. "And a list of doctors she was seeing. Plus any other medical conditions or allergies she might've had. Any scars or tattoos or distinguishing marks . . ."

"She had slash marks on her wrists from when she tried to kill herself once."

"Both wrists?"

Daisy nodded. "She gave up after a few cuts because it hurt so much."

He opened his notebook and jotted it down.

Daisy recalled her sister's first psychotic break. Anna was thirteen, Daisy was sixteen, and they'd gone upstairs to the attic to fetch some old board games that their mother had put away the previous spring. *Boring games,* Anna called them. It was summer, a stifling-hot August afternoon, and the stand-alone fan kept blowing the hot air from one corner of the attic to the other. They'd propped the only window open with a stick in order to get some fresh air circulating, when all of a sudden a bird flew inside—a sparrow or a starling, one of those mousy-looking birds that was always everywhere, pecking at the grass seeds, darting across the lawn. The girls screamed and chased it, and after a while, the bird grew tired and clung to the dusty curtains. "It's infected," Anna hissed. "It's infected with bugs!" Before Daisy could stop her, Anna grabbed a tennis racket and beat the bird senseless with it, then threw it into the fan, where it exploded in a squib of blood and feathers.

Still, no matter how shocking her behavior, Daisy felt immeasurable sorrow for her sister—Anna's illness was punishment enough. It was her life sentence.

"Anything else you can tell me?" Jack said.

"Just that I have her diary."

"Diary? What diary?"

"I found it in her room back home. I was going to give it to you, but since it's in code, I thought you'd want me to translate it first."

"What kind of code?"

"Anna's Language. She makes up words."

"Like what?"

"*Sizzle* means 'sister,' *see-ya-later* means 'elevator.' Stuff like that. But it's last year's diary, so it might not be helpful. I'm sure she started a new one once she got to L.A."

"We didn't find any diaries or journals inside the apartment."

"Really? Maybe she took it with her."

"Okay. Let me know what it says. I'm looking for a total view of the situation. What was going on in her life before she disappeared. I'd like to have her dental charts, too, just in case." He removed his sunglasses and squinted at her. "When was your brother born?"

"Twenty-five years ago. Why?"

"Last week's missing person, Colby Ostrow, was forty-five. That means he would've been nineteen or twenty when Louis was born. Old enough to father a son."

"You can't be serious," she said. "My mother is sixty-three years old."

He shrugged. "Stranger things have happened."

"You obviously don't know my mother."

"All I know is, Anna was looking for Louis's father when she disappeared. We found a copy of your brother's birth certificate inside the apartment." He pulled something out of his pocket, unfolded it and handed it to her.

Daisy gave an involuntary shudder. The birth certificate said that Louis Hubbard was born on March 5, twenty-five years ago, to Lily Hubbard and John Doe.

"I want you to do me a favor, Daisy. I want you to find out who John Doe is."

"Oh really? How would I go about doing that?"

"Ask your mother."

She scowled and handed the birth certificate back. "Fat chance."

"It would save us a lot of legwork and pointless speculation."

She shook her head. "Look, I can clear this up right away. What color are Colby Ostrow's eyes?"

"Blue. Why?"

"What color is his hair?"

"Blond. Before it turned gray and fell out."

She crossed her arms. "All right. I'm ninety percent certain he isn't Louis's father."

"And you know this how?"

"Let's start with the eyes. It takes three pairs of genes to control eye color, a combination of dominant and recessive genes. Basically, when the 'bey 2' gene on chromosome 15 has a brown allele and a blue allele, the brown allele will be dominant over the blue allele. But there are two other gene pairs that can influence the outcome. Simply put, you only need one dominant allele to express a dominant trait, but you need two recessive alleles to express a recessive trait. My mother's eyes are blue. But Louis's eyes were brown. In rare instances, two blue-eyed parents can produce a brown-eyed child, or vice versa, but it's safe to assume that Louis's father had brown eyes. And Colby Ostrow's eyes are blue, you said?"

He nodded.

"Okay, hair color is determined by the presence of melanin in the hair shaft. Melanin is produced by pigment cells in the hair follicles. There are two types—eumelanin, which ranges from light brown to black, and phomelanin, which ranges from pale yellow to dark red. There are four copies of the gene for eumelanin in human DNA, and each one is found on a different chromosome. Each gene has two alleles—one producing melanin, the other producing no melanin. The more functional copies of the melanin gene you have, the darker your hair will be. The same is true for phomelanin. So it's a good bet that Louis's father had dark hair, whereas Colby Ostrow has fair hair. Of course, you can always dye your hair a different color, but that won't affect the outcome."

"Wow."

"More importantly, I can't picture my mother with a man twenty years her junior. I just don't see it happening."

His beeper went off. "Excuse me," he said, frowning down at the number. "Gotta take this." He left her standing on the balcony and ducked inside.

Daisy could pick up fragments of conversation: ". . . fucking asshole's circling the drain . . . I hope they fry the bastard . . ." Tough talk. Daisy wondered what he said about her sister when she wasn't there? Had he been reining in his dark sense of humor for her sake? As soon as she was gone, would he loosen his belt and become a tough-talking cynic again?

"Listen, I've kept you long enough," he said, coming back outside and glancing at his watch. "There's nothing more you can do. Will you be staying in L.A. for a few days?"

She nodded. "Until I find Anna."

"Okay." He ran his hand through his hair, and some of the greasy strands stood on end. "Call me tomorrow, and I'll tell you what I've got."

"Thanks."

"I can't share everything," he said, putting his arm around her and escorting her to the door. "But I'll do what I can."

5.

When Daisy got back to her motel, there were four messages waiting for her on the motel phone—two from Truett, one from Fiona and one from Lily. She sat on the edge of her bed and ate her tasteless club sandwich, going over the morning's events like over a sore tooth she couldn't stop poking. It was almost noon. It would be three o'clock back in Boston. She picked up the phone and dialed her mother's number.

"Hello?" Lily answered tensely.

"Hi, Mom, it's me."

"I've been thinking about you all day, sweetheart."

"I met with the lead detective. He's working very hard." Her clothes had looked fresh that morning. The air conditioner labored industriously, but the room was still warm. So warm she wanted to soak her head in a bowl of ice water. "I went to her apartment today, Mom," she said. "It was so depressing. I looked through her closet and touched all her things."

"Do they know what happened yet?"

"No. But they're doing the best they can."

"She'll get tired of hiding," Lily said. "She always does. Then we'll get a phone call."

"Mom." Her head hurt. She rummaged through the drawers of the bedside table, looking for a bottle of aspirin. "I think we should prepare ourselves for the worst."

"Don't be silly," Lily insisted. "Anna will find her way home. She always does."

"Two other people have gone missing from De Campo Beach in the past year. The police say Anna makes three. They think these disappearances could be related. Mom? The police need to know who Louis's father was."

"What? Why?"

"Because Anna was looking for him."

"What?" The upset in her voice was audible.

"She had a copy of Louis's birth certificate with her. She was trying to find out who Louis's biological father was." Daisy clutched the receiver. "I know it wasn't Mr. Barsum."

Lily sighed. "No, of course not."

"Who, then?"

There was a long silence. Then her mother started weeping softly on the other end of the line. Just the thought of her mother hoarding all her precious secrets inside that drafty old house made Daisy feel disgusted and angry.

"Mom, please. Don't cry."

Lily was making a clogged, constipated sound.

"Mom? The police have asked me to find out . . . but I really want to know."

"Did they check the homeless shelters and halfway houses? Have they tried the local churches? Are there any real churches in California, Daisy, or just those New Age places?"

She experienced a level of anxiety she'd rarely felt before. "You're not going to tell me, are you? Not even when Anna's life is in danger."

"Would you please stop yelling at me?"

"Nobody's yelling!" Her head hurt. "Listen to me, Mom. Supposing for a minute that Anna didn't run away, what if she needs our help? What if her search for Louis's father has something to do with her disappearance?"

"It couldn't possibly have anything to do with that. Why are you harassing me?"

"I'm not harassing you, Mom."

"It wouldn't make a bit of difference, Daisy. Not even if I told you everything, it wouldn't help you find your sister. Do you understand? It's completely irrelevant."

"Fine. I'm exhausted. I'll call you tomorrow." She hung up and noticed that her hands were shaking.

She lay down on the bed and closed her eyes. Her heart rate was right up there. She was afraid she'd pressed her mother too hard. She was angry at herself for not staying in closer touch with her sister. She was feeling guilty about the thing with Truett. She never should've have taken him home the other night. Yesterday she'd snuck into Professor Julia Truett's classroom and had secretly watched her work. Holding a piece of chalk, Julia flicked her short honey-colored hair out of her face with the back of her hand, a gesture both efficient and wildly appealing. She was funny and articulate, and her students burst into applause at the end of her lecture. Why did Truett want to leave her? She seemed like a remarkable woman.

Now the phone rang, and she leaped for it. "Mom?"

"Just me," Truett said. "Sorry to disappoint."

She collapsed back against her pillow. "Hello, Truett."

"What a tepid response. Your physiology should go nuts at the sound of my voice. Your face should flush. Your heart should do flip-flops. Your arms should break out in sweaty goose bumps . . ."

"My arms *are* breaking out in sweaty goose bumps." She was actually happy to hear his voice.

"I'm having a love affair with your voice mail, you know."

"Sorry. I'm having a shitty day."

"Bad news?"

"Nothing good."

"I wish I could help somehow, Daisy."

"They don't know anything yet. I'm just sitting here in my motel room staring at the four walls. Eating a stale sandwich."

"Sounds like a party."

"Yeah." She smiled. "Me and the minibar. Me and the complimentary soap."

"Careful." He laughed. "I can only have one serious discussion per day."

"Are you taking care of my mice?"

"Of course."

"How are the myelin levels?"

"Near normal."

"Good."

"If there's anything I can do, you let me know."

"Thanks. Talk to you later." She hung up and stared at the ceiling.

Daisy knew she couldn't just lie there. She had to do something. She took a shower, put on some fresh clothes, found a photograph of Anna she'd brought with her from Vermont, then took a cab back to De Campo Beach.

Her first stop was a nonprofit soup kitchen, but the woman in charge wasn't very helpful. "I don't recognize her," she stated flatly. "Sorry."

"Are there any homeless shelters nearby?"

"You might try the church on Pleasant Avenue."

She visited several churches and homeless shelters, but nobody recognized Anna from her photograph. Finally, an old priest with crinkly eyes pointed her toward the strand, where a large throng of homeless men and women were giving off a recreational-chemical vibe.

"They come here for the social services and the weather," he explained. "Lots of these abandoned buildings were damaged in the 1994 Northridge quake, and now we've got a big problem with squatters."

Daisy spent the rest of the afternoon wandering in and out of abandoned buildings and trudging up and down the strand, asking drifters and runaways if they'd seen her sister. The sand wasn't white like the sand of tropical beaches; it was pink mixed with chips of mica that made it sparkle. In places, it wasn't so much a beach as a sand-filled ashtray, with lots of discarded cigarette butts and a few hypodermic needles thrown in for good measure.

Nobody recognized Anna from her photograph, so

Daisy left the beach and headed north along the boulevard, passing bike shops and boutiques and organic
cafés. "Have you seen this woman? She's twenty-eight
years old. Her name is Anna Hubbard."

Most people were too busy to stop. Unable to concede
defeat, she strolled along the boulevard until she came to
the Santa Monica Promenade. "Excuse me, but have you
seen my sister? She's five foot eight. She has red hair
and blue eyes. Do you recognize her?" She followed a
crowd of tourists from Sweden and Japan down to the
end of the pier. Behind her, a little girl shrieked,
"Mommy, a bee stung me!" The sky was the color of a
blue party balloon inflated to the breaking point. Rap
music grunted from a boom box, and a teenage boy
swung his head to the beat as if the drums were pum-
meling him from inside.

Daisy had been walking for hours. Her feet were
swollen and aching by the time she reached the arcade at
the end of the pier. The large, open space was filled with
the sound of kids' laughter and the jingle-jangle of pinball machines. It smelled like the inside of a grocery bag.
It smelled of mustard and hot dogs and lemonade and
floor wax.

She approached a small group of teenage girls and
showed them Anna's picture. "Have you seen my sister?" she said.

The girls wore looks of intense disinterest, snapping
their gum and rolling their eyes.

"I have," the skinniest one volunteered. "I used to see
her with Roy all the time."

"Who's Roy?" Daisy asked.

The girl shrugged. "Just some guy." She looked like a

rag doll with green button eyes. She had terrible posture for a teenager, a tattoo of a Japanese character on her arm and green polish on her nails.

"What's your name?" Daisy asked her.

"Christie."

"When was the last time you saw my sister, Christie?"

"I don't know." The girl made a face. "Back in January, I think. She used to hang out on the promenade a lot, but I haven't seen her in ages."

"What about Roy? Have you seen this guy Roy around lately?"

Christie shook her head.

"Do you know where he lives?"

"Nope."

"Does he have a phone number? A last name?"

"I only know him from the promenade." Her eyes grew big and round. "Why? What happened?"

"I'm trying to find my sister. Would you help me find my sister?"

Christie wore a peach-and-white-striped T-shirt over purple bikini bottoms, and there were green streaks in her short dark hair. The green in her hair matched the green on her nails and the green of her eyes. "I don't know," she said cagily. "Could you loan me some money?"

"How much?" Daisy asked, and the other girls became keenly interested all of a sudden.

For fifty dollars, Christie agreed to accompany Daisy back to the De Campo Beach police station, where Jack interviewed her for about twenty minutes. Then a sketch artist made a composite of Roy based on Christie's best recollection.

When the sketch was completed, Jack asked Daisy if she recognized the man in the drawing. Roy had pock-marked skin, shoulder-length dark hair and the kind of bland, police-sketch stare that made her fear him instinctively. His nose was long and straight with slender nostrils. His jaw was square. His forehead was tall and bony, and narrow coils of dark hair wound down on either side of his head. He was just the type of powerful-looking loser Anna would fall for.

"I've never seen him before in my life," Daisy said.

"Can I go now?" Christie asked impatiently.

After extracting a promise from her that she would let him know if she ever saw Roy or Anna on the promenade again, Jack let her go.

"What are you going to do now?" Daisy said.

"Distribute the artist's composite to the media."

"But there must be other people who've seen Roy, right? Are you going down to the promenade to look for other witnesses? Can I help?"

"It's better to go through the media," Jack told her firmly. "I'll handle it from here."

She felt a burst of resentment and went back to her motel, where she got dressed for bed, brushed her teeth, braided her hair, then stood staring out her window at the courtyard. The night was very still, not a breeze stirring the palm fronds. The empty pool was all lit up. You could count the leaves floating on its surface. She took two aspirins and crawled into bed, then stayed up late reading her sister's diary.

Daisy found herself delving once again into Anna's troubled world. She needed a magnifying glass to read the minuscule handwriting. After an hour, she had translated several pages: *"I got that tingling sensation on the back of my arms, that stroking sensation like pussy willows, and I thought about calling Daisy again. I can't remember the last time we spoke. I miss her so much. She once told me that people are made out of the same things as rocks and gas and dust. But a rock won't curl up on the sofa with you. Gas can't kiss you. Dust doesn't sing you lullabies. I think Daisy needs somebody. I think she's as crazy as I am, in her own demented way."*

Anna tried to explain what it was like being her: *"My thoughts will split off from my mind and become these jagged pieces of glass that cut into me and torment me. They burrow under my skin and dig deeper and deeper, so I won't ever forget. It's like I'm not allowed to forget. Like I can never forget who I am. It's like being held hostage by my own memories."*

Often she focused on her obsession with Mr. Barsum: *"Where did he go after Mom found out what he'd done to us? Where is he now? He's probably still a bank teller. He's probably out there somewhere, getting away with things."*

Around ten o'clock, emotionally drained and still jet-lagged, Daisy turned off the light and went to bed. At some point as she was drifting off to sleep, she imagined Anna's breath against her cheek. The two sisters had once been so close they could finish each other's sentences. They sometimes spoke Anna's Language. They played *Monotony* when it rained. They shared *DNA secrets* late at night, whispering to each other from their twin beds. *DNA* meant Daisy and Anna. Sometimes they conspired against their mother, and Lily would feel ganged up on. Eventually, the girls grew so close they felt *close-trophobic*.

Daisy could picture her mother inside that big old house, lying under three or four blankets. Tonight the wind would be howling. The snow would be falling. Sometimes it got so cold in Vermont you thought you were going to die. You'd have to bundle up whenever you ventured outside and not expose even an inch of skin. A vicious twenty-mile-an-hour wind in the dead of winter could peel your scalp right off your head. She saw her mother's dusky, shivering form. Lily wore pale pink lipstick and a few swipes of rouge on her withered cheeks. She liked to read books and drink tea. She volunteered at the local hospital and had her bridge game.

Tomorrow, Daisy decided, she would call her mother and apologize. Then she'd contact a group called the Los Angeles Center for the Missing. Somebody had told her about it today. They helped family members print and distribute missing-persons posters, coordinated search teams and provided hotline services. Daisy realized she could no longer count on the police. She would go back to the beach tomorrow. She would find her sister no matter what. The blinking red sign outside her window kept waking her up with its fiery neon glow. It was as if the whole world had gone nuclear, only she was somehow safe. She closed her eyes and tried to drift like a leaf on the surface of the motel pool.

6.

The De Campo Beach crime lab occupied the first three floors of a drab five-story building on Thomasius Street. The building's facade clung to its 1970s veneer like an aging movie starlet clutching a makeup kit. The plumbing needed a major overhaul. The walls needed a new coat of paint. The fingerprint lab was located down in the windowless basement, a large partitioned space full of evidence waiting to be processed—everything from postage stamps to ATMs. The floor was sticky with chemical spills and covered with about a pound of dust.

"Did you hear about Bryner?" Ramona Torres asked Jack as she placed an eight-ounce water glass inside the superglue-fuming chamber.

"What about him?"

"Ha! I know something you don't know. Na na na na na na."

"Okay, you got me." He cracked the flimsy lid of his carryout coffee. "What happened to Bryner?"

"He quit."

"No kidding? That shocks the shit out of me."

"Exactly. I thought he was a lifer."

"For chrissakes, I stand in awe of him. Maybe I should quit, too."

"And do what?"

"I dunno. Have lots of frantic, wheezing sex."

"You are too hilarious." Ramona never wore her contacts when she was superglue-fuming, since exposure to the fumes might've glued her contact lenses to her corneas. Instead, she wore a pair of spinsterish wire-rim eyeglasses that made her look owlish and conceited.

Jack got a big kick out of Ramona's fresh-scrubbed earnestness. The rest of the techies who roamed the bowels of the crime lab were a grizzled, middle-aged bunch, but Ramona was young and unpretentious. Today her Gap jeans and tailored blouse were neatly pressed, and she wore a silver pin in the shape of a horse. There was a horse etched into the buckle of her belt, too. He liked that she had a horse theme going and wondered how long she'd thought about it while getting dressed that morning. Jack hadn't thought about anything while getting dressed that morning; he considered just throwing on a suit and tie to be a major accomplishment.

"The question is, Makowski . . . will you ever find true love with anybody other than yourself?"

"Speaking of true love, Ramona, when are we getting married?"

She had a lovely laugh. "You are truly demented."

"Oh, right. I forgot. You're way too 'edgy' for me."

"Do me a favor," she said. "The next time you get the urge to commit matrimony, just go out and find a woman who can't stand you, give her your paycheck and be done with it."

The superglue-fuming chamber was a large cabinet about eight feet long and four feet high with various access doors and storage compartments. Next to the control panel on top of the unit was a glass bell jar. The bell jar was eighteen inches tall and allowed Ramona to process smaller items without having to use the entire chamber, thereby saving on cyanoacrylate, or CA, also known as superglue. Arranged on a tray were some of the items Jack had tagged in Anna Hubbard's apartment the other day. Ramona had been lifting prints for eight hours straight without any luck. Most of the latents were "elimination prints," which meant they matched either the victim or others who had legitimate excuses for being at the scene.

Now she deposited a few drops of glue into a glass dish in the bottom tray of the bell jar, then secured and activated the unit. Two small fans blew the dispersing CA fumes throughout the bell jar, evenly coating the evidence. A latent print was made up of natural skin secretions—perspiration, sebaceous oils and dirt. Although the sweat in a latent print dried fairly quickly—making it impossible to trace—the amino acids could last for months. Since superglue had an affinity for amino acids, all you needed was a few drops of glue, any brand, heated inside an airtight chamber. After a few minutes of exposure, the dispersing fumes would stick to the amino acids and leave a visible print behind.

Now Ramona switched off the fans and vented the

gas. "Hm," she said, taking out the water glass. "Good palm print. Large. Possibly male."

"Is he right- or left-handed?" Jack asked.

She turned it over. "See these top ridges? The way they flow inward toward the body? He's right-handed. Definitely." She chose a dark red powder from her dusting kit, dusted the water glass and lifted the palm print off with a piece of transparent tape.

"Any fingerprints?"

"Let's see," she said, examining the water glass, tilting it sideways, turning it upside down. "Uh-oh. Looks like he wore Band-Aids, Jack."

"Shit." It was an old burglar's trick. To avoid leaving your fingerprints at the scene, you simply cut the adhesive tape off ten Band-Aids, trimmed them to the shape of your fingertips and voilà. Instant anonymity.

"I doubt he left any latents at the scene," she said. "Oh well. At least we've got a decent palm print."

"Which won't be on the database."

The fingerprint database of known criminals dated back to 1972, when the FBI first introduced a standard system of print classification. The National Crime Information Center served to expedite the exchange of information between most state and local agencies. Once a print was lifted, it could be compared to a specific suspect or else entered into a computerized database like the Automated Fingerprint Identification System (AFIS), and in less than a second, the computer would be able to scan a set of prints against half a million others.

Decades ago, when the bad guy was arrested, he would be compelled to press his inky fingers onto a ten-card. After that, his entire hand would be inked, including the palm. But with the advent of scanning technology, the old ink-based systems were gradually being abandoned, and now everybody used digital devices that took only fingerprints, not palm prints. Unless a convenient palm print scanner was developed soon, countless cases would go unsolved. It was a serious problem, since palm prints made up 30 percent of the evidence pulled from all crime scenes.

Jack's cell phone rang, and he checked the number. It was his partner, William Tully. "Hey," he answered.

"I got the results off that answering machine," Tully said in his slow, methodical way. No matter what was going on, he always had a smile in his voice. "Fourteen messages were from the victim's mother. Six were about the rent. Four were from telemarketers and one was a hang-up. I had it traced back to a pay phone on the corner of Third and Rodecker."

"What's at Third and Rodecker?"

"A car wash."

7.

The owner of Rubba-Dub Car Wash was a short, compact man with a moon-shaped face and a military haircut. Miguel Estavez shuffled from foot to foot, impatient to get back to his customers. "Yeah, that's him," he said, handing Jack the police artist's sketch. "That's Roy Gaines."

"Are you sure?" Jack had to shout to be heard above the roaring sound of the high-pressure hoses. On the roof of the car wash was a huge rubber duck. Beneath the ALWAYS OPEN sign was a coffee shop where customers could wait their turn while a dozen industrious employees vacuumed automobile interiors and hand-waxed hoods in the noisy bays between the divider tarps.

"Yeah, that's definitely him," Miguel asserted. "Roy Gaines is one of my best customers. He always goes for the works. Pre-soak, triple-foam brush, high-pressure rinse, undercarriage wash . . ."

"What kind of car does he drive?"

"Vintage '66 T-Bird, completely renovated. Black with a red interior. It's in excellent condition. Not even a broken taillight. I've done detail work on it myself."

"Where do you keep your records?"

"Follow me." Miguel led the way past the automated wash with its foaming brushes and spray nozzles. "How about a freebie, Detective?" he hollered, nodding at Jack's 1988 Ford Topaz with its balding tires and sandblasted finish. "I could check out the suspension for you, gratis."

"Nothing's more expensive than a freebie, Miguel. Just get me Gaines's address."

It was four o'clock by the time Jack had the search and seizure warrant signed by the duty judge. He followed a maze of quiet side streets toward Paradise Road, where the stucco ranch houses were built too close together on their narrow lots, the whole world wanting to share the good life. He parked in front of a nine-unit apartment house on the corner of Paradise and Foxtail, less than a dozen blocks from the beach. These units would be pricey. The sea breeze was strong and hot, and the apartment house was built wide and low to the ground in accordance with the state's earthquake regulations. Jack took the outer staircase to the second floor, where he knocked on a glossy white door.

Nobody answered.

He knocked again, louder this time.

It looked as if Gaines wasn't home. Jack skipped back down the stairs and found the landlord in his ground-floor unit. "LAPD. I've got a search warrant," he said.

The morbidly obese, ponytailed Silvio Fortunata barely glanced at the warrant before escorting Jack back up the stairs to the one-bedroom apartment. The fat man in painter's pants and a ripped *Zardoz* T-shirt looked as if he might be moments away from a heart attack. He huffed and puffed all the way up the stairs, then stood red-faced and sweaty in the doorway.

The apartment was as hot as a barbecue pit. On the wall of the front foyer was a poster of the ocean. In the living room, Jack noticed a dried-mud footprint on the floor. He could see the rest of the neighborhood through the single-pane windows. Flowering magnolias and Chinese bottle-brush grew in the exquisitely sculpted garden next door, and the lawn sprinklers were on. Gaines's nearest neighbors apparently failed to recognize that Los Angeles was in the middle of a drought, one of the worst on record. Various parts of Southern California had been declared water emergencies, so what were these people thinking?

"Yeah, it's like the laws of nature don't apply to some people," Silvio said, following Jack's gaze. He stood wheezing in the doorway and wore glasses with narrow frames that made his plump face look even fuller.

"He live alone?" Jack asked.

"Far as I know."

"Does he get many visitors?"

"A few."

"Could you describe them for me?"

"I don't pay much attention."

"Male? Female?"

"Have you ever owned a building, Detective?" Silvio said loudly. "I'm on the phone twenty-four-seven, dealing with sublets and vacancies and complaints about the noise, or else I'm fixing toilets and changing lightbulbs. To each his own, is my motto. Just as long as the rent gets paid, you know?"

"So you never saw any of these visitors come and go? He lives right above you."

"I'm not the curious type."

"Ever hear any strange sounds coming from the apartment? Raised voices? Loud parties?"

"He's pretty quiet. Like I said. My only complaint's the smell."

"What smell?"

"A squirrel must've gotten trapped in the wall and died or something. It's worse back there."

Jack nodded calmly. "Would you mind closing the door on your way out?"

After the big man had lumbered off, Jack prowled through the kitchen and found two forks, a knife and no spoons in the silverware drawer. There was a coiled length of rope and a rusty garden hoe underneath the kitchen sink. There were potted plants on the windowsills, mismatching dishware in the cabinets and a topological map of Southern California in one of the built-ins, along with plenty of heavy-duty trash bags. Jack counted eleven boxes. That was a whole lot of trash bags.

The bathroom's plumbing was old but in good working order. The tiles were Mexican-influenced. The mirrored door of the medicine chest had been unscrewed and removed, and now Jack stood examining the contents—a can of shaving cream, a package of razor blades, a pair of scissors, a box of Band-Aids. He shoved the mildewy shower curtain aside and noticed that the tub was ringed with flecks of dried mud and leaf debris. That was odd. You'd expect to find sand this close to the beach, not mud. Not leaf debris. He made a mental note of it, then went to check out the bedroom.

The bedroom housed a collection of gym equipment, an art deco bureau and a simple frame bed with a box spring and mattress. The *slush-slush* of sporadic traffic on the street below radiated through the open windows. The bulky weight-lifting equipment had worn grooves in the hardwood floor. About a dozen medical textbooks were stacked on a rickety table next to the bed. Sifting through them, Jack noticed that these books were decades out of date, from the fifties and sixties, with random passages underlined.

A decomposing body could be detected from ten to twenty feet away. Jack pulled out his handkerchief and clamped it over his nose, then stood staring at the closet door. A floor-length mirror had been removed, and only six screws and the unpainted wood remained. He thought about the missing medicine-chest mirror. Somebody didn't like having his image reflected back at him.

The bedroom windows were open wide, letting in a salty sea breeze that failed to mask the underlying odor of decay. Jack took a few steps toward the closet, and the smell became overwhelming. He kept the handkerchief clamped over his nose as he tested the closet door. It was locked.

He glanced around the room, settling on the art deco bureau as the most likely place for keys to be stashed. He opened the sticky top drawer and pushed aside a jumble of Jockey shorts and rolled-up socks. He scooped up the coiled plastic key chain with several skeleton keys attached and unlocked the closet door.

The stench of putrefaction was unbelievable. It was coming from an old steamer trunk pushed against the far wall. Jack tried the lid and found that it, too, was locked. He inserted the key, and the lid popped open.

He drew back from the smell. The body was in an advanced state of decomposition. Colby Ostrow was bent almost double so that he could fit inside the trunk. He wore a dark blue shirt, khaki pants and loafers—the same outfit he'd last been seen wearing. His face was discolored and bloated, the lips nearly black. The body was cold. There was some upper-torso rigor. The hands were fisted shut, a few strands of hair clutched in his fingers—medium-length gray hairs that probably belonged to the victim himself, not an uncommon occurrence in strangulation cases. Jack figured the remains were about forty-eight hours old.

He got on his cell phone and, with an impatience bordering on panic, waited for Tully to pick up. "Come on, come on." Tully was the kind of guy who would do anything for you, if it came to that. When Jack was old and dying, Tully would be at his hospital bed. When they were seventy and retired from the force, they'd go to the deli every day and have Sable 'n' Eggs and shoot the shit. They'd catch up on the Lakers game. Maybe they'd even have floorside seats. Jack envisioned that kind of thing.

He paced back and forth in the suspect's bedroom. "C'mon, Tully. Pick up. Pick up." He glanced out the window, a band of perspiration forming on his upper lip. The heat was making the asphalt glisten. He glanced at the half-eaten sandwich on a paper plate on the rolltop desk. There was a neatly folded napkin, plastic silverware and a can of soda. All the pencils were back in their pencil cup, and the paperwork was stacked nice and neat. Bills mostly.

He heard the sound of tires on asphalt and looked up. A vintage black T-Bird pulled over to the curb, and the driver got out. Roy Gaines stood over six feet tall, with dark hair and a waxy complexion. He wore black sweats, red athletic shoes and mirrored glasses. He locked his car with his keys the old-fashioned way, then glanced up at the apartment house.

"Shit." Jack drew away from the window. Too late. The suspect had already seen him.

Gaines took off like a shot.

Jack pocketed his cell phone and bolted out the door.

8.

Jack was sprinting southbound on Tripalo Street, beads of sweat dripping down his neck. "In foot pursuit of a white male wearing black sweats and red athletic shoes," he panted into his portable as the suspect rounded a stucco house about thirty yards ahead of him. Gaines had led him into a family neighborhood, full of gingerbread cottages with peaked roofs and dormer windows, where the tidy homes were backed by asphalt alleyways. Jack hurtled across somebody's front yard, kicking up scuffs of dust, then vaulted over a child's tricycle. During drought season, the coyotes would follow their prey down into the suburbs, where the delectable fruit trees and lawn sprinklers and swimming pools were. Jack was chasing a coyote now, a carnivorous animal. He sidestepped a lawn chair, then darted past a baking tennis court before catching sight of the suspect across the street.

"Hey!" He crossed the road, dodging cars and drawing his service revolver, then chased Gaines up a long alleyway, grateful for the shade of the spreading sycamores and cottonwoods behind the wood-shingled homes. The alleyway mounted a long, easy grade that ended in a chain-link fence. "Hold it right there!"

Gaines grabbed hold of the top of the fence and, denting the garbage can lids, hoisted himself up and over. He landed on the other side like a cat.

"Stop! Freeze!"

Gaines slowly raised his hands.

Jack slipped the safety off his service revolver and held the suspect's eye through the chain-link. Roy Gaines was tall and trim, wild-eyed and bristling with confidence, the type of tattooed character who, if he moved in next door to you, would surely scare your dog to death. His face was damaged but beautiful, as pockmarked as the surface of the moon, with prominent cheekbones, a straight nose and thin mouth, the aggressive line of his jaw disappearing into a strong neck and square shoulders. His upper body was impressive. He'd cut the sleeves off his sweatshirt in order to show off his biceps, and those prison-hard muscles made Jack feel like a fat, lazy toad.

"Don't you move!" Jack aimed his gun and saw the world through a lens of adrenaline where everything was a threat, even the California laurel bordering the alleyway. "Stay right where you are!"

Gaines showed no reaction.

Jack was conscious of everything around him—the willows and sycamores, the older tract homes, his shortness of breath, his racing heart. He looked up at the top rail of the eight-foot-high fence and wondered how he was supposed to scale it and still keep the suspect in his sites. He held the gun with a stiff, urgent grip and craned his neck, trying to figure it out, when all of a sudden Gaines turned and fled in the opposite direction, heading for a parallel street.

"Jesus Christ." Jack holstered his weapon and clambered up and over the fence, toes digging into the wire mesh. He dropped down, landing hard on his hands and knees in somebody's driveway. "Oof!"

He couldn't see Gaines anywhere, but the sound of footsteps rang out. Jack searched the shady areas between house lots, and after a moment, Gaines burst from the shadows into the light, his dark hair lifting in spikes and spines.

Jack streaked after him, weaving through the late-afternoon traffic like the skinny kid in gym class who had a lot to prove. "Police! Police!" He stabbed out his arm and flashed his badge while brakes squealed all around him. He dodged car hoods and narrowly missed a passing motorcycle before a BMW right-angled sharply in front of him, the distracted driver dropping his cell phone and screaming, "Is that why you became a cop? So you could cross the street anytime you fucking feel like it?" There was no forehead, just a disappointing fringe of hair and a pair of power shades.

"My heart bleeds!" Jack shouted back before heading east on Laurel, his feet drumming over the cracked asphalt as he circumvented an old man out walking his dogs and almost tripped over their leashes. The afternoon sun was high and intense, and the flesh of his face jolted up and down with every pounding stride.

Huff, huff, huff.

Thirty yards ahead of him, Gaines scaled another fence, dropping down and running through a series of backyards. Up and over fences. Seriously, who was this guy? Jack legged it past an audience of rusty lounge chairs and blackened barbecue equipment, then circumvented a swimming pool where a bunch of kids were having a birthday party.

Huff, huff, huff.

He stubbornly chased the suspect, refusing to give up despite his lousy physical condition. Too much Stoli, not enough spinach. A little kid spidered out of his way as he chose a parallel yard, beautifully landscaped with rosebushes and lemon trees. He crashed through the garden, crushing the magnificent birds of paradise underfoot, then flipped over a fence and landed directly in front of the suspect, his feet slamming like brakes.

Jack aimed his gun center mass and waited for his breathing to normalize. "Put your hands up," he said hoarsely. There was no fence between them now. "Come on. Up."

Gaines slowly raised his hands, his eyes trained on the man with the gun.

Jack liked it when they obeyed him. "Don't let me misinterpret your actions." He had the suspect pinned between an empty garage and a cement-block wall. The Spanish-style stucco ranch house was hastily constructed, and already there were cracks in the foundation. He could hear the suction of a sliding glass door, could feel a curious pair of eyes peering down at them from behind the miniblinds.

"Mind your own business!" Jack hollered up, and the window slid shut. To the suspect, he said, "Turn around."

A police car braked in the driveway behind them.

Gaines lowered his arms and moved calmly forward. Jack couldn't believe it. "Don't come any closer!"

Gaines took another aggressive step.

"Stop or I'll shoot!" he warned, speaking with the narrative speed of a two-year-old. "Don't come any closer! Stop . . . stop . . ."

Gaines grabbed Jack by the shirt and jerked him sideways, then spun him around. He landed a vertical fist to the nose that snapped Jack's head back.

Jack's hands scrabbled for a grip. Shots rang out, high and wide. Spent shells fell to the ground and pinged over the asphalt. Bluish smoke whirled in the air above their heads.

Tully came racing toward them. Jack had never been so happy to see this big, beautiful, middle-aged black man in his entire life. Tully barreled up the driveway, and soon the three of them were grappling.

They dropped to the pavement and rolled around in the dead grass. Jack punched Gaines in the nose, and the suspect screamed. His face was spiked with blood. His eyes were insane. Jack pried the gun away and twisted his arms around behind his back, then pitched him over onto his face and crushed his head so deep in the grass he imagined that Gaines could see the antennae quivering on a grasshopper.

Tully kept the suspect pinned while Jack ran his hands over his body, searching for hidden weapons. It was over. He tried to feel good about it. His mouth was filling with blood. He grabbed Gaines's left hand and snapped on a cuff, then reached for his other arm and wrenched it backward.

"Ow."

"Shut up!"

Once the suspect's hands were cuffed, a little twist could be torture. Easier to control that way. He would surrender to them willingly. Jack hoisted Gaines to his feet and recited his Miranda rights.

Roy Gaines listened solemnly. He had the kind of quiet stare that made you seriously doubt yourself. There were cloudy spots like bacterial colonies suspended in the brown irises.

Jack had a sudden memory of his father doing lines in his trailer while on location with *Freddie the Fuzz*. Jack was only seven when Dick Makowski told him, "Freddie's just make-believe, okay? I hate the fucking police. They're all on the take. And this show? This stupid show that you love so much? It's bullshit, Jack. It's ratings crap. Don't buy any of it."

But he had bought it. Despite his father's cynicism, Jack grew up wanting to be just like Freddie and the police officers he'd met on location, and now here he was, putting away the bad guys. Would his father be proud of him? He doubted it, even though Jack's job was to keep shallow, bitter men like Dick Makowski free from harm.

Tully wiped the blood off his chin and grinned. "Good work," he said, and that was all the validation Jack needed.

9.

Around 1:00 A.M., after wrestling for hours with her insomnia, Daisy got out of bed and stared out her cabin window. The scenery hadn't changed. The palm trees still looked freeze-dried. The pool was a blue bubble. The stars twinkled brightly in the sky. There were 200 billion stars in the Milky Way alone, the same number of neurons as were in the human brain. All those neurons, and yet nobody could figure out where Anna was. Daisy wanted finality. She wanted closure.

The motel phone rang, startling her out of this unhappy reverie. "It's Jack Makowski. We need to talk."

Her mouth tightened. She turned on the light. "What's wrong?"

"Can we meet in person?"

"What, now?"

"Yes. Now."

She understood perfectly well what he meant—at

least her body knew before her brain did. "Okay," she said.

"Pick you up in fifteen minutes."

He took her to an all-night diner, where the vinyl booths were the color of candy apples and C&W lullabies wafted from the jukebox. The tired-looking detective ran his thumb down a tall plastic menu, hunting for something to eat. There were spider veins around his nose and a hollow look to his face, as if he'd seen the inside of too many cocktail lounges. His shoulders kept slumping forward, and he straightened them every couple of minutes, and she couldn't help pitying him. He looked so solitary and serious beneath the fluorescent lights.

Now a waiflike waitress with a headful of split ends came over to their table, and Daisy ordered a decaf coffee.

"Is that all?" the girl said sweetly. "We make the best burgers in L.A., bar none."

Daisy shook her head. "No thanks."

"Sure you don't want anything?" Jack said. "It's on me."

"I'm not hungry." She slumped way down in her seat, the sound of her own voice grating on her nerves.

"Apple pie a la mode," Jack told the waitress, handing the menu back. "I like my coffee strong. Espresso if you have it, three shots with lots of cream." He folded his hands on the place mat. His brow was lined with tension above a pair of deep-set eyes. His mouth was wide and fleshy, and his nose curved in at the tip, leading to a strangely sculpted upper lip. She liked his upper lip. It was soft and vulnerable-looking, in contrast to his tough-guy stance. "So," he said, "we arrested a suspect today."

She nodded, in a heightened state of alert.

"I'm gonna be up-front with you," he said, assuming an authoritative air. "A case is considered cleared when the D.A. files murder charges and the suspect is in custody. Roy Gaines is being held on several charges, including first-degree murder."

She tried to stay focused. "First-degree murder?"

"The body of Colby Ostrow was found inside a steamer trunk in Gaines's apartment. Now what we've done is, we've questioned him extensively about your sister, and he . . ."

The waitress delivered their orders and took her time rearranging the cream and sugar on the table. She smiled flirtatiously at Jack while the seconds ticked past with excruciating slowness.

After she'd sashayed away, Jack said, "So . . . I had a talk with Gaines."

Daisy inhaled sharply, the room beginning to lose its hard edges. "And?"

"He told me that he was willing to take us to your sister's grave." He reached for her hand. "I wanted to tell you in person."

She fought off a wave of seasickness. "Her *grave*?"

"I'm sorry, Daisy."

Garth Brooks faded from the jukebox, only to be replaced by a loud humming sound in her ears. "You mean . . . he killed her? Roy Gaines killed my sister?"

"Now, wait a minute. He didn't say he killed her, not in so many words. But he's agreed to take us to her grave, just as long as . . ." He paused to search her face. "As long as you accompany us."

"What?"

"Don't worry, Daisy. You'll be well protected."

She couldn't escape the terror that was grinding away inside of her now. She stared at a sign on the wall that promised pancakes the size of your head. The after-club crowd was beginning to fill the diner, an eclectic group of drifters with body piercings and multicolored hair. "Wait a minute," she said, his words not quite catching up to her reality. "Wait a minute . . ."

"You'll be protected every step of the way."

"Where is this grave?"

"Somewhere in the Angeles National Forest."

"And he killed her?" She clutched herself in a fretful hug. "My sister's dead?"

"He didn't exactly confess to killing her . . . but he's willing to show us where the body's buried. He wants credit for the information. It's a legal maneuver. He gets brownie points for cooperating. Everybody wants to avoid the death penalty."

She could feel pins and needles in the extremities of her body. "Why me?" she asked desperately. "Why does he want me there?"

"Because, for whatever twisted reason . . . that's the deal. It's what he wants. Believe me, he won't cooperate otherwise."

"But this could be a trick, right? What if she's still alive?"

"Daisy . . ."

She could hear him breathing steadily through his nose, could sense his eyes following her when she wasn't looking. She heard the fabric move on his body, felt the tension in his muscles as he took out a mug shot and showed it to her. "Take another look. Do you recognize him at all?"

She silently counted to ten before she studied the black-and-white photograph. It was slightly different from the police artist's sketch, but the same basic features were there—the prominent brow, the thin, well-defined lips, those oddly unresponsive eyes. It was the eyes that made him inhuman, she decided. What animal did he resemble? What animal could do this? "No," she told Jack, handing it back. "I don't recognize him."

"Okay." He slipped the mug shot into his shirt pocket. "Look," he said softly, "I want to end your vigil. Bring peace to you and your mother. I'll be there the whole time. Plenty of other detectives will be there. There's absolutely nothing for you to worry about, Daisy. You'll be surrounded by armed officers."

"But what does he want from me?" she almost shrieked.

A few heads turned.

Jack held her hand, his grip firm but comforting. "Look, I've appealed to his sense of decency. I've told him that you and your mom deserve closure."

"And that's when he confessed?"

"He didn't exactly confess, but yeah . . . that's when he agreed to show us to her grave."

She couldn't breathe. She needed to focus on her air intake. "So where is this place? This forest?"

"Northeast of here, in the mountains above the suburbs."

"But . . . he could be lying, right? It's possible she's

still alive, isn't it?" She gazed at him for a puzzled moment. "You just said . . ."

"Look, let me lay it all out for you. We've asked for help from the L.A. Sheriff's Department. They sent out a search team about an hour ago, along with some tracker dogs. We've got the forest rangers involved. This is a multiple-agency investigation now. Believe me, there are plenty of people out there right now looking for your sister."

"Can I go with them?"

"No. I don't want you involved at this juncture."

"Why not?"

"Because the tracker dogs might pick up your scent."

Her pulse would not slow down. "Can't you make him tell you where she is? Can't you force him to?"

He shook his head. His clothes were very practical-looking—sneakers and jeans and a cotton T-shirt with sweat rings under the arms. "Doesn't work that way," he said.

"Why not?"

"Because this is his call. It's his show, however much I hate that. And believe me, I can be pretty persuasive. But unless we get lucky tonight, this is as good as it gets. He'll take us there tomorrow morning. That's the deal."

"I don't give a shit." She threw down her napkin. "I want to go looking for her."

He leaned forward. "This is difficult terrain we're talking about. A vast area. There's some concern for people's safety. Like I said, three different agencies are coordinating their efforts. Trust me, Daisy, we all want to find your sister tonight. But we may not be that lucky. Come on now. Eat something. You'll need your strength.

I'm picking you up at four-thirty. We'll get there around dawn tomorrow."

She tried to swallow, but her swallowing mechanism wasn't working right. "How is he getting there?" she asked.

"Gaines? By helicopter." Jack dug into his apple pie. "Mm. Sure you don't want a bite?"

She stared at him. How could he be hungry at a time like this? He stored food in his cheeks like a squirrel. She could feel her whole body twitching with adrenaline. "You never told me how he killed his other victim," she said.

He shook his head.

"Tell me."

He reached for her hand. "Not for you to know."

She didn't speak. She felt humiliated.

"You don't want that inside your head. Trust me."

"Did he stab him? Shoot him? What?"

"Look, in truth . . . we won't know until we've found the body . . . you know what I'm saying?"

She realized she was shivering and sweating at the same time. Her arms felt as weightless as prosthetics. "I want to see her."

"Excuse me?"

"When we find the body. I want to see her."

He nodded. "We'll need you to ID her."

"And don't let him get anywhere near me."

"Don't worry," he said. "I won't let that prick within thirty yards."

10.

Waiting for 4:00 A.M. to roll around was like waiting for granite to form. Just minutes before her travel alarm clock was set to go off, Daisy crawled out of bed and snapped open the blinds. The sun wouldn't rise for another two hours, and the predawn sky was dark. She could see Venus, the brightest of all the planets, glimmering beside the waning crescent moon. Only one side of the moon was visible, since the earth's gravity held it fast and kept it from displaying all its faces. This phenomenon was called captured rotation. Daisy sympathized with the moon. She felt captured forever in the gravitational pull of her sister's planet-size drama.

She needed a gallon of coffee just to prop her eyes open. She made a cup of instant, then got dressed in shorts and a T-shirt and sat on the edge of her bed, sipping terrible-tasting coffee until Jack picked her up at 4:30 and they headed east into the rising sun. They rode along in silence while the sky gradually faded from deep purple to a windswept pink along the horizon. Daisy put on a pair of dark glasses to hide her red-rimmed eyes.

"How're you holding up?" he asked. "You holding up okay?"

She nodded.

"It's not anybody who would do this, you know. Takes a brave person."

"I don't feel so brave." She stared out the window and tried to shrug off this encroaching, surreal uneasiness. She was beginning to get a sense of the vastness of L.A. The freeway was twelve lanes wide and mostly free of traffic this morning, but she could picture the bumper-to-bumper nightmares that probably occurred here every day, huge traffic jams that loaned the air its opaque quality.

She swept her hair off her neck into a loose bun—the temperature was already in the eighties, despite the early hour. As the sun rose steadily above the horizon, the stars blinked out like distant cars rounding a bend. "It's so hot already."

"By noon, it'll reach the mid-nineties," Jack told her.

"The radio mentioned something about a drought."

"Driest year in Southern California in a century. We've had less than a third of our normal rainfall. It's affecting everything, except for the lawn sprinklers in Beverly Hills."

She knew she should smile. She shivered instead. *I'm going to find my sister today. I am going to Anna's grave.*

The 1988 Ford Topaz howled as they drove along, wind whistling through little holes in the rust. Mardi Gras beads dangled from the rearview mirror, and a tiny beer bottle swung from the key chain. On the floor were scattered maps and traffic tickets, rumpled paper napkins from various fast-food joints. The engine kept jarring her with its strident, mechanical sound.

"There are advantages to owning a shitbox." He glanced at her as if he could read her mind. "For instance, I can leave it in a vacant lot overnight with the doors open and the keys in the ignition, and nobody will steal it."

She smiled. "And you never have to wash it."

"Fender benders don't bother me."

Her smile faded, and she drew numbly into herself. Just then the sun broke through the smog, and she could see the snowcapped mountains in the distance, beautiful natural barriers that kept the suburbs from sprawling infinitely in all directions.

"We're almost there," Jack said.

The foothills were dry and barren, a series of twisting slopes covered with dead-looking chaparral. They finally left the freeway and took a winding route into the slate-colored canyons, where the waterfalls were dying. They drove past clear mountain streams that trickled instead of poured down the sides of the wrinkled canyons, and after about fifteen minutes they reached high country with its dense woods of spirelike cedars and pines. The serious lack of rainfall had forced the plant life to bloom much earlier than normal, and now a startling assortment of wildflowers grew along the banks of the thinning streams— yellow lilies with fringed petals, perky blue flowers, shy white ones. The foraging animals would exhaust the habitat if it didn't rain soon and grant this parched earth some relief.

At the Red Box Forestry Station, they took a right onto Mt. Wilson Road and climbed steadily uphill, past a craggy cliff on one side and a pine forest on the other. As they crested the top of the next rise, a dozen parked police cars came into view. Jack pulled in behind them while a hot gust of wind rocked the trees all around them, their crowns pitching and swelling like ocean waves. Perspiring heavily, Daisy got out of the car, and they walked up a slight incline toward a knot of detectives from the L.A. County Sheriff's Department and the De Campo Beach Police Department.

Jack introduced her to his partner, Detective William Tully, who stood leaning against an unmarked Skylark with his ankles crossed. Tully was overweight and balding, a big black man in an ill-fitting suit who reminded Daisy of a plump, sad-faced little boy. He shook hands with exceeding politeness—part of his technique, she figured. "How are you?" he asked with an old-school display of concern. "You doin' okay? You feelin' up to this?"

"I'm a nervous wreck," she admitted.

He smiled warmly at her. "You'll do fine."

"Where's the prisoner?" Jack asked him.

"Down at the ranger station. They just flew him in."

"So they'll be heading this way soon?"

Tully nodded. "He's waived his rights to counsel. The Sheriff's Department wants credit."

"Fuck." Jack drew Daisy aside. "I don't know how long this is gonna take. Would you like to wait in the car?"

She nodded, and he escorted her back to the car, so formal and stilted her body squirmed in protest. Normally, this dismissive attitude would've pissed her off, but now it just made her want to cry. She felt so weak and useless. He opened the door for her, and she slid inside, then wrenched her window shut. She turned on the A/C full blast and sat wondering how long her sister had been buried underground. One square foot of soil could contain thousands of insects and millions of microscopic life-forms. During a drought, these populations declined somewhat, but even very dry soil was home to countless bacteria, fungi, algae and protozoans.

She sat shivering for what felt like an eternity while Jack and the other detectives milled around, talking in low voices, their noisy portable units squawking like exotic birds. Jack stood with his back to her as if he were trying to shield her from something.

Now a string of police cars came speeding along the fire road toward them, four cruisers with their lights strobing. As they zoomed past, Daisy craned her neck and caught sight of a man in the backseat of one of the squad cars—pale skin, dark hair, just a blur.

Jack jogged back and shot in behind the wheel.

"What's going on?" she asked, her adrenaline surging.

"We follow them."

"Where to?"

"Wherever he takes us."

They roared after the other police cars over a confusing network of roads while a helicopter hovered above the foothills, its rotor blades whirling. They veered up a steep rise, where she could see a mass of mountains in the distance, jagged elevations riddled with turquoise shadows. They drove along a narrow ridge, then down another canyon; next they took a little-traveled road through difficult terrain, past pine trees and dense under-brush, until at last they came to a meandering fire road that wormed its way deeper into the woods. After ten minutes of bumpy travel, the armada of cars gradually slowed to a crawl, and the road abruptly ended. A cloud of dust rose up.

Daisy didn't wait for Jack to open her door for her. She got out, and they headed into the woods together while everybody else hung back.

"I don't like this," she said.

"Try to relax."

Her lungs would not expand to accommodate the amount of oxygen her body needed. The helicopter had followed them. It hovered above the treetops, then banked north. Ten yards behind Daisy and Jack trailed a small battalion of armed officers, casually dressed detectives and uniformed deputies with their captive in his orange jailhouse jumpsuit.

Jack held her firmly by the arm and wore the face of the jaded detective who wasn't about to share anything significant with her. He would dish out the truth in small, controlled doses, and she could see she was going to have to wrestle him for the rest.

"Why do we have to go first?" she said in a loud, unhappy voice.

"I don't want you to have to look at him."

"But he can see *me*. Right?"

Jack glanced back at the prisoner.

"That's even worse," she said. "And please stop steering me around, Jack. I don't like being steered places."

He released her arm, and they veered off the dirt trail into a bevy of golden wildflowers. "Watch it," he cautioned. "Tick heaven." They stood beneath the enormity of the forest while the contingent of law officers shuffled past. The man in the orange jumpsuit approached them with long, purposeful strides, and she could feel his eyes on her. It was horrible, as if he were pushing a pillow into her face. Daisy wanted to run away, but her body was frozen in place.

Roy Gaines was broad-shouldered, over six feet tall, with elegant, almost feminine features and black shoulder-length hair. She couldn't tell what color his eyes were, but they observed her with an unmatched curiosity. His gaze both frightened and appalled her. Two cops with rifles bracketed the prisoner, who was handcuffed to a waist chain. He seemed subdued, or rather quietly composed, as he strolled silently past them on a trail that'd recently been cleared of brush. Daisy swallowed back the words she wanted to scream at him: *What have you done with my sister, you sick fuck?*

He broke off eye contact and headed north along the trail while she and Jack got back on the dusty footpath and followed the others through the woods. She kept catching glimpses of the prisoner's Sunkist-orange jumpsuit in between the prison bars of the trees up ahead, her anger flaring as she listened to the sound of many feet crashing through the dry brush. The hike was unrelenting, the sun surprisingly intense.

"Where's he taking us?" she asked moodily.

"God only knows."

Her legs kicked out. The air felt like dirty milk against her skin. The trail curved to the west and crossed several dry creekbeds, then headed northwest along the wall of the canyon. Soon they came upon a clearing, where the prisoner and several detectives paused to discuss something. A negotiation was taking place.

"What's going on?" Jack asked irritably.

After a moment, Tully said, "We're taking a five-minute break."

Daisy hung back in a shady spot along the trail, safe in the shadow of the woods, while Roy Gaines stood out in the open with his face tipped toward the sun. He asked for a cigarette, his voice deep and lulling.

Tully pulled a pack of cigarettes out of his shirt pocket, tapped one out for the prisoner and tucked it between his thin lips. There was the flick of a match being struck, then a small flame illuminated the prisoner's face.

Daisy could see his eyes. They were shiny black like water bugs. Revulsion rose in her. "Why are they being so nice to him?"

"Shh, it's okay," Jack said. "Don't let him see you lose your cool."

She'd noticed the fire regulations posted back at the forestry station. Smoking was supposed to be restricted to an enclosed vehicle or building, or else limited to a campsite with a three-foot brush clearance. "Why are they letting him smoke?" she asked. "I thought this place was a tinderbox."

"He's cooperating, so we're cooperating," Jack explained. "And we're well aware of the fire restrictions."

It took her several minutes to get her hostility in check. The day was hot and awful, like summer wrapped in cellophane. Nobody said a word. Nobody moved a muscle. Roy Gaines smoked his cigarette and glanced at the towering pine trees while a meandering breeze ruffled Daisy's hair. The vastness of the forest was humbling. The hot wind stirred the pine branches, needles drifting down like snow.

Her stomach hurt. Lethargic bees just waking up from a long winter's hibernation buzzed in lazy circles around her head. The constant hum of the insects was making her nauseated. There were too many ticks, too many spittlebugs, too many flies and moths and bees and wasps and beetles and gnats. The forest teemed with life—not just in the air but underground as well. A spoonful of soil contained more bacteria than there were human beings on the planet.

She felt a vague apprehension and caught the prisoner staring at her again. Her scalp jumped. He was standing in the full blaze of the sun, studying her. It was obscene. His mouth was thin and hard, and his limbs were loose and muscular. He shook his head sideways, knocking a few inky strands of hair out of his eyes so that he could see her better.

"What?" she screamed.

Heads turned.

Her body grew taut with waiting. She was furious, heartsick, but Gaines said nothing. He just smoked his cigarette down to the filter.

"Why is he looking at me?" she asked Jack shrilly. She didn't realize her voice could get that high.

Jack's eyes narrowed. He turned to Gaines and said, "You gave me your word." He planted himself between them. "This is bullshit. I'm not gonna put up with it."

The prisoner held his eye. "I haven't broken my word."

"No contact means no eye contact!"

There was a dreamlike quality to the scene.

"Give this woman some peace, for God's sake!"

The prisoner said nothing. He tipped his head and squinted at the sky while the sun's rays slashed down on him.

Jack took a few steps forward and slapped the cigarette out of Gaines's mouth. "Break time's over," he said.

"Hey, hey." Tully crushed the cigarette underfoot. He made sure it was out before pocketing it, not wanting to leave any evidence of their rule bending behind.

"Break's over," Jack told the others.

After a tense moment, they got back on the trail and continued walking under the full blaze of the sun. After a quarter of a mile or so, they took a right fork that skirted the western edge of a meadow, then descended into another small canyon. Gaines nodded toward a section of forest that the park crews hadn't pruned yet. The trail was marked with little flags of orange plastic and overgrown branches. "Over there," he said.

"Where?" Jack left Daisy's side. "Off the trail there?"

Gaines pointed with his chin into the far reaches of the woods beneath the shadow of the mountain. A hot breeze stirred the dried-out leaf mulch at their feet as the officers and their prisoner left the footpath and moved in a northeasterly direction. They stopped beneath a stand of towering ponderosa pines, where the earth had recently been disturbed. Broken branches and telegraph weeds were crushed under a few carelessly placed rocks, and the soil emitted a repugnant smell.

Daisy could feel the air being sucked out of her lungs as she moved toward the lip of the grave site. *Oh, Anna, are you really buried in this forgotten part of the world?*

Several officers took out their emergency shovels and began to dig. Soon Jack and Tully joined in, rolling up their sleeves and bending to this gruesome task.

Daisy backed away, a bitter taste rising in her throat. She watched the shovels tunnel into the earth, and after a few minutes, a human foot came into view.

11.

Jack asked one of the officers to take Daisy back to her motel before they exhumed the body from its shallow grave.

"I don't want to go," she said. Her eyes were glazed, and her skin was translucent.

"You're in shock," he told her. "It's better this way."

"No."

He held her eye. He wanted her to trust him, not just now but in the future. Knowing how incredibly vulnerable she was made him feel even more responsible for her. He'd heard the low primal moaning of too many family members not to want her gone from the scene. "I'll call you later, okay?" he said.

A uniformed officer escorted Daisy back down the unmarked trail, and Jack watched as she disappeared behind the tree line. Then, sensing a commotion behind him, he turned in time to see two County Sheriff's

Department officers hustling Roy Gaines onto the waiting helicopter. He displayed little emotion as he glanced back at Jack, his eyes clear and seemingly bemused. This was no evil genius. Without a whole lot of pressure from the police, he'd given it all up—the body, the dump site, his connection to the victim. A detective's best friend was the perpetrator's tendency to brag. His desire for the spotlight.

As the chopper buzzed away, Jack knelt on the ground and studied the corpse. *Hm. Not much good news here.* A body outdoors in warm weather immediately began attracting hordes of insects looking for a good place to lay their eggs. At first glance, it would appear that Anna Hubbard had been moldering in her grave for three or four months now, since there was very little left of her but leather, sinew and bones. However, Jack knew that as far as dead bodies were concerned, looks could be deceiving. The state of decomp depended on several variables—weather, soil conditions, insect activity. In Anna Hubbard's case, she'd been alive five weeks ago, according to her mother. Five weeks, and this was all that was left of her. The maggots had long since crawled away from the corpse and burrowed into the ground, taking with them over 80 percent of her total body weight.

The smell was hard to take. He breathed in through his open mouth while Dr. Theodore Swanzy of the Los Angeles County Medical Examiner's Office knelt in the weeds and brushed the dirt off the victim's skull. Because the body had been buried during a drought, mummification had occurred. The twenty-eight-year-old woman's eggplant-colored skin reminded Jack of a wet T-shirt that had dried over bones. The corpse's skin was shoe-leather tough, and the scalp with its long auburn hair had slipped off the skull and lay coiled in the dirt. The hands had sloughed off their bones like gloves, and clinging to the skeletal fingers were bits of decayed flesh that the beetles hadn't run off with yet. The victim wore a faded denim dress, a bra and white cotton underpants. Her shoes were missing. In the folds of the dress were stray fly pupae that reminded Jack of rat droppings. A beetle scuttled across an anklebone, and Jack's heart twisted for an instant as he imagined her laughter. He saw her eyes sparkle. Funny how death could reduce you to nothing—all those dreams, all those longings, gone in an instant. How was that possible?

"What's the time of death?" he asked Ted Swanzy.

"Hard to tell." Fast approaching his seventh decade, Dr. Theodore Swanzy was in dire need of a nose hair trim. He had a face like a mottled paper bag and a voice as high and rasping as an electric razor from yelling at his medical students and residents all day long. "Judging from the state of preservation and the number of larvae I've counted so far, I'd say at least a month."

Jack nodded. It fit with the timeline.

"See this area of the victim's neck where it's badly degraded?" Ted said, pointing it out as if he were back in the classroom. "See this area of trauma around the throat where the scratch marks have opened up all this underlying tissue? Now, that's what I'd call prime blowfly real estate. A female blowfly will choose the quickest route into the underlying fat and muscle tissue. In this instance, they left the face intact and went for the open wounds on the neck. You can see that the victim's face has remained relatively untouched, because the flies have chosen to lay their eggs where the major trauma took place."

Jack glanced up. "Are you saying she was strangled to death?"

He gave a curt nod. "I'm guessing it was a two-handed attack to the front of the neck, where the maggot presence is most prominent."

An hour later, they loaded Anna Hubbard's remains onto the morgue van for transport to downtown L.A., where the body would be held in cold storage. After the van had pulled away, Jack stood for a moment and assessed the scene. The case had to be airtight. Never mind that the suspect had led them directly to the body, most criminal defense attorneys were sharks. They'd do anything to win. It wasn't so much about their client's rights or serving justice as it was about them winning a case and getting their faces plastered all over the six o'clock news.

The mountain's shadow had moved. Jack could feel the sun against his shoulders now, could sense the big blue dome of the sky beyond the treetops as he breathed through his nostrils, full of the stench of decay. The stink molecules clumped together, sticking to your nasal passages long after you'd left the scene. The only way to get rid of them was to sniff water, an old trick.

Jack knew that an official release of the findings from the Medical Examiner's Office could take weeks. Anna Hubbard's dentist back East was shipping her dental charts via UPS, and print matching could take several days due to backlog, but Jack wanted a positive ID this afternoon if possible. He left the tech team to complete its grid search, got in his state-of-the-art junk heap with its broken side mirror and rattling suspension and drove down the mountainside in the steadfast glare of late afternoon. Once he was on the freeway, he activated his cell phone and dialed the number of Daisy's motel.

"Hello?" She sounded groggy.

"It's Jack. Sorry to bother you." The sun reflecting off somebody's rear windshield stunned his eyes, momentarily blinding him. "I need you to ID the body for me, today if possible."

"Oh God . . ."

"Before we can proceed with an autopsy. I'd like to get a jump on things."

"All right," she said weakly.

"Daisy, I'm sorry about your loss." He had been proud of her; she had not reacted hysterically the way some family members did. "Meet me there in half an hour. I'll give you the address."

Everything gleamed inside the autopsy suite—the stainless-steel organ scales, the instrument trays with their sharp-edged scalpels and rib cutters, the cold metal autopsy tables. The Los Angeles County Medical Examiner's Office was open 24/7, and today every station bustled with preoccupied pathologists and medical students hovering over dead bodies.

"Busy week?" Jack asked the mortuary technician.

"April's the worst," he said with a shrug. "One good thing about the dead, though. You never lose a patient." Already a hard-core cynic in his Office of the Medical Examiner T-shirt, the young blond mortuary tech escorted Jack and Daisy past the autopsy stations toward the back door.

"Where are we going?" Daisy asked, her voice sounding leveled off.

"The decomp morgue." The tech pushed open a heavy metal door.

"Step right up." Jack held the door for her, and they crossed the loading platform into a separate, smaller building where the badly decomposed bodies were housed. Daisy moved gracefully past him, looking particularly frail beneath the sodium-vapor lighting. He could tell she was suffering, but there wasn't much he could do about it.

Brightly lit and recently renovated, the decomp morgue contained some of the newest forensics technology in the country. They followed the mortuary tech over to the cooler with its capacity for seventy-four bodies—double rows of thirty-seven refrigerated units. "Take a deep breath," Jack told her. "Don't think. Just look."

The refrigerated units were kept at one degree above freezing. A blast of frigid air hit them as the mortuary tech rolled a drawer open and unzipped a body bag.

Daisy's initial instinct was to draw back, but Jack held her firmly in position. "Is that her?" he said.

Anna Hubbard's mummified corpse lay pitifully inert on the cold steel table, her face a ghoulish Halloween mask. It took a few moments for the shock to wear off, but then Daisy shook her head vigorously.

"What?" he said, startled by this response. "Daisy. I need you to stay focused."

"That dress . . ."

"What about it?"

She shook her head again. The dress was sleeveless

with a pattern of tiny pink flowers on denim fabric. "I've never seen it before," she said. "I'm thinking . . ."

"Take your time."

"It's not her."

"What?"

"That isn't Anna's hair," she said, pointing at the scalp curled inside the body bag. "Anna's hair is longer and redder than that."

"Redder?"

"Coppery red."

He took out his notebook and riffled through its pages. He thought she'd said auburn, but he couldn't find it anywhere in his notes. He hadn't even questioned the fact that this was Anna Hubbard. "Okay, hold on." He examined the leathery wrists, looking for slash marks from an old suicide attempt. He couldn't find any.

"It's not my sister!"

It hit Jack all at once. "The bastard lied to us."

Jack drove Daisy back to her motel, preoccupied by a puzzling question. Why had Gaines led them to the wrong body? Was it a deliberate act of deception? Jack doubted the prisoner had gotten the bodies mixed up, since most serial killers remembered every detail of their crimes. No, Roy Gaines was playing mind games. But why? What purpose did it serve? They had him on two first-degree murder charges now. It was self-defeating.

The stop-and-go traffic reminded him of that old joke: *What do you call a car that's stuck in rush-hour traffic? A stationary wagon.* He glanced over at Daisy. He wanted to comfort her but didn't know how. Old jokes probably wouldn't do it. As his car bumped over the patchwork parking lot of the Shooting Star Motel, Jack realized he'd never been so thirsty in his life. His tongue felt like a dried apricot. He would drop Daisy off and go to Bugg's Place. Bugg's was a cop bar. Drinking was Jack's way of blowing off steam. He would go to Bugg's and get drunk and joke about today and talk about *us versus them*. Outsiders never understood *us versus them*. His three ex-wives certainly hadn't understood it. Other cops were the only ones who understood *us versus them*, and going to Bugg's would make Jack feel less alone.

Now he parked his car and got out and escorted Daisy to the door of her cabin.

"Would you like to come in?" she said, fear flickering in her eyes. "Just for a minute?"

Jack recognized the fragile state she was in. As a courtesy, he stuck his head in the door and glanced around the room—cerulean-blue walls, double bed, an old wooden bureau with lots of drawers, a minibar. He licked his dry lips.

"I don't want to be alone," she told him, standing too close. "I'm afraid."

A cop could so easily take advantage of a person in this condition. "Lemme check it out for you," he offered, stepping inside. "Then I've really gotta go."

The sun's electrified rays slanted into the room through the smoky, half-closed blinds. He walked around the room and opened the bathroom door. The shower stall was empty. The closet was empty. "All clear," he said.

"So where do you think she is? My sister."

He was feeling more compassion than usual. They

were both restless. There was nothing to do but pretend. "She may very well be alive," he told her.

"Really?"

It pained him to go on. He could tell that her sense of boundaries was beginning to unravel. "No," he admitted. "I doubt it, given the circumstances."

"But that's just your opinion, right?"

"Yeah. That's just my opinion."

Her rosebud mouth drew taut.

"Hey," he said in an emphatic way. "What the hell do I know? I can't read the future. I just stick to the facts."

"I can't stop shaking," she said, hugging herself.

"I should go."

She made a sudden unexpected move, leaning against him with her soft-swaying body, and Jack grew tense beyond belief. A heavy sweat broke out on his face as she touched the cracked leather holster underneath his left arm. "So what happens next?" she murmured.

Next was nightmares, loss of appetite, withdrawal from loved ones. The pattern was inevitable. But he responded evenly, "We're going to keep looking. We're going to do everything we can."

She searched his face. It was bullshit. He knew it. She knew it. She closed her eyes and gave him a lingering kiss, then drew abruptly back. "I'm sorry," she said, looking almost as startled as he was, her eyes shiny bright with tears.

"It's okay," he said.

"No, I shouldn't have done that."

"We're not supposed to fraternize."

There was a delicate, haunted look about her. He was puzzled by her behavior, by her inability to define her boundaries. He recognized the wide-open vulnerability of a damaged psyche, but that only made him want to protect her more. "Don't worry about it," he said gently.

"No, seriously. I shouldn't have done that." She rubbed her tired face as if she wanted to rearrange her features. "I'm just scared. I don't want to be alone."

"I promise I will find your sister," he said, heading for the door. "One thing about me, I am unrelenting."

12.

Daisy lay in bed, feeling sluggish and out of breath. Completely flat. She buried her face in the motel pillow, wanting to fall into a dreamless sleep, since only in sleep did the possibility of Anna still exist. She recalled her sister's snorty laughter, the funny words she used to invent, like *cargoyle* for an ugly car, or *eu-five-ia* (which came after *euphoria*), and she wanted to laugh. Her body grew tangled with emotion as she recalled her sister's violent mood swings, the way she'd get mad and throw things at the TV whenever *The Brady Bunch* theme song came on. When they were little, Anna used to ask her all the time why the sky was blue. It was a question that obsessed her. She wouldn't let go. "Why's the sky blue, Daisy? Why not red or green?" And Daisy, who didn't have a clue back then, would say, "Because." Just "Because." Now that she knew why the sky was blue, Anna wasn't there to ask her anymore.

The sky was blue because the sun's light waves interacted with the earth's atmosphere in such a way as to scatter the white light. Since blue wavelengths were the shortest of all wavelengths, a larger portion of them got scattered. Bouncing off air particles, they became visible to the naked eye. "The sky is blue because of the rejected wavelengths, Anna."

But if her sister were there today, she would've said, "I think 'Because' is a better answer."

The heat was unrelenting. Daisy told her body to move, but it refused to obey her brain. She was extremely bothered by this lack of response from her body. She lay there with her tongue exploring the inside of her cheek and scowled at the furniture, her anger twisting around inside of her. She hated herself for being so naive. The world was a dangerous place. She used to think that everything would be okay, but that was a joke. Life was a joke. It was funny what we thought was true. For instance, there was a time long ago when the scientific community believed that the atom was an impenetrable sphere, like a ball bearing. Now they knew it to be composed of moving parts—ions, neutrons, electrons. Daisy wondered what else people "knew for a fact" that would later be proved false and antiquated.

She stared at the motel walls, wanting to obliterate her grief. With an enormous burst of energy, she got out of bed, crossed the room and emptied out the minibar. Then she crawled back into bed and drained the little liquor bottles one by one. The combination of drinks tasted like turpentine going down. A fly buzzed lethargically past her head. Back in Vermont, during the summertime, troops of carpenter ants and stray flies would mysteriously find their way into the house, and Lily would become obsessed with killing them. She set traps for the ants and would run around the kitchen with a plastic fly-swatter and a can of Raid, smashing the flies against the white walls. The girls would snicker while their mother folded the morning paper in half and swatted any fly that landed on the breakfast table, then wiped up the remains with a paper napkin. "Eww! Gross!" The girls would keep score. Mom 3, Flies 0.

Daisy swallowed the dregs of the last bottle like medicine, then pulled the covers over her head and closed her eyes.

TWENTY-TWO
YEARS AGO

1.

From the very first day that Orson Barsum moved into the house, he attempted to father the Hubbard girls. To love them. To nurture them. They could see it in his eyes, this repressed tenderness that went beyond a sense of duty or obligation. Louis called him Da-Da, but the girls called him Mr. Barsum. He was a big-boned, gentle man with solemn eyes and a five o'clock shadow, and there was always an olive-drab aura about him. After he'd finally ruined everything and had left Edgewater in shame and dishonor, Daisy's mother had told her, "You can never reap the rewards of love unless you accept all the pain and rejection and loss that go along with it."

When Louis was two years old, he began to develop many ticks that wouldn't go away. He underwent several operations and had to stay for weeks at a time at Children's Hospital in Boston. When he came home from his trips to the pediatrics ward, he was bald. "There are no words to describe what I'm feeling," Lily told Daisy at the time. "I am simply heartbroken."

Eight-year-old Daisy loved her little brother more than she loved anybody else in the whole wide world. Louis Hubbard believed in everything—the Easter Bunny, Tinker Bell, the Cookie Monster. He had a great big undiscriminating heart and loved party balloons and brightly colored toys and would listen to any kind of music. He had a cavernous laugh and would pat any dog or cat that came within range of his stroller.

It was Mr. Barsum who first discovered Louis's childhood illness. It happened the year after he had moved in. One night they all woke up to a terrifying sound—a low rumble that vibrated the beds and rattled the plastic beads on Daisy's bedside table. She sat up searching for her sister's shadow across the room. "Anna?"

"I heard it."

"What was that? Thunder?"

"More like an earthquake," Anna said dramatically.

Daisy dug her hands between her knees to keep from shivering to death as the rumbling grew louder and the whole house shuddered before finally settling back into stillness. Outside her window, everything was black. "Mom?" she called. *"Mom?"*

Their mother opened the door. "Girls? You okay?"

"What was that?" they asked in unison.

"The dam broke. That was the lake whooshing away."

"What dam?" Anna said angrily, as if she should've been informed of it earlier.

Lily swept into the room, smelling of mango perfume and coconut hand lotion, then floated past Daisy toward Anna's bed. Elusive as a butterfly.

"Will the lake come here?" Anna asked as their mother sat down beside her.

"No, honey. We're on high ground," Lily said. "It's the people who live below us in the valley who might have problems."

"I'm scared," Daisy whispered. "Mom?"

Her mother crossed the room and sat on the edge of her bed. She smoothed the hair away from Daisy's face with the gentlest of touches. They lived out in the boondocks, surrounded by rolling green hills and woods and cornfields and farms, and the lake down the hill had campsites and docks for boating and fishing, and every Saturday, Mr. Barsum would take the girls rowing on Mohawk Lake. They'd wear their soggy tangerine-colored life jackets, and Daisy would rake her hands in the cold black water while Mr. Barsum fished off the bow or else rowed them around. The girls would shade their eyes and search for fish in the water—schools of sunfish or trout that reminded her of sleek strands of seaweed caught on fishhooks. Sometimes Mr. Barsum would row them out to the island in the middle of the lake, where the painted turtles sat sunning themselves on the flat rocks and the black king snakes lay coiled in the grass like warm inner tubes. Frog eggs floated in the water near the shore, along with paper cups, which Mr. Barsum would dutifully scoop out of the lake, practically tipping the boat and making the girls squeal. "Why do people do this?" he'd say, collecting trash at the bottom of the rowboat. "We live in a throwaway society, girls."

"What about Hickory Street?" Anna asked now. She was sitting up in bed and had her sunglasses on. She kept her sunglasses on her bedside table, right next to her headless Barbie. "Maranda lives on Hickory Street!"

"I'm sure Maranda's fine," their mother said.

Maranda was Anna's best friend, a plump little girl with a wide face and turnip-yellow hair.

The radio was on in their mother's bedroom across the hall, and through the open doorway, Daisy could see Mr. Barsum's shadow on the wall—his silhouette and the rounded back of his favorite chair. Far away, sirens were whining. Their mother wore a long nightgown, and the ribbons at her throat were the same color as the tiny red hearts all over the flannel fabric. Daisy reached out to touch her mother's arm, which was the softest thing she knew.

"The dam broke," Lily explained, "and all the water rushed down into the valley. We're lucky it happened in the middle of the night when nobody was swimming in it." She shuddered, probably thinking about her girls getting sucked away. She parted the gauzy curtains and looked out at the blackness.

"Can we get up?" Daisy asked.

"No, sweetie." Lily tested her forehead for a fever, and Daisy reached for her mother's palm, which felt rougher than the skin of her arm but softer than a callus.

Anna had one foot on the floor. "Hey, Mom?"

"Get back in bed."

Anna tucked her leg back up.

Across the hallway from them, the radio was droning, while outside, the birds were singing like it was the middle of the day. Two owls made separate songs, and a moth brushed up against the window screen, pressing its whiteness to the wire mesh in an attempt to get closer to the hallway light. In the woods outside their house, a thousand summer leaves rustled in the wind.

Anna was crying now—her cries were always the same, soft and wheezy, like an allergy. Sometimes she swallowed air and got the hiccups.

"Lily?" Mr. Barsum said. He was standing in the doorway in his boxer shorts and nothing else, and Daisy bet a million bucks his feet smelled. "There's something wrong with Louis," he said.

Lily bolted out of the girls' room, and Daisy stared at her sister, who was standing on her bed with a frightened look on her face.

"Get back in bed," Daisy said.

"I am in bed, stupid."

"Lie down, numbnuts!"

Two shadows stirred the light outside their door while the thread of the announcer's voice unraveled from the radio. *"Louis? Louis?"* their mother whispered harshly.

Daisy kicked her covers off and hopped out of bed.

"Don't," Anna hissed. "You'll get into trouble."

"Shut up, pip-squeak." Breathing softly through her open mouth, Daisy tiptoed across the room and stood in the doorway, fear spreading in little ripples down her legs. Her mother's gasps were songlike, all part of a single breath. The bedroom across the dark hall was full of light, and Lily and Mr. Barsum were bent over the baby's crib, their backs toward her, and all she could see was Mr. Barsum's jerking shoulders. A strange sound came from his lungs, like an engine that wouldn't start. *Sputter, sputter.* "What should we do?" he gasped.

Her mother's hand wandered into Mr. Barsum's hair, over his ears and down the back of his neck, the same way it wandered over Daisy's and Anna's heads whenever they needed comforting.

A bitter taste filled Daisy's mouth. She was afraid to move. It felt as if everything were suddenly busting up right in front of her; as if they were all cracking apart and falling to pieces. Mr. Barsum's shoulders heaved, and she watched the top of his head with all his thick dark hair bouncing up and down as he sobbed. She'd never seen him cry like that before, and she hated his guts worse than ever.

That night, they whisked Louis away to the hospital, just like the lake had been whisked away. Daisy felt a lethal ache around her heart, scared that her brother might be dead, only nobody would tell her about it. The following morning, while their mother was at the hospital, Mr. Barsum took the girls down to the lake, where they kept their rowboat tied to the dock.

At first, the trees were too thick to see through, but as they took jogging steps downhill, the trees began to thin out and Daisy could see that the lake was empty. Flushed. As they stood on the piney shore, she couldn't believe it—the lake was gone.

"Wow," Mr. Barsum said, scooping Anna up in his arms. "Would you look at that?"

"Is Louis okay?" Daisy asked him.

"He'll be fine. You'll see."

She knew he was lying. She wondered how he could be so strong and so weak at the same time.

"Will you look at that?" He whistled. "What a sight."

The wharf extended out into nothing. The drop was deep into water-speckled mud, and the dock's legs were black and hairy and covered in slime. Small fish splashed around in the shallow pockets of water, and way out in the middle of the lake, blue sky reflected off the remaining puzzle pieces. On the opposite shore, saplings shot up from the banks, their lime-green limbs bending over muddy drops. Plenty of litter mucked the lake bottom—tar-colored fishing poles and bright plastic buckets, half-buried flip-flops and boards with the nails sticking out, the red rust like crusted ketchup.

"Holy cow," Mr. Barsum said, taking in the view.

"It's all splashed out like a big bathtub," Anna lisped. She didn't actually have a lisp, but she liked to pretend she did for certain grown-ups. "Maranda's family had to wait up on the roof for the rescue boat," she said, playing with Mr. Barsum's hair.

He tested the wharf by jiggling it with his foot, then walked the girls out to the very end. From the muddy bottom came a strong smell. Dead fish floated belly-up in the puddles while live fish twitched their fins and snapped their snouts, trying to wriggle into the deeper pools of water.

"Poor fish!" Daisy cried.

"Yuck!" said Anna.

Daisy remembered how scared she used to be of the cold, dark lake bottom; but now that it was empty, she could see that this was all there was—mud and goop and limp plant life and everybody's dropped things. She'd never be afraid of it again.

"Should we go investigate, girls?" Without waiting for an answer, Mr. Barsum set Anna down on the wharf, his hand brushing her backside as he released her.

"Yay!" she said, hurrying back to Daisy, her yellow

sundress catching the light in between breaks in the clouds.

Daisy took her sister's hand, and together they climbed down onto the lake bottom, where the mudflats bore their weight like sandbars at the beach.

"Hey, look. Somebody's shoe." Mr. Barsum picked up a lady's white high heel. Next to it was a dead fish with blackened gills that smelled rotten in the strong sun. "We pollute our water, we pollute our air. Pretty soon they'll have to bottle the air and sell it. Maybe I should get in on the ground floor, huh? We could make a million bucks."

The girls had to struggle just to keep up with him, he was going so fast. More than once, they found themselves surrounded by knee-deep pools of water, where fish the size of Daisy's hand skittered and darted in all directions at the exact same instant together.

"What kind of fish are those?" Anna lisped.

"Sun."

"Huh?"

"*Sun*fish," Daisy said. "Well . . . maybe they're bluegills."

Anna made a sour face as if it didn't matter what they were called.

Mr. Barsum was moving away from them fast, striding across the lake as if he were crossing a big floor, his work boots coated with mud.

"Mr. Barsum!" Anna hollered. "You're going too fast!"

He stopped long enough to scoop her up in his arms, and Anna flashed a superior smile back at Daisy, who kept hopping from dry spot to dry spot, falling further and further behind. Her mother was at the hospital. She felt enormously sad. What would happen to Louis? They were heading for the vast middle of the lake. Daisy glanced back at the shore, the wharf very far away now.

"Mr. Barsum?" she cried. "Should we be out this far?"

"We can do whatever we like." He smiled at her. "C'mon, Upsy-Daisy. Where's your sense of adventure?"

Anna squirmed in his arms, but he held on tight and continued moving swiftly toward Turtle Island. He took long strides, and Daisy had to jump from mudflat to mudflat in order to keep up. The mud was reluctant to let go of her feet, and soon one of her sneakers slogged off, but Mr. Barsum still wouldn't slow down. He was on a mission. Walking through the mud was like pulling on and off a pair of winter boots, over and over again. Sunlight glittered on deep pools of water where the fish swam around like bugs inside a windowless room. Daisy could just make out their shadows in that underwater world.

"Mr. Barsum?" she gasped, her stomach tingling like a peppermint. "Can we go back now?"

"Shh. Almost there," he said cheerfully.

When they got to Turtle Island, they had to climb up a slippery bank that smelled of creatures dying in the hot sun. Mr. Barsum carried Anna onto the island, put her down, then came back for Daisy. She could hear him breathing hard in her ear as he scaled the greasy bank. Finally, the three of them were standing on the little island that used to be in the middle of the lake.

"Wow," Anna said. "Look how far out we've come!"

"We have indeed," Mr. Barsum said.

The island trees grew tangled together, and Daisy could just see the shoreline from here. Dozens of sunning turtles and snakes stirred all around them, and Mr. Barsum laughed as he shooed them off their warm rocks. "Hey," he said. "Let's go check out the house."

Daisy looked at the old ramshackle house, which the girls had explored countless times. Leafy vines swallowed up the windows, and the front door stood open. Mr. Barsum took their hands, and the three of them went inside, where the furniture was bleached of color and most of the paint had flaked off the walls. High school kids had had lots of parties here, and the floor was littered with beer cans.

"Let's go upstairs," Mr. Barsum said, and they climbed the creaky staircase together, then entered a bedroom that smelled of rain and growing things. Their feet disturbed the dust as they crossed the floor, motes of dust drifting in the sunlight, and they could hear something rustle in the walls. *Rustle, rustle.*

"What was that?" Daisy asked.

"Bats," he said.

Anna shuddered. "I hate bats!"

"Bats are good," Mr. Barsum told her. "They eat mosquitoes."

"Oh. I love bats!" she lisped.

"You don't love bats," Daisy groaned, exasperated.

Mr. Barsum cleared a space for them on the moldy mattress, sweeping aside the muddy sneakers and little rubbery things. After he had brushed it all off, he sat down and pulled the girls onto his knees. One for each knee. "There," he said, looking at them and smiling.

Daisy got so jittery she just had to stand up.

"What's wrong?" he said.

"Nothing."

"Sit down, Daisy."

"No."

"Okay, fine." Mr. Barsum sat there hugging Anna until her face grew very pale. Then he did a strange thing. He pulled off her panties and reached his hand up underneath her yellow sundress. He kept his hand there for a minute.

Anna's eyes popped wide open, and she stared at Daisy, who didn't know what to do. She just stood like a statue, frozen and silent, while Anna's mouth drew into a taut little bow.

Mr. Barsum reached for Daisy next and pulled her down on top of him, and the three of them lay on the musty old mattress for a while. The mattress smelled of pee. "Will you give me a kiss?" he asked Daisy, but she shook her head no. "Just one little kiss?"

She lay very still, barely breathing, and when he kissed her, it felt as if she were sinking, as if her pockets were filled with stones. His breath smelled funny. His lips were wet. She figured that by saying yes to a kiss, she had given him permission to do anything else he wanted to do. There was a butterfly on the wall above her head, and she stared at its huge false eyes, one on each wing. On the wall near the butterfly, somebody had written in pencil, "Promise not to erase this." All right. She promised. She would never erase it, just as long as Mr. Barsum let them go.

The butterfly flexed its wings and flew away, and the wall dissolved into the stinky mattress, and suddenly, Mr. Barsum's hands were all over her. His fingers were sticky. She felt stuck in his stickiness. Would she ever be unstuck?

Daisy could feel her heart thumping, her blood buzzing, her stomach bubbling as he touched her all over. She turned away and stared at the things on the floor—a dusty syringe, an old textbook gnawed on by mice, a beetle walking across a crusted T-shirt, a football spray-painted with a bright red *X*. The football was flat, all the air leaked out, and the stitches in the leather were like angry little mouths. *Xxxxxxx.*

Now Mr. Barsum rolled her over and planted a big kiss on her face. He tilted his head like an insect, like a praying mantis, and Daisy started shaking. What did he want from her? She closed her eyes, and her eyelids rotted shut. It felt as if she were falling backward off the mattress. When she opened her eyes again, all she could see was the football, something written on its side. *Wilson NFL.* She squinted at the pebbled leather—it was old and cracked and had a big hole in it. She stared at the red spray-painted *X*.

X means no.

X means stop.

Daisy rolled away from him, then crawled with frantic movements toward the edge of the mattress and stood up. "Anna, c'mon!" she cried.

Her sister was a scared rabbit, folded in Mr. Barsum's big hairy arms.

"Anna! Hurry!"

Mr. Barsum shushed her. "C'mere, sweetie," he said, but there was fear in his voice now.

She realized just how far they'd come and ran down the stairs and out the door. She scurried down the slippery bank, but when she got to the lake bottom, her feet sank so deep in the mud she couldn't move. She took another step forward and sank even deeper into the wet muck. Terrified, she screamed, "Help! Help me!"

Mr. Barsum came running out of the house.

Daisy fell forward into the mud, her hands disappearing like two spoons in cake batter. She was sinking into the lake. The lake would swallow her alive. "Help!" She wept hysterically.

Mr. Barsum yanked her out of the mud, and she hugged him gratefully around the neck. "Shh. You're safe now. You're okay," he said, but she wouldn't stop crying. She sobbed like a baby, like Louis in his crib. The mud kept sucking the footprints out of Mr. Barsum—*squish, squish, squish*—as he walked a few yards away, then set her down on a mudflat where it was safe.

"Stay here," he said, then headed back inside for Anna.

But Daisy didn't wait. She ran as fast as her legs would carry her back to the dock. She had to get out of there. She jumped from mudflat to mudflat, leaving squishy footprints. She was quick as a flash. Nothing could hurt her. Nobody would ever catch her. She was super-fast.

"Daisy!" Anna screamed, her voice echoing across the lake. "Wait for me!"

But Daisy didn't wait. She saw the shore, she saw the wharf and she ran. The faster she ran, the further away the wharf seemed to get. She tripped and fell on her hands and knees, then picked herself up, brushed herself off and ran for the wharf as if her hair were on fire.

"Daisy, slow down!" Mr. Barsum hollered behind her. "I want to talk to you."

She spun around and looked at him. He was carrying

Anna on his shoulders, and Anna had her arms wrapped around Mr. Barsum's head. His squinting face reminded Daisy of the worried look he'd gotten last night when he first discovered Louis was sick. She hated him. She didn't feel so brave anymore. She felt sick to her stomach.

Mr. Barsum let Anna down, and she ran toward her sister, and the two girls hugged, then washed themselves off in a clear shallow pool near the wharf. Anna splashed a few minnows ashore with her cupped hands, then watched as they flipped back into the water.

Mr. Barsum squatted beside them and silently rinsed his arms and neck. His face was beaded with sweat. He said, "You're okay now, aren't you, Daisy?"

She nodded.

"Here, use this." He took off his T-shirt and handed it to her, and she wiped her arms and face with it. When she handed it back, he said, "Don't tell your mother, okay?"

"I wouldn't," Daisy said, ashamed.

"Okay, Anna?" Mr. Barsum said. "This'll be our little secret."

Anna scratched her arm, lost in thought.

"Our secret. What happened on the island."

Anna nodded absently.

"We got carried away."

Daisy looked at him, at his lips and eyebrows and those big pores on his nose. He was strange. She didn't know him anymore. She took Anna's hand, and together they headed back up the hill. "Don't tell Mom," she whispered harshly.

"Why not?"

"Just don't!" She glanced over her shoulder. Mr. Barsum was picking trash out of the lake. He heaped things in a soggy pile near the wharf and whistled a song she'd heard plenty of times before. "In the Good Old Summertime."

When their mother got home from the hospital that afternoon, she didn't have Louis with her. "He's staying overnight. The doctors need to do more tests."

"What's wrong?" Daisy wanted to know.

"They think he's very sick, sweetie."

"How sick?"

"Don't worry. I'm going back there tonight."

"When's Louis coming home?" she asked.

Her mother put her hand on Daisy's head. "Will you do me a favor?" she said. "Will you be the woman of the house while I'm gone?"

Daisy looked away.

"I need you to be brave, okay? For me. Can you be my big strong girl?"

Anna came downstairs just then. She was crying.

"Honey, what is it?" Lily asked in a voice as soft as butter. She plucked a tissue from the box and made Anna blow her nose. "Louis is going to be just fine," she said. "Don't worry. We're all going to be fine."

Mr. Barsum stood in the doorway. He leaned against the door frame and watched them silently while Anna mumbled something to herself.

Lily bent close. "What, sweetie?" she said.

"My tummy hurts."

"Come here."

Lily hugged Anna until she stopped crying, and Mr.

Barsum went back into the living room. Daisy could hear the TV playing low while Lily lit a cigarette, puffing smoke rings thick as bracelets into the air.

Louis was sick for four long years with a rare disease that slowly erased him. He seemed like a perfectly healthy baby until he was two. Then the night of the flood, Mr. Barsum had noticed that Louis was having a seizure. His eyes rolled up in his head, and he couldn't stop twitching. When the twitching stopped, he couldn't grasp anything with his hands. A few months later, he stopped responding to certain words. Over the years, Louis's motor skills worsened, and he never learned to walk. The disease weakened him in slow increments, gradually forcing his head to one side. Toward the end, he had to take medicine for the pain. First Valium, then morphine. Lily injected the morphine herself. One day, Louis lost the use of his legs and had to be wheeled around in a stroller like a toddler.

The summer Louis turned four, there was an invasion of Japanese beetles. Iridescent-green beetles were everywhere—in the roses, in the fields, devouring the grapevines, gnawing on the pansies. Louis had a pet guinea pig named Yoda, and the girls would pick handfuls of Japanese beetles from the garden and feed them to Yoda, then watch with fascination as he crunched on them like peanuts. To the Japanese beetles, Yoda was a hideous monster with an unquenchable appetite.

One day after school, while the grown-ups were still at work, Daisy and Anna went a little nuts, running around the house like a pair of wild ponies. They played hide-and-seek and wheeled Louis around from room to room, hiding him in the pantry, then inside the closet, when all of a sudden, Anna ran up to Daisy and said, "There's a man at the door!"

"What man?"

"I don't know. I didn't ask."

"So? Go answer it."

"You!" Anna was looking scared. "He's just standing there."

Daisy peeked around the corner and saw the man through the screen door, which was latched shut. He was standing on the porch, glancing at his watch. She ducked behind the kitchen counter again. "What a weirdo," she whispered.

"Told you," Anna said.

There was another knock, and the girls held their breath and waited, but the man didn't go away.

"Why doesn't he just leave?" Daisy hissed after a minute.

"Maybe he saw us. What should we do?"

Daisy shrugged. Very carefully, she peered around the corner again and could see the man's silhouette. He stood in the great open furnace of the day, dressed in a rumpled black suit. He had dark hair and a dark beard and mustache and wore dark glasses, and he looked like a tall shadow.

He knocked again. *Bang, bang, bang.*

Daisy ducked behind the counter and squatted next to the refrigerator. "Go away," she whispered fervently, like a prayer. "Go away, go away, go away."

"Should we ask him what he wants?" Anna said.

"No." Daisy grabbed her sister's arm.

"Why not?"

"Because."

"Well . . . we can't stay here forever."

"Shh. Lemme think." She squeezed her brain, but nothing came out. She felt blank and empty, like the lake that had never come back. It was a terrible feeling, not to be able to think of a plan. Just then Anna stood up and went around the corner before Daisy had a chance to stop her.

Daisy stayed hidden in the shadows while Anna unlocked the door and opened it. "Hello?" she heard her sister say.

The man mumbled something. He had a soft voice.

Daisy pressed herself flat against the wall. She didn't know what she was so scared of. Why was she so afraid? She could hear Anna and the man talking, their voices low and muffled. The conversation went back and forth while Daisy craned her neck. Then Anna said good-bye, and the door banged shut.

"What was that all about?" Daisy asked when her sister came back.

"Nothing," Anna said.

"Nothing? What were you two blabbing about?"

"I'm not telling."

"You're crazy."

"I am not!" Anna pouted. "Take it back!"

"Not until you tell me what he said."

She rolled her eyes. "Okay, I'll tell you. But only if you promise not to laugh."

"I won't."

"Promise, Daisy?"

"Cross my heart. Now tell me."

"He wanted to see Louis."

"He did?"

"But I told him Louis wasn't here."

"Good thinking."

"Then I asked him what he wanted to see Louis for, and he told me that he was an angel, and he was coming to take Louis away."

"What?" Daisy frowned. Her sister *was* crazy. "Don't be an idiot. Tell me what he really said."

"Go look!" Anna hollered. "Go see for yourself if you don't believe me!"

Daisy ran to the window, but there was nobody there. No man, no car pulling away. She squinted up the street. "It was just a salesman," she said.

"No, he was an *angel*," Anna insisted.

Daisy could almost imagine a pair of wings tucked underneath the man's rumpled black suit. "There is no such thing as angels, you big baby. That's totally make-believe."

"Why are you so mean to me?" Anna cried, looking deeply hurt and crestfallen. She ran away and hid with Louis inside the vacuum cleaner closet.

The following day, Daisy found three guinea pig poops mashed into the plastic bristles of her toothbrush. She studied her toothbrush with growing disgust, then threw it away in the wastebasket and stepped back from the sink. There were four more Yoda poops on the tiled floor. She checked the bottoms of her sandals and found another dropping squished against the heel. She cleaned up the poops and washed her hands but didn't tell her mother. She deserved to be punished. She'd been mean to her sister yesterday.

* * *

"Louis died," Lily told anyone who'd listen, "feeling no pain." Since she was in charge of the morphine, she'd made sure of it.

At the funeral, Daisy began to understand that when somebody you loved died, you reached for the most minuscule things to be grateful for. And so, at Louis's funeral, Daisy kept focusing on one thought: *Louis is feeling no pain. He's in heaven now, sitting on a toadstool in some forest glade, contemplating the birds and the butterflies. Yeah, that's right. Louis is in heaven now, and he's feeling no pain. No pain at all.*

The coffin was so small it hurt to look at it. Louis's face was soft and malleable, like hot wax cooling. His hands pressed an invisible book to his chest. His lips were closed forever on the last words he'd ever say: "Don't forget to feed Yoda." His hair was slicked back off his face, like at Sunday school. He was poised, Daisy realized, between light and eternal darkness. It took her breath away, how brave her little brother was. Far braver than she'd ever be.

Although he'd been sick for a long time, the end came suddenly. Nobody was ready for it, least of all Daisy's mother. Lily sat stricken and inconsolable while friends and relatives came and went, dispensing words of comfort, or so they thought. They held her hand and whispered things that flew right over her head. Daisy knew instinctively that nothing would ever assuage her mother's grief, that she would be forever fearful for her two remaining children. There were so many dead Hubbards, she kept saying. Her eyes were red. Her face was drawn.

After the funeral, Daisy and Anna spent the afternoon in their room, playing checkers.

"So what happens now?" Anna asked.

Daisy didn't look up from the board; she was winning. "To what?"

"To Louis."

"He just lies there," she said.

"Underground?"

"That's the rumor."

"Do you have to be so mean about it?"

"Well, what d'you think?"

"I think he's up in heaven now. Don't you?"

Tired of this line of questioning, Daisy scattered the checkers.

"Hey!"

"Hay is for horses." She flopped back in bed and lay there thinking about Louis. "He's floating on a soft pink cloud . . . eating ice cream . . . chocolate swirl."

Anna smiled.

"And whenever Yoda falls asleep, he goes to visit Louis up in heaven, just like a vacation. And all the dead Japanese beetles are up there, too, so Louis can feed their poor little butts to Yoda all over again . . . and Louis and the beetles and Yoda are feeling no pain."

"No pain," Anna agreed. "Ever again."

That spring, when the last of the winter snows began to melt, all the rivers and streams overflowed their banks. It was a warm, sunny mid-March afternoon when the girls went running through the woods behind their house and suddenly found themselves sucked off the flooded footbridge into the swollen stream.

It all happened so fast. Daisy went under and felt herself being pushed and pulled at the same time by the icy current. She grasped for twigs, swallowed water and somehow managed to keep her head above water. She bobbed downstream, then hooked onto an old tree trunk that had fallen across the stream and was half submerged in the rushing water. "Anna?" she shrieked. "Anna!"

Anna came floating toward her, spinning around and around. "Help me!"

"Take my hand." Daisy reached for her. "Take it!"

"I can't!" Anna's eyes grew big as silver dollars.

Daisy's feet slipped over the rocky bottom. The current was very strong. She held on to the soggy tree and reached for her sister's hand.

Anna was coming toward her fast. "Mommy!" she screamed.

Daisy snatched Anna's hand and held on tight, then braced herself against the rushing current. It was hard, like trying to fly a thousand-pound kite. She grew hot all over while her muscles strained to hold on to her sister.

Dog-paddling frantically with her free arm, Anna gulped for air. "Help," she screamed. "Don't let go of me!"

"I won't!" But Daisy could feel their fingers beginning to slip apart. It was so hard, and she was so tired of fighting the current. So tired of hanging on.

"Daisy?"

"I know. Shut up." She clasped Anna's hand and thought for a minute. Then she said, "Stop dog-paddling!"

"What?"

"Quit dog-paddling! Just float!"

"Float?"

"Grab this branch and keep holding my hand and float! Go on. I got you!"

Anna stopped dog-paddling and reached for the branch, and they clung to one another in the freezing-cold water while the current kept trying to push them apart.

Anna blinked at Daisy through her wet eyelashes. "Now what?" she said.

"Whatever you do, don't let go." It was easier, much easier, to hold on to her hand now. Daisy tried to find her footing, but the streambed was treacherous and the current kept smashing her against the fallen tree. They had to get to shore somehow. They couldn't stay there much longer or they'd freeze to death, and Daisy didn't want to visit Louis up in heaven just yet. She wasn't ready for that.

"Anna?" she said. Her younger sister had closed her eyes and looked like she was about to fall asleep. "Anna!" Daisy screamed in her face.

"What?" She sounded churlish.

"Wake up! We have to move."

"No, we don't."

"Yeah, we do. Wake up! Come on. Pull yourself out of the water!"

"No."

Daisy slapped her face.

"Ow!"

"Follow me." Daisy didn't falter. Struggling for a handhold, she gripped the fallen tree's soggy branches and hauled herself across the fast-moving current, slowly pulling herself up the length of the trunk. She pulled and pulled until she thought her arms might fall off. She pulled until she was standing in just a few feet of water, then she turned to Anna and said, "Move it!"

"I can't."

"Yes, you can. Pull yourself up!"

Anna reached for the biggest part of the branch. Her fingers were bright pink. Very slowly, she pulled herself out of the swirling water, and now the sisters were up to their knees in the foamy cresting water. It splashed and danced around their shivering legs.

"Come on." Daisy grabbed Anna's hand, and they slogged their way to dry land.

The girls squealed with delighted laughter. Anna wanted to lie down in the grass and get warm in the sun, but Daisy wouldn't let her. She dragged her sister through the woods.

"Quit pulling me!"

"You'll get hypothermia."

"What's hypothermia?"

"It means you'll freeze to death." Daisy towed Anna behind her through a sunny splash of freckles. "Hurry!" she cried.

"My feet are frozen!"

"That's why we're running home."

"I can't feel my hands."

"Shake them. Like this. We have to get home before hypothermia sets in."

"Hey," Anna said suddenly. "You rescued me."

"I know, stupid. Move!"

"Daisy, promise me—"

"What?"

"Promise me you'll always rescue me. Okay? That you'll always rescue me when I get into trouble."

"Don't be silly."

"Promise me!"

"Okay," she said. "I promise. Now run!"

Five minutes later, they burst out of the woods and saw their home not fifty yards away. The house seemed so remote and self-contained it radiated a kind of warmth. It glowed. Daisy had never wanted to get home so badly before in her life. She could taste the gingersnap cookies her mother had baked the night before. She could almost hear her mother's voice.

"Come on!"

They streaked across the front yard, laughing and cheering gleefully, when a figure emerged from behind the barn. It was Mr. Barsum in his army jacket and boots, a skunk stripe of white in his dark hair. "Girls?" he said with great concern.

"Mr. Barsum!" Anna ran wildly into his arms.

He picked her up and held on tight. "You okay?"

"I am now!"

He looked at Daisy. "You're all wet. What happened?"

"We got knocked off the footbridge."

He took Daisy's hand. "You're stiff as a board."

She let him hold her hand, too exhausted to resist.

"Come on inside," he said.

He took them into the house, which was warm and welcoming.

"Where's Mom?" Daisy asked.

"Out shopping." He stomped his boots on the worn

floorboards. "Do this to get the blood circulating again," he told them. "My little drowned rats."

Daisy pulled away from him and stood by the kitchen door, ready to bolt.

"C'mon in," Mr. Barsum told her.

"What for?"

"Don't be pigheaded, Daisy."

"I'm not pigheaded."

He sat on a kitchen chair and held Anna in his lap. Very gently, he took off her wet clothes. He removed her soggy T-shirt and rubbed her bare hands between his. Every once in a while, he breathed warm air onto her skin.

"When's Mom coming home?" Daisy asked.

"In a while, crocodile."

It was warm inside the house, while outside, the snow was slowly evaporating, sending the meltwater rushing downhill into ditches and ponds. Daisy dug her hands into her wet pants pockets and hunched forward, shuddering violently. She didn't care how wet she was, these clothes weren't coming off. The spring meltwater made a cascading sound, like music that didn't belong here on earth, but up in heaven with Louis, where he was feeling no pain. No pain at all.

Mr. Barsum took Anna's sneakers and socks off and began to rub her feet.

"Ow," she said, "pins and needles."

"I know." He lifted her small foot to his mouth and blew on it. "Here. I'll warm them."

Daisy's stomach hurt. She didn't know what to do.

"Come inside and close the door," he told her. "I'll

make us some hot cocoa. Would you like that?" His
voice was soothing, like the voices on the radio.

Daisy's hair was wet and tangled, her clothes were
soaked through. They dripped onto the kitchen floor, like
meltwater melting off of her.

"Come here, sweetie." He snuck his hands around
Anna's middle and pressed his rough cheek against her
rosy one.

Daisy felt her scalp shivering beneath her damp hair.
"We got lost," she said. "But I found the way home."

Mr. Barsum's face was hidden in the folds of Anna's
body, and Anna seemed to be a million miles away.

"We got lost," Daisy repeated. "In the woods."

Anna licked her bluish lips.

Daisy's face flushed. A spring breeze was coming in
through the open doorway. It blew long strands of her
hair forward over her eyes, long blond strands that
whipped back into her face like rat tails. "We got lost in
the forest," she said, but it wasn't any use. Nobody was
listening. She wriggled her toes around inside her sneakers and noticed they made a squishy sound.

"Close the door," Mr. Barsum said, and finally, she
did.

BLUE
WAVELENGTHS

1.

Jack found Daisy in a dive bar across the street from her motel. She was slumped over her drink like a wilted houseplant, her long blond hair done up in a sloppy ponytail. She wore vintage jeans and a high-tech T-shirt, and something was different about her. Or maybe he was the one who had changed. He slung his leg over the cracked vinyl stool and said, "What are you doing here?"

She looked at him briefly. "Drowning my sorrows."

"Drown a few for me while you're at it."

"You've got sorrows, Jack?"

"No, Daisy. Us police officers are perpetually happy creatures."

The aging male bartender had an oddly youthful hairdo, poufed out to the sides and dyed a lusterless brown. "What can I get you?" he asked Jack.

"Splash of Coke. I'm the designated driver."

The bartender nodded and filled a glass with cola, then slapped down a coaster. "Two bucks."

"For sugar water?" Jack got out his wallet.

"So this is the human face of the police, huh?" Daisy glanced at his off-duty attire—old jeans, a Billy Corgan T-shirt and a scruffy pair of basketball shoes.

"You'll never catch me wearing a polo shirt."

She smiled and nodded. "Can I ask you something?"

"Sure."

"What happened to your three marriages?"

He shrugged. "I suffocate people, apparently."

"What do you mean?"

"I keep wanting to rescue people, even when they're perfectly okay. I have no off-switch, I'm told."

She frowned. "You must have an off-switch someplace."

"Be my guest."

She eyed him curiously. "So none of your ex-wives needed rescuing?"

"In the beginning, they all did. Tess had a terrible family situation. She was nineteen, I was twenty-one. She was a true innocent who never should've married me. Then there's Margot, a runaway from a middle-class family in Birmingham and a hard-core junkie by the time I met her. I got her into rehab, made her go back to school and get her degree. She turned out splendidly. Became an attorney and fell in love with her law partner. Penny was a six-month mistake. A very disturbed person. I got her into therapy, and her therapist talked her into dumping me."

"Ah," she said. "You like victims."

"I guess you could say I'm a victimaholic."

"Well, Jack . . . you're safe with me."

He wasn't so sure about that. He had tracked her down for a reason. He had a grim favor to ask of her.

She was drinking a dark liqueur mixed with cream. He knew what she was doing. She wanted the grief to somehow magically disappear, only it wouldn't disappear. It would sit inside of her like a bed of embers, burning dully for months, maybe even years. Jack of all people knew that you couldn't put out a fire with alcohol. "Why don't you tell me about your family," he said gently.

Daisy was quiet for a few minutes. A cigarette smoldered in a glass ashtray, never too far from her fingers. "My brother, Louis, died of Stier-Zellar's disease," she said.

He took a swallow of soda. "Never heard of it."

"You wouldn't. It's very rare. So rare the carrier frequency hasn't even been measured yet. Less than a hundred children in the United States have the disease at any given time. So it gets lumped in with all the other orphans."

"Orphans? What orphans?"

"Stier-Zellar's, Huntington's, hemophilia, Tourette's syndrome, narcolepsy, Tay-Sachs . . . the list goes on. Any disease or rare disorder that affects fewer than two hundred thousand Americans is called an 'orphan disease.' About six thousand of them fall under this category. Once you add it up, though, you're talking about twenty-five million suffering Americans."

He let out a low whistle. "Twenty-five million, huh?"

"That number really gets the politicians' hearts pumping. It's how we finally got congress to pass the Rare

Diseases Act. It provides incentives for companies to fund research into orphan diseases."

Something was different. Something had changed in his feelings toward her since yesterday. He was tempted to touch her silky blond hair. She had such a sad flower-bud mouth and was encumbered by the most beautiful face imaginable. "How old were you when Louis died?" he said.

"Twelve. Anna was nine."

Jack waited. He breathed in, he breathed out. He sensed she was about to tell him something important. He could see her trying to hold back the pain.

"My sister and I were molested by a family friend." She sat for a moment with her heavy heart. "I believe that the sexual abuse contributed to my sister's illness in a big way. She was molested between the ages of five and nine, then had her first psychotic break when she was thirteen."

"Who was this person?"

"A bank teller. We called him Mr. Barsum. My mother met him through her job. She's a CPA. My father died several years earlier, and I think Lily—my mother—was lonely. She loved my father very much. She didn't want to get married again."

"So this guy . . . this Mr. Barsum . . . lived with you?"

"Me and Mom and Anna and Louis."

"When did it first happen? The abuse?"

She took a long drag, then put out her cigarette. "When my brother was two years old, he started showing the classic symptoms of Stier-Zellar's. We'd never heard of it before, so it came as a complete shock. Mr. Barsum ended up taking care of us while Mom shuttled

Louis back and forth between hospitals. I should've told her what was happening. I should've put an end to it, but I was deeply conflicted. I didn't think she'd believe me, for one thing. He made plenty of threats. I was terrified the whole time it was happening. The weird thing was, Anna grew very attached to Mr. Barsum. She loved him, in a way. When my mother finally found out what was going on and sent him packing, Anna became traumatized. It was as if we'd lost our father all over again."

"How old was she when her real father died?"

"She hadn't been born yet. I was three."

"Do you remember him at all? Your father?"

"I think I have false memories of him. I've seen so many pictures, you know? I have images of him in my head that could've come from home movies."

He didn't like toying with her emotions. He wanted to be up-front with her, to come clean and ask her for this favor, but he was afraid she would refuse him. So he hesitated.

"Schizophrenia's still a mystery," Daisy went on. "They don't know exactly what causes it, but they think there's more than one gene involved. It's not purely genetic, this disease. Environmental factors play a big role. Unlike Huntington's, where a single faulty gene can doom you." She stared into her drink, lost in thought. "Each of us is born with a biological life sentence. We have three trillion cells in our bodies, and each cell carries all of our hereditary information. Go back in time and find your ancestors—these people hold the key to your genetic makeup."

Jack found himself gazing at her lips. They were

generous and curvaceous and showed very little of her teeth, even when she smiled. Even when she spoke.

She looked up. "What?" she said.

"Nothing."

"What're you thinking, Jack?"

He liked it when she called him Jack. Too quick to see, since he concealed it so well, was the way his body jumped at the mention of his name. An old song was playing on the jukebox. "Billy, Don't Be a Hero" by Bo Donaldson and the Heywoods. It took him back to the mid-seventies, when Jack wanted to be a hero, too, just like the cops on *Freddie the Fuzz*. He would call himself Jack the G-Man. "What's Vermont like?" he asked her.

"Wet in the spring. Cold in the winter." She paused to swallow. "Did you know it's against the law in Vermont for a woman to wear her false teeth without her husband's permission?"

He cracked a smile. "I did not know that."

"And it's illegal to whistle underwater."

"I'll remember that the next time I'm passing through."

She heaved a sigh. "How about you, Jack? What's your sad story?"

"You want my saddest story? Or my second-saddest story?"

"Oh, the saddest. Please."

"My first wife," he told her, "was a good person. I'd come home from work, and Tess would ask me about my day, and I would usually make the mistake of telling her." He finished his soda. "So one day she gets pregnant. We couldn't be happier, right? Everything's fine. Everything's great. Then I almost get shot on the job. I almost get killed on the job, and she hears about it. She sees it on TV. There's been a mix-up, and they tell her I'm dead. It's a terrible mistake, but she files for divorce shortly afterward. She divorces me because of this faulty information."

She looked at him pityingly.

"She moves to Toronto and marries a dentist. Very safe, you see. Dentists don't ordinarily get shot on the job. So now I see my kid every summer for two weeks. I don't even know my own daughter. She's growing up without me." He studied his hands. "It's the hardest on weekends. Whenever I have too much time on my hands, my thoughts will turn morbid. So I pour all my energy into my cases. Dead bodies consume my every waking moment. If you don't believe me, ask my ex-wives."

"No, I believe you," she said.

"It's tough on a relationship when you can't wait for Sunday morning to roll around because there's a fresh batch of bodies down at the morgue, you know. Truth is . . . I like whiskey way more than I like people."

"I don't believe you," she said. "I think your whole problem is that you care too much."

He picked up a black matchbook that spelled out BOO YAY'S in red lettering. "When Tess was pregnant, we couldn't decide about a name. So we called the baby BOLO."

"What's BOLO?"

"Be on the lookout for. It's cop code. Cute, huh?"

"What's your daughter's real name?"

"Bonnie Lou. The BOLO influence is still there."

"That's a pretty name."

He dropped the matches and said, "Colby Ostrow was strangled to death."

The nod was a reflex.

"He was dead two days when we found him inside a steamer trunk in Gaines's apartment. We think Gaines was about to bury him in the Angeles National Forest."

Her eyes never left his face. "What about the woman you thought was my sister?"

"Her name is Katja Webb. She's a Hollywood prostitute."

"Was she strangled, too?"

He nodded.

Her eyebrows lifted, supple as green twigs. Her face was delicate-boned. Snub nose, the better to snub you with. Wise blue eyes behind the pain. "How old is Katja?" she asked.

"Nineteen when she died. A teenage runaway who got caught up in drugs and prostitution. Colby Ostrow, Katja Webb . . . both were victims of opportunity. But with your sister, it's a whole new ball game."

"What do you mean?"

"Remember our teenage witness, Christie? She saw your sister and Gaines on the promenade together, several times. And there's a tenant who recalls seeing them in the building as far back as eight months ago."

She stared at him. "Eight months?"

"They were friends or acquaintances. Maybe he was her drug dealer. I don't know. But it's unusual, because the other victims had no connection to Gaines. These were classic stranger killings. Victims of opportunity."

She cupped her hand over her mouth, and her eyes filled with tears. The jukebox in the corner was playing

Chet Baker's "Let's Get Lost." Every time somebody came in the door, smoke poured out of the bar.

"Why don't you ask him?" she said in an anguished voice. "Ask Roy Gaines what his relationship with my sister was."

"He won't elaborate." He narrowed his eyes against the glare of the sun coming in through the plate-glass window. "He refuses to say anything else."

"So she knew him for eight months, and then one day he just killed her? Is that what you think?"

"I don't know. Maybe she went off her meds. Maybe that triggered a reaction in him. Whatever, Gaines isn't talking. Not to me, at any rate."

"Can't you do something? Can't you force him to tell you?"

"Daisy," he said as gently as possible.

"What?"

"I went to see him this morning. We have his full co-operation now, if only . . ."

Her eyes narrowed.

"If only you'd accompany us again."

Her pain was visible in every pore.

"He promises to take us to her grave this time."

"No." She shook her head. "No way. He's lying."

"Daisy. Even if it turns out not to be Anna . . . you realize that some other mother or sister wants to find their loved one. Do it for them, if not for yourself."

She fell silent, and he watched this new thought worm its way through her consciousness. He knew that she would cooperate. She was a good person. He felt like a complete asshole, taking advantage of her goodness like that.

2.

The following morning, Daisy found herself tromping along a dirt trail worn down by foot traffic, the boots of at least twenty law officers kicking up dust in front of her. They paused at the crest of a hill to observe the mountains and ocean in the distance. She could see the high-rises of Hollywood from here and was glad she'd remembered to bring her insect repellent. The deerflies were thick and left painful bites. Now the group headed down a gently sloping hill, where the chaparral grew over the trail in places, and continued past a firebreak down the right-hand side of the canyon. At the head of this grim procession, Roy Gaines moved easily, a man supremely comfortable in his own skin. His shoulders were thrown back and his orange jailhouse jumpsuit looked freshly pressed. She was too tired to hate him. Too tired to fear him. She just wanted it to be over with.

Halfway down the canyon, they followed a horseshoe

bend in the trail and crossed a dried creekbed into a wild meadow ringed with pine trees. Gaines launched a loogie of bacteria-laden saliva into the grass and said, "Can I have a cigarette?"

They stopped on a slight rise near the dried-up creekbed, where the plants were struggling to grow out of the baked soil, their leaves interlaced with spiderwebs. The sun was blazing hot, and the rocks at their feet were stratified from untold freezes and thaws. Detective Tully put away the map he'd been marking with a pencil and took out a pack of cigarettes.

"Be right back." Jack left Daisy's side to powwow with Tully, and she felt abandoned and adrift. She couldn't see the prisoner's eyes behind his mirrored glasses, but she sensed that he was watching her.

Gaines drew thoughtfully on his cigarette while the rest of the men stood around talking. The hairs on the back of Daisy's neck prickled as she noticed the smoke unfurling from his nostrils, those mirrored glasses reflecting her miniature form back at her. "Even if you find a cure," he said in a low, steady voice, "it won't bring your brother back."

She gave a convulsive start.

"Meanwhile, where'd your life go?"

She felt the shock reverberating down to her fingertips.

"I bet you spent half your life with your head in a book," he continued, his calm voice tearing at her composure. "You can cure a mouse, Daisy. But what about a human being? Do you honestly think you'll achieve that in your lifetime?"

Jack strode over and slapped the cigarette out of

Gaines's hand, then stomped on it hard. "Shut the fuck up," he said.

"Chromosome 4. C-A-G repeated a hundred times," Gaines said, still watching her. "That's destiny, right? That's fate."

"Whatever you have to say, you say to me," Jack insisted.

"Daisy knows what I'm talking about."

Jack gave an animal growl and shoved the prisoner, who stumbled backward into the weeds.

"Hey!" Tully said. "Jack. C'mon."

Daisy's heart folded in on itself. The sequence C-A-G, repeated over and over, was the gene on chromosome 4 responsible for Huntington's disease. If this gene repeated thirty-five times or less, you'd be normal. Any higher than that, and you'd die from a disease that took your mind before it slowly killed your body.

"Fucking animal," Jack spat.

The prisoner's face showed no reaction.

"C'mon, Jack," Tully said. "Let it go."

He stood in the clearing with his hands fisted.

Tully knelt down to pocket the butt, and the men formed a tense procession and headed back into the woods.

Jack lagged behind until he rejoined Daisy's side. "You okay?" he asked, his ice-blue eyes full of concern.

"Fine." She was quivering like a mouse. "What did he mean by that?"

"He's just trying to rile you."

"Why? What's the point?"

"Do you want to stop? Because we can put an end to this charade right now."

Her mouth grew defiant. "No."

"Are you sure?"

"I don't want him to think he can intimidate me."

"Good for you. Screw him."

Beneath the graceful oak trees were boulders the color of thunderclouds. There were indentations in some of the rocks where Native Americans used to grind their acorns. The pestles would be buried in the ground, long abandoned.

"C-A-G repeated a hundred times." She turned to Jack. "He's talking about the gene for Huntington's disease. I wrote about it in my article on genes and destiny. It's one of the articles you found on Anna's computer."

"Genes and destiny?"

"Our genes determine everything from hair color to eye color, but what we do in our lives also affects the way our genes perform. Heart disease is a good example. Smoking, stress, high blood pressure . . . all these things can contribute to the advancement of the disease. On the other hand, Huntington's is an example of how one gene can literally seal your fate. Once you have Huntington's, it doesn't matter what your lifestyle is. You can quit smoking, quit drinking, start an exercise program . . . it won't make a bit of difference. Nothing's going to help you. Most human diseases are more complex than that, but if you're unlucky enough to have the gene for Huntington's, then sadly enough, biology is destiny."

"So what's his point?"

"I don't know. But it sounds like he doesn't believe in gene therapy."

"You can cure a mouse, but not a human being?"

"Exactly."

"Is that true?"

"We've had our share of setbacks, Jack. We've still got a long way to go, but gene therapy has already been used to cure human beings. It works on bubble babies . . . children born with such deficient immune systems they have to be isolated inside a plastic bubble or they'll die."

"What about Stier-Zellar's?"

"The results have been remarkable so far . . . in mice."

He nodded. As they trudged along, he seemed to be contemplating something. "Exactly what is gene therapy anyway?" he finally said.

"It's when a healthy gene is inserted into the body so that it can proliferate and repair any serious genetic defects. That's the theory anyway. Usually, you clone a gene using a bacterium. The gene is spliced onto the bacterium's DNA, so that every time the bacterium reproduces, it makes an exact copy of itself. Bacteria multiply so rapidly that billions of copies can be produced very quickly. You can also use polymerase chain reaction. The weird thing is, all living creatures share the same genetic code. So the genes from one species can be expressed in another."

"That is fucking weird."

"With Stier-Zellar's, you need a viral vector system in order to transport the genes into the brain cells of a human being. We plan on introducing healthy genes directly into the brains of our patients using a real or synthetic virus that will infect the neurons and express the normal human gene that these children lack."

"How successful do you think you'll be?"

"Nobody knows. Results are unpredictable. For example, they've managed to implant in mice the gene that makes jellyfish glow. And guess what? The mice glow. But they tried it with monkeys and failed. The monkeys didn't glow."

"Mice that *glow*?"

She nodded. "Talk about giving science a bad name, huh? You don't know whether it's a miracle or a sign of the apocalypse. But it is science. Good or bad."

A few yards past another firebreak, the trail led down the side of the canyon, and one by one they skidded toward the bottom, their feet kicking up sand and gravel. Daisy banged her elbow on one of the rusty metal pipes that were propping up the eroded hillside and could feel a sharp throbbing in her arm as she tried to make sense of it all. Anna had obviously told Gaines about her work with Stier-Zellar's disease. He'd read her article on Huntington's and seemed to know enough about genes to discuss certain details. Her sister had known Roy Gaines for as long as eight months, which meant that the timeline went like this: Anna moved to L.A. last June, met Gaines in August, quit therapy in October and disappeared in February.

It appalled Daisy that a complete stranger could know so much about her. She wondered what other secrets Anna had told him. Did he know about Mr. Barsum, for instance? It made her feel dirty, as if somebody's finger were dragging across her face.

They found the trail again and pushed deeper into the woods, where the towering pines grew so thick in places that the sun was almost completely swallowed up. You could barely make out people's faces in this false dusk. Daisy brushed against a plume of sagebrush, and it released its aromatic scent into the air. The footpath wove steeply downhill through a span of kindling-dry cedars that were spread across the slope.

"Okay," Gaines said as they reached the bottom of the canyon. "There it is."

They banked down an erosion ditch and came upon a grave site that was partially hidden from view, covered under rocks and dead pine branches. Daisy stood a few yards back, her worst fears crowding in on her.

"I'll have one of the officers take you back to your motel," Jack said.

"No," she told him. "I want to stay this time."

His tone was skeptical. "I don't think so."

"I need to honor whatever it is she's been through."

"All right. Just don't sue me later."

She stood shivering in the shade of the tall trees while the officers got out their emergency shovels and began to dig. As their blades bit into the dirt, a small cloud of flies puffed up. One of them landed on her arm, and Daisy frantically brushed it away. She felt an alarming palpitation as the golden-brown dust rose up and shimmered in the air.

The grave was fairly shallow, and soon they'd uncovered a body. Jack snapped on a pair of latex gloves and scooped some of the dirt off the mummified face. The rubbery nose was mashed to one side, and the puttylike mouth was frozen in a snarl. Daisy stared uncomprehendingly at that unrecognizable face. The short, curly white hair didn't belong to her sister. "Oh God," she whispered.

"What?"

She took a staggering step back. "Look at her hair."

"Fuck." Jack stood up. "Get him out of here!"

Daisy caught the prisoner's eye, his face narrow and expressionless. "Why are you doing this to me?" she screamed.

"Because," he told her as the officers led him roughly away, "you should know the truth."

"What?"

"Only you," he said. "I'll only talk to you!"

And she fell into a black hole so dense, nothing could escape from its gravitational pull.

3.

The first thing Jack surrendered was his gun. Next he signed a waiver stating that he absolved the psychiatric prison of any responsibility in case he was held hostage or killed. He handed the waiver back to the guard, and the steel blast doors opened with a mechanical whir. He walked inside, where another armed guard escorted him down the wide, unfriendly corridor toward the conference room set aside for lawyers and their clients just off the main cellblock. The uniformed guard with the bullet-shaped head slid a perforated key-card through an electronic trough, and the steel-plated door snapped open.

The conference room was narrow and claustrophobic, with double bars on all the windows, a bolted-down table and chairs, and the kind of flat bright lighting you'd find in a supermarket. "There's the panic button," the guard said, pointing at the steel-plated buzzer panel next to the room's only exit. "If you need me, just press it."

Jack nodded. He understood perfectly well that he would be left alone with the prisoner, unarmed and unobserved.

Roy Gaines was facing arraignment on charges of first-degree murder in the deaths of Colby Ostrow, Katja Webb and now his latest victim, Irma Petropoulous, the elderly woman who had disappeared from her De Campo Beach home over a year ago. Jack's first missing person. The attorney appointed to represent Gaines had asked the court to suppress the arrestee's initial confession, due to the fact that the attorney hadn't been present at the time of said confession, ignoring the fact that his client had repeatedly waived his rights to counsel and had even signed a waiver to that effect. Fortunately, the judge rejected the attorney's request, and Roy Gaines had been transferred to Francois-Giroux Prison for psychiatric testing in order to determine his competency to stand trial.

Now Jack took a seat and waited with a readiness bordering on agitation. After a few minutes, two armed guards ushered the suspect into the conference room and sat him down in the only other chair. Gaines wore horn-rimmed glasses and a black T-shirt under the standard orange jumpsuit, his hands cuffed to a waist chain. He sat passively while the guards did a quick check of the room for contraband, then locked the door behind them.

Jack frowned. Seated in front of him was a sociopath, a man who knew the difference between right and wrong but who killed for deeply selfish and malevolent reasons. "You lied to me," he said calmly, belying the tension inside of him.

Gaines didn't respond.

It was as quiet as a block of ice in here. Shafts of sunlight slanted through the prison-bar windows, striping the floor. The space between bars was about the width of a human forearm. The entire facility had been designed to drive a grown man crazy; it was as dull and functional as a public school building, only there would be no escape from the boredom.

Gaines looked older than his thirty-four years, prematurely aged but still physically imposing with his powerful shoulders and ripped upper pecs, his monster triceps and his greasy black hair, each inky strand as thick as piano wire. The cement walls had been painted a mind-numbing beige, and Roy Gaines sat staring at them.

"Hello?" Jack said angrily. "You still with me?"

The prisoner didn't seem to be listening.

"You tried to engage the victim's sister in conversation," Jack said. "You lied about the corpse's identity. You've broken all the rules."

Gaines just floated there in front of him. Sitting and staring.

"So what's your game plan, Roy? Huh? You enjoy killing people, that's obvious. You like playing mind games. What else?"

This elicited a thin smile. "I didn't kill anyone."

"No, of course not. You just told us where the bodies were buried, right?"

"I shouldn't be in here. I'm an innocent man."

"We're all fucking innocent, Roy. Everybody on death row is innocent." Jack gave him a stony look. "I know exactly what you're doing."

The prisoner's jaw muscles tensed.

"C'mon, Roy, think about it. Acquittals on insanity

pleas are extremely rare, you know that. We'll find Anna Hubbard's body sooner or later, with or without your help. We've got tracker dogs out there right now, scouring the woods. Once we find the body on our own, all bets are off. No more plea bargains. You'll be facing the death penalty for sure. So unless you decide to cooperate and tell me where she is right now . . . unless you show some sort of compassion or remorse, then I truly can't help you."

He watched Jack with flat dark eyes that already seemed set apart from the world. "I'll tell her sister," he said.

Jack shook his head. "Ain't gonna happen."

A far-off siren sounded.

"Can I have a cigarette?" Gaines asked. "In my pocket. I can't reach." He indicated his helplessness by moving his shackled arms in a limited fashion, the clunky waist chains rattling against the seat of his chair.

Jack got up and removed a pack of cigarettes from the prisoner's jumpsuit pocket, then put them on the table in front of him and sat back down. "Maybe you should quit."

Gaines smiled. In this light, he had a feral face with teeth like kernels of corn. "Prison is no place to give up smoking, Detective."

"So tell us where you buried the body. Point me in the right direction."

Gaines glanced at the cigarettes on the table.

"End her sister's suffering. End her mother's suffering." Jack waited, an eerie silence enveloping them like a fine spring mist that comes and goes quicker than a daydream. He noticed he was perspiring lightly. He had yet to see Gaines break a sweat.

"I need to explain a few things to her," the prisoner said, shifting in his seat.

"Who? Ms. Hubbard?"

The seconds ticked past.

"Y'know, Roy, we don't need to know why you did what you did. We've already got the hows and wherefores. So screw the whys. I don't give a damn why."

"She will."

In his mind, Jack fed a bullet into the chamber of his service revolver, aimed it at Gaines's stubborn skull and pulled the trigger. In reality, he laced his fingers together on the metal tabletop. "The California death penalty gives you a choice between gas and lethal injection." He leaned forward. "No jury's gonna buy this insanity crap. Come on, Roy. You're a big boy. You know that most juries are merciless when it comes to the insanity defense."

Beneath the glare of the prison lights, Gaines's boil scars and dog-yellow teeth were prominent, but the attitude, the arrogance, the false calm, were all part of a carefully crafted facade, Jack knew.

"Are you even listening to me? Or should I just shut the fuck up?"

Gaines blinked.

Inhaling deeply through his nose, Jack said, "Okay, so why'd you agree to see me without a lawyer present? What's the fucking point of this little tête-à-tête?"

"Because," he said, "you can bring her here. She trusts you."

Jack's trigger finger twitched. "I should've shot you back when I had the chance," he said.

4.

Daisy could feel her heart pounding in her chest as she collapsed on top of her motel bed. *C-A-G*. Roy Gaines's words kept echoing inside her head. *C-A-G repeated a hundred times . . .*

She'd published an article in *Science Now* called "Genes and Fate." In it, Daisy had posited that, although a person's genotype determined everything from eye color to inherited diseases, we were not robots programmed by our genes. Citing the work of Matt Ridley, she'd explained that *how* a person dealt with his or her stress could affect the entire immune system, since it was now believed that stress was responsible for switching on or off certain genes. Both the body and the mind had influence over genes.

In her article, Daisy had used Huntington's as an example of the ways in which destiny could sometimes not be altered. No amount of medical intervention or vitamin pills would stop Huntington's disease from manifesting itself. If the gene repeated thirty-nine times, you'd get the disease at age sixty-six. If it repeated forty-one times, you'd get the disease at age fifty-five. Any more than fifty repeats, and you were doomed to develop Huntington's in your twenties. A terrible fate.

Genes also played a role in intelligence, but not personality. A study on the genetic influence of mental ability showed that over 50 percent of memory capacity could be attributed to genes. But whether a person was passive or assertive, easygoing or temperamental, had mostly to do with environmental factors. In her article, Daisy concluded that genes, for the most part, did not equal destiny.

Now she stared at the ceiling from a prone position on her motel bed. There were several messages waiting for her on her answering machine, but she couldn't summon the energy to play them back. Her eyes were open, but she felt as if she were dreaming. She tried to shake off today's nightmare, but the harder she tried, the more vivid it became. She told herself to get up, but her body refused to cooperate. "Come on, Lazy Daisy. Do something."

She got out of bed and found Anna's diary in her suitcase. She cracked the binding and studied Anna's minuscule handwriting: *"Momster & i fite, awf stuff, bitt n wrd. Cnt w8 gt outtahere."* Daisy translated the passage to read: *"Mom and I had a fight, awful stuff, bitter and weird."* Or maybe *"bitter words."* *"I can't wait to get out of here."*

She kept reading. *"March 24: So many wolf spiders in the house today! I found this HUGE one in the bathtub and freaked out. I killed it with my shoe, smashing it over and over again until it was nothing but dust. Then I scrubbed out the bathtub with bleach and Ajax, and soaked it in Lysol and sprayed it with Raid until I couldn't breathe. It totally creeped me out."*

"April 3: I hate my life. I can't wait to leave. I hate this fucking town! I hardly ever sleep at night anymore, but even when I manage to catch a few hours, I'll sleep past noon the next day. It's not like I'm full of grooviness or anything, going to all these wild parties and staying up late every night and having lotsa groovy fun. No, I'm so boring! I stay inside and eat cookies. I'm dead tired half the time. When am I ever going to catch up on my sleep? Maybe when hell freezes over. I'll have some cheese and crackers with that whine . . ."

"April 12: 50 more days, and I'm outta here! Mom was so awful today, I couldn't stand it anymore, so I got stoned and drove downtown for some reason. Then I parked and got out and walked around Main Street for a while. It's so pretty there. I walked up and down until everything seemed to fly right past me at a very high rate of speed. The sun was beating down so hard against the brick walls of the buildings it had the effect of creating these weird visual hallucinations, these optical illusions or something. I kept staring at this one particular window in front of a bar, and my mind started to whirl and dance. It was doing things with the neon signs, creating these liquid animations. I must've stood there forever, and finally I went in, had a few drinks, got dizzy and drove back home. Wouldn't you know it, MOM WAS STANDING ON THE PORCH WAITING FOR ME!"

Daisy's eyes began to droop. So far, nothing in her

sister's diary was going to be of much help to the police. Like a cheating mystery buff, she skipped the middle part and turned to the very last page. Written on June 2, just a few days before Anna had flown off to L.A., she had written: *"i C Dr. E. H. Hilt sn & cnt w8!"* Daisy shot up in her chair. *"I'm going to see Dr. E. H. Hilt soon and I can't wait!"* Finally, they had a name to pursue.

She got on the phone and called the 411 operator, but there was no Dr. E. H. Hilt listed in Edgewater. As a matter of fact, there was nobody by that name in the entire Vermont phone book.

Next she called Los Angeles information and asked for Dr. Hilt. There was no such person listed in Los Angeles County, either. She dropped the diary on the bed and reached for her bottled water, took two aspirins, then noticed the diary had fallen open to a specific page in the middle of the book. A page with Anna's signature written all over it. There were doodled daisies and smiley suns, but mostly there was Anna's cramped, girlish signature—once, twice, three times . . . ten altogether. Only it was her first name combined with a different last name. *Anna Hildreth.* What was that supposed to mean? Was it code for Hubbard? No, wait. Hubbard was *Cup,* short for Cupboard, as in "Old Mother Hubbard went to the cupboard." The girls together were *DNA* (Daisy and Anna), but individually, they were *Banana Cup* and *D-Cup* (*Banana* from Anna Banana, and *D-Cup* from Daisy Hubbard or Cup). And their mother was simply *L.*

Hildreth must be code for something. Then again, it could signify nothing at all. Anna's fondness for wordplay, when combined with her increasing paranoia, often had little to do with reality. It all depended.

Feeling like an empty sack, Daisy packed her sister's diary away and picked up her cell phone. She would've done anything to avoid making this next call. She lay inert on the bed and listened to the flatline of the dial tone, wondering what she was going to tell Lily. She couldn't begin to explain how surreal her day had been, how cut-out-of-cardboard everything seemed.

Lily picked up on the third ring. "Hello?"

Daisy took a deep breath and said, "Hi, Mom, it's me."

There was no response. She could sense her mother reeling in her emotions, girding herself for the worst.

"It wasn't her," Daisy said.

"Oh my God." Lily sobbed with relief.

"Mom?"

"Thank God."

"Mom, I don't think . . ."

There was a long pause. "What?"

"I don't think this means that Anna is okay."

"Daisy," her mother said. "You have to believe in something."

5.

Jack found Daisy in the bar across the street again, seated at a knotty-pine table perfect for solo drinking and self-pitying reflection. He ordered a beer and sat down beside her, then stared at the stubborn, slotlike set of her mouth.

"Watch it," Daisy said. "I'm drunk enough to insult you."

"I think I can handle it."

She was working on a pack of cigarettes and a large red wine. Her third, by the looks of things. "I've been sitting here nursing my rage," she told him. "And tomorrow I'll be nursing a walloping hangover."

He swallowed some of his beer. "What you're experiencing," he said, "is perfectly normal. It's what you have to go through."

"Oh fuck you."

The sun coming in through the plate-glass window

warmed his face and arms. "Good," he said. "Let your anger out."

She smiled, tears springing to her eyes. She quickly wiped them away and said, "Can I ask you a personal question, Jack?"

"Sure, go ahead. Now that we're on a fuck-you basis."

She gave him a sad little smile. "What makes you cry?"

"Me? Nah. My tear ducts shriveled up a long time ago."

"I'm serious."

He leaned back in his seat, creating a pocket of distance between them. "My little girl makes me cry," he said, and she looked enormously sorry she'd even brought it up.

A tender lull kicked in.

He watched Daisy drink her wine and smoke her cigarette. Then he said, "Gaines wants to talk to you."

Her eyes glazed over. "Forget it."

He glanced around the bar at the license plates nailed to the walls, the pineapple-yellow jukebox in the corner, a small group of women with their feet hooked around the rungs of their stools, their leather pants darkly gleaming. He wondered if the motorcycles outside belonged to them. Girls in packs. Foster's on tap. The silver disco ball was spinning around, sending flashes of mirrored light dancing across the walls, a touch of nostalgia for the *stayin' alive* seventies.

"He'll only talk to you," Jack said.

Daisy shook her head. "I can't go through that again."

"I don't blame you. You've shown exceptional courage this past week, Daisy. Exceptional fortitude.

There'd be no dishonor in declining the invitation. No dishonor at all."

She frowned, her lips so full and wet they were sexually distracting. "What would I have to do?" she asked.

He wasn't expecting this. "I'd take you over to the prison, where you'd sit behind a pane of Plexiglas and communicate through a handset. I'd be in the next room, monitoring your every move. Security is tight. You'd be in absolutely no danger."

She gave him a hard look. "Not physically anyway."

"It's a lot to ask."

She leaned forward, carrying the weight of the world on her face. Her eyes had that hundred-yard stare. "Did she suffer much? My sister?"

Jack did what he had to do. He lied. "She was probably unconscious in seconds."

"Honestly?"

"Yes."

This seemed to satisfy her. "Tell me about the woman in the grave," she said. "The one with the curly white hair."

"Irma Petropoulous? She had five grandkids and a drinking habit. She was well on her way to cirrhosis of the liver. Her daughter reported her missing about a year ago."

Daisy blew out a thoughtful plume of smoke, then tapped her cigarette in the ashtray. Her tongue was purple from the red wine. It was the histamines in the wine that gave you such a walloping hangover. Jack had read about it somewhere.

"And there was a prostitute? Katja somebody?"

"From Minnesota originally. She came to Hollywood

to be a movie star, wouldn't you know it. Her mother contacted the LAPD six months ago."

"She didn't live in De Campo Beach?"

He shook his head. "Katja cruised Sunset Strip, spreading goodwill and disease wherever she went. Turns out she had a full-blown case of AIDS. She weighed less than ninety pounds when she disappeared." Remnants of anger slipped into his voice. "Colby Ostrow had a sister in the Valley and a nephew and niece who loved him."

She nodded sadly.

He swallowed the rest of his beer. He liked it here. He wanted to idle away the afternoon with her, forget about the case. Forget about the variety of horrors man visited upon man. She looked so lovely in the lavender light. He liked her plainness, her honesty, the lack of paint on her face. She was like some rare, beautiful flower growing out of a crack in the sidewalk.

"I found something in Anna's diary," she said. "Something that puzzles me. She had a doctor's appointment before she left home last June. Only there is no Dr. Hilt listed in the Vermont phone book. He doesn't exist, as far as I can tell. I think it might be code for something else. Anna likes word games. She enjoys toying with the meaning of things."

"For example?"

"Waste product."

"Excuse me?"

"Instead of saying, 'When the shit hits the fan,' she'd say, 'When the waste product hits the air-circulating rotational device.' 'Oh shit' becomes 'oh waste product.' Ugly curtains are 'cretins.' Mom's the Momster."

"So what's 'Dr. Hilt' mean?"

"I have no idea." She stared at the drink in her hands. "Anna could be too enigmatic for her own good sometimes."

There it was again—past tense. Daisy Hubbard was beginning to accept the inevitable.

They sat staring at one another. Then she reached out and touched his face. It was an awkward moment, both innocent and dangerous. He closed his eyes, giving in to the coolness behind the lids. Her hand smelled slightly sweet. Slightly tart. He opened his eyes and said, "This is not unlike stepping off a cliff."

"It's funny. I trust you."

He lowered his gaze. He wasn't sure she should trust him. He'd come here for the express purpose of persuading her to talk to Gaines. Now he realized he could be playing into the bad guy's hands, delivering her like a lamb to the slaughter. "Look," he said, "I'll handle this thing without you, okay?"

"No," she said. "I've changed my mind. I want to do it."

"Daisy . . ."

She stood up. "Let's get it over with."

6.

Jack and Daisy were greeted by an escort team of cheerless mental health professionals in the lobby of the main building. The hospital administrator was a pasty specter of a man who walked with stiff little steps, as if his legs were made of glass. "We allow noncontact visits only," he said. "The prisoner will be escorted into the visitor's room by two correctional officers, who will remain in the secure area for the duration."

Francois-Giroux Psychiatric Prison held a distinct smell that Daisy would never forget. She felt smaller and smaller as they walked through a maze of corridors monitored by closed-circuit TV. The maximum-security prison consisted of a dozen enormous cement-block buildings set on approximately thirty acres of land, the entire complex surrounded by perimeter walls topped off with razor wire. They followed the administrator down one oppressive corridor after another, their footsteps echoing behind his little clippety-clops.

"The entire control and communications is handled from a centralized area," he said, pulling a squawking walkie-talkie off his belt. "The officer at the front desk operates the doors electronically, controlling all entrances and exits." He spoke into the walkie-talkie for a moment, then said, "There'll be nobody else inside the visitor's room with you today. Detective Makowski and I will monitor the proceedings from an adjacent room, and I can assure you, Ms. Hubbard, your personal safety is guaranteed."

"Famous last words," she said with a laugh.

He didn't even crack a smile.

She felt her level of anxiety rising as they followed this humorless man into the empty visitor's room, where the floors were tacky from years of foot traffic and the overhead skylights flooded the area with a diffuse light. She took a seat at one of the dirty white booths, then stared at the telephone handset. The Plexiglas had grease marks on it.

"See those surveillance cameras?" Jack pointed at the video cameras in every corner. "I'll be watching you the whole time. He'll come in through that door over there. He'll be handcuffed and manacled. Two guards will escort him over to his seat, and you'll be protected by this barrier. He'll pick up his handset. You pick up yours. You can stop talking—or listening—anytime you like, Daisy. Don't let him bully you. If you feel threatened in any way, just call out to one of the guards. Ready?"

"Wait," she said, losing her nerve.

"Relax. You're doing great." He started to leave, but

she grabbed his hand and held on to it for a moment. "It's okay," he said gently. "I'll be right next door."

She nodded.

"He can't hurt you."

Watching him walk away, she felt a growing uneasiness. He didn't look back as he opened the heavy perforated door, then let it slam shut behind him. She sat with her terrible fears, and after a moment, she could hear footsteps—a door thudding shut, the *clink-clink* of chains.

Two armed guards escorted Roy Gaines into the secured area behind the Plexiglas. She felt sparks of hatred for him, sparks of fury. His eyes really got to her. They held an awful knowledge. As she looked into those eyes, she could sense an oiliness spreading over her, thick and suffocating. He wore his standard-issue jumpsuit, a white T-shirt and the horn-rimmed glasses of a college professor. The length of the chain between his legs was about twelve inches, and crossing the floor in leg irons looked difficult.

Good, she thought. *Suffer.*

The armed guards escorted him roughly over to his chair, then sat him down in front of her. They uncuffed the prisoner's right hand and cuffed his left hand to a metal hook on the tabletop. Their movements were very fluid and mechanical, but she could detect something else in their demeanor—a thinly disguised fear that made her feel less safe. They barely acknowledged Daisy's existence, and something primitive in her wanted to run away.

Gaines sat just a few feet away from her now, behind a thick Plexiglas barrier. He picked up his handset and indicated that she should, too. He seemed relatively low-key, self-effacing and polite, but it made her recall Jack's warning: *Sociopaths can be charming. Be careful. He might trick you into thinking he's normal, Daisy. Don't fall for it.*

She picked up the handset, dreading the moment of contact.

"Thanks for agreeing to talk to me," he said.

Funny, she'd expected him to breathe fire. She couldn't stop looking at him and grew extremely self-conscious. She felt like a mental patient, observed from all angles. She was keenly aware that Jack and the prison authorities were watching their every move. "You've got something to say to me?" she asked, afraid he might not hear her over the hammering of her heart.

He nodded vaguely.

"Well?"

"I wanted you to know a few things," he said. "I'm not crazy. I don't hear voices in my head. I don't run around naked, screaming at the top of my lungs. I don't throw my own feces or drink my own urine, like some of the winners in this establishment."

She didn't argue with him.

"I figured you'd understand what I'm about to say, since she's your sister."

Her heart wouldn't stop pounding.

Gaines leaned forward, and she could see his acne scars in great detail through the scratched Plexiglas. "I shouldn't be here," he said calmly. "I didn't kill anyone."

She blinked. "You didn't?"

"No. I'm an innocent man."

"But you led the police to two bodies," she said angrily. "Three, if you count Colby Ostrow."

"I only buried them. I didn't kill them."

"Who killed them, then?"

"Think about it," he said.

She was going to be sick to her stomach.

He sat there staring at her.

"I don't understand . . ."

"Your sister," he said, enunciating every syllable, "killed those people."

"What?"

"I *buried* them, but Anna *murdered* them."

She could feel the flesh quiver on her bones.

"She's still out there. Killing people."

"I don't believe you. You're lying."

He gave her a stony look.

It made her think of a recurring nightmare she used to have as a little girl—piles of blankets, frightful anguish. The more she kicked the covers off, the more blankets were piled on top of her. "Look," she said, "Anna may be many things, but she'd never murder anyone. Ever!"

"It's just curious, isn't it?" He gave her such a sincere look it didn't feel like a con. It felt genuine. "The idea that somebody like your sister . . . a person as beautiful as that, with a Virgin Mary complex and everything . . . could turn to murder?"

Revulsion rose in her. "You're full of shit," she said. "What are you saying? Are you saying that *Anna* killed these people? My sister? Why would she do such a thing? She may be sick in the head, but she's not crazy! You're the monster! My sister wouldn't hurt a flea. And even if it were true . . . why would you bury the bodies for her?"

He looked away, his face darkening.

"You know what I think?" she said. "I think you're lying. I think you killed those people, and you killed my sister, and now you're trying to confuse me."

He stabbed his finger on the tabletop. "I never loved anyone . . . like I loved her. The second Anna came into my life, I knew . . . I just knew we belonged together. She didn't feel sorry for me. She didn't humor me. And most important of all, she wasn't afraid of me."

"Yeah, well, Anna can be really stupid when it comes to the men in her life."

He stared at her.

"Forget it," she said, ready to hang up. "This is bullshit."

"You really don't know, do you?" he said.

She hesitated.

"When the mice die, and you put them in the freezer?" he said impatiently. "When your brother couldn't lift his head off the pillow anymore?"

It was as if they were talking through a bad connection.

"You try to save lives. That's your job. This is Anna's." He sat forward, suddenly anxious to unburden himself. "She found the gene."

"What gene? What are you talking about?"

"On chromosome 24."

"There are only twenty-three chromosomes."

He shook his head. "Anna has twenty-four."

"What? Jesus . . . I don't understand what you're saying."

"She has the gene for death."

Her mind was reeling. "What?"

"She says they never leave her, not completely. Not the essence of who they are. She says that when she takes them, sometimes they fight it. Sometimes they fight it, but eventually, they give in. They all give in eventually . . . rich or poor, doesn't matter. She says she can feel their bodies begin to relax when they suddenly realize it's not as bad as they thought it would be. She says it's like plugging into an electric outlet, all this energy comes charging into you and . . ." He stopped talking and sat back in his chair.

Her emotions grew wild and tangled. "What do you mean? She thinks she has twenty-four chromosomes, and this makes her kill people?" Her heart would not stop thundering in her ears. "I don't understand. Are you saying that the two of you are in on this together? That you and my sister conspired to kill these people?"

He glanced around at the security cameras. "I never admitted to killing anyone. I simply told the police where the bodies were buried. It's part of the plea agreement."

"Okay, fine. So tell me where Anna is."

He didn't respond.

"Tell me where she is if she's still alive!"

"I don't know. I thought you could find her."

"What?"

"I don't know where she is anymore."

"You're full of shit, you know? Anna was sweet and funny and bright, and you killed her." She swallowed back the tears. She didn't want to cry in front of him.

"I don't kill people," Gaines said evenly. "I thought we covered that."

"But you said—"

"She's Death, is what I said . . . Anna is Death. Don't you get it? It's my duty to help her."

"What?"

"I said, what I said was . . . she takes them when they're ready to go. She takes them because that's her job. She's Death, and it's my job to help her, okay? It's my job to bury the bodies. I'm no murderer. I already told you that."

"So she's *alive*?"

He nodded moodily.

"And she thinks she's *Death*?"

"Until she found out who she really was, Anna didn't have a life," he said. "She was just alive and breathing."

"What do you mean?"

"Do you have a life, Daisy? Do you consider yourself to be truly alive?"

She froze.

"Those mice you experiment with can't choose," he said. "They can't plot their escape, and neither can you. When your time is up, it's up."

She turned toward the guards. "I'm done!"

"Listen to me. You can't stop her, Daisy. You can't stop Death."

She dropped the handset. "Guard?"

Jack slammed into the room. "Are you okay?"

"He's insane!" She stood on shaky legs.

He stroked her face and hair.

"Get me out of here," she whispered.

He was there, and that was all that mattered.

7.

Back in Daisy's motel room, Jack held her in his arms and tried to shake off the image of Roy Gaines behind the Plexiglas barrier, his delusion like a river they'd all been swept into. "He's lying," he told her. "He's building an insanity defense. I've seen this before."

"So you think he killed her?"

"Yes."

"But what if you're wrong?"

"He's trying to confuse you. He's only pretending to be crazy, but he's crazy like a fox. Think about it. He gets to blame the one victim who has delusions of grandeur. He knows her history. It's not such a big leap from the Virgin Mary to Death, is it? Don't you see what he's doing? He's buried her somewhere up in those mountains, convinced we'll never find her. So he tells you she's still out there, running around killing people. He wants to plant doubt in the jurors' minds."

Daisy stood moodily in a shaft of sunlight. "So it's all a scam? Him showing us those other bodies? Everything?"

"What else could it be?"

"Folie à deux."

Jack frowned. "What's that?"

"It means shared psychotic disorder. It happens sometimes when two susceptible individuals become involved in a mutually dependent psychotic relationship. One person has delusions, which the other one comes to share, and together they create a whole new belief system. *Folie à deux.*"

"I don't buy it."

"Why not?"

"Because I know this guy. He's smart. He's manipulating you. He's playing off your desire to find your sister alive. Think about it, Daisy. It's the perfect alibi. 'I didn't kill them. She did. She thinks she's Death.' So where is she? 'I don't know. She's crazy. She ran away.' "

"You don't think they could both be delusional?"

"I think he's a sociopath. Sociopaths are different from psychotics. Psychotics hear voices inside their heads. Sociopaths don't feel anything. They're soulless."

She sagged with defeat on the edge of the bed. "I didn't ask the right questions," she said dejectedly.

He sat down beside her and wrapped his arm around her. "It's okay. You did good."

"No. I should've asked him the obvious. If she's Death, why didn't he fear for his life? I could've tripped him up."

"You did better than ninety percent of the population would've, under the circumstances."

She shook her head angrily. "I should have protected her. Anna was three years younger than me when Mr. Barsum molested us. My sister was just a little girl, and I should have protected her. Why didn't I protect her?"

"Hey," he said, turning toward her. "There is no possible scenario in which you are to blame for any of this."

"Don't you see? I couldn't save her then, and I can't save her now."

She sat in a patch of sunlight, her face so sad and lovely it astounded him. He slid the straps of her batik-print dress off her shoulders and planted little kisses across her throat, making the beads of a necklace.

He could sense her giving in, but then something happened, because she slid the straps back up. "Please don't," she whispered. "I can't."

"Lie down with me," he said, drawing her onto the bed with him. He ran his fingers along her backbone, feeling the little bumps there. "I like your body," he said. "You're so beautiful. Do you like how this feels when I touch you?"

"Yes," she whispered, but the muscles of her back kept tensing up.

"We can stop if you want." He withdrew his hand.

She watched him solemnly, her eyes rounding a little. "I'm afraid," she admitted.

"Don't be. There's nothing to be afraid of."

"I don't like feeling vulnerable."

"Okay. We'll just lie here," he said. "We'll just lie here together."

Her face relaxed, and he realized that she trusted him. He wanted her to trust him, not just with her mind but with her body. She kissed him with a slack willingness, and they fumbled out of their clothes. Their bodies moved rhythmically together while the headboard bumped against the wall. He was brown from the sun, and he liked the way his brown hands explored her pale skin. She was paler, even, than the palest parts of himself.

"I haven't floated away yet," she said, looking at him with a kind of wonder. "I keep expecting to float away."

"Float away?"

"Out of my body."

"It's okay," he told her.

"I can't believe I'm still here in the room with you."

He could feel the tension in various parts of her body beginning to release its hold. He could tell it was painful for her to let go of this tension. He could feel her body relaxing against him, and as she relaxed, he could feel other areas of her beginning to stir. These different feelings and sensations held him fast. They moved him deeply.

"Is it okay?" he asked. "Does that feel good?"

"I like you inside me," she said in a hushed whisper.

A curl of blond hair settled in the hollow of her throat. The motel bed made a *creak-creak* sound. The wind blew through his heart an unexpected echo. It scared him to think that he might be falling in love with her.

Afterward they lay together, wrapped in a soft, warm silence. Her reclining body made a curve like a breaker coming toward him. A wrinkle in the bedspread felt like a finger tracking along his spine. As he watched her, his mind grew blank as a clean sheet of paper. "I'll come back tonight," he promised her.

"Yes," she said. "Come back."

He waited a beat, then said, "I want this like I've never wanted anything before in my life."

She nodded and looked into his face, the truth about them finally registering.

"I know all about you," he said. "I know how it is to lose somebody you love."

She burst into tears, her grief flooding forward, and he held her for a very long time. She was hot and human. She moved and breathed beside him.

"I'm coming back tonight," he said, sitting up and getting dressed. He pulled on his sticky clothes. He zipped and buttoned up.

"Wait," she said, reaching for her bedside table. "I've been meaning to show you something."

He nodded as he pulled his T-shirt down over his head.

She opened the diary to a specific page. "See where she wrote her name a bunch of times? Only that isn't her last name. Anna Hildreth. It's like she's a schoolgirl, dreaming about getting married to a man named Hildreth. See?"

He looked at the cramped signature. *Anna Hildreth, Anna Hildreth, Anna Hildreth . . .* She had scrawled it a total of ten times. "Is it code for anything?"

Daisy shook her head.

He frowned down at the page. It made him wonder. "So who's Hildreth?"

"I don't know anyone by that name. Wait." Daisy searched for a pen and piece of paper. "It's an anagram," she said, sitting up.

"You lost me."

"It just hit me. It's an anagram!"

"Again," Jack said. "Lost."

"Remember when I told you about her appointment with Dr. E. H. Hilt?"

"Yeah?"

Her tongue poked out between her lips as she wrote something down on a piece of motel stationery, then held it up for him to see. She'd spelled out: HILDRETH = DR E H HILT. "It's an anagram. Dr. E. H. Hilt *is* Hildreth."

"Okay, so who the hell is Hildreth?" Jack rubbed his jaw. "Wait, lemme ask you something. Why did your sister move to Los Angeles in the first place?"

"I'm not sure."

"Why not Chicago or New York?"

"She said she wanted to get as far away from Lily as possible. She was only half joking."

"Did she have her own Internet account at home?"

"Yes. Why?"

"Okay, bear with me a minute. Of all the victims, Anna's the only one who had a relationship with Gaines. He told you back in prison that he was in love with her, right? 'I never loved anyone like I loved her.' *Loved*, by the way. Did you notice that? He used the past tense. What does that tell you?"

Daisy frowned. "He knows something we don't know."

"Exactly. But getting back to my other point. Let's just suppose your sister met Roy Gaines over the Internet . . ."

"I thought you said they met eight months ago."

"According to one witness, they met *at least* eight months ago. They could've met earlier. Is there any other reason she chose L.A.?"

"Just that she was sick of living in Vermont."

"No other reason?"

"Wait," Daisy said. "They might've met while she was surfing the Internet, going on all those chat rooms and Web sites in search of Louis's father. Don't you think Gaines is the type to look for his victims that way?"

"If they did meet over the Internet," Jack said, taking it to its logical conclusion, "then he's the reason she decided to move to L.A."

"So he's Hildreth?"

Jack scratched his chin. "Either Gaines is Hildreth, or Hildreth is Gaines. Can I take this?" He indicated the diary.

She nodded. "So then, her saying that she couldn't wait to see Dr. Hilt meant she couldn't wait to see Roy Gaines. Oh God. She fell into his trap."

He took her hand. "I've got to go."

"What are you going to do?"

At the door he gave her a lingering kiss. "I'll take care of everything, Daisy," he promised. "Don't worry anymore."

8.

Even if there was only a slight chance that her sister was alive, Daisy had to find out. She had no choice. She picked up the phone. "Mom?" she said. "I need you to do me a favor. Go to Anna's computer and open it."

"What for?"

"You have to trust me. Just turn on her computer and open her hard drive."

"All right. Hold on." It took Lily several minutes of fumbling and mumbling to get the computer started.

"Are there any saved e-mails?" Daisy asked her.

"Six."

"Would you read off the addresses to me?"

"Father-Finders-at-Yahoo-dot-com, Orphan-Diseases-at-AOL-dot-com, three e-mails from Maranda . . ."

"Would you read those aloud?"

"I'm not comfortable doing that, Daisy."

"Mom, please. We're trying to find Anna, okay?"

She opened the e-mails one at a time and read them out loud to her daughter. There was nothing important on any of them, nothing about Roy Gaines or Roy Hildreth or a doctor named Hilt.

"Is that all?" Daisy asked.

"One more. It's to Tanya's Friends."

"What?"

"Tanya's-Friends-at-Excite-dot-com."

"Open it."

Lily did.

"Read it to me."

"Just read it?"

"Mom. Please."

"Okay, it says, 'I'll be moving to L.A. next month. Can't wait to meet you in person. I'll give you a call when I get there. Your friend, Anna.' "

Daisy called Truett at the neurogenetics lab. "What's the number for Tanya's Friends?" she asked as soon as he'd picked up.

"Who is this?" he said playfully.

"I'm in a hurry, Truett. My sister was in touch with a local chapter of Tanya's Friends and I need the number . . ."

"Okay, hold on. Let me look it up."

At the lab, they had a computer database containing the names of every organization and support group for orphan diseases in America. They used the database to notify family members about current clinical studies or promising breakthroughs and other pertinent information. They also used the database to find volunteers for their clinical trials.

"Okay. Got it. Tanya's Friends." He gave her the address and phone number, then said, "Listen. Two cannibals are eating a clown. One says to the other, 'Does this taste funny to you?'"

She smiled.

"It's my one and only cannibal joke."

"Talk to you later, Truett."

"I miss you, Daisy," he said and hung up.

Daisy rented a car using her Visa card, then drove to a residential neighborhood in the Valley where the houses were built too close to a major freeway. She parked in front of a stucco building with a manicured lawn and neatly trimmed hedges and got out. Her hair was plastered to her face with sweat. She could hear the steady sound of traffic on the freeway. It sounded just like the ocean.

She knocked on the door, and a woman with sunken cheeks and large ears set far back on her head answered. She wore turquoise shorts and an indigo tank top that showed off her sagging breasts.

"Kathy Lansky?"

"Yes?" the woman said.

"My name's Daisy Hubbard. I think you know my sister, Anna?"

The woman squinted. It took her a moment. "Oh yes. C'mon in."

"Thanks."

Daisy sat in the living room while Kathy fetched her a glass of iced tea from the kitchen. Daisy could see the stove through the open doorway, a bean pot simmering on the back burner.

"Sugar and lemon?" Kathy asked.

"Sounds good."

The wooden floorboards squeaked as Kathy carried the tray of drinks back into the living room. She handed Daisy an ice-cold glass of iced tea, then took a seat in the rocking chair beside her. "Anna was a member of our group," she said, "but I haven't seen her in months."

"When was the last time you saw her?"

"November, I think." She gave a rigid yawn. A tear rolled down her cheek, and she wiped it away with her hand. "Why?" she said. "Did something happen?"

Daisy took a sip of tea, wondering what to say. She set the glass on the coffee table next to a vase of wildflowers. "How often does your group meet?"

"Once a week."

"And how often did Anna attend before she stopped coming?"

Kathy rolled her eyes. "Um . . . three months, maybe four. Never missed a session, except for that one time when she went home."

"Went home?"

"You know. To Vermont. I think it was last September."

"She went home last September?"

"For two weeks."

Daisy didn't bother correcting her. Anna hadn't been back to Vermont since she'd moved out to the West Coast.

"Why? Is something wrong?" Kathy said.

"My sister has disappeared."

"Oh no."

"We don't know where she is."

"I'm sorry to hear that."

"I'm trying to track her whereabouts these past ten months. Retrace her steps and find out what she's been up to."

"I see." She nodded. "Well, she came to almost every meeting, from August through November, I think. Except for those two weeks in September. We originally met through NORD, you know."

"NORD?"

"It's a networking program for families of patients with rare diseases. She was looking to join a local group. This was back when she lived in Vermont. She said her brother . . . your brother . . . died of Stier-Zellar's disease?"

Daisy nodded.

"Well, that's why we're Tanya's Friends. Tanya had S-Z." She stood up and handed Daisy a glossy brochure, then sat back down and started rocking. "We give people an opportunity to share their experiences and exchange information. A chance to chat, vent and unload. We're one of the biggest S-Z groups in the country. Some of our members have even testified in Washington."

"Did she ever bring anybody to the meetings with her?"

"Just once. Some guy with pitted skin. He was a real gorilla, that guy."

"Roy Gaines?"

"I don't remember his name. She only brought him once."

Daisy sat forward. "Who else is in your group?"

"Sorry. That's confidential." Melancholy had settled into the woman's square, flat face, as if she'd seen too much suffering. "I can't give out names."

"Was Colby Ostrow in your group?"

"Yes. Why?"

"Did you know that he was murdered last week?"

Her face grew pale. "What?"

"Was Irma Petropoulous in your group?"

"No," she said, "but her daughter is."

9.

Daisy couldn't reach Jack on his cell phone and left a message for him to call her as soon as possible. Then she ran the scenario through her head: Anna had brought Gaines to one of her meetings, where he'd used the opportunity to target a couple more victims. That certainly blew Jack's theory that Colby Ostrow and Irma Petropoulous had been victims of opportunity, chosen at random. But why kill these people? And what if Jack was wrong about Gaines? What if Anna had killed them? What if she actually believed she was Death now?

Anna was schizophrenic, not a sociopath. The two disorders were leagues apart. Daisy's sister was no killer, but she could be delusional. Anna believed in angels and miracles, and there was no reason to think that, having gone off her meds, she might not delude herself into thinking she was Death, or that she had a death gene on chromosome 24. Daisy knew one thing for sure—she would not stop until she found her sister. She owed Anna that much.

A wave of heat hit her as she crossed the sun-scorched asphalt toward the pier. She'd spent the better part of the afternoon walking up and down the strand, dogging complete strangers and showing them Anna's picture. "Have you seen this woman? Her name is Anna Hubbard, she's twenty-eight years old . . ."

It was five o'clock by the time she arrived at the arcade again, where a dramatic orange sunset splashed across the white pine floor. She approached a group of teenagers playing pinball and said, "Have you seen Christie? I'm looking for Christie."

One of the girls turned her head, her earrings catching the light. Her golden eyes were placid, and she was smoking a hand-rolled cigarette. The dangly earrings, silver feathers inlaid with turquoise, were just like the ones Daisy had given Anna for her Sweet Sixteen.

Daisy stared at the girl. "Those look like my sister's earrings," she said. "Anna Hubbard. Do you know her?"

The girl couldn't have been more than sixteen and had bronzed, flawless skin and long unkempt hair. Her heavily lined eyes were sunk in her face like submerged gems, and her clothes were dirty, as if she'd spent the night under a traffic overpass.

"Hey," Daisy said, walking swiftly toward her. "Where'd you get those?"

The girl flicked her cigarette on the floor and scowled.

"Do you know Anna Hubbard?"

The girl turned and ran.

"Hey!" Daisy chased her out the door. "Stop!"

She followed the girl down the pier toward the strand, then across the street into a quiet residential neighborhood, where the cottages were wrapped in shawls of purple bougainvillea.

"Wait!" Daisy grabbed the girl by her tie-dyed T-shirt and spun her around.

"What?" the girl shrieked. "What do you want?"

"Those are my sister's earrings," Daisy told her.

"They are not!"

"Where is she?"

"I don't know what the fuck you're talking about!"

"Do you want me to call the police?" Daisy clutched the girl's arm with one hand and took out her cell phone with the other.

"No." She quickly removed the contested earrings and handed them over. "Here," she said. "Take them."

"I don't want the stupid earrings, I want my sister!" Daisy tightened her grip around the girl's arm. "If you don't tell me where Anna is right now, I'm calling the police. Do you understand? They'll arrest you for stealing."

The girl twisted violently out of Daisy's grasp, and they traded jabs.

"Just tell me where you got them!" Daisy screamed.

The girl turned and ran down the sidewalk, her shoes making staccato sounds.

"Hey!" Daisy tore after her. "Come back!"

Quickly gaining speed, the girl rounded the corner and disappeared.

Daisy tripped on a buckled part of the sidewalk and went sprawling. She scrambled to her feet and limped down to the corner, but the girl was nowhere in sight.

10.

It was six o'clock by the time Jack got a copy of Anna Hubbard's credit card transactions faxed over to him. In the past year, she'd used her credit cards to purchase things like clothes, gasoline, dinners and automobile repairs. Last August she'd bought two round-trip tickets to Boise, Idaho, for the first two weeks in September. During this trip, she and an unknown traveling companion had rented a car and stayed at two different hotels—one in Boise, the other in Pocatello. Okay, Jack wondered, what was so fucking alluring about Idaho? The credit card bills showed that Anna had purchased a pair of binoculars, along with some bed linens and a few gifts from the Spud Shop, and there were charges for meals in restaurants from Boise to American Falls.

Next he phoned his contact over at the Department of Motor Vehicles. It was late, but Harold Bregman owed him a favor. Harold liked to party, and last year Jack had caught him with a pound of marijuana in his possession. Much to Harold's relief, Jack had given him a pass, but now Jack owned his ass. That was the way it worked.

"I need a driver's license for a Roy Hildreth or a Dr. E. H. Hilt," he said, spelling them out. "He's thirty-four, six foot three, brown eyes, black hair."

"Do you realize that I'm just pulling into my driveway?" Harold whined.

"So turn your fucking car around."

"Jesus . . . do you know what time it is?"

"It's *you-owe-me* time, asshole."

"Shit. Okay. Lemme see what I can do," he grumbled. "Gimme an hour."

Jack hung up and stared at his hands. His palms looked yellow in this light. He was acting on mere suspicion alone, since he had nothing concrete to go on, but the what-ifs were beginning to pile up. Looking back, it made sense. Roy Gaines's driver's license was out of state. Louisiana didn't require fingerprints the way California, Colorado, Georgia, Hawaii and Texas did. They'd found cash and money orders stashed away in his funky De Campo Beach apartment. His car was in excellent condition—no expired stickers, no broken taillights. He hadn't gotten so much as a traffic ticket. And he'd moved around a lot—six different locations in the past four years. Which seemed harmless enough, but when you added it all together, it pointed to a false-identity scam. People with false identities were constantly relocating. They drove with extreme caution in order to avoid getting ticketed. They kept a lot of cash around and carried out-of-state licenses.

It was approaching seven o'clock by the time Harold

called him back. "There is no E. H. Hilt," he said. "But there's a Roy Orion Hildreth. I'm sending it to you now."

"Thanks." Jack waited for the e-mail to arrive, then opened the attachment. Roy Orion Hildreth was Roy Gaines, only with shorter hair and without the horn-rims. He'd somehow managed to retain his own history while resurfacing as an entirely new person.

Unfortunately, even nowadays, creating a false identity was no big deal. All you needed was a cemetery. Find a child who had died prematurely who'd be approximately the same age as yourself, then apply for a birth certificate using the information from the death announcement in the local paper. Once you had a birth certificate, you could pretty much get a driver's license and a passport. From that point on, you could avoid detection by keeping a low profile and a clean driving record, moving around a lot, always paying for things in cash and never applying for life insurance or credit cards or anything else that could be skip-traced. Jack bet a thousand bucks that Roy Gaines had more than one alias, more than one residence and multiple sets of IDs for every contingency. Why Los Angeles? Because the best place to hide a leaf was in the forest.

Feeling a surge of adrenaline, he picked up the phone and called his contact over at the Criminal Records Unit, interrupting her in the middle of her dinner. Harold Bregman wasn't the only one who owed Jack a favor.

11.

Daisy had been searching for over an hour now for the girl with the bronze skin and the golden eyes, poking into hair salons, skateboard shops and art galleries. Too many tourists were out on the promenade tonight, getting drunk and buying things. Parking was a nightmare. The palm fronds quivered in the sultry heat as she gritted her teeth with determination and approached complete strangers in her quest to find the girl who had Anna's earrings. She walked past a group of teenagers hanging around outside an ice cream parlor and said, "Do you know Anna Hubbard? Have you seen this woman?"

She could smell incense in the air. Nobody had any idea who Anna was from her picture, and Daisy was beginning to suspect that there would not be a feel-good ending to this story. She pointed out the earrings in the picture. "What about these?" she said. "Have you seen a girl wearing these earrings? She's in her teens, she's got these gold-colored eyes . . ."

One of the boys flashed his bad teeth. "You mean Gillian?"

"Who?" Daisy said.

"Long hair? Rolls her own cigarettes?"

"That's the one."

His face had a remarkably timeless, weathered look. "I know where you can find her."

Down by the bike path, several yards away from the dollar-a-slice pizza shop, Daisy found a drum circle in the sand. A dozen or so shabbily dressed beach bums sat around drumming and getting stoned.

Too tired to stand another moment, she flopped down in the sand and watched the drummers for a while. The sky blazed with pink and orange streaks. The air throbbed with drumbeats. Two boys played Hackey Sack, kicking a small ball around. A teenage girl was taking self-portraits with her camera phone. Her hair was tucked under a scarf, and she wore granny glasses and a peace T-shirt, but Daisy recognized her just the same. "Gillian?" she said.

The girl shot up and ran away.

Daisy chased her down the boardwalk and onto the beach. "Gillian, wait!"

Down by the water, the sound of the surf was like the drum circle, booming and receding. The setting sun cast a rosy glow over everything, and you could see the pink mountains in the hazy distance. Daisy bounded after her. "Gillian!"

The girl tripped and fell in the sand, and Daisy caught up with her, grabbed her by the hands and hoisted her to her feet. "Where's my sister? Where's Anna Hubbard? Do you know?"

She just stood there, looking hungry and scared.

"Do you know Roy Gaines?"

The girl let out a small cry and lobbed a fist at Daisy's sternum. Daisy grabbed her thrashing fist and twisted her arm around, and they landed clumsily in the sand, tangled together and exhausted. Breathing hard. Too tired to run anymore.

Gillian curled herself up in a fetal position and just lay there, scooping handfuls of sand and letting them spill through her fingers.

"I want to find my sister," Daisy told her softly. "That's all. She needs my help."

Gillian stopped scooping sand.

"Will you help me?" Daisy pleaded.

And she gave the smallest of nods.

FOLIE À DEUX

1.

Jack had everything he needed. It was a warm night, around eight o'clock by the time he pulled into the parking garage of the psychiatric prison. There were plenty of spaces to choose from, since most of the staff had gone home. He reached for his briefcase and got out, then paused for a moment with his keys in his hand. He was having second thoughts. Maybe he should turn around and go home. After all, he could lose his job for what he was about to do. *Think, Jack. Is this what you really want?* He slammed the door and locked his car, then headed for the elevator, his footsteps echoing throughout the underground garage.

Inside the main building, he approached the reception desk. "I'm here to see Roy Gaines," he said.

Corrections Officer Bob Barrows was a Joe Lunch Bucket kind of guy, an ex-football tackle with beefy layers of muscle who belonged to that brotherhood of wayward guards who sometimes beat their prisoners and often fired their weapons into the recreation yard whenever a fight broke out. Jack's heart rate soared as he produced his badge.

Officer Barrows scanned the appointment book and checked Jack's name off a list. "Surrender your weapon," he said.

Jack gave up his gun and signed the waiver.

"Put your briefcase on the counter." The officer had a broad, impassive face and a holstered steel-blue 9mm Beretta. An idiotic song was playing on the radio on his desk, some boy-band dreck. On the wall behind him was a row of plaques commemorating the eight prison guards who'd died during a riot in the 1960s. Twitching with adrenaline, Jack placed his briefcase on the marble countertop.

Officer Barrows spun it around and opened it, his eyes ticking back and forth as he rummaged through the storage pockets. After a moment, he lowered his chin and studied Jack over his bifocals.

The bile-green walls began to ululate. Not a word was spoken between them, not a syllable exchanged. Jack could feel the sweat building on his brow as he slouched beneath the weight of the enormous risk he was taking. There were things inside his briefcase that any other guard would have confiscated immediately.

"You look like your dog just died," Barrows said with a conspiratorial smile.

Jack didn't know how to respond to this.

"Relax." The big guard closed the briefcase and handed it back to him. He was giving Jack a pass, just like Jack had given Harold Bregman a pass. *Congratula-*

tions, you're my bitch. He'd just joined the brotherhood of corrupt prison guards.

Never in his life had Jack considered crossing that line before. Now he took a deep breath and blew the hair out of his eyes, feeling no remorse. No shame. He was surprised how little emotion he felt. After all, why shouldn't Roy Gaines or Roy Hildreth or whoever the hell he was . . . why shouldn't he suffer the way his victims had suffered? Why shouldn't justice be served for once?

"Step over to the door," Officer Barrows said, and Jack did as he was told. But before buzzing him in, the guard paused and said, "Say hello from me while you're at it."

Jack turned. "Excuse me?"

"The guy's an eight-cylinder psycho. That son of a bitch told me I've got six months to live. Says my pump's gonna give out." He spit the next word. "Cocksucker."

Jack made a vague gesture of sympathy.

"So go on. Do your worst. You have my blessing."

The big steel blast doors opened with a mechanical hiss, and, gripping his briefcase by its leather handle, Jack walked inside, where a tired-looking armed guard escorted him down the wide corridor toward the attorney conference room.

The room had no monitoring devices. You could literally get away with murder in here. There was nothing but a bolted-down table, two chairs, a wrought-iron grate on the floor and an overhead fluorescent light strip. Jack could see the full moon through the barred, wire-reinforced windows. He set his briefcase down on the table and waited for his heart rate to slow to normal. The last thing he needed was to show Gaines a crack in the armor.

After an interminable couple of minutes, the door thunked open and two officers carrying an assortment of Berettas, pepper spray, blackjacks and stun guns on their utility belts escorted the prisoner inside. Handcuffed to a waist chain and manacled with leg irons, Roy took shuffling steps across the floor.

Jack swallowed back his revulsion as he held Roy's eye. It was quiet as feathers in here. The prisoner's waxy complexion suited his new environment. The prison was designed to prohibit daylight, and patients lived in a constant netherworld of solar neglect. The guards plopped Roy down in his seat, then quickly retreated. Something was wrong; they feared him. Jack didn't like that.

Roy snorted derisively. "What're they so scared of?"

Jack stood up too quickly, his head going light, then waited for his equilibrium to return. "Notice where we are, Roy," he said quietly. "There are no monitoring devices in this room. No closed-circuit TVs. No guards. It's just you and me, pal."

Roy watched him closely as he spoke, observing his face and lips with narrowed eyes. He would react critically, Jack was sure, to any hesitation on his part.

"My job calls for an unusual amount of restraint," he went on, "but I draw the line when it comes to the victim's family. I've given you plenty of chances, my friend, and what have I gotten for my troubles? More bullshit. More games. I won't allow it."

Roy's shoulders lifted as he took a shallow breath.

"You really had me fooled, Roy. I honestly believed you wanted to clear your conscience and end this family's suffering. But whenever I think you're about to co-operate with us, you go ahead and prove to me how wrong I am." He fed off the prisoner's discomfort as he opened his briefcase and produced a roll of duct tape. "So. Here we are. Now it's my turn to fuck with *your* head."

Roy stirred. "Touch me, and I'll sue your ass."

"Ask yourself: Do I look like I give a shit?" In one swift move, Jack unwound a generous length of tape—it made a sticky sound coming off the roll—then looped it around the prisoner's chest, binding his upper torso to the chair. He slapped another piece of tape over Roy's mouth and pressed it shut. "Officer Barrows says hello, by the way."

Roy bucked in his chair, straining at his binds. He made strangled guttural sounds from behind the duct tape, but nothing happened. No guards came running. No lights flashed. No alarm bells rang.

It gave Jack a nasty thrill. He removed the file folders from his briefcase—quite a healthy stack—and slapped them down on the table. "Luckily for me," he said, "I know people who know people. People who owe me favors. People who don't necessarily follow life's little rules."

Breathing hard through his nose, Roy glanced at the stack of paperwork.

"You know, it's curious," Jack said, wiping the slippery sweat off the back of his neck. "You respond to physical threats the way most ex-cons do. Only you aren't an ex-con, are you, Roy? Your record is clean."

Roy gave him a blank, unfriendly stare.

"You're innocent. Right?"

He didn't react, except for the slightest uptick of an eyebrow.

"Well? Are you or aren't you?"

He stared at Jack, sweat beading visibly on his forehead. It was the first time Jack had seen him sweat, and he considered that to be a small triumph.

"Maybe this'll help." He took a cheap plastic hand mirror out of his briefcase, the kind you'd find in any drugstore, and held it in front of Roy's face. "Take a good look."

He averted his gaze.

"Look at yourself, Roy. Is this the face of an innocent man? Does this sweaty, pitted, pathetic-looking creature seem innocent to you? Does he?" He grabbed the prisoner by his hair and held the mirror close. "You don't like looking at yourself, do you? Is that why you removed the medicine chest mirror and the full-length mirror from your closet door? Whatsamatter, Roy? Your conscience bothering you? I'm surprised you even have a conscience."

The prisoner swung his head from side to side, but Jack held him fast by the roots of his hair and forced him to look at his reflection.

"Is that why you took all your mirrors down? Because you hate peering into those guilty eyes of yours? Or is it simple vanity? It's probably vanity."

The prisoner let out a muffled groan.

"I hate to ruin your strategy, my friend. But I know who killed those people. And it wasn't Anna Hubbard. Not even close. So what's really going on here, boys and girls? Anybody? Oh, wait. I get it. You're 'psychotic.'"

He made quote signs with his fingers. "You have a 'mental illness.' It's called 'antisocial personality disorder.' "

Roy inhaled deeply through his nose and stared at Jack, who put the mirror down and picked up a file.

"You left quite a trail of bread crumbs behind you, Mr. Hildreth. I have here copies of your juvenile records and psychiatric evaluations going back thirty years."

The prisoner's face looked like it was about to hatch. He bucked and jerked in his seat, but the duct tape held him fast to the bolted-down chair. Behind the iron bars, the room's windows were painted shut.

"You were born thirty-four years ago to Benny Hildreth and Linda Pratt."

Roy stopped fighting and closed his eyes, his muscular body sagging against the chair.

"Born in Arizona, an only child," Jack went on. "Your mother died when you were eight, and over the course of the next three years, you ran away from home a total of twenty times. At thirteen, you started dipping into your father's prescription drugs."

Roy tried to form words through the tape. He rolled his eyes and made poignant gagging sounds, which Jack ignored.

"You dropped out of high school your sophomore year, then bounced in and out of juvenile hall until you were nineteen, when . . ."

Roy's body strained against the tape.

"You got a girl pregnant. She was seventeen and Catholic. She didn't believe in abortion, so she went ahead and had the baby, which later died. A year later, you did time for check forgery. Two years after that, you were busted for a parole violation. At twenty-three, you did a stint in a mental institution after slashing your wrists with the sharpened edges of your driver's license."

Roy emitted a miserable groan.

"At the hospital, you ate your own fingernails, then claimed you'd been poisoned." Jack looked up. "Should I go on? Yes? No? Maybe?"

The prisoner shook his head no.

"Want me to stop?"

Roy nodded, his eyes wet with defeat.

Jack put the folder down. "Okay. So tell me. Where did you bury her?"

Roy gave a loud grunt.

"Are you going to tell me where she is? For real this time?"

He snarled behind the tape.

"Let's put a fucking end to this charade."

Roy tried to break free again.

"No? You're not going to cooperate?"

His gaze grew defiant.

"Fine with me." Jack picked up the file and continued. "Your mom was a hypochondriac. She used to lie around in bed all day long, and the only way you could ever get close to her was by reading her medical textbooks out loud to her. You learned about diseases that way. The two of you would discuss her symptoms and diagnose her imaginary ailments, but in the end, she failed to diagnose the one thing that ultimately killed her—overmedication."

Roy stared at Jack, seething with hostility.

"Your father was a bone trader," he went on, "which means he sold and traded the remains of dead people for a living. Fingers, skulls, blood samples, eyeballs . . . *eyeballs?* What a great guy your dad must've been.

Fucking Father of the Year. Says here there's a huge underground market for this sort of crap." Disgusted, Jack turned the page. "Your father sold photographs of dead celebrities and videotapes of necrophilia. Lovely. He sold slides of Marilyn Monroe's blood and slices of President Reagan's polyps. He retailed in snips of hair, bone fragments, pieces of brain matter, the list goes on. Gee whiz. Sounds like you had a real *Brady Bunch* upbringing."

The prisoner's head sagged. He refused to look up.

Jack noticed this. He relished this. He selected a psychiatric file from the stack on the table. "At the hospital, when you tried to slit your wrists . . . why'd you want to die, Roy? Was it your bone-trader father? Your miserable past? What?"

Roy hissed through his nostrils like a cornered animal. He coiled like a snake, then raised himself up as far as he could in his seat, leg muscles quivering, and shook his head in an exaggerated way, all the tendons in his neck popping.

"Should we find out? I've got all your psychiatric records, going back to the early eighties. We can do this all night long if we want to. I brought a thermos of coffee. Nobody's gonna bother us. Should I go on? Yes? No? Maybe?"

Roy shook his head vehemently.

"Want me to stop? For real this time?"

He nodded.

Jack put the folder down. "Where'd you bury her?"

Roy gave a loud grunt.

They stared at each other.

"Where'd you bury Anna Hubbard?"

His chest heaved up and down.

"Look, Roy," Jack said, moving in close. "Give it up, and we'll cut you a deal. Life without parole. You want to avoid the death penalty, don't you?"

The prisoner's eyes welled with tears.

"You'll tell me everything?"

He nodded.

"No more bullshit? No more games?"

"Mmf," came the muffled response. "Mmf!"

Jack took out a topological map, then ripped the duct tape off Roy's mouth, leaving a band of reddened skin where the tape had been. "Okay. So. Where'd you bury the body?"

"High country," he gasped. "East of Pine Canyon."

Opening a map of the San Gabriel Mountains, Jack flattened it against the tabletop. "Show me."

Roy pointed. "Around this area here . . . just off an unmarked trail."

Jack handed him a pencil. "Mark it on the map."

Roy shook his head. "I can't."

"That's not the response I wanted to hear."

"I don't remember. I can only identify the specific location when I'm there. On the ground. In person."

Jack grabbed him by the collar and squeezed. "Daisy's not gonna be there. You're not dragging her through another one of your fucking dramas, understand?"

Roy gave an abrupt nod.

"No more bullshit, or your ass is grass." Jack released him. "Okay, let's go."

2.

Daisy fished her car keys out of her pocket and headed for the promenade. Gillian had given her an address. Was it a lie? Was it a false lead? The frightened girl wouldn't even tell her if Anna was okay or not. She'd just scribbled the information on a scrap of paper and run off. Now Daisy's head was spinning. She was in shock, but she had to stay focused. Anna needed her. The heels of her shoes crackled over the gritty sidewalk as she hurried back to her rental car, got in behind the wheel and started the engine. *Anna's alive.* She could feel it in the pit of her stomach. Her sister was alive. She could hardly believe it.

Daisy seriously doubted that Anna had killed anyone. She believed instead that, in a delusional state, her sister might've helped Roy Gaines with his grisly acts. She didn't want to think about that right now. She had to find Anna and get her back on her meds, just find her sister safe and sound. There would be plenty of time to figure out the rest of it later on.

The engine rumbled like one of those machines that tumbled pebbles, and she got back onto the boulevard and joined the steady stream of traffic. She rolled her window down, letting in a rush of hot gritty air. Traffic was slow, but the wind whipping into the car created the illusion of speed. She had a few prescription bottles in her backpack—Anna's medication, her antipsychotics and antidepressants. If it was true that Anna was alive, then Daisy would have to coax her sister into taking some pills tonight. It reminded her of all the times she'd tried to reason with Anna by pretending to believe that there was a conspiracy against her, a tactic that seldom worked.

Daisy took the 405 south. Time passed like liquid mercury, the elusive way it slipped over your palm. The sound of the hot gritty wind rushing into the car grew deafening, and she rolled her window back up, unsure of where she was going. Directions had been sketchy.

After fifteen minutes, she eased off the freeway, then came to a stop at the bottom of the exit ramp. To her left was a cement divider, to her right the ruins of an empty parking lot. She took a left and shivered, wondering what was in store for her. What if this was a trap? What if Roy Gaines had other accomplices? What if Anna was being held against her will in this desolate part of town? Or worse, what if Anna was bouncing-off-the-walls psychotic? What if she *had* killed those people? What would Daisy do then?

She drove through an industrial section of town, past the grisly bones of California poverty—burned-out crack houses, gutted strip malls, graffiti-covered cars. A pickup truck was stalled beneath an overpass, and the frustrated driver stood waving his arms as if he were conducting a symphony.

"Hold on," Daisy whispered, catching sight of her perspiring face in the rearview mirror. "I'm coming, Anna. Hold on."

3.

The Angeles Crest Highway was the longest canyon drive in L.A. County, rough on the suspension but well worth the trip. The view was spectacular. The route was tight and winding, with very little traffic at this late hour and just an occasional falling rock or two. Jack wound his way uphill into high country, the Ford's rebuilt engine rattling, while the prisoner stared at him through the rearview mirror, never once averting his gaze.

"Take a right." Roy sat quietly in the backseat, his cuffed hands folded in his lap.

Jack took a right off the highway onto an unposted road that twisted up through the forested canyon, where they drove past tall pines and little else—no gas stations, no stores, no telephone poles. He reduced his speed and checked his tank, which was less than half full. He reminded himself that the area was never patrolled at night.

"Take this next left coming up," Roy said.

Jack turned down a one-lane, dirt and gravel road, then glanced in the rearview mirror. The prisoner was looking out the window now. He seemed to have regained his composure and was calm in his defeat. Jack was confident he'd lead him to Anna Hubbard's grave this time. Roy Hildreth's past was a nightmare he didn't want to relive.

The car climbed up the next canyon, and on its way down, they passed a run-down cabin surrounded by weeping willows. Across the street from the overgrown cabin was a dried-up streambed where the canyon opened onto a sand wash.

"Stop," Roy said.

Jack braked and got out.

The full moon was high in the sky and would provide them with enough light to hike by. Jack opened the back door and yanked the prisoner out by his jumpsuit. The leg irons made him walk like a penguin.

"I can't move with these things on."

Jack was fully aware that Roy might be setting a trap for him in this isolated section of forest. "Turn toward the car. Lean over the hood. Don't make any sudden moves." Roy did as he was told, and Jack knelt in the dirt and unlocked the leg manacles, then tossed them into the backseat, where they clanged together noisily. Then he got his heavy-duty flashlight and emergency shovel out of the trunk.

"Okay, let's go." He pushed Roy in front of him and kept his gun aimed at the prisoner's spine. They were way out in the middle of nowhere, surrounded by pine trees and little else. A feverish wind rushing through the dry needles made the treetops creak and sigh, while high overhead, Jupiter and Venus twinkled distantly in the hazy night sky.

"Where to?" Jack said.

"That unmarked trailhead across the street."

"Try anything, and I'll shoot you in the back."

The air was gummy hot. The trail skirted the western edge of the canyon. Jack could feel the hum of many insects, even though he couldn't see them. They occasionally buzzed around his ears and landed on his sweaty face. The trail turned sharply at the elbow before wandering deeper into the woods. Soon the trees became behemoths, and through their distant upper branches, he could make out the Big Dipper. The North Star, although not the brightest star in the sky, was the easiest one to locate—you just followed the two "pointer" stars on the Big Dipper. Soon Jack got his bearings. They were heading east.

Roy spoke. "Aren't you even curious?"

"About what?"

"Why I did it."

"Sure, Roy. Why'd you do it?"

"Justice," he said.

"Uh-huh." Jack pointed at the trail ahead with his flashlight beam. "Keep moving."

The heavy-duty handcuffs were positioned at the navel, allowing Roy limited use of his hands. The carbon-steel waist chain had been designed for high-security transport and featured steel swivels for extra strength and durability. The handcuffs were fitted with oversize rivet heads and double locks so that you'd need two keys to open them. Jack kept his service revolver aimed at Roy's back as they continued moving along the trail.

Above them, high in the night sky, heavenly bodies shone faintly down through the smog layer—distant stars and ice planets and restless asteroids. Inwardly, Jack was beginning to have his doubts. Tonight's actions could mean the end of his career, although it wouldn't be the first time he'd risked everything for a woman. Earlier that evening, he'd filled out a Prisoner Escort Record. Due to time constraints, he'd managed to get only one of the required signatures, and so, in one of those rash acts of desperation he was known for, Jack forged the other signature. Hours later, he'd used the phony Prisoner Escort Record to dispatch the prisoner out of the facility.

"It's over there," Roy said.

A dozen yards or so down the slope of the canyon was a mound of earth covered in dry branches. Jack could smell cedar on the stagnant air as they crossed a wooden plank that'd been placed horizontally over an eroded ditch. They stumbled down the incline. "Stay in front of me," Jack said. "Easy. Okay, stop. Spread your feet."

Roy stood before him with his hands cuffed and his legs apart while Jack aimed his light around at the trees. He needed to find a branch that was secure enough to handcuff the prisoner to.

Centuries of gravity and wind had shaped these ancient conifers, their branches growing outward rather than upward. Jack chose a particularly gnarled giant, then aimed his gun at Roy's head and said, "Walk over there. Slowly."

Roy did as he was told.

"Okay, stop," Jack said. "Legs apart. Your back to me."

Roy turned around.

Jack got the keys out of his pocket and approached the prisoner with caution. "Don't even think about it," he said, testing a couple of branches before he found a nice sturdy one. He grabbed Roy's left hand, unlocked the handcuff, unraveled the belly chain and cuffed Roy's right hand to the conifer tree. The prisoner's left hand was free now, but he wouldn't be going anywhere soon. Jack took a step back and holstered his weapon.

Roy put his free hand to good use by plucking a pack of cigarettes out of his jumpsuit pocket. "Got a light?" he said, knocking a cigarette out of the pack and slipping it between his lips.

Jack lit the cigarette for him, holding his eye a cautious beat. Then he walked over to the grave site and, extending his emergency shovel, began to dig.

He dug and dug, and soon the heady smell of overturned earth filled his nostrils. There would be nothing left of Anna Hubbard's corpse but leather and bones. *Justice.* What kind of justice was that? Justice for whom? He felt bad for her aborted life.

He dug for several minutes more before the blade of his shovel hit something soft. He dug with focused energy until a small object knuckled out of the ground. He picked it up and dusted it off. It was a brown leather wallet. He opened it and took out the driver's license.

The California license belonged to a man from Fresno named Andy Johnson. He was twenty years old. "What the . . ." Jack looked up. "What the hell is this?"

Roy stood in silhouette, the orange ember of his cigarette circling the dark. "Keep digging," he said.

A chill ran along Jack's spine. He retrieved his shovel and dug until he'd unearthed a skeletal hand with a man's wristwatch attached. The message was clear. He'd been set up. "You lying bastard."

"Keep digging."

"What is this? What's going on?"

Roy's voice was emptied of all feeling. "Just dig," he said, blowing out a trail of smoke.

Heart going like gangbusters, Jack knelt in the dirt and dug frantically with his hands. He had vastly underestimated the prisoner's capacity for deception. The corpse wore a dove-gray suit and a checkered tie. Jack staggered to his feet and roared, *"Where is she?"*

"Jesus Christ!" Gaines was on fire. He must've dropped his cigarette, because the underbrush was ablaze around him, withered wildflowers and last year's dry leaves creating a tinderbox that whooshed outward from Roy Hildreth in all directions.

"Jesus, help me!" The prisoner stood handcuffed to the tree, stomping his feet and trying to put out the fire that was licking up his pant legs now.

One match, one flame, one second—that was all it took. Wind and fire made a deadly combination. The dried-out pine needles littering the ground had gone up with a whoosh, and smoke filled the air as the flames spread rapidly.

Jack didn't think; he reacted. He grabbed his emergency shovel and raced over to put out the fire. He shoveled dirt on the flames and smacked at the burning grass with the flat of the blade while a thick toxic smoke clogged his lungs.

"Jesus! I'm on fire!" Roy's pant legs were still burning.

Jack knelt in front of him and slapped at the smoldering jumpsuit with his hands, not wanting to bring Roy back to prison with third-degree burns. He patted the smoking fabric and sucked air so fast he started to hyperventilate. The smell of soot and dirt covered everything. He coughed, then gasped in surprise as the belly chain looped down around his neck.

4.

Daisy was driving along a residential side street where the potholes were so deep and so numerous it looked like a bombed-out landing strip. She stared with nervous fascination at the weed-infested lawns and cracked foundations. The houses in this neighborhood suffered from serious neglect. A cold dread washed over her as she swung into the oil-stained driveway of a faded bungalow partially hidden from view behind a vine-choked fence. She switched off the ignition and sat listening to the ticking of the engine. The mailbox looked as if somebody had walloped it with a baseball bat, and the front yard's only tree stood like a proud amputee sadistically removed of its limbs. She could make out the faded impression of an "88" on the front door where the house numbers had once been.

Daisy got out of her car and headed up the crumbling walkway toward the bungalow, its stucco exterior riddled with hairline cracks. The caulking around the windows was so dried out you could easily push in the panes of glass. There was water damage around the front door, and the metal doorknob was pitted and dinged. Dread folded down on her as she pushed the front door open, its creaking hinges coming loose on their rusty screws.

"Hello?" She paused on the threshold.

The darkened house didn't respond.

Daisy proceeded down a windowless hallway, reaching for the walls in order to steady herself. The floor felt wildly uneven, as if the house had slipped off its foundation during an earthquake. Everywhere you looked were little piles of scrap plaster and plaster dust. Her foot hit a hammer that hadn't been touched in decades. She passed a narrow doorway and caught sight of the kitchen's cheap particleboard cabinets, its faded linoleum countertops and a sticky tiled floor with the grout buckling up. The stove had been painted with several coats of grease and grime.

The living room walls were the color of melted bronze. The ornamental plaster was fissured with cracks like baked soapstone, and the ceiling was low and sagging in the center, as if some quantum singularity were pulling the house inexorably toward it. Unlit candles hogged all the flat surfaces of the room, and the useless smoke detector on the ceiling had a bunch of wires sticking out of it.

"Hello?" Daisy said, her voice echoing back at her.

"Gillian?" came the faint reply. "Is that you?"

Goose bumps rose on her arms. "Anna?" She followed the sound of her sister's voice toward the back of the house, where the hardwood floors had been overvarnished, clumps of dark stains like melanomas on the floorboards. At the end of the hallway was a plyboard door, unsanded joint compound filling the many holes in the drywall, plaster patches held in place by sloppily applied drywall tape.

She opened the door, and a sharp musty odor hit her. Anna lay curled on a messy bed, her head resting on a sausaged towel, her long coppery red hair splayed across the mattress. She wore a yellow sundress—the missing yellow sundress with its pattern of fuchsia flowers. On her feet were those beat-up black Nikes that she liked to kick around in.

"Anna?"

Her sister peered over her shoulder and smiled at her with instant recognition. "Daisy?" She seemed really pleased to see her but not altogether surprised.

"Oh my God, are you all right?"

Anna rolled over to greet her, a sense of discomfort in the way she moved. Her face had filled out. Her thighs had widened. Her ankles were swollen. Her belly was huge.

Daisy swept into the room. "My God, what's wrong?"

"I'm pregnant." Anna smiled, her hands resting on her big belly, supporting it. "Where's Gillian?"

Daisy stood in raw disbelief.

Anna craned her neck. "Gillian?"

"She's not here. It's just me."

"Oh." Anna reached for her hand, waving a tissue like a little white flag. "Look at you. You're so skinny!"

"How pregnant?" Daisy asked with some urgency.

"Eight months and two weeks."

Kneeling down beside the bed, Daisy felt her sister's

forehead, then took her hand. "You're feverish. Are you having any contractions yet?"

"I don't know." Anna frowned. There were circles underneath her eyes—dark, scary circles. The floor was littered with food wrappers and empty soda cans, and it looked as if she'd been eating some kind of gaudy purple breakfast cereal straight out of the box. "I feel so fat," she groaned. "Look how fat I am, Daisy."

"Jesus, Anna. How long have you been living here?"

Her face was soft all over, like a big cat's. "I'm just so happy to see you."

"Have you seen a doctor?"

"No!" She grew instantly terrified, her milk-engorged breasts and enormous belly stretching the spaghetti-stained fabric to its limits. She wouldn't let go of Daisy's hand. "I'd rather eat bugs than go to the hospital, Daisy. You know how I feel about hospitals!"

"Okay. Calm down."

"I hate doctors!"

The implications were grave. Besides the baby's overall health, the fetus hadn't been screened yet to make sure that it was free of Stier-Zellar's disease.

"We've got to get you to a doctor," Daisy explained, "for the baby's sake."

"No doctors!"

"Shh, it's okay." A blunt overhead light gave the room its abbreviated shadows. "I'll be with you the whole time. Don't worry, Anna. Nobody's going to hurt you."

"Where's Gillian?"

"At the beach. She gave me your address."

"She takes care of me. She brings me things. We've

been staying here awhile. The owners moved away. Can you blame them?"

"How long have you been living here with Gillian?"

"I won't go to the hospital, Daisy. You know how much I hate hospitals!"

"Okay, shh. Lie back down." Daisy drew the blankets up over Anna's stinky, shivering body. She got the pill bottles out of her backpack, then ducked into the bathroom and filled a dirty-looking glass with tap water. She came out and sat on the edge of Anna's bed. "Here. Take these."

"What are they?"

"Something to make you feel better."

Anna sat up again while Daisy gave her her meds. She looked at the little pills in her hand and said, "Tell me the truth, Daisy. Is cyanide brown?"

"What? No. Those are your meds."

"Because I read somewhere that cyanide is brown, like these," she said with a nervous intake of breath.

"Anna, I'm your sister. I'm not trying to kill you. Just take them. They'll make you feel better. Here." She handed her the glass of water. "Go on."

Anna's dark blue eyes welled with tears. "Tell me the truth," she said. "Are these cyanide pills?"

"No. They're tranquilizers, Anna. Remember? They'll help calm you down and make you feel better."

She still wouldn't take them.

"Anna. Look at me."

Anna looked up.

"It's Daisy. I love you. Take your pills."

"I love you, too," she whispered.

"Good. Then take your pills."

"They're not cyanide?"

"No. Trust me."

"Okay." She swallowed the pills with water, then handed the glass back and lay down on the filthy bed. "I had a dream about us," she said. "Remember the lake in the wintertime? We were in Mom's car, and we were driving across the ice, when all of a sudden we saw this other car getting stuck and spinning its wheels. It sank through the ice, and I thought our car was going to sink, too, Daisy. So we tried to get out of there, but it was too late. Because we were already underwater and everything was green. And all these gems were arranged on the backseat, perfectly arranged for everyone to see. So I put them in my pocket for safekeeping." She kicked at the suffocating sheets and blankets and clutched her swollen belly. "God, it's so hot. Is it hot in here?"

Daisy took out her cell phone.

"Who are you calling?" Anna whispered fervently.

"Shh," she said. "Hush. Lie back down. I'm here. You're going to be okay."

5.

Jack clawed at his throat in a desperate attempt to re-move the chain and relieve some of the pressure. He couldn't breathe but kept telling himself not to panic. If the carotid arteries were constricted, the blood supply to the brain would be cut off, causing brain death in min-utes. He staggered forward on his knees, eyes bulging with incredulity, fingers pawing at the earth.

Roy held him in a death grip, the steel chain encir-cling his neck. Jack could feel cold metal digging into his flesh and told himself not to move. His carotid arter-ies were compressed due to horizontal pressure to the front of the neck. He'd be unconscious soon. If Roy re-leased him, he might regain consciousness again in ten or twelve seconds, but what were the chances of that? Jack could picture himself crouched at Roy's feet—cowering, helpless, pathetic. How had this happened? How had he gotten himself into this situation?

Jack told himself to hold still. He might survive the attack if he managed to slip one hand under the waist chain, thereby alleviating some of the pressure on his windpipe. Maybe—just maybe—if he didn't panic, if he didn't struggle, he could survive this thing. The neck was pliable. By slipping his hand underneath the ligature, he could loosen the chain and protect his windpipe. He held very still and tried to push his fingers up under the chain, but it was wrapped too tightly around his neck.

He could see the smoldering grass and tinder-dry leaf mulch in front of him. A small blue flame flared up. The fire wasn't completely out yet. Little orange flames swelled toward them across the forest floor, and the wind made these flames dance and shiver.

The chain went loose for a second as Roy paused to adjust his grip, and Jack took the opportunity to slip one finger under the loop before Roy tightened his grip again. Jack thought he'd heard something snap in his larynx or trachea. That couldn't be good. He sagged forward slightly, sensing a drop in blood pressure. He could feel his tired flesh hanging off his bones; he could feel his blood pumping sluggishly through his veins, and the clunky clock in his chest going *tick, tock, tick*.

His hands grew cold and numb. His chest was on fire from the effort of trying to breathe. *Life sucks and then you die.* He was losing altitude fast. He knew from the many autopsies he'd witnessed that people who died of strangulation usually had reddened ligature marks around their necks and claw marks on their throats from their own desperate fingernails.

Roy was dragging him underwater. Jack realized with

sudden clarity that he was going to die. He was going to die in this sylvan forest—the only forest in Los Angeles. Now his cell phone rang. There was no way he could reach it. It chirped in his shirt pocket. It chirped incessantly. He wanted to answer it, but his hands would not leave his throat. He tried to speak, but there was a disconnect between his mind and his tongue. He tried to answer through telepathy. *Hello?* he would say. *I'm dying here.*

All around him, the forest floor was smoldering, and the wind kept playing with the fire, pushing little flames this way and that, making them swirl and dance and flare. His brain felt like hot soup. His tongue was so relaxed it lolled out of his mouth and overlapped his bottom teeth, and he chewed on it like a piece of meat.

Jack hovered on the edge of consciousness, all hope dwindling in the distance like a fast-moving truck. His index finger was numb, but he kept trying to pry the chain away from his throat. He was proud to have been a cop. He had loved many women, including his first wife, Tess, and his last love, Daisy. De Campo Beach had been his home for more than twenty years—sunlight bouncing off the waves, roller skaters coasting along the boardwalk, sand under his feet, hot dogs at sunset. He loved the little white blossoms that grew in the spring and winter's purple twilight bouncing off the many windows of the office buildings along Main Street. He loved his little girl, light as a thought cloud . . . Bonnie Lou Makowski . . . his little BOLO . . . be on the lookout for. Jack could feel himself drifting away, his mind beginning to unravel. His jaw went slack. His neck felt oddly distended.

Above his head, the tree branches made a net that captured the moon. Jack could feel himself floating toward that lovely moon. Then the fear went away, and his mind was wiped clean.

6.

The detective thrashed around on his hands and knees in utter silence. Perfect silence. Roy pulled the body closer, pressing it against his leg and twisting the chain with all his might. He wouldn't let go until the detective was dead.

Roy was a patient man. He had waited very patiently for this moment to arrive. He had planned for this moment. He had studied Jack Makowski. He'd sized him up right away.

Jack was the type of loose-cannon cop who would go to extreme lengths to solve a case. He would do almost anything to get to the truth. He would break all the rules. He would lose control.

Roy had deliberately baited the police, showing them to the shallow graves of his victims but not to Anna's grave, knowing full well that it would infuriate Jack. Knowing that he would be led by his heart, not his head.

Yes, Roy was a patient man. But he was also an angry man. The anger burned in him still. It had burned in him all these years. Nobody was going to stop him. Nobody was going to get in his way. The hate was there. It ran deep. The detective's cell phone kept ringing. It made a chirping sound. It chirped and chirped and suddenly stopped chirping. It was as if the detective's heart had stopped beating.

Now the wind changed course, swinging out of the west and fanning the flames all around them. Flickering flames gusted around Roy's feet, and he brought his boot heel down in the dirt and twisted the chain tighter, while the moments ticked past with monstrous slowness.

Roy waited for it. When the bolt hit, it blew a huge hole in him. It knocked him out of his shoes. He felt almost physically ill. He went cold all over and saw flashing lights, as if he'd been slammed between two Mack trucks. His brain became fascinated with the fire, with the body slumped in front of him, with his own hands gripping the steel chain. All this tension welled up in him, and then his whole body whipped violently to one side. He felt a weird tingling sensation, like cold water being poured all over him. He felt cold and incredibly hot at the same time. His tongue tasted like pennies. His arms and legs weighed a hundred pounds each. His eyelashes hurt. He could feel the hot air blowing across his body. The detective was almost dead. He could smell it. The air had a sulfuric, burning smell to it. He breathed it in and squeezed the chain until he could feel the detective's will collapse. Until he could feel his heart give out and his mind give up. Until the body flopped forward in the dirt.

Roy let go, feeling all floaty. He released the chain, hands throbbing, and the detective sagged into the charred grass like a dead deer. Roy noticed that his pant legs were still burning. He slapped at the fabric, trying to extinguish the fire with his free hand, but the hot flames came licking up his legs. He jerked his right arm forward, but the steel handcuff bit into his wrist. "Shit!" He'd forgotten he was still handcuffed to the tree.

Roy tugged and pulled, trying to bring the branch down, but it held fast. It was a sturdy old tree. He scraped the handcuff along the gnarled tree branch as far as it would go, then he yanked on it until his wrist bled.

His left leg was sizzling like acid now, the fabric releasing a thick acrid smoke that made him want to gag. Fingers clawing at the air, he reached for the detective's body, but the detective was slumped too far forward. The tree branch shivered as he stretched his arms wide and finally caught the waistband of the detective's pants, hooking a belt loop with two fingers. Straining every muscle in his back, he dragged the body backward across the smoking ground. He dragged the dead weight toward him. The detective was heavier than he looked. Roy inched the body closer, then dug around one-handed in the detective's back pockets for the keys.

Unlocking the handcuffs, Roy dropped to the ground and rolled around in the dirt. He screamed and pounded his legs until he'd snuffed out the flames, and then everything went quiet. He took a deep breath. He let it out slowly. His left leg throbbed where some of the orange jumpsuit had turned to ash.

He stood up and rubbed his sore wrist. He opened and closed his stiff fingers, getting some of the circulation back. He smoothed his hair behind his ears, then turned the body over and found the cell phone. There were several messages waiting for the detective on his voice mail. Roy put the phone to his ear.

7.

Daisy put her cell phone away, frustrated that she hadn't been able to reach Jack. As the moon rose above the city, she sat on the edge of her sister's bed and watched her sleep. Anna's lower lip was thicker than her upper lip, and she had a faint mustache. Her short, square teeth had little spaces between them, and her hooded eyes fluttered delicately in their dream state. Now her body jerked awake. "Daisy?" she said, opening her eyes.

"Shh. You're safe. I'm here."

"Hi."

"Hi."

"How come you're looking at me funny?"

"Am I?"

"Yes."

"All this time, I thought you were dead," Daisy told her. "But now here you are. I still can't believe it."

Anna frowned. "I don't get it. Why'd you think I was dead?"

"It's a long story."

Anna smiled. "I was dreaming about my angel, Daisy. Remember my angel? The one who came to our door? You said he was a salesman, remember?"

"Yes, I remember."

"In my dream, I felt loved. Indescribably loved. Daisy? Remember my angel?"

"Yes," she said.

"He told me I'd have the Son of God."

The bedroom was papered with pictures torn out of art books and magazines—classic depictions of the Virgin Mary holding Baby Jesus. Daisy got it. Anna was going to have the Son of God. The Second Coming. More proof that Roy had lied to her. Anna was delusional, but it was just an extension of her old obsessions. She didn't think she was Death. Roy Gaines had lied to her, and Jack had been right all along.

The headlights of a passing car streaked through the slatted blinds and pinwheeled across the ceiling, and Anna's face contorted in pain. "Ow," she said.

"What is it? Anna?"

Her cheeks burned. She rubbed her shoulder. "Don't let her take my baby away from me," she said.

"Shh. You're feverish."

"Don't let Mom take this baby away from me, Daisy."

"Why would she do that?"

"Promise me."

"Okay, I promise. Now calm down."

"Daisy?"

"What?"

"Why are you wearing that?"

She looked at her vintage jeans and her sopping-wet T-shirt. The jeans were slightly torn at the knees, and there were spots of blood on the denim fabric from her little scrape with Gillian. "Why? What's wrong with it?"

"You're dressed to depress."

She smiled. "I look fine."

"You look like a bum. If you want to go to some pizza parlor, then fine. Off with you."

Daisy laughed. "What are you talking about?"

"I want to go someplace nice. I'm hungry. I want to eat a steak."

"Okay," Daisy said. "I'll buy you a steak, but first get some rest."

Anna closed her eyes.

Daisy went into the adjoining bathroom, sat down on the closed toilet seat and listened to stray sounds coming through the open window. There were so many questions she wanted to ask. Who was the baby's father? Why hadn't Anna come home? Why hadn't she called and told them she was in trouble? The outside air smelled faintly of gasoline. She got up and washed her hands in the sink while the radios of passing cars pounded out clashing rap songs.

Daisy rinsed a washcloth in cold water, then wrung it out and stood over the sink for a moment, pressing the cool cloth against her forehead. She could hear Anna talking to herself and cocked her head. She heard the sound of a door creaking open. She put the washcloth down, went back into Anna's bedroom and found Roy Gaines standing in the doorway.

He raised his arm. He held a gun. A shot rang out, a sound so loud it blew her eardrums out.

Daisy screamed and dove behind the bed. He was trying to kill her. She got flat on her stomach and stayed there. "Anna, get down!"

He had them trapped. He was standing in the doorway.

Daisy tried not to panic. "Anna, get down!" she cried.

Anna reached into the top drawer of her bedside table and pulled out a gun. Gripping it in both hands, she aimed it at the door and fired.

Bang, bang!

Small red jets shot out of the barrel.

Roy fired back. Bullets ricocheted.

Daisy flinched.

Pop, pop, pop.

Then there was silence.

Daisy had a difficult time swallowing. The air smelled faintly sulfurous, like rotten eggs.

"I'm bleeding!" Anna screamed.

Daisy scrambled to her feet. "Oh my God—"

"The baby." Anna's hands were covered with blood.

Daisy looked at the doorway. Roy was gone.

"Daisy, help me!"

"Stay there," she said. "Don't move."

She grabbed a straight-back chair from the corner and jammed it underneath the doorknob. Then she hurried back to her sister's side. "Where are you bleeding?"

"I don't know."

Anna's belly was warm and sticky. Daisy could hear something go *glug-glug-glug*. She knew that acute blood loss of 35 percent could be fatal. She swiped a towel off the floor and pressed it to her sister's abdomen. "Here, hold this."

Anna held the towel and said her Hail Marys.

Daisy got on her cell phone and dialed 911. Her hands were covered in blood. They were trembling. "Hello? I need an ambulance right away. My sister's been shot. I'm at 88 Westland. She's eight and a half months pregnant."

"Where is she bleeding?" the operator asked.

"I don't know. Somewhere on her belly."

"You need to hold something over the wound."

"All right."

"You need to locate the entrance wound."

She glanced out the window and saw Roy Gaines clutching his shoulder. He was bleeding. He got in Jack's car, that old shitbox Ford Topaz, and burned away from the curb. Why did he have Jack's car? Where was Jack?

She sat cradling the phone to her ear, holding the dirty towel against her sister's belly and trying not to panic. Trying not to scream. The silence inside the house was like the surface of a pond, drops of tension reverberating outward in concentric rings.

8.

There was blood all over the sheets, all over Anna's yellow sundress. Daisy applied pressure to the wound.

"He found me," Anna said hysterically. "How did he find me?"

"Shh, try not to talk." Daisy pressed her hands over her sister's bleeding belly.

"He didn't want this baby. He told me to get rid of it!" Anna cried. "Get rid of it, can you believe that? It's his fucking baby!"

Daisy was stunned. "Roy Gaines is the father?"

"His name is Roy Hildreth. He went crazy. He tried to push me down the stairs, Daisy. He tried to kill this baby. That's why I left him. That's why I ran away. I thought he was going to kill me! I don't know how he found out where I am . . . but he's trying to kill my baby. Please don't let him kill my baby!"

"Shh," Daisy said. "The police are on their way."

There were sirens in the distance. "Why didn't you call me, Anna? Why didn't you come home? We could've helped you."

She had lost so much blood she looked like a porcelain doll. "I'm sorry, Daisy. I messed up."

The sirens grew louder. Now flashing red lights flared into the room, and Daisy got up and removed the chair from the door, then ran outside to greet the ambulance.

"My sister's eight and a half months pregnant," she told the female paramedic. "She was shot in the abdomen."

"How many times?" the square-faced woman asked as she and a male coworker got their medical equipment out of the ambulance and wheeled a gurney inside.

"I don't know," Daisy said, following them.

"How many gunshots did you hear?"

"I didn't count them all. Maybe four. Maybe six."

"Any other medical conditions we should know about?"

"She's schizophrenic. I just gave her two Repaxins."

"Is she having contractions yet?"

"I don't think so."

"How old is she?"

"Twenty-eight."

They went inside and found Anna groaning on the bed, clutching her swollen belly. The female paramedic lifted her sundress and looked for an entry wound. She turned Anna onto her side, and Daisy could see the blood spurting out a little bullet hole in her back.

"It's in the upper abdomen and out the back," the

female paramedic said. "When was your last prenatal care visit?" she asked Anna directly.

"No doctors. No hospitals!"

"Shh." Daisy leaned forward. "Anna, have you been to a clinic yet? Anything?"

She rubbed her distended belly and moaned. "No."

The female paramedic didn't seem too happy about it. "Is this your first pregnancy?"

"Yes."

"Any vaginal bleeding?"

"Ow. It hurts."

Daisy stood out of their way as the paramedics worked frantically to save her sister's life. They stemmed the bleeding, hooked Anna up to an IV line and lifted her onto the gurney. Then they wheeled her outside to the waiting ambulance.

"Can I come?" Daisy asked.

"Sure, hop in." The female paramedic helped her up, and Daisy sat in the jump seat while the ambulance swerved away from that awful house, sirens wailing.

"Daisy?" Anna said groggily.

"Shh. Save your strength."

"I thought it would bring me peace, but it didn't."

"What didn't?"

"End 70."

She felt a tightening in her gut. "What d'you mean?"

"It's a gift for you."

"A gift?"

"You'll find out when you get there." Her voice faded, her eyelids fluttered shut and the mood inside the ambulance suddenly shifted.

"Abdomen feels rigid," the female paramedic said.

She listened to Anna's belly with a stethoscope. "I can't find the fetal heart tone. I just had it a second ago . . ."

The male paramedic leaned forward and spoke to the driver. "Tell them to meet us in the ambulance bay for an immediate C-section," he said.

9.

Daisy followed the paramedics as they wheeled her sister down the hospital corridor. Anna was dazed and drenched in sweat, paler than Daisy had ever seen her, flailing around on the gurney. Daisy chased them around the next corner, where a hospital team was waiting outside the emergency room doors.

"Whaddya got?" the diminutive doctor said.

"Twenty-eight years old, first pregnancy, thirty-six weeks of gestation," the female paramedic rattled off. "No vaginal bleeding. Pulse is one thirty and weak."

The doctor lifted the blanket and examined Anna's abdomen, palpating it with his fingers. "Push a bolus of normal saline," he said as they wheeled her through the swinging doors. "I want five hundred millileters of normal saline to run wide open. Let's get a CT scan."

There was a dramatic uptick of activity as the staff began prepping Anna for a crash C-section. They swabbed her belly with antiseptics and gave her a shot to slow the contractions, then hooked her and the baby up to separate heart monitors.

"What's happening?" Anna's voice was weak.

"Don't worry," Daisy said. "I'm not leaving your side."

During the next painful contraction, Anna's eyes went flat, and she suddenly and dramatically lost consciousness. Her heart monitor flatlined as she slumped back against the gurney.

The doctor placed his hand on Anna's neck. "She's in cardiac arrest. Get the Cardiff wedge."

They rolled Anna onto her side and placed the Cardiff wedge behind her back, then bent her knees slightly to support her weight, keeping her at a thirty-degree angle. Daisy knew that if a pregnant woman was left lying flat on her back for any length of time, the gravid uterus could press down on her vena cava and prevent the blood from returning to her heart. One of the nurses was gently pulling the uterus to the left now in order to relieve some of the pressure.

The doctor tilted Anna's head back, breathed twice into her mouth and began vigorous chest compressions against the backboard. "Get ready to intubate," he said. "One milligram epi IV bolus. One milligram atropine."

The nurses started a second IV line and performed bag-valve-mask ventilations while the doctor continued with the chest compressions. A resident monitored the separate heartbeats while an anesthesiologist made preparations for endotracheal intubation.

"Blood pressure's zero," a nurse said. "The baby's

heart tones are slow . . . ninety per minute. Fetal heart rate is slowing."

"Clear!"

Daisy stood by and watched helplessly while they zapped Anna's chest with the paddles. Her body convulsed, and the doctor glanced up at the heart monitor, which started to make those reassuring bleeping sounds again. "She's back," he said. "We need to take this baby out. Now."

"What just happened?" Daisy asked.

"Please wait outside," he told her, then turned to one of the nurses. "I want the neonatal resuscitation equipment down here now!"

The waiting room was infinitely white beneath a bank of artificial lights. The walls were white, the ceiling was white, the floor had been buffed to such a high degree that the waxy sheen was brighter than the overhead lights reflecting off its surface. Daisy sat hugging herself, trying to find some island of comfort, some refuge from all this whiteness. She knew now that her sister was innocent, that Roy Gaines had killed those people himself. He wanted to kill Anna's baby. He must've escaped from prison, and now he had Jack's car. A monster was on the loose. She had to call the police.

She looked around for her backpack, then realized she'd left her cell phone back at Anna's place. She got up and went to the nurses' station, where she found several slammed-looking hospital employees sitting around on swivel chairs behind the glass-paneled wall. "Could I use your phone?" she asked. "It's an emergency."

A heavyset nurse with triple chins slid the push-button phone across the counter. "Dial nine for an outside line."

Daisy called the De Campo Beach police station and asked to speak to Detective Tully. It took a moment or two for the desk sergeant to connect them. "Hello?" Tully said.

"This is Daisy Hubbard. Do you remember me?"

"Of course, Daisy."

"My sister's in trouble. I don't know who else to turn to. I can't reach Jack, but I saw Roy Gaines get into Jack's Ford Topaz and drive away. He must've escaped from prison. I have no idea where Jack is, but Gaines shot my sister in the abdomen. She's almost nine months pregnant and—"

"Whoa, slow down," he said. "Where are you?"

"Landon Meyers Hospital."

"Sit tight," he said. "I'll be right over."

She thanked the nurse, then took her seat again, the hush of the hospital crushing her eardrums. It was quieter than she expected. She thought she liked quiet, but she didn't. Not now. She wanted bustle and activity. She wanted to be blown away by the nurses' professionalism, but she wasn't. They looked tired and harried on this busy night shift.

Roy Gaines had tried to kill her. He'd tried to kill Anna's baby. Anna was innocent. Her sister was innocent, and Roy Gaines had lied to them. He'd deceived them all. Colby Ostrow, Irma Petropoulous . . . these people were members of Tanya's Friends. Why had Roy killed them? Was he so jealous of the people in Anna's life that he'd resorted to murder? Was he pathologically jealous? Even of the baby? And what about Katja Webb?

Did Anna know her somehow? Had she met Katja during her quest to find Louis's father?

Daisy couldn't keep her teeth from chattering. A young Hispanic nurse hurried past, pushing a warming bed on wheels toward the emergency room. When the doors swung open, Daisy caught a glimpse of frenzied activity before they flapped shut again. The controlled atmosphere inside the E.R. had dissolved into panic and uncertainty.

She went over to the nurses' station again. "What's going on?" she asked. "Is my sister okay?"

"I don't have that information," the heavyset nurse told her.

"Could you please find out?"

She eyed Daisy with pity. "Take a seat. I'll get somebody out here to talk to you."

"Is the baby okay?"

"I'll send someone out."

She sat down on the faded white sofa again. There were two middle-aged women seated opposite her. "My husband's appendix burst," one told the other. "He's never had his appendix out, and look what happens."

Daisy chewed on a thumbnail, then glanced at the E.R. doors. She could hear muffled voices, along with a few strident commands. *"Suction!"* She ignored the twinge this created inside her. If Roy Gaines had Jack's car, then he probably had Jack's gun. That was probably Jack's gun he'd shot at them with. If Roy had Jack's car and Jack's gun, then he must have Jack's cell phone as well. An hour ago, Daisy had called Jack on his cell phone and left Anna's address on his voice mail. If Roy had Jack's cell phone, then she was responsible for telling him where her sister was hiding out. It was all Daisy's fault that her sister had been shot.

"My daughter fell and bumped her head," one of the middle-aged women was saying. "She found out her husband was cheating on her and got drunk and fell. I told her a million times to leave the jerk. Now she's got a cheating husband *and* a concussion."

"Ms. Hubbard?" The diminutive doctor was headed her way.

Daisy stood up. "Yes?"

"Let's talk over here."

She followed him into a corner of the waiting room. "I'm Dr. Jarvaska," he said, shaking her hand. He had warm hazel eyes, a furry upper lip that was trying to be a mustache and a surgical scarf wrapped around his head. "Please have a seat."

She sat in a wooden chair that was painted with sunflowers and rainbows. There was a white silence. It drifted down like snow. The exhausted-looking doctor smiled at her. He got down on one knee like a man about to propose marriage.

"I'm afraid there were complications," he said. "I'm sorry. We did everything we could."

The news was like a necklace breaking, beads scattering every which way so that you'd never find them again. "What do you mean?" Daisy asked.

"I'm afraid she's gone."

"Gone?" The waiting room grew bigger and bigger, until it became enormous and overwhelming. "Who? The baby?"

"No, he's in good health. It's your sister. I'm sorry."

There was a churchlike silence. She tried to absorb

what he'd just told her, but nothing registered. The air began to dim. Her hands went to her face just as everything in her field of vision shrank to the size of a keyhole.

"We had to perform an emergency C-section," he continued, "because the placenta had separated from the uterine wall. She was bleeding into her uterus, and no blood was going to the fetus. We did a crash C-section in order to save the baby's life, but I'm afraid your sister didn't make it."

Her veins filled with Freon. She was in shock.

"Fortunately, at this stage of pregnancy, the uterine wall is very thick. As a result, the bullet didn't penetrate into the womb. It missed the baby, but there were intra-abdominal injuries . . ."

She didn't hear him anymore. Everything fell away, leaving her dancing on the edge of the universe. She came back slowly. He was still talking. She watched his mouth move and his tongue click against his teeth.

"Is there anything I can do for you?" he asked. "Anyone I can call?"

She shook her head.

"Are you all right?"

"Can I see her?"

"Yes, of course." He stood up. "Follow me."

The doctor left her alone in the operating bay. All the machinery was turned off—the X-ray view box, the overhead lights, the crash cart, the resuscitation equipment. There were stray needles on the floor, along with discarded bandages, medical wrappers and bloody footprints. A thin hospital sheet was drawn up around Anna's shoulders, and her eyes were closed. Her eyelashes made two neat rows of commas.

Gazing down at those peaceful features was like slipping down a mossy bank. It broke Daisy's brain. It tore her up like paper. She stood for a long time holding her sister's hand, unable to cry. She couldn't seem to cry. Why couldn't she cry? There were no tears left in her tear ducts. No moisture left anywhere in her body. She knew she should be crying, and it made her very angry that her throat would not produce a single sob.

10.

Detective William Tully directed his center-mounted spotlight at the 1988 Ford Topaz parked in front of a dead eucalyptus tree in the middle of the hospital parking lot. He would've recognized that crap color anywhere. He got out and approached the stolen vehicle with caution, then checked out the interior—Mardi Gras beads, junk-food wrappers, a tiny beer bottle dangling from the key chain. It was Jack's car, all right. "Shit." Tully had been trained to show no emotion, but his heart beat out a nasty vibrato as he holstered his weapon. One thing was certain—if Roy Gaines had escaped from Jack's custody and stolen his wheels, then Jack was probably dead. "Jesus, Jack. What the hell happened here?"

Tully's partner was the smartest cop he knew. Jack Makowski might bend the rules a little, but he would never deliberately put himself in harm's way. Tully held on to a thread of hope as he keyed his portable. "30H24 to dispatch, where's my backup?"

"On its way," dispatch responded drily.

Tully wiped his face and blinked the sweat out of his eyes. It had reached ninety-nine degrees in downtown Los Angeles today, breaking the day's 1926 record. Nobody smiled in this heat. He stood in the dark and noticed that half the parking lot was in shadows. He'd read somewhere that of the thousands of streetlights in the Greater Los Angeles area, at least 10 percent went out each week. That was a whole lot of darkness. The night sky was starless. You could probably see stars if there were any, but there weren't. Not in this desolate part of town.

Tully had grown up in a neighborhood much like this one, where the backyards bordered the freeways and a long thin strip of smog settled over buildings like a permanent bad mood. As a boy, he used to hold his mother's gin and tonic while she drove them to the supermarket in her rust-bucket Chevy. The wipers didn't wipe anymore. You could play only one side of any cassette in the broken tape player. They would listen to *Gary Lewis and the Playboys* or *Love Unlimited Orchestra*. The glove compartment was jammed shut from the time his mother's boyfriend had kicked it in. Who knew what was inside that battered glove compartment? You couldn't pry it open. Young Tully had tried.

Now a black-and-white pulled up behind him, and Tully stood squinting into its brilliant high beams. The lights cut out, and two LAPD officers stepped out of the vehicle. The older cop had a pinched expression, as if he didn't have anything to be excited about. The rookie was jittery. "Whaddya got for us, Detective?"

"There's a fugitive at large. I want you to sit on this vehicle. If he comes back, I want you to grab him."

"What's he look like?"

"Male Caucasian, six foot three, black hair, brown eyes. Goes by the name of Roy Gaines."

The officers eyed one another. The De Campo Beach Strangler arrest had been in all the papers, and Jack was a local hero.

Now Tully heard a small thunk on the side door panel. There was another thunk on the windshield. June bugs. They were early this year. It was this heat. The mercury had shot up to August levels. He felt a tap on his arm— another June bug—and a chill ran through him. *Goddammit, Jack, what the hell happened here?*

11.

Daisy sensed a presence in the operating bay with her and turned around. The young Hispanic nurse was standing in the doorway, the same nurse she'd seen wheeling a warming bed into the E.R. earlier.

"Sorry to interrupt," she said softly, "but whenever you're ready, I've got something to show you."

Daisy nodded absently.

"I'll come back later."

"No. I'm ready." Daisy released Anna's hand, a twinge of pain shooting up the right side of her body. After one last look, she followed the nurse back through the swinging doors and had no idea where they were going. She didn't ask.

They took an elevator up to the eighth floor. The nurse's right eyelid drooped a little, the only flaw in her otherwise pretty face. Her hair was the color of powdered cinnamon. When the polished metal doors whooshed open, Daisy followed her down another corridor and into a nursery full of wailing babies.

The screams of the newborns were like paper cuts—sharp and clean and slow to bleed. Most babies were born with day and night reversed. They slept during the day and became very lively at night, and that was certainly true now. These babies cried and squirmed and waved their little arms, wanting their mothers' attention. There were colorful posters on the walls and lots of pamphlets about breast-feeding. A small crowd had gathered behind the viewing window—anxious fathers peering in through the glass and pointing out the new arrivals to their excited siblings and proud grandparents. One man held his five-year-old up to the glass so that he could see into the warming beds.

"It's a boy," the nurse said, bending over one of the beds and cradling a bundle in her arms. "Six pounds. His Apgar score is 8, which is excellent."

Daisy didn't understand.

"Would you like to hold him?" The nurse handed her the baby wrapped in a blue blanket. The blanket had snowflakes and polar bears all over it.

Daisy's heart pushed into her throat.

"Go on," the nurse said. "Hold him for a while."

The baby squirmed in protest. The skin around his mouth looked pale, a sure sign of stress. She couldn't begin to comprehend this tiny trembling existence and wanted to hand him back immediately, but the nurse's arms were folded across her chest. The baby clung to Daisy's finger with his perfect little hand. Her finger was like a log compared to his tiny grasping ones. After a moment, he settled down and, gazing up at her, gurgled pleasantly. There was a pink tinge to his cheeks.

"Does he have a name?" the nurse asked.

"I don't know. I don't think so."

"Ooh, so handsome," the nurse cooed, chucking him under the chin. "Ooh, so big and strong."

The baby burped, and Daisy drew back, utterly lost. His dark blue eyes would take a few weeks to show their true color. Her thumb was the size of a tree trunk, and he clung to it with his perfect little hand and watched her with his deep-seated eyes. His thick dark hair had little bearing on what his hair would eventually look like. Most Caucasian babies were born with dark blue eyes and thick dark hair.

He shook with his whole body, as if he were excited to be there. She wanted to put him down, but the nurse had walked away. "Hello?" These overworked nurses were very good at ignoring people.

Daisy rocked her sister's baby gently in her arms. He had the Russian roulette of genotypes, with two bullets in the chamber. If Anna was a carrier of Stier-Zellar's disease, then her son might also be a carrier. That was the good news. If both parents turned out to be carriers, then they could transmit their two mutated genes to their infant, possibly giving him the fatal disease. But Stier-Zellar's was extremely rare, so the odds were on his side. Looking at him now, Daisy decided that the chances of both parents being carriers were remote. Still, he'd have to be tested right away, just to make sure.

The genetics of schizophrenia was much more complex. The role that genes played in the disease was still being debated. Daisy shivered, not wanting to think about that right now. It was too much for her to handle.

No wonder the babies were shrieking. It was chilly up here in the nursery. She walked over to the plate glass and stood bouncing the baby gently up and down. He seemed to like that. He had a button nose and seashell ears and gazed at her with such questioning eyes she couldn't help falling in love with him.

"Hello, Anna's baby," she said tenderly. "You can go to sleep now."

She caught sight of their reflection in the plate glass and realized that she had become Anna's vision of the Madonna and Child. Her sister had left her with a brand-new worry, like a shadow she couldn't shake. Here in her arms was a tiny human being, and somebody was going to have to take care of him.

12.

The hospital's facade of metal and glass evoked the bland industrial forms of the 1970s. Tully tripped up a series of broad cement steps into a large lobby the color of twilight at dusk and quickly located the information kiosk. He got directions from a crusty-eyed clerk whose makeup had caked in the cracks of her smile.

Up on the eighth floor, several tired-looking nurses pointed him into a quiet corner of the nursery, where Daisy Hubbard sat rocking a baby. "Get up," he said, breathing harder than he should have as he moved swiftly toward her. "Roy Gaines is on the premises."

She glanced up. "What?"

"Come with me."

There were fine lines of despair on her face.

He escorted her into one of the birthing rooms, where everything was done up in Easter-egg colors. She sat on the edge of an adjustable bed with the baby in her arms. "He's in the hospital?" she asked anxiously.

"You'll be safe in here. See those two officers?"

Outside the door, he'd posted a pair of security guards.

"They'll protect you. Just tell me what happened."

She drew her slender shoulders together. "I found Anna in an abandoned house on Westland Avenue, so I called Jack to tell him where I was. When he didn't pick up, I left a message on his voice mail and gave him the address. Half an hour later, Roy Gaines showed up and started shooting at us. But Anna had a gun. She shot him in the shoulder, I think, and he left."

"She had a gun?"

Daisy nodded. "We'd both be dead otherwise."

"Then what?"

"He took off in Jack's car. The ambulance brought us here, but the doctors weren't able to save my sister's life." She wiped her nose with the back of her hand. "Where's Jack?" she asked with shiny eyes. "Is he all right?"

"Let's not worry about that right now."

"Did something happen to him?"

Tully's hands were fisted shut. She would probably find out about it sooner or later, so he said, "Look, he got the prisoner released to his custody this evening. We think they drove out to the Angeles National Forest to look for your sister's grave. Now, I don't know if you've heard, but there's a forest fire raging in the canyons east of L.A. It's spreading fast. We don't know if he's up there or not. We don't know anything for certain."

"Oh my God."

"Stay put." He turned to leave, but she stopped him.

"He'll be looking for Anna," she said. "If Roy Gaines is here in the hospital? He doesn't know she's gone yet. He'll be looking for her."

Tully nodded and went back out into the corridor, where he got on the phone and called the E.R. After talking to three different nurses, he found out that Anna's body had been transported to the hospital morgue, which was located in the basement. He also found out that a man fitting Gaines's description had been looking for Anna Hubbard, and that the nurses had directed him to the morgue.

Tully hurried along the corridor, the odor of disinfectant reaching his nostrils. A maintenance engineer was mopping the floor with some strong germicidal detergent, and Tully felt a tightening in his chest. He had to get to the morgue. He stood impatiently in front of the elevators, pushing the Down button over and over again, his thoughts falling flat on the polished floor. Jack must be dead. It hadn't hit him until just this moment. Jack was probably dead. "What's taking you so long?" he snapped at the slow-moving elevators.

Stairs were faster. He pushed through a fire door coated with about fifty layers of paint and left the eighth floor without a clue as to where he was going. His legs carried him down a flight before his knees buckled and he had to lean against the railing. A grim scenario kept playing in his head: Jack got the prisoner released to his custody using the falsified PER form, then drove him to a remote canyon, where Gaines somehow wrestled the gun away and shot Jack dead. The prisoner then started a fire before fleeing the scene in Jack's car. They would find his body tomorrow or the next day, burned beyond recognition. They'd locate it only after the fire crews had put out the flames. *Burned beyond recognition.* Jesus. He'd just seen Jack yesterday, that charming idiot.

Tully smiled sadly to himself while standing in a pool of yellow light. *Dammit, Jack. You threw it all away, and for what?* Jack loved to solve things. He loved to rescue people, especially pretty women. He believed in fair play. He believed in justice. Stand back. Step aside. Here comes St. Makowski, sacrificing everything for principle.

Now Tully heard an echo in the stairwell. It sounded like footsteps. He leaned over the railing and caught a glimpse of a figure disappearing through the fire door directly below him. "Hey!" he shouted as the door slammed shut with a whump.

He grabbed the banister and chased down another flight of stairs, then wheeled for the landing. He pushed through the heavy fire door in hot pursuit of . . . nobody. There was nobody there. Still clinging to his suspicions, he moved swiftly down the brightly lit corridor, chasing phantoms into each room.

The hospital rooms were dark, since it was after midnight and most of the patients were sound asleep. Some were still up, though, restlessly roaming the corridors, senior citizens pushing their walkers with irritable defiance. He hurried past the sixth-floor waiting room with its TV monitor mounted on the wall and its Day-Glo color scheme. He flew past the nurses' station, where he caught snippets of conversation, then glanced at the directory as he ran past—*Medical, Pediatric, Surgery, ICU.* The lettering was eye-chart small. He was on the geriatrics ward.

Tully approached a bank of elevators where a few elderly insomniacs shuffled on and off, then spotted a dark-haired male pushing a laundry cart. The hallway was only eight feet wide, and there was a serious traffic flow problem due to colliding wheelchairs. The suspect was a dozen yards ahead of him now, his shoes squeaking on the rubber tiles.

Tully's heart hitched. He drew his weapon and held it close to his side, not wanting to alarm anyone. He trailed the suspect past rushed-off-their-feet nurses and orderlies. Ahead of him, several large columns bracketed the lounge area, and now the suspect made an abrupt right turn.

Tully drew his weapon. "Police! Freeze!" His booming voice sent shock waves throughout the corridor, senior citizens piling to a stop all around him, their eyes rheumy with bewilderment.

The suspect turned with distress on his face. His laundry cart rolled into a water fountain. "Don't shoot!" He raised his hands in the air.

It wasn't Roy Gaines.

"Shit." Tully holstered his handgun and made for the stairwell again.

13.

The morgue smelled sickeningly sweet—of organ meats and burnt bone from the mortuary technician's saw. Roy touched Anna's smooth face and felt a slight resistance beneath his fingertips. There was a pearly translucence to her skin, but the underlying muscle tone was gone. Her body was a battlefield where the retreating army had left evidence of its defeat—obstetric forceps, clamps, IV lines, bloody gauze swabs. The doctors hadn't even bothered to sew her back up again, and the uterine cavity lay exposed, layers of tissue peeled back like the petals of a dark flower. An abandoned retractor widened the walls of her womb, and the baby's umbilical cord came trailing out like a sad little piggie's tail, ligated at one end. The doctors and nurses had scooped Anna's baby out like a mound of cherry ice cream. Where was it now? What had they done with it?

Air scudded into Roy's lungs, the pain like a thousand

wasp stings as he touched the hollow of her neck and stroked the heavy loops of her hair, then bent to kiss those sugary, grainy lips. She did not kiss him back. Where was Anna Hubbard? Where had she gone?

He tried to close the womb back up with a soft-pawed groping. He wanted to put it all back together again. He wanted to reverse time. An itchy flush crawled up his neck. Anna wasn't supposed to die. He'd been aiming for her sister, but everything had happened so fast. They were supposed to be together forever, and now this had happened, and he couldn't figure out what had gone wrong.

He plucked out the suction apparatus and threw it on the floor. He removed the retractor, the forceps, IV lines, the gauze swabs. He picked up the clipboard and glanced at the Authorization for Disposal of Body form. He scanned the pathology request. This was not the way it was supposed to be. He noticed the stamped tag on her ankle and touched the coolness of her skin. Her leg was soft and pliable. He compared their hands. Anna's fingers were like his—only smaller and more delicate.

He took shallow, wheezing breaths, then retreated into some crawly corner of his brain where he couldn't see Anna anymore, only his dead mother. Roy's mother had died when he was eight years old, from alcohol poisoning and five different medications. He'd grown up in the deserts of the Southwest, a lonely, troubled boy. Linda Hildreth would show Roy affection only during those occasions when the two of them would discuss her symptoms together. The rest of the time she'd be semiconscious.

His father started out as a medical equipment salesman but soon stumbled upon the bone trade when he met an unscrupulous doctor willing to off-load body parts. Mercenary morticians and photojournalists soon followed. Benny Hildreth would go to the ends of the earth for a snip of celebrity hair, a dead president's bone fragments or a rare photograph of Lee Harvey Oswald's rotting head. He bought and sold gruesome crime scene pictures from European police archives and rare collectibles from the Holocaust. Roy wasn't supposed to tell anyone what his father did for a living. He could only say he was in the medical profession. Roy wasn't supposed to go into his father's office, either; but one day he snuck in and raided the forbidden file cabinets, snagged a file at random and smuggled it up to his room. That night, he read the whole thing. Inside were black-and-white photographs of a woman who'd decapitated her husband. There was a newspaper clipping accompanying the pictures that described the gory details. On June 12, 1943, after stabbing her husband repeatedly in the chest, Cissy Cregg laid his face on the kitchen breadboard and hacked off his head. She did this because she thought he was the devil. She even took pictures of herself killing the devil, arranging each shot with great care, since she wanted to document it for her minister. The minister, of course, had called the police immediately.

After his mother had died, Roy started to accompany his father on his cross-country trips. Posing as a medical equipment salesman, his father would have access to all sorts of places other people could never get into. The doctors who sold him this stuff, especially in Los Angeles and New York City, always wanted to meet far away from the hospital. They picked tacky all-night diners or burger joints on the seedy side of town to meet clandestinely in, and Roy loved the wisecracking waitresses and exaggerated claims of *Best Burgers in the Universe!* The men who met with his father in these places always looked uncomfortable to find Roy sitting there, but his father would say, "Don't worry about him." The men would turn red and glance over their shoulders, as if they were doing something bad.

Sometimes when people came to the house to buy something, Roy would listen at the door. Before his father showed them anything, he would say, "What I'm about to show you could cause lasting emotional distress, so I'm going to have to ask you . . . do you hereby swear that you will not hold me responsible for any of the things that may occur as a result of your viewing these photos and collectibles?" And the person would say "I do," just like in a wedding ceremony.

Back in the hospital morgue, Roy kicked a swivel caster, disturbing the cart, then staggered to one knee. He touched his face and noticed there was a strange wetness on his cheek. He looked at his wet fingers while heavy sobs erupted from his lungs. Where were these animal sounds coming from? Anna's arm dropped off the cart and slapped him gently in the face. It frightened him. He took her cold hand and gave in to another uncontrolled outburst. Now that she was gone, would the sun ever rise again? Or would this be the end of the world forever? She wasn't supposed to die. He laced his fingers through hers and felt a stabbing pain in his left arm. It was bandaged with his T-shirt, and the bleeding had finally stopped. The wound wasn't serious. He would survive. Why hadn't Anna?

Now he heard footsteps approaching and struggled to his feet. Somebody was in the outer office. The police would be looking for him. Roy knew the ins and outs of medical institutions. He knew exactly what to do. He glanced around the room and spotted the stainless-steel door behind which the dead bodies were stored. He snatched a pair of surgical pliers and a skull chisel from an instrument tray, then checked the clipboard for the body release schedule. He found the body tag number for the next release and, inching off his sneakers, walked barefoot into the refrigerated room.

14.

Thirty-year-old slacker Chuck Dozoretz worked for Callaghan Funeral Homes and was used to dead bodies by now. Nothing fazed him, except for this heat. It was hot all over. "Once the sun goes down, shouldn't the temperature go down with it?" he complained as he entered the morgue through the loading bay. "Is that too much to ask?"

The only employee inside the morgue tonight wasn't young, he wasn't old, he was just Kent the Morgue Tech. Ageless Kent was a zero in the personality department.

"What's that on your chin?" Chuck asked him.

"I'm growing a goatee."

"You don't say? Trying to butch yourself up for your girlfriend, huh?"

Kent took the clipboard off the wall and handed it to him. "Sign at the bottom."

"Hey, if I was a girl, I'd do you." Chuck signed with a flourish. "How about those Lakers, huh?"

"Go, Lakers." Kent tore off a copy of the signed release form and handed it to Chuck, who folded it and put it in his pocket.

"I'm in a real bad mood," Chuck admitted. "My boss informed me today that I don't have a winning attitude. Can you believe that?"

"A can-do attitude?"

"Exactly. A can-do attitude. Hello? I work for a funeral home. How much of a winning attitude do you need? But hey, you gotta pay the rent."

"Rent doesn't go away." Kent wore the kind of cheap cologne that smelled like an electrical fire. He put the clipboard back on the wall, and Chuck followed him into the refrigerated room where the dead bodies were stored.

"So I decided okay, I'm getting drunk tonight. That's why I'm in such a hurry." He looked at his watch. "It's closing in on beer-thirty."

Kent checked the body-bag tags and slid one of the stainless-steel trays out.

Through the opaque plastic, Chuck could see the corpse's feet and hands, the ghostly outline of a head. "Pyramid Snowcap ale," he said. "Great mahogany color. What's your brew, Kent?"

The prick didn't answer him. "Ready?" Kent said, and together they lifted the body onto the lightweight aluminum transporter cart. "He's all yours."

Chuck didn't want to leave the refrigerated room just yet. It was so frosty in here you could see your own breath. "Later, dude." He pushed the cart back down the hallway toward the loading dock, where he'd parked the hearse.

"Up you go." He loaded the body into the back of the wagon, fished out his keys and slipped in behind the wheel of the hearse. How depressingly predictable his life was. He paused to comb his thinning brown hair with his sweaty fingers, then started the engine. The CD player burst to life. The speakers throbbed, the bass line pounded, and Chuck backed out of the reserved space and drove away.

15.

Tully went tumbling down the stairwell until he came to the ground floor, where he smashed through a series of doors and flashed his badge at the startled orderlies. "Which way's the morgue?"

They pointed him in the right direction, and he sprinted down the eastern corridor, then punched through another fire door before taking a flight of stairs down. The morgue was right in front of him now. He paused to slow his racing heart, then went inside. "Hello?"

In the silence that followed, he thought he could detect the ghostly echoes of past activity—the clink of a steel scalpel being dropped on a tray, the sucking sound of internal organs being pulled out of a body cavity. It smelled awful down here, like burnt rubber and disinfectant. "Hello?"

Silence.

His calves had knotted up. He walked past modular storage racks full of surgical equipment and a large scale used for weighing dead bodies, then turned the corner and stopped. Anna Hubbard's body lay naked on an autopsy table. His first instinct was to cover her up. He looked around for a sheet or a towel.

"Can I help you, sir?"

He spun around. A pasty-faced young man stood in the doorway with his arms crossed. He had materialized out of nowhere, setting Tully's heart racing again.

"Detective Tully, LAPD." He flashed his badge. "I'm looking for a white guy, six foot three, black hair, bad complexion. You seen him?"

The morgue tech shook his head.

"Any activity recently?"

"Yeah, I just released a body to Callaghan Funeral Homes."

"When was this?"

"Five minutes ago."

"Which way?"

"Out the loading dock." He pointed. "That way."

Rattling off a string of obscenities, Tully flew across the room and ran into a tray of instruments. "Shit." The steel instruments went clattering across the floor.

He raced out the back door and stood on the loading dock, staring into the vast parking lot. Hundreds of cars gleamed beneath the sodium-vapor lights. The heat was suffocating. The smog hung in the air like curtains. He radioed the two cops staking out Jack's car. "Any activity?" he asked.

"No sign of him yet, Detective."

"Did you see a hearse pull out of the parking lot?"

"Yeah, a few minutes ago."

"Go after it."

"Why?"

"Just go. I'm right behind you."

16.

Roy could barely breathe. He was lying on his back inside the plastic body bag, loud rock music reverberating throughout the floor pan of the hearse. He could feel the bass line pounding up his spine as he wormed his index finger into the zipper seam of the body bag and pushed it down a few inches. Just enough for him to squeeze his hand through. He felt around for the pull tab, then slid the zipper all the way down and took a deep breath. He could feel the brakes squeezing against the brake drum as the hearse came to a stop. While the driver distracted himself with a little off-key yodeling, Roy took the opportunity to crawl out of the body bag, open the lift gate and hop out of the hearse.

His bare feet hit the warm asphalt as he ran across the road. He was in a residential area—not a great one—the surrounding city blocks shabby and anonymous. The hearse was stopped at a red light, and the driver continued to rock his head to the beat and wait for the light to change. He didn't even realize his cargo was gone.

Roy's left arm throbbed, and he cradled it close to his body, then picked a direction and ran full out, legs pumping. Somewhere in the distance, a mutt was barking at a phantom. He turned down a commercial street and jogged past a closed-for-the-night fruit stand and a shoe repair shop. A cloud of steam whistled out of the Laundromat vent, wisps of smoke dissipating into the moonlit air. Only the Chinese restaurant was open at this hour, emitting an intoxicating aroma through its windows and doors. There were no customers, just a bunch of tired-looking cooks and waiters clustered around the wobbly tables. To the left of the restaurant was an alleyway.

Roy darted around back into a narrow parking lot, where four cars stood in front of a smelly Dumpster, the buckling pavement strewn with broken glass. A fishy smell saturated the air. Roy paused for a moment. These cars were no good. Too new. He needed something vintage. He continued up the alleyway, then took a left onto a quiet residential street full of darkened houses and made his way east. He eyeballed the driveways. There. The gold Chevy Impala, circa 1975.

Roy followed the concrete walkway around behind an aging ranch-style house, then paused at the hummingbird feeder strung from a gutter with a coat hanger. It contained sugar water, but the ruby-throated hummers had long since stopped coming. Instead, a troop of metallic-green beetles marched through a crack in the basin to sip at the artificial nectar.

He moved into the depthless shadows of the broad overhanging eaves behind the house and peeked into a rear window. He could see a drab room, small by anyone's standards, full of nondescript furniture carelessly arranged—a desk with a pockmarked surface, a pink-shaded lamp, a broken swivel chair. Everything had lost its luster. His throat grew parched, and his scalp tightened. This was one of those places that made him almost physically ill.

He moved out of the shadows and nearly tripped over a barbecue grill, where two black lumps were stuck to the grillwork. *Gut grenades.* On the back porch was an American flag on a pole, looking sad around the edges. The car was parked in the gravel driveway. Roy liked Chevy Impalas best. This one was big and roomy with a gold-leaf paint job, dual exhaust, a CD player with a punch amp, 56K on the odometer. Not bad. His hair lifted in a humid breeze as he moved toward it and opened the hood.

Just as he'd suspected. A chromed-out V-8 engine. He followed the plug wires to the red coil wires, then ran a wire from the positive side of the battery to the coil, giving power to the dash. Next he located the starter solenoid, which on most GM cars was on the starter. Using the surgical pliers he'd ripped off from the morgue, Roy crossed the small wire with the positive battery cable, and the engine roared to life.

He slammed the hood shut, then went over to the driver's side door, where he jammed the skull chisel into the keyhole. He worked the chisel hard until it broke the pins, allowing him to turn the chamber and open the door. He got in behind the wheel and adjusted the rearview mirror. Then he unlocked the steering column using the flat blade of the skull chisel, shifted the car into reverse and backed out of the driveway.

Upstairs in the house, a light blinked on. "Hey!" Somebody stuck their head out the window. "What's going on down there?"

Roy nosed onto the quiet street and sped away.

17.

The baby was sound asleep in Daisy's arms, exhausted from the birth experience. Whenever he yawned, she could see the short tight band that connected his tongue to the wet floor of his mouth. This band would stretch over time. She touched the diamond-shaped soft spot on his skull, the one that pulsated with each beat of his heart. If this had been a natural birth, the baby's soft spots would've allowed his skull to compress just enough to fit through the birth canal. But unlike most newborns, C-section babies weren't misshapen. They had round heads and normal facial features.

Daisy glanced at the birth certificate on the beside table. She'd already filled in the date and time, but there was a blank space for the baby's name. She had no idea what to call him. He stirred in her arms. His limbs seemed oddly foreshortened, but that, too, was normal. After all, he'd just spent eight and a half months curled up inside his mother's womb. In time, his arms and legs would uncurl from his body. His ears were soft and floppy, but the cartilage would harden after the first few weeks of life. He was pink all over from a profusion of red blood vessels showing through the delicate skin. He was so helpless, so dependent on the goodwill of others, she feared for him. She feared for herself. Daisy had been left caretaker of this little miracle and didn't quite know how to feel about it.

She gripped a tissue in her hand until it was molded to the shape of her fingers. Anna hadn't mentioned any names during the grievously brief time they'd had together. So little time, and now she'd left Daisy with her precious infant. Poor Anna.

Exhausted and grief-stricken, Daisy closed her eyes and could picture her sister's skirts and blouses and designer jeans folded neatly over their hangers in that sad apartment of hers. She saw Anna's motorcycle jacket. She saw her fuzzy bedroom slippers—lions and monkeys and bears—some so decrepit they had to be ducttaped together. Slippers grouped together like the passenger list of Noah's ark. *Noah.* Now there was a solid name for a boy.

Daisy had a feeling of sudden, strong empathy for her mother as she wrote *Anna Hubbard* beneath "Mother" on the birth certificate, and *John Doe* under "Father," just as Lily had done twenty-five years ago. Now she understood. Sometimes the truth was simply too painful, too hurtful, to be told. She would never speak of Roy Gaines again. From now on, she would tell people she had no idea who the baby's father was.

In the distance, she could hear the newborns crying

and looked at the sleeping infant in her arms. She studied his pinched little hands. He was more than a bundle of molecules. More than a combination of oxygen, carbon and nitrogen. He was a burning force. A vessel of raw power and pale delicacy. Looking at him was like watching a fiddlehead fern unfurl on the forest floor. It was primal and awe-inspiring. It was like facing the sky with your eyes closed. Like falling awake. How was she ever going to give him up? How could she possibly do that?

His name, she decided, was Noah.

"Hello, Noah Hubbard," she whispered. "Sounds good, doesn't it?"

He displayed sucking reflexes in his sleep.

"I can't even keep a goldfish alive," she told the baby. "How am I supposed to take care of you?"

It was impossible. A serious problem. She couldn't keep a baby, not with her busy schedule. What was she going to do? She glanced at the dark green push-button phone on the bedside table and did a quick calculation in her head. It would be 5:00 A.M. back East. That was early for Lily, but the news was grave. She cradled the receiver in the crux of her neck and dialed her mother's number.

"Hello?" Lily answered sleepily.

"Hi, Mom. It's me."

"Daisy? What time's it?"

"Mom?" Her stomach did flip-flops. "I've got bad news."

18.

Tully chased the fugitive through the grape-colored canyons east of Los Angeles, where a forest fire was raging. Months of low humidity and high temperatures had cured the dog hair on the forest floor, creating the perfect fuel for these wind-driven flames. He gripped the steering wheel of his department vehicle, a standard-issue Ford (Fucker Only Runs Downhill), and found himself surrounded on all sides by a ferocious, unpredictable inferno as he dogged the Chevy Impala through the winding hills. Twenty minutes ago, witnesses had reported a stolen vehicle and described a white male, six feet plus, black hair, et cetera. A BOLO had been issued. Now a fire truck came speeding toward him from the opposite direction, blasting its horn.

"Fuck!" Tully's stomach lurched as he swerved to avoid it. The fire truck roared on by, rocking him violently and taking with it one of his nine lives, while up ahead the Chevy Impala left the valley bottom and climbed steadily eastward, its taillights cutting steeply up the side of the canyon.

Tully tore after Roy Gaines, pressing pedal to the metal. He pierced a wall of rolling black smoke and found himself on a hairy S-curve. The drop was steep. He veered up the side of the canyon while high overhead, fixed-wing tankers and local news helicopters circled and buzzed, tracking the fire's progress through the sparsely populated area. The LAPD air unit had an infrared tracking device that could locate heat sources on the ground—people in vehicles or on foot. It was great for hunting down fugitives. The city was laid out on a grid pattern, making it relatively easy to pursue a vehicle from a thousand feet in the air, but Tully worried that the fire and smoke might be interfering with that.

He reached the crest of the ridge, where the road grew suddenly long and straight. The ridge was covered with unearthly rock formations, and the full moon cast crazy shadows over the landscape. Freak gusts of wind fanned the flames, making torches out of the crowns of the Douglas firs as the fugitive sped along the ridgeline, then took a hard right after the water tank and disappeared. Tully followed suit, turning sharply at the water tank and experiencing a slow-rolling wave of terror as his tires began to lose their traction. He sat bolt upright in his seat, tires locking as he hit the brakes.

The car skidded all over the road. "Oh shit!" He practically stood on the brakes, gravel pinging against the wheel wells as the car came to a hair-raising stop a few feet short of the precipice. His stomach clenched. The Ford shuddered frighteningly.

Across the valley, he could see columns of smoke rising up from the distant hills. He'd lost sight of the air unit. Where the hell were they? They were supposed to be tracking the Chevy for him, but in places the fire had become so intense they'd had to bank away. Now Tully wrenched the Ford into reverse, eased away from the drop and pulled back onto the road again. He accelerated hard down the canyonside.

These fire roads were loosely packed with gravel and rock and made for a bumpy ride. Choppy. Noisy. He clutched the steering wheel while all around him, trees swayed in the heat-stoked winds and intermittent bursts of sparks shot across the hood of his car. The fire crews were out there in droves tonight, cutting fire lines and struggling to contain the volatile flames into controllable stretches of rugged terrain. A choking smoke hung in the air. It made Tully shudder to think about his partner's fate. He loved Jack like a brother. Sometimes he hated Jack the way brothers hated one another—in a jealous, competitive way. He hated Jack's ability to charm the pants off everyone he met. He hated that he sometimes used his father's old cop show to his advantage. Jack was slightly arrogant, slightly smug; he'd always been that way. He was born with a certitude about who he was, and nobody and nothing could shake it from him.

Burned beyond recognition. Tully had seen charred bodies before, their arms raised in front of them like a boxer's. Flexion of the limbs, it was called. The human body, when exposed to intense heat, assumed a pugilistic attitude. *Poor Jack.* When they found him tomorrow or the next day, his muscles would be exposed, the seared skin split open, and the flesh of his hands would be completely burned away, leaving no fingers to take prints off of, just the crumbling bone.

The next couple of miles were excruciating. Tully's hands grew rigid on the wheel as the shock of the rough road migrated up his arms. By the time he'd caught up with the Chevy, a sick fury had risen in him. He could make out the back of Gaines's head through the charred pine needles lacing the windshield and wanted to put a bullet through that ignorant skull. Detective William Tully wanted his kill shot. Now. His rage was quiet, but it would express itself soon enough.

The road became even more winding and dangerous. He passed several Department of Transportation signs warning him to watch out for falling rocks and chased Gaines around the next corner. He reached for his revolver and set it on the seat beside him. Here the road abruptly turned to dirt, and the Chevy's wheels kicked up so much dust Gaines vanished in a fog of dancing particles.

Dust swam before Tully's high beams. He was dripping with sweat, delirious with adrenaline. He tried to avoid the worst of the holes and rocks in the road and felt like a man in a minefield. As he rounded the next curve, the rabid squeal of brakes reached his ears. He could see the red glow of the Chevy's taillights turning sharply and then disappearing into a cloud of dust.

"Shit!" A massive oak tree materialized out of nowhere like a mirage. Tully hit the brakes and tried to swerve out of its way, but the tree had fallen across the road, dragging several power lines down with it. Dull shock hit him as he slammed into the tree with a bang, the impact propelling him forward and nearly knocking his eyeballs out. The front end of the Ford collapsed in a shower of sparks while his chest hit the steering wheel and the air bag exploded. All the oxygen evacuated his lungs, and he was plunged into a world of darkness and hissing steam.

Moments later, Tully emerged from deep shock with his ears ringing. The car horn wouldn't stop blaring. He turned with slow scrutiny to assess the damage. The front seat had buckled forward. There was broken glass everywhere. He could smell the gasoline. *Drip, drip, drip.* That couldn't be good.

Soon the car was filled with a thick, caustic smoke. He tried not to panic, but the door was jammed shut. He slammed against it with his shoulder, then realized he would need to use more force than that. Turning sideways, he gave the door a swift kick. The locking mechanism rattled, but nothing happened. He was trapped inside the wreck, and the gas tank was leaking. *Drip, drip, drip.* The interior of the car was becoming as hot as the mouth of a furnace.

"Jesus help me." Rummaging frantically through the glove compartment, Tully found a screwdriver and aimed it at the window, then threw a well-placed punch that shattered the glass. He wriggled his way out through the broken window—oof, he was fat. Since when had he gotten so fat? Tully squeezed himself out like a thick squirt of toothpaste and landed in the dirt, then crawled away on his hands and knees, screaming for his life.

The gas tank erupted behind him. A huge blast ripped through the air, and an enormous shock wave hurtled him headlong into a pine tree. "Shit!" The soft-needled branches cushioned his fall, and he landed on the ground and stayed low. He couldn't see a damn thing. He was choking on smoke. The blast had ignited a fireball almost twenty feet high, and every window in his car had shattered, setting off the car alarm.

There was a change in air pressure as the air got sucked back inside the vehicle due to a partial vacuum created by the blast, then another explosion buckled the carriage. Tully ducked and rolled while the car rose up in the air, then plunged back down to the ground with a sonic boom. A series of gritty rollovers propelled him into a ditch. He unlocked his fingers and looked up just as the vehicle pancaked with a whoosh and a dance of embers. He shielded his face from the intense heat while fiery fragments showered down from the sky.

"Oh God . . . oh my God . . ." His car was totaled. Gone. The department car was on fire. The heat was so intense the tears dried almost instantly on his face.

He looked around as embers the size of marbles came whirling out of the sky. Burning embers struck his face and arms. "Ouch," he said, stumbling to his feet. "Ouch, ouch!" He couldn't stop coughing. The burning car sent plumes of thick black smoke billowing in all directions, and he tried to outrun it.

There was a series of small explosions. *Pop, pop, pop.* It was his service revolver going off. He had left it inside the car. He crouched in a defensive posture and covered his head, trying to make himself less of a target. A stray bullet flew past his head, and he dove for the ground.

Pop, pop, pop.

Silence.

Dazed but okay, he stumbled to his feet. He brushed himself off, shook the glass out of his hair, then realized he was bleeding. His scalp and arms were cut. Now he heard a whirring sound. *Rrr, rrrr.*

It was coming from somewhere behind him.

Rrr, rrrr.

Tully turned around.

The Chevy Impala had fishtailed into a culvert, narrowly averting disaster, and now Roy Gaines was trying to get away. He sat behind the wheel of his stolen vehicle and keyed the stalled-out engine, his face lit by the green dashboard lights.

Rrr, rrrr.

Tully reached down into his leg holster for his off-duty weapon. His hands were shaking. Keeping his .38 aimed at the fugitive's head, he slowly approached the car.

Behind the glass, Gaines's face was fish-belly pale, and his eyes watered in the hazy heat. He keyed the ignition one more time, and the engine turned over.

"Stay right where you are," Tully said hoarsely. "Get out of the vehicle. Now!"

Gaines stomped on the gas, and the car jolted forward, pinning Tully in its high beams. Blinded by the glare, the detective fired. The windshield fractured.

The car screamed forward and hit Tully as he tried to roll out of the way.

He landed hard on the ground, then twisted around and fired at the fleeing vehicle, unloading three wild rounds into the dancing taillights. The Chevy was a squid, escaping in a cloud of ink.

Tully lay on the ground, his breathing shallow and fast. He tried to increase its depth and slow its rate, to breathe from the abdomen, not the chest. He wanted to prevent himself from hyperventilating. He couldn't believe he'd lost control of the situation like that. Everything in the vicinity was catching fire—trees, underbrush, weeds. He had to get out of there.

A single-engine plane buzzed aimlessly overhead, and he listened to its mosquito whine as he assessed the damage—two broken fingers, a cracked rib, possible wrist fracture, sprained ankle. He limped down the sloping road, then reached for his portable unit and called it in. He was beyond sick now. He'd let the fugitive get away.

19.

Roy was speeding up the side of the canyon while an LAPD air unit circled above him, big blasts of candlepower from its spotlight striking him in the eyes and nearly blinding him. He kept a firm grip of the wheel as he took the next hairpin turn, feeling the helicopter's rotor blades shuddering against the hood of his car. He twisted through a cloud of dust, tunneling deeper into the woods and looking for any hot spots where the swirling flames and thick black smoke might drive the chopper away. Over the next rise, the road fell steeply downhill, and Roy hung on tight while his front wheels lost their grip and started to slide. He tapped the brakes, slowing the car to a more reasonable speed, his heart thumping just ahead of him. At the bottom of this hairy descent was a paved road.

Roy got onto a remarkably smooth two-lane byway and quickly accelerated to eighty, heading north. He listened to the steady hum of the blacktop and looked out his window at the sky. The chopper was gone. The stars were mostly hidden behind a layer of smoke. The asphalt had a pleasant cadence and rhythm. He turned on the radio, and the jazz music held him with its kinetic, spiraling energy. He basked in the full-throated richness pulsating out of the car speakers, then remembered: *This is Dad's favorite album.*

He could feel his father's unnatural energy like a spray of static electricity inside the car. "How's it goin', Roy Boy?" The voice was exceedingly familiar to him, but the signal was faint. His flesh crept as he recalled the conversation they'd had seventeen years ago.

"You think I liked being married?" his father said. "Do you think I liked being chained to that crazy woman? Your mother used to lie there like a petrified dog turd. Is that what you want in your life, Roy?"

"No, Dad."

"Huh?"

"I said no."

"Think about it very carefully."

On the day of Linda Hildreth's funeral, hundreds of people had shown up to pay their respects; half of them were complete strangers to eight-year-old Roy. After it was over and everybody had gone home, when it was just Roy and his dad inside the empty house, his father had said, "You hungry?"

Roy spun around and stared into the empty hallway. "Dad?"

"In here," his father said. "Grab a seat. Dinner's ready."

Roy followed the sound of his voice into the dining

room. On the sideboard was an impressive array of liquor bottles—tequila, vodka, bourbon, rum, Scotch. Two places had been set at the antique dining table, and Roy recognized the polished chrome utensils that his mother rarely used, the lit candles, the bone china plates heaped with mashed potatoes and expensive cuts of steak.

"How are you, son? You okay?" his father said from the doorway. Benny Hildreth was a tall, slender man with brown hair and brown eyes, impeccably groomed. He had his look down—mustache, Rolex, sharkskin suit, very seventies.

"Yeah, I guess." Roy shrugged and dipped his finger into the mashed potatoes, tasting butter, salt and pepper.

"I sold off that World War I collection. Got a good price for it, too." His father reached for a pack of cigarettes next to the beveled-glass ashtray on the sideboard, shook one out and lit it. He paused to enjoy the taste, then said, "Imported ale. Want one?"

"Yeah, sure." Roy followed him into the kitchen, then glanced at the wine rack. "I'd rather have some of that."

"Ooh. Classy." His father wiggled his eyebrows at him, and Roy laughed. Benny selected a bottle of Chablis, filled two long-stemmed glasses and handed one to Roy. "Bottoms up," he said with a grin.

"Peas on earth . . ."

". . . and good tall women."

They lifted their glasses, clinked them together.

Roy took a sip, then watched the sky's reflection in the infinity pool outside their kitchen window. The wine tasted sour, like tainted grape juice. He didn't like it. "Dad?" he said.

"Yeah, son?"

"If you knew you were going to die soon, and you could only make one phone call, who would you call and what would you say?"

His father reached into his pocket and took out his wallet. He removed the picture of Roy's mother and said, "I'd call your mother and tell her what a cunt she was." He tossed the picture into the wastebasket. "C'mon. Let's eat," he said.

The memory faded, a tapestry of cobwebs settling for a moment into a perfect imitation of his father before it teetered and fell, scattering in the diffuse light.

Now the LAPD air unit swooped out of the night sky, nosing down until it was almost on top of him. It made big looping turns in the air, its rotor blades whipping up clouds of dust so thick that Roy could barely see where he was going.

He pulled a U-turn in the middle of the road and headed in the opposite direction. He had to find another fire road, fast, or he'd never get rid of them. After two miles of frantic searching, he took a sharp right onto a hard-packed road that snaked up into the woods. He drove for miles with the whine of the rotor blades ringing in his ears. Good-size rocks banged against the wheel wells, while the road gradually degraded to dirt and the kicked-up dust cocooned him in a yellow haze.

He was surrounded on all sides by crackling flames. These trees had survived centuries of lightning strikes, but now the fire would spread swiftly through the dry woods. Even the upper reaches of the old-growth ponderosas were on fire. The chopper followed him until the fire grew so intense it had to lift away. It banked wide to the east, then circled in a steady northbound ascent.

Roy drove deeper into the burning woods, until the roar grew deafening and the steering wheel became almost too hot to touch. When a blistering heat radiated into the car through his rolled-down window, he hit the brakes. He put the Chevy into reverse and stepped on the gas, but the rear wheels spun around uselessly. He eased his foot off the accelerator, then slowly turned the steering wheel from side to side as he reapplied power. The car reared back, then dropped down into the sand wash.

It was no use. The vehicle was stuck.

He got out and shielded his face with his hands. Behind him, the wind-fueled flames blew brilliant yellow gusts from one side of the road to the other. In front of him was a dirt trail, well maintained and fairly free of underbrush. Covering his head with his shirt, he made a dash for the trail, then broke into a sprint.

The Chevy went up with a whoosh behind him. Roy glanced back in time to see the LAPD air unit hovering above the burning wreckage, tracking this major heat source on its infrared scope. He heard a loud bang, and a bright orange ball of flame shot into the air and rocked the chopper sideways. Even from a distance, Roy could feel the blast of hot, sticky air.

He turned and ran full tilt, the sound of the rotor blades gradually fading into the distance. Reality fell away. After about a mile, he couldn't hear anything anymore.

He came upon a road that was well graded and passable by automobile. He paused for a moment, then crossed the road barefoot and stood on a rocky cliff overlooking the foothills of East Los Angeles. Sporadic fires swirled through the sparsely populated area, isolated fires that rivaled the stars in their lonely, twinkling beauty. He could see the entire panorama of the night sky—moon, stars, planes, choppers. Slurry bombers swept down to unload their cargo, and news helicopters hovered like hummingbirds, their blue beams crisscrossing through the smoke. When the air tankers dropped their slurry, it fell vertically onto the fire like rain from the belly of a thunderstorm.

Roy took a deep breath and got back on the road, heading north. Hate kept him going. Hate kept one foot moving in front of the other. All-consuming hate. He walked until the concrete knot of Los Angeles had faded from memory.

20.

Jack fumbled for a handhold in the wildly carved limestone, cursing and stumbling, while high overhead the moon wore a yellow ring. He hugged the inner edge of the canyon and paused to catch his breath. The uphill climb was slow going. He reached for a sandstone slab, then slid a few feet down the wall of rock, yelling, "Shit!" as he descended. These gravel-strewn ridges were difficult to surmount. The loose pebbles gave little grip. The cracked limestone crumbled and splintered as he attempted to regain his footing.

It took him over an hour to inch his way up the inner canyon, clinging to rock formations in a difficult and steep ascent. His breathing grew labored as he hoisted himself up over the top of a granite ledge, striated with colors like the growth rings on a tree. He lay there for a few minutes before he struggled to his feet and stood on shaky legs.

The moon was bright enough to read by. Less than forty yards away was a road. Jack licked the salt off his lips and took several painful breaths. It hurt to swallow. He touched the lesions around his throat, wondering if there might be any underlying neck injury. A person could survive manual strangulation, only to die from complications a few days later.

He crossed the dry creekbed, where an ashen salamander slithered past his feet. The air smelled of soot. Blackened sagebrush edged up to the footpath. He didn't have his cell phone with him. He didn't have his gun. He probably didn't have a career anymore. He had fucked up royally. He could hear a car coming and tried to holler for help, but nothing came out of his parched throat. Just a hiss. Just a wheeze.

He hobbled toward the road, only twenty yards away now, feeling dangerously dehydrated. He waved his arms in the air, but the next car drove past without stopping or even slowing down. He heard a droning sound and turned to look at the foothills and beyond. Distant choppers made dizzying orbits as they dredged the night sky, their spotlights sweeping through the smoky air. They buzzed like bumblebees, each note spun into dissonance by the gusting wind.

His index finger was badly bruised and swollen. "Thank you, thank you." That finger had saved his life tonight. He'd managed to slip it underneath the steel chain and alleviate some of the pressure on his windpipe. At least he was alive. How lucky was that?

Lucky, yes. But he wasn't exactly elated. Roy had beaten him. Roy had deceived him. Roy was still out

there with Jack's car, Jack's gun, Jack's cell phone.
Jesus. He could feel his career circling the drain.

He limped along an erosion ditch and approached the
road. Another car would be coming soon. He would
stand and wait for it.

ONE WEEK LATER

1.

Daisy was back in her old childhood room, the one with the cobwebs in the corners and the Golden Books on the pine shelves, the very room where she'd once plotted her escape from Edgewater, Vermont, population 12,000. It was early in the morning, and she lay in bed with the covers pulled up to her neck, so chilly for mid-April. Just down the hallway was the sleeping baby. They'd put his crib in the guest bedroom, since it was easier for Daisy and her mother to take turns that way. Meanwhile, she shared her old room with Anna's ghost.

She studied the too-small closet and cracked vanity mirror, the other twin bed pushed into the opposite corner. Gathered around the headboard were Anna's Raggedy Ann and Andy, a harem of Barbies, an army of Troll dolls. Dolls that talked. Dolls that burst into song when you pulled their strings. Wonder Woman, Spanish flamenco dancer, Madame Alexander, too many eerie dolls' eyes staring at Daisy from across the room. Watching her accusingly. *Where's Anna? What have you done with our mother?*

She closed her eyes, not wanting to look at them, not wanting to think about Anna anymore. She felt stuck in a time warp, with Anna's final hours playing over and over inside her head. Every morning she felt it—the seizure grip of fear. She'd fight the morning's first light, bury her head in her pillow and try to run away from the truth, but the truth would always catch up with her eventually, spinning her like a centrifuge. Her heart would race and her body would drag like an old tire hooked to a fishing line, and she would move reluctantly, exhaustedly, into the light of another day.

It helped to have the baby to take care of. His needs were so immediate, so urgent, there was hardly any time to grieve. *Noah Hubbard.* The name had just popped into her head. Maybe because this baby, with all his genetic baggage, was sailing into unknown territory. During the day, she walked around doing the things that had to be done, pretending to be okay. She put on a false face for the baby's sake, for Lily's sake, but every so often the grief would slam into her and she would just have to sit down. Anna's funeral was in three days. Arrangements were being made with the help of Lily's friends. They knew all about such things, these intrepid old ladies.

Outside, a pair of mourning doves kept cooing back and forth. Daisy liked the way the light fanned out across the rug. On the floor beside the bed was a stack of poor-quality photocopies of Anna's phone bills and recent credit card transactions. Daisy had spent half the night trying to piece together her sister's life in L.A. She'd

gotten maybe three hours of sleep altogether. Jack was
back in Los Angeles, recovering from his injuries. He'd
been suspended from the department pending an internal
investigation into his alleged misconduct. He'd called
her late last night to say that he would be flying out to
Vermont in a few days. "Hildreth knows where you
work," he told her bluntly. "He knows where you live.
He knows where your mother lives. Keep your doors
locked, Daisy. I've informed the local police about the
situation, and I'll be there soon. But first I've got some
business to take care of." His words sent shivers slithering down her spine, but more important, she missed him.
She wanted him nearby.

At the foot of the bed was the girls' old Scrabble
board game. Last night Daisy had tried to make an anagram out of *END 70*, just as *Hildreth* had been an anagram for *Dr. E. H. Hilt*. She'd played around with the
letters *E-N-D* but only came up with *DEN* and *NED*.
Next she'd turned the zero into the letter *O* and got:

> *END O*
> *DE ON*
> *DE NO*
> *ED ON*
> *ED NO*
> *NODE*
> *DO EN*
> *DONE*

Done? Had Anna *done* something? Was she *done?*
Done 7? Was Anna trying to say that she was *done, done,
done, done* . . . seven times? Was that the hidden mean-

ing behind the message? It made no sense. Daisy gave up.

Now a plunking sound interrupted her thoughts. Strange sounds often emanated from the old house—groaning water pipes, hissing radiators, sheets of snow sliding off the roof in the wintertime, the floorboards expanding and contracting. Years ago, Mr. Barsum had painted the girls' hardwood floor dark green for some inexplicable reason, and Anna used to joke that the floor was a river and their beds were two life rafts, and she would fall off her bed onto the floor, crying, "Help me!" And Daisy would have to rescue her from the raging river all over again.

Outside the leaky bedroom windows, Holsteins grazed in the alfalfa fields and gackles settled like fat black leaves on the tree branches. April was usually a lime-green tribute to spring, but everything had arrived a little late this year. During Vermont's long winter months, the snow would slowly accumulate, layer upon layer, until huge drifts reclined against the sides of buildings, burying the cars and trash cans under a dirty white blanket. By mid-February, the mailman would have to dig the mailboxes out with his gloved hands. The house was always gray and icicled in the wintertime, heat from the radiators melting peepholes in the frosted windowpanes. But now that spring had finally arrived, the snow would melt rapidly, and the meltwater would flow downhill and turn the ditches into miniature streams. Daisy could hear the meltwater now—that lively cascading sound, like the tinkling of many bells.

She reached for the bottle of sleeping pills on her

bedside table. Dr. Slinglander had prescribed them for her. She couldn't eat, couldn't sleep, could barely choke down the tea her mother was constantly bringing to her. She was tempted to take two pills and knock herself out, but that would only make tonight's sleep more elusive. She herded the impulse back into a dusty corner of her brain while Anna's final words replayed inside her head: *I thought it would bring me peace, but it didn't. End 70 is a gift for you. You'll find out when you get there.*

Now she heard footsteps on the stairs and a rustling sound outside her door, accompanied by a soft knock.

"Enter at your own peril," Daisy said as if she were twelve again.

Her mother stepped into the room as tentatively as if she were entering a shrine. "How'd you sleep?" she asked.

"Not so great. Noah woke up a bunch and . . ." Her voice trailed off.

"Me, too," Lily said quietly. "Breakfast is ready."

"No thanks, Ma."

With a long-suffering sigh, Lily crossed the room and tugged on all the window shades, letting them rattle upward so that sunlight filled the room and gradually took the chill out of the air.

"Don't," Daisy groaned, covering her head with her pillow.

"I made your favorite. Sausage and eggs."

She could smell the tantalizing combination of sizzling maple sausages, hash browns and green peppers wafting up the staircase, her mother's idea of heaven. "I'm not hungry," she said. "But thanks."

Lily paused at the window to take in the sight of the

budding burdocks in the front yard. "Well, I guess spring is officially here."

Daisy tossed her pillow aside. "And five billion years from now, the sun will expand into this red giant that's going to burn our planet to a cinder. So enjoy it while it lasts."

Her mother scowled. "And you know this how?"

"Eight years of higher education and the loans to prove it."

"You can't go on like this, you know. Not sleeping. Not eating. Are you trying to starve yourself to death?"

"Maybe," she said. Through her bedroom windows, Daisy could see the utterly blue, utterly empty sky.

"You're just trying to get my goat," Lily said irritably.

"Your goat? Exactly where is this goat located, Ma?"

Lily's light-colored hair fell in wisps around her temples and cheeks, and her smile was broad but faded. The colors that composed her seemed to merge with the old wallpaper; she was like a once-colorful sundress that had been washed too many times. The back of her beige dress was wrinkled, and she wore running shoes and athletic socks as if she were about to dash around the block a few times. A thought so alien it made Daisy giggle.

"What's so funny?"

"Nothing."

"All right. Fine." Lily frowned at the pink tissue bunched in her fist. They'd run out of white tissues because of the baby and were down to their last box of pink, perfumy ones, the kind that made Daisy sneeze. "What's all this?" Lily kicked the paperwork on the floor with the toe of her running shoe.

"Don't mess it up, Ma."

"Were you up all night reading again?" She picked up a book on chaos theory and held it at arm's length. "Wow." She squinted. "Either my eyesight's getting worse, or my arms are shrinking."

"Mom?" Daisy said, feeling a nervous jump in the pit of her stomach. "Remember Wednesday when I took the baby to the doctor's office?"

Lily put the book down. "Yes?"

"I paid to have him tested."

"What for?"

"I got him genetically screened for Stier-Zellar's."

Lily pursed her lips. "All right. And what if he tests positive? What if he turns out to be just like Louis?"

"Ignorance isn't going to save us, Mom," Daisy told her, sitting up and crossing her legs on the bed. "We can't stick our heads in the sand. We've got to find out."

"Oh God." She sat heavily on the edge of her daughter's bed. "I can't go through it again, Daisy. I'm sorry."

"Nobody's asking you to."

"Oh really? Who's going to raise him, then? You?"

She honestly hadn't thought about it. DNA was a book with a beginning and an end. There was the book of Daisy. The book of Lily. The book of Anna. The book of Noah. It would take only one gene—one sentence in Noah's book—to seal his fate. We all had glitches in our DNA, hereditary predispositions. Changes in the sequence of a gene could change the action of a protein, just like a single misplaced word could change the meaning of a sentence.

"What are we going to do? Put him up for adoption?" Lily said, the anger sitting on her face. "Who in their right mind would adopt a child with Stier-Zellar's?"

"I just assumed—"

"What? That I'd do all the child-rearing?"

Daisy hadn't thought about an alternative.

"I mean it, Daisy . . ."

"Mom. We don't have the results back yet. And besides, Stier-Zellar's is an autosomal recessive condition."

"In English, please."

"Anna's father wasn't an obligate carrier, but you are. Anna was never tested, but we can assume that her risk of being a carrier is about one in three. That's fairly low. And the chances of the baby's father being a carrier are extremely remote, maybe one in a thousand. Anna was clinically unaffected by the mutated gene, which means that out of the remaining possibilities, there's only a zero to thirty percent chance she inherited the mutation from you."

"What if you're wrong? What if Roy Hildreth just so happens to be a carrier, too? What then?"

"Even so," Daisy said calmly, "if both parents are carriers, there's only a twenty-five percent risk. It's not a gimme, Mom. You need two mutations for the disease to manifest itself."

"Well, that's all very impressive-sounding. But if Noah turns out to have that awful disease, I'm not going to be the one to take care of him. I mean it, Daisy. I never want to go through that again."

"There are new therapies, Mom. New treatments. We could get him into clinical trials right away."

"But that's not a cure, is it?"

"Not yet," Daisy admitted. She didn't know what she was going to do. The baby occupied every waking second of every hour of their day. She and Lily took turns bottle-feeding him, changing his diapers, burping him, bathing him. It was a humbling experience, at times exhilarating, at times exhausting. He woke up, looked around, went back to sleep. He woke up, screamed a lot, went back to sleep. He woke up, looked around, pooped in his diapers and went back to sleep. He couldn't stop drooling. His drool was everywhere.

"I did it once. I won't do it again." Lily stood up. "And neither should you."

"Mom?"

"What?"

"Do we know anyone in Boise, Idaho?"

"What?" Confusion spread across Lily's face. "No. Why?"

"American Falls doesn't ring a bell?"

"No." There was a brief pause. "Why, sweetie?"

"I've been looking through Anna's credit card records. She went to Idaho last September, but she told people she was coming home for two weeks. She hasn't been home in ten months, has she?"

"No, she hasn't." Lily sighed, her hands clasped in front of her like a disapproving schoolteacher's. The way she scowled reminded Daisy of all the times her mother had sat in judgment of her decisions and choices. "Does it matter?" she asked.

"I'm just trying to sort it all out."

"When is your detective friend supposed to get here?"

"His name is Jack. I know you don't like strangers in the house, Mom, but he's a nice guy. He just wants to protect us."

"Do we need protecting?"

"Yes, Mom," Daisy told her. "We do."

"How long will he be staying?"

"I don't know. Until he feels the house is secure."

Lily looked down at the tissue in her hand. "After Gregory died," she said softly, "I must've lost twenty pounds. I had such terrible stomachaches. If you'd told me at the time that I'd get over it eventually, I never would've believed you. I remember hugging him before he took off for work that day. I don't remember what we talked about. I hope I said, 'I love you.' I think I did. Afterwards I missed him so much, but there was nothing I could do about it. He was gone."

Prisms of light touched the bureau, the footboard of her bed, the salmon-colored blankets—magic fairies, Anna used to call them. *Quick, make a wish.*

Suddenly, Daisy's cell phone rang. She'd left it in her backpack at the foot of her bed, and now she scrambled to answer it. "Hello?"

"Ms. Hubbard? This is Dr. Brown's office. We got the results back from Noah's newborn screen."

"Yes?" she said breathlessly. Maybe Lily was right. Maybe they were better off not knowing.

"He is a carrier, but he doesn't have Stier-Zellar's."

She could feel her whole body relax. "Really? Honestly?"

"We also have the results of your genetic test," the nurse went on. "You have one mutation for the gene, so that makes you a carrier as well."

"Thank you." Daisy hung up. It stung for only a second. "He's fine, Mom. He's a carrier, but he's perfectly healthy. He's going to be fine."

Lily's face became so raw and nakedly vulnerable that Daisy almost feared for her health.

"Mom? Are you all right?"

She emitted a high, shivery laugh. Tears clung to her eyelashes. "I'm just so happy."

"Me, too." Daisy gave her a lingering hug.

2.

Jack's gutless rental car didn't have enough horsepower to get it over the next hill, let alone the next mesa. It was sluggish as a snail gliding along on a slimy, muscular foot. The interior was so cramped his knees were jammed up somewhere near his skull. There was something on the windshield, a speck of something. He'd been trying to scrape it off with his thumbnail, but he couldn't seem to get rid of it. No wonder. It was on the outside of the glass. This car would drive him insane.

He was in a lousy mood. He'd been in a lousy mood for days. The wildfire had scorched fifteen thousand acres, and over fifty homes and cabins had been destroyed. The damage estimates continued to climb. Erosion and mudslides would be a big problem in the fall when the rains came. A homeless man had died in the blaze. The cause of the fire was still under investigation, but all fingers pointed to Jack's reckless behavior. The investigators had found a set of charred handcuffs at the point of the fire's origin. Did they need any more proof?

He regretted his actions. He lamented the destruction of so much property and the death he'd apparently caused. He went to bed at night wishing he could turn back time. He woke up wishing he could go back to sleep. He carried the guilt on his frame and in the way that he moved. He was ashamed on more levels than his tormented psyche would ever admit. He was currently on suspended leave with pay and had hired a lawyer to handle the Internal Affairs Division investigation into his "egregious misconduct." Only Tully was standing by him.

The drone of the rental car's tires thundered in his ears as he cruised through southern Arizona in search of the small town where Roy Orion Hildreth had grown up. A hot desert wind rushed into the car, blowing his hair around in streamers. He passed a bar. He passed another bar. He was hungry. He should eat. He took out his cell phone and dialed Tully's number.

"Hey, Jack," his ex-partner answered.

"Just tell me you love me, and I'll go away."

There was a pause. "Where are you?"

"Waltz Lake. Only there is no lake. And nobody's dancing."

"I'm in charge of this investigation, Jack. Don't go running interference. You're on suspended leave, remember?"

"Relax. I'm taking a vacation."

"Uh-huh."

"Think of all the money I'll be saving the department."

"Uh-huh."

He glanced in the rearview mirror at his own defeated-looking eyes. "Look, I'll share whatever I find with you, Tully. I just want to help you catch this guy."

"Stay out of it, Jack."

"The paperwork alone could take weeks. Don't look a gift horse in the mouth."

There was a long pause. "No," Tully finally said.

"Okay."

"Okay?"

"We didn't have this conversation."

"You have a weird and unique way about you, Makowski," his friend said, and hung up.

Half an hour later, the road Jack was on went from gravel to loose rock, and after a few minutes, this bumpy ride ended in a chalk driveway. The two-story house was made of wheat-colored concrete and hovered in the morning mist like a fortress overlooking its own deteriorating grounds. The windows were all boarded up, and there were no other buildings around for several miles. So this was where Roy Hildreth had spent his miserable childhood?

Jack reached into his leg holster for his off-duty gun and approached the house up a series of stone slabs built into the graduated ground. He pried open the rusty wrought-iron gate and took the flaky flagstone pathway across a sunbaked front yard. The coyotes had finished their night wanderings, and if you looked real hard, you could see them scampering into the dusty hills. The surrounding desert held hundreds of plant species—creosote, chuparosa, jojoba, lavender, mesquite. He was burning up in this heat. The mercury had already hit one hundred. The ancient rock garden in front of the house contained a weird topography, barrel cactus growing next to desert-varnished boulders.

In the garden, partially hidden beneath a tangled mass of vines, was a marble slab with FATHER etched on its pale pink surface. Jack had ingested every bit of data he could find on Roy Hildreth. Twelve years ago, Roy's father had died of a massive heart attack. According to Benny Hildreth's wishes, he'd been buried on the property. He'd gotten permission from the state to be interred in his own front yard, since he refused to be buried in a cemetery. Benny knew all too well what went on in those places. He'd been a bone trader for far too long to trust the men who handled dead bodies.

A strong odor of mulch filled Jack's nostrils as he leaned over the marble slab and parted the weeds. There was an enormous hole in the ground. The grave had been dug up recently. The coffin was down in the hole. The lid was off the coffin, and the body was missing. Jack clapped his hands, knocking off the dust, and gripped his gun. It looked like Roy had been here recently. He'd stolen his father's corpse.

Jack walked toward the house and mounted the creaky wooden steps, then turned the brass doorknob and gently pushed the door open with his spread-apart fingers. At the end of the formal entryway was a shattered floor-to-ceiling mirror. Jack could see his reflection in the broken shards—he looked like a madman with his hair blown wildly about his head. The bruises on his face were healing nicely, and his singed eyebrows were beginning to grow back. He smoothed his wind-whipped hair behind his ears with his bandaged hands. He'd burned them pretty good. His index finger was in a splint, and the waist chain had left behind a string of dark red welts on his neck. A few years ago, Jack would have told you that he knew himself and his place in the universe, but as he slipped toward thirty-nine, he was beginning to distrust this perception of himself.

His scalp shivered as he heard a skittering sound. It was coming from the living room. He crossed the water-damaged parquet floor, where the rotten wood felt as soggy underfoot as an enormous hot dog bun. The entryway's heavily varnished moldings were alligatored with neglect. This was exactly the kind of house the neighborhood kids would insist was haunted. Step across the threshold, and you'd hasten your own death. Bring a plant inside, and it would shrivel in seconds.

The living room at the heart of the house was barely beating. The vents and light fixtures were congested with dust. A decade's worth of cigarettes had been snuffed out along the edges of the flat-wood molding. Jack trained his gun on a skittering sound. It was coming from behind the dusty leather recliner peppered with shotgun blasts. He could feel the tension in him diffracting like cracks on thin ice as he circled slowly around it.

A dozen rats scattered in all directions, abandoning the corpse that was propped up on the leather chair. The body was spiffily dressed in a gray flannel suit, a blue silk tie and black shoes. The smell was repugnant. The corpse's face and hands were covered with a disgusting yellow waxy substance that could've been adipocere. Adipocere happened when the body's fat turned to wax as a result of a wet burial. Caskets were like cars; they deteriorated in much the same way. Once the enamel was breached, the metal casket would begin to rust and leak. That might account for the skin's soapy appearance. Around the corpse's neck was a hand-lettered sign: BONE TRADER BLOWOUT SALE—TAKE ME HOME FOR $5!

Repulsed, Jack took a step back and trained his gun on the smallest of sounds. Was Roy watching him? Was he there inside the house?

He could just imagine embers glowing in the wood-burning fireplace. Benny Hildreth used to keep the A/C on full blast, no matter what the season. Jack had read about it in one of the files. It was usually a cool sixty-six degrees in here. Benny ran the A/C hard and lit a fire every night, talk about extravagant. The house had been passed from father to son, and now Jack glanced at the ruined furniture—the brown leather sectional sofas, the Barcelona chairs, a tipped-over candelabra on the tarnished copper mantelpiece. Built in the 1950s, this house had once been the envy of the entire town with its Palladian windows and illuminated backyard. A pathway lined with Grecian urns had led from the house to the octagonal gazebo. There was a patio with café umbrellas, stainless-steel gas heaters and a dark stone Buddha. Jack had seen pictures in the court files. Beyond the patio was a sleek rectangular pool with an infinity edge. Roy's parents used to hold parties year round, sometimes wife-swapping shindigs during the Swinging Sixties. Linda would retire early, however, due to her delicate health. Then she and young Roy would sit in the master bedroom and look out the window at the colorful paper lanterns and listen to the party noises below. Now the house smelled of rot creeping up the foundation, of mold permeating the ductwork, of mildew drifting through the heat registers.

Aiming his gun around every corner, Jack left the living room and stood on the threshold of Benny Hildreth's office. Lingering in the doorway, he felt many things— apprehension, excitement, curiosity. He believed that the place must be holy to Roy. A touchstone of sorts. He would come back to remind himself of who he was. He would stash things here—fake identity papers, credit cards, a getaway car.

Now Jack studied the cracked faux-leather sofa, the sun-damaged chairs with their delaminating finishes, the heavily varnished table with its water rings and natural oils gone all dark and wavy, the stack of out-of-date *Fortune* magazines crazed with cobwebs. This room was a coffin. He spotted the Pooped Pussycat jewelry box on top of the black filing cabinet and crossed the room. There was a collection of silver keys inside. He selected a key and fitted it into a lock, and the top file drawer rolled open.

Jack scooped out a handful of yellowing manila file folders with stick-on labels from a manual typewriter: *Police Archive Photos, Autopsies, World War II, Famous People.* He set the files down on the scratched wooden desk and opened another file drawer. It screeched like a child. He randomly selected a folder, its contents smelling of dry rot. The manila folder spread apart like the dusty, translucent wings of a carefully preserved butterfly. In his hands were eight-by-ten glossies of dead people—a headless man who'd been struck by a train, red chunks of human body parts taken from the belly of a crocodile, stacked Holocaust victims labeled

BREMHOLZ—*firewood*. He slapped more folders down on the desk, dust rising from the wormy wood. He removed all the files and found what he was looking for— a rumpled paper bag. Inside the bag were some phony ID papers and a few hospital name tags, which he spilled out. *Henry Wendell, M.D., Evan Baker, Behavioral Pediatrics . . .*

He heard a noise. It sounded like footsteps. Jack's limbs filled with an unnatural energy as he hurried back across the hallway into the living room. A dog glanced up from the corner, then trotted away. It left through a broken window.

With a shiver of residual anxiety, he looked around at the toppled, broken furniture and mentally reviewed the history he'd pieced together from the commitment files and psychiatric evaluations, years of accumulated recommendations and court assessments. Roy had grown up in this house surrounded by the pornography of death. His hypochondriac mother had died when he was eight years old. His bone-trader father had taken him on gruesome business trips from hospital to morgue, trading and selling death memorabilia. When he was a little boy, Roy wanted to become a doctor. He told his psychiatrists later on that he'd wanted to cure his mother of her elusive illnesses. But then after she had died, so did his dream. He dropped out of high school during his sophomore year and was in and out of juvenile hall from that point onward. He impregnated Kerry Pearl but never married her. She raised the baby with her parents' help, and it died later on. At twenty-three, he did a stint in a mental institution after slashing his wrists in jail with the sharpened edges of his driver's license. At the hospital, he told the doctors he wanted to die. Why did he want to die?

Upstairs in Roy's bedroom, the walls were painted Utah-sky blue. The frogs in the dusty terrarium had hardened to shoe leather. The plants had withered to straw. Jack dug around in Roy's bureau drawers, groping through moldy Jockey shorts and Spider-Man pajamas sprinkled with petrified rat pellets. He stepped back and studied the room for a beat, then noticed a cardboard box hidden under the bed. He got down on his hands and knees and slid it out. He sneezed from inhaled dust balls.

The box contained a bunch of scientific magazines, some of them over a dozen years old. Jack leafed through the top periodical, stopping wherever the pages had been turned down. He scanned an article on genetics, an article on DNA. Then a picture fell out.

Jack scooped it up. The snapshot had been folded and unfolded so many times it was almost torn in half. A cute toddler sat in a wheelchair. She had a thin face, pronounced cheekbones and dark eyes that seemed to drift in and out of focus. She had curly dark hair and dimples and looked very frail. Jack turned the picture over. Written on the back in girlish script, it said *Suzy Pearl Hildreth, 1991*. Roy and Kerry Pearl's daughter, Suzy, would've been three years old at the time this picture was taken.

A nauseating feeling came over him. The little girl's head was tilted to one side, giving her a lopsided look. This was Roy's baby, Jack realized, the baby who'd died. She looked as if she was very ill. As if she had a disease. An ugly thought chugged through his brain—

could it be that this innocent child had triggered a string of brutal murders?

He flipped through more of the magazines and found several articles on Stier-Zellar's disease. Jack suddenly recalled what Daisy had told him about Tanya's Friends, how Anna had brought Roy along with her once. And Roy had all those hospital name tags. He knew his way around metropolitan medical centers. He could've easily gotten access to people's medical files. He could've gotten into their confidential records and found out who were carriers and who weren't.

Jack put down the magazine and pocketed the picture. He had to get to Vermont right away.

3.

Driving along Woodpecker Road, Jack took in the sight of the soft spring colors blanketing the fields and woods. The house was white with red trim, perched on top of a hill like something out of a fairy tale. He stepped out of his car and stood on stiff legs, feeling the warmth of the sun on his face. Then he winced when Daisy ran head-long into his arms, his taped ribs still tender. "Ouch."

"I missed you," she said, kissing him.

"I missed you, too."

The very air changed. It became charged.

"Come on inside and meet Lily. I hope you like meat loaf."

"I love meat loaf."

"Good answer." She took his hand. "You won't believe how much the baby has grown."

They went inside. Noah was a pink, squirming bundle of needs. Lily Hubbard was wound tighter than a bee's bum, but Jack could appreciate the pain she was in. He was gracious and charming, and twenty minutes into the visit, he figured he'd pretty much won her over.

During dinner, he told them of his plans for their safety. He was going to change the locks on all the doors and install an alarm system along with automated yard lights; he'd already spoken to the local authorities and had faxed the town sheriff pictures of Roy Hildreth; he told them they should alter their schedules and always carry pepper spray around with them wherever they went. He could see that he was making Daisy and her mother uncomfortable, so he changed the subject and told a few stories about *Freddie the Fuzz*.

"They hired a real cop to show up on the set and tell my father how real cops did things. Dad wanted Freddie to slide across the hood of a car, but this cop—his name was Carl—said no . . . not only would his gun belt scratch up the paint job, but a person could get seriously injured that way."

Lily laughed. "I've always wondered why the police on TV stick their finger into the white powder and then taste it."

"Yeah, well . . . real police aren't that stupid. It could be cyanide," Jack said. "Also, real police never give up their guns for the hostages. If they did, nobody would ever get rescued. Anyway, Dad wasn't too thrilled with his advice."

"So what did he do?"

"He fired the professional police officer and went back to make-believe."

Lily laughed, and Jack could see where Daisy had gotten her pretty blue eyes.

They had coffee and dessert in the living room, then Lily excused herself and went to bed. Daisy took Jack's hand and led him into the den and closed the door. He kissed her on the neck. "God," he said, "you smell like fresh-baked bread."

They made love on the plaid sofa in the downstairs den, and he felt like a teenager again. She kissed him, and he kissed her back. The couch had rusty springs that squeaked, and Daisy kept shushing him while he fumbled with the buttons of her blouse.

Afterward she clung to him. "I feel safe with you," she whispered.

He wanted her to feel safe with him. They lay together on the sofa, staring into one another's eyes, while outside the snow melted and the wind did its drifting routine. "I brought you something," he told her. He got up and rummaged through his overnight bag, then pulled out the gun he had purchased for her in Rutland.

She just looked at it and wouldn't touch it.

"You'll need protection," he insisted. "Just in case."

"Are you kidding me?"

"Here. Take it."

"Absolutely not."

"A heavier gun soaks up a lot of recoil, but I figured, since you don't shoot that often, you'd do better with a medium-barrel thirty-eight. A revolver suits an occasional shooter."

"I don't want a gun in the house," she said.

He could see the veins pulsating in her temples.

"You can keep it under lock and key," he said. "This is just in case."

"Just in case what?"

"He gets inside the house."

With great reluctance, she took the gun and hefted it in her hand.

"It's a revolver. Easy to load, easy to store. You don't have to maintain it the way you would an automatic. You can just throw it in a drawer until you need it. Then you aim and shoot, using your dominant eye."

"Which one's my dominant eye?"

"I don't know. They're both so lovely."

Her smile was sweet.

"Want me to show you? I'll show you."

He took her outside, where they practiced aiming and firing pretend bullets in the backyard. She was right-handed, but her dominant eye turned out to be the left one. Jack showed her how to take the safety off, how to load and empty the cylinder. "The official policy of most police departments is . . . don't encourage civilians to fight back," he said. "Give the carjacker your car, don't fight off the rapist. But that's a politically driven policy. You wanna know what I'd recommend? Fight, scream, scratch, claw, kick, shoot . . . do anything you have to to thwart the bad guy."

"Now you're really scaring me, Jack."

"I'm paranoid," he admitted. "I'm suspicious. Try being a cop for fourteen years, see where you grow your calluses."

Goose bumps rose on her arms. "Do you honestly think he's going to come after us?"

"Yes."

"Why? Because of Anna? Does he want to kill the baby?"

He took the picture of little Suzy Pearl Hildreth out of his wallet and handed it to her. "I found this in Arizona."

Daisy studied it. "She's got Stier-Zellar's," she said after a moment.

Jack nodded. "He got a girl pregnant when he was eighteen. She was seventeen. She raised the baby with her parents' help. I don't know how involved he was in the child's upbringing, but I think it messed with his head."

"So he's killing off the carriers?" Daisy said, the truth finally registering. "C-A-G. Biology is destiny. He doesn't believe in gene therapy. He doesn't believe we'll ever find a cure. Not in his lifetime, at any rate."

"So he's 'curing' the disease himself . . . by killing off the carriers."

"Which means that *he's* a carrier," Daisy said. "It takes two parents with the mutated gene to produce an afflicted child." She looked at the picture again. "She probably died a lingering death. He must've started killing people shortly afterwards."

"Shortly after she died, he tried to slash his wrists. He did a stint in a mental institution." Jack nodded. "They're reopening missing-persons cases all over the country, trying to see if any of the victims were carriers. See if there's a connection."

She handed him the picture. The steel revolver looked burdensome in her hands. "I have to call Truett. We need to warn our patients."

"Right now all he's thinking about is that little girl. He doesn't want history repeating itself."

"So he's coming after Noah?"

"And you. And your mother."

She nodded. "We're all carriers."

"You want to be safe?" he said. "Put new locks on the doors, get an alarm system, learn self-defense, get the neighbors involved and keep this gun handy. You'll need a firearm for protection, Daisy. That's not an opinion, it's a fact."

She looked at the gun in her hand in a detached manner, as if it didn't belong there. "I read somewhere that the human heart is like a machine gun," she said. "After each contraction, the heart rests as it fills with blood like a new round filling the chamber of an automatic."

He smiled. "Be careful where you aim that thing."

She lowered the gun, but he'd meant her heart.

4.

The day was overcast by the time they arrived at the church. Daisy settled the baby into his stroller and wheeled him across the parking lot, her hands gripping the handle as if she were afraid that the stroller might rear up and bolt away. People were milling around the church doors, and Daisy recognized a few families she hadn't seen in a while. She and the baby and Lily and Jack walked down the aisle and sat in the front pew. Lily took the baby and held him; Jack took Daisy's hand and held it. She remembered the last time she and Anna had been inside a church together, for Maranda's wedding, and how Anna had joked, "You are bound together in holy acrimony. I mean holy monotony . . . I mean . . ."

Despite the minister's thoughtful eulogy, Daisy couldn't feel Anna's presence inside the church with them. All she felt was five kinds of numb. Anna was gone. Anna was someplace far away, just as she'd been in real life. Anna Hubbard was never where you expected her to be—emotionally, physically, psychologically.

Outside, it was raining, and they raced back to the car. Jack helped Daisy collapse the stroller and put it in the trunk, then they drove to the cemetery, where everybody stood around in a big circle with their umbrellas open and took turns tossing flowers onto the casket. Daisy started to cry, a mourner's cry, heavy and heartsick. She sopped up the tears with a fistful of tissues, hunching her shoulders and weeping quietly into her hands. Sorrow shook her and wouldn't let go. She wanted to know— what had interrupted Anna's path from the happy child she'd been twenty years ago to the troubled adult she became? The two sisters had reacted to the twin traumas of their childhood in very different ways—Daisy had become an overachieving scientist, hell-bent on finding a cure for the rare disease that'd taken her brother's life, whereas Anna had spun out of control while fighting for her right to an independent life. The sense of responsibility and the urge to escape had played differently on each sister's psyche.

Loss was written on Lily's face in heavy lines. It made Daisy sad. Her mother reminded her of a hawk that had lost the ability to fly. An image popped into her head—Anna in labor, the doctors and nurses working frantically to save her life. Had she understood what was happening to her? Had she been in any pain? Had she at least realized that her baby would survive? Daisy's entire body worked to push away the image as if it weren't any part of her, as if it hadn't seeped into every fiber, muscle and bone of her being. Snip off any portion of her, and there, like a hologram, would be Anna.

Her voice trembled when it came her turn to say something, and she recited one of her sister's favorite poems, "Remember" by Christina Rossetti: *Remember me when I am gone away, gone far away into the silent land; when you can no more hold me by the hand, nor I half turn to go yet turning stay . . . For if the darkness and corruption leave a vestige of the thoughts that once I had, better by far you should forget and smile than that you should remember and be sad.*

Back home, Daisy helped her mother prepare the food while Jack checked out the house and grounds.

"Does he honestly think that man is going to try to hurt us?" Lily asked with a condescending frown.

"Stop criticizing him, Mom."

"I'm not criticizing."

"Yes, you are. I know that look."

"I'm just saying . . . what do you really know about him, Daisy?"

She wheeled around. "You don't understand what Jack's been through, Mom. What he's given up. We should be grateful."

"I'm just saying . . ."

"He's protecting us. We need protection, okay?"

Lily fell silent, and Daisy was glad that she hadn't told her mother about the gun. Outside, the wind was blowing the sopping-wet trees around, and soon people started to arrive from the cemetery, old friends and distant relatives Daisy hadn't seen in years. Lily hugged everybody who came through the door, then sat in a thronelike armchair in the living room, basking in all the unexpected attention. She laughed and chatted happily as if nothing terrible had happened, until Daisy entered the room. Then she grew silent and offered solicitous glances, or else urged her daughter to have a glass of wine or a piece of cake.

"You should eat," Lily said, and so Daisy took a few bites of something without really tasting it. She ate because that was what was expected of her. She hadn't eaten, and so she should eat. Her hands shook at the thought of Roy Hildreth and the Angeles National Forest. It seemed so far away now, like a childhood nightmare. She wiped her lips on a paper napkin, sipped her wine and greeted the thought of her sister's death with a deepening sense of guilt. She tried to finger-massage away a newly blooming migraine, then recalled her old paralysis in the face of Mr. Barsum's many sins, how she would freeze and stay frozen.

Dr. Slinglander arrived, looking very comfortable in his red cardigan sweater, his khaki trousers and worn brown Hush Puppies. He took Daisy's hand in his gigantic paws and studied her face. "So," he said, looking at her with the world's kindest brown eyes. "How's the baby?"

"Fine. We got fantastic news yesterday."

He showed great concern. "You had him tested?"

"He's a carrier, but he doesn't have the disease."

He shook with relieved laughter. "That's the best news I've heard all week."

She watched him for a curious moment. His teeth were far too perfect in a slant of light, and there was something oddly familiar about the creased corners of his mouth and the soft triangular shape of his nose. He took out a handkerchief and mopped his shiny face. "So, then, Daisy, you haven't made a decision yet?"

She frowned. "Decision about what?"

"Whether or not you'll be bringing the baby to Boston with you?"

"Who said I was thinking of doing that?"

"Lily mentioned it."

She chewed on a thumbnail and studied his face. Dr. Slinglander was around the same age as Lily. He had snow-white hair and crinkly brown eyes, but his hair used to be brown, she recalled. Dark brown hair and brown eyes, just like Louis.

A chill enveloped her as she recalled her mother's pain and suffering after Gregory Hubbard had died. During the days and weeks that followed his funeral, Lily had become almost catatonic with grief, her sadness seeping into everything she said or did. Eventually, she went to see Dr. Slinglander for counseling. She was still seeing him three years later when she came home from the maternity ward with Louis.

"How long had you been treating Anna?" Daisy suddenly asked.

"Oh," he said with a thoughtful frown. "Years. Let me think."

She couldn't help staring. Could it be that, after all this time, Louis's father was standing right in front of her? But why hadn't he told Anna? Anna, of all people. The person he'd treated for years. It was either the world's biggest betrayal, or it couldn't in fact be true.

"Daisy," he said, "it might be a very positive thing for you to keep this baby."

She shook her head. "I'm not sure I could handle it, knowing who the father is."

"Don't invest Noah with the baggage of his parents. You can both move on, you know. Think about it," he said, and walked away.

She stared after him. The house was full of people she didn't recognize. She finished her wine, then had another glassful, and another, and soon she was drunk. She stumbled around in a state of liquid suspension like a million-year-old swamp mummy, like a barnacled shipwreck, drunk the whole time, her heart in her throat. All those faceless neighbors milling around inside their house—Anna's friends and coworkers, and two strange little girls, two little sisters whose eyes shone with mischief, whose faces were soft and round as pieces of fruit; two little girls she wouldn't let near her, for fear they'd be swept into the whirling vortex of her grief.

At some point, Jack took her hand and said, "Follow me."

"Where are we going?"

"You need some fresh air."

The back porch faced a sloping backyard. Beyond the old stone wall, the woods came right up to the property line. These poplars were the first to green up in the spring. Daisy and Jack sat drinking coffee from Styrofoam cups and listening to the rush of the wind through the trees. Goose bumps rose on her arms as the wind gave shape to the rain. Back inside the house, it sounded like a party going on. "I hate this," she said. "They're having too much fun."

"I know." He played with her fingers.

She looked at him. She was glad he was there. There

were three little scars like flatworms on his throat, and his suit was slightly rumpled. He looked good to her anyway. "People think I'm helpless, don't they?" she said.

"Nobody knows what to think, Daisy."

"Well, I'm not."

"Okay."

She held his eye. She wanted to be honest with him. "My boss is coming today," she said. "You'll probably meet him. I just wanted you to know that he and I had this thing . . . this . . ." She stopped short.

Truett appeared in the doorway just then, holding a tall glass and looking frazzled. His timing couldn't have been worse. "Just got here," he said. "Sorry I missed it. Feels like I've been driving for centuries."

"Truett!" Daisy stood up and kissed him on the cheek. She could smell the lab on him, that wonderful chemical odor.

"I'm not interrupting anything, am I?" He joined them on the porch, scraping a chair forward. His tennis shoes, baggy shorts and Celtics T-shirt made him look as if he'd wandered into the wrong house by accident. "Remind me never to ask you for directions again," he told Daisy, flashing that charmingly off-center smile of his.

"My directions were very clear," she said.

"I don't wish to quarrel with a respected scientist. Hey, I know you," he said, shaking Jack's hand. "You're that detective she keeps talking about."

Jack narrowed his eyes. "Jack Makowski."

"Marlon Truett."

"My boss," Daisy explained. The two men seemed to have an instant chemical aversion to one another.

"Got a minute?" Truett asked her.

Jack stood up. "I'll go get some coffee."

She squeezed his hand before he left.

Once they were alone, Truett leaned forward in his chair and planted a wet kiss on her cheek. "Daisy, I'm sorry I missed the funeral. Careless of me to head out so late. How'd it go?"

"It was sad, Truett. Really sad."

"I imagine all the clichés have been used up?"

"Every single one."

He smiled. "So. When are you coming back to us?"

"Soon."

"How soon? Soon when?"

"I'm not sure," she hedged. "I've got to see about the baby."

"Baby? Don't tell me you want to raise a baby, Daisy."

"Why not?"

He made a face. "You can't be serious."

"What, a scientist can't raise a baby?"

"Not if you hope to win the Nobel someday."

"I think the Nobel Prize is overrated," she said, only half joking.

"Ha." He gave a disapproving smirk. "You don't want my advice, then. Anything that doesn't contribute to my career is expendable."

"I didn't say I was going to keep him. I said I haven't decided yet."

"Good. Because there's a distinct lack of wattage in the lab at the moment," he said. "I need some of your candlepower, Daisy."

The overcast sky was no color really, just a widening brightness the rain kept falling from. She could hear the sound of the meltwater all around them, a welcome sign of spring.

"You know Evelyn Prentice?" Truett said, and Daisy nodded. Professor Prentice taught biology and had twins, but she'd gotten pregnant only after she was tenured. "She's a master juggler, a brilliant scientist," he said, "but even she can't handle it. She spends all her mornings at home. That's a significant amount of time to be away from the lab."

"Give me a few weeks," she said.

He rubbed his eyes, then peered at her through his elegant fingers. "I want you, Daisy. I can't lie about it anymore. I want you in more ways than one, but I promise to be a gentleman about it. I can only complicate your life, I'm afraid. Clinical trials start next week," he said, standing up. "One way or the other, your future is with me. Think about it."

5.

That night, Jack watched over the house after Daisy and her mother had gone to bed. He sat out in his parked car like a man on a stakeout. Upstairs in her room, Daisy opened the drawer of her bedside table to make sure the revolver was still there. It was like a dark secret tainting the room. She hated the fact that it was there at all. She slept on her stomach with her face pressed into her pillow and fell into a void where no light could penetrate, where no shadows could possibly form.

In the middle of the night, she awoke to a strange sound. A rabbit was crying somewhere in the woods. No, wait a minute. Rabbits squealed. This sounded more like a human child. She shivered and checked her alarm clock—1:30. She lay listening to the world from some foggy, woolly place. Her pillow was hot. In her half-sleep, she couldn't figure out why a child would be crying all by itself in the woods. Then she realized that was the baby screaming. She could picture his tiny body shaking with inner drama and got out of bed, stuck her feet into a pair of Anna's fuzzy slippers and shuffled down the hallway toward his room.

"Shh. Daisy's here." His diaper was dry. "What's the matter, big guy?" She lifted him out of his crib.

He paused long enough to stare sadly at her, as if he were incubating solemn thoughts.

"Are you hungry? Is that it?"

He gazed at her with his intense dark eyes and then shit his diaper before letting out another exaggerated scream.

Daisy changed his poopy diaper, then took him downstairs for his bottle. He drank with epic thirst, and when he was done, he curled up his fingers and toes and screamed with his entire body.

"Shh. You'll wake the whole neighborhood." She tried everything—rocking him, holding him, singing to him. But even his stuffed toys seemed to unnerve him. She shook his favorite mint-green bunny in his face, but he only yelled and blew snot.

She snagged a pink tissue from the box and wiped his nose with it. They were forever wiping liquid substances from his body. They must've gone through a landfill of diaper wipes, a mountain of paper towels. Now she strapped Noah in his baby seat on the kitchen table and went over to the sink to rinse out his bottle. She accidentally dropped it, and it crashed to the floor.

The baby reacted by shrieking.

She cleaned up the mess using an old newspaper. She tore out some of the pages to sop up the glass with, and he fell silent.

She glanced up. "What?" she said, tearing another page out of last Tuesday's paper.

He listened with rapt attention.

She ripped another section in half, and he gurgled happily. She went through last Sunday's edition and was on yesterday evening's by the time he finally nodded off.

Lily came shuffling into the kitchen just then.

"Shh," Daisy said. "Baby's sleeping."

Her mother nodded. "Want some ice cream?"

"Sure."

"Couldn't sleep," Lily whispered. "Such a racket."

Daisy could hear the distant cries in the woods.

"Sounds human, doesn't it?" Lily shuddered, then took a pint of sugar-free chocolate ice cream out of the freezer and fetched two bowls from the china cabinet.

Daisy rubbed her nose fiercely. "It's a cat," she said. "Only cats sound that human."

As the cries grew louder and more pronounced, Lily said, "I wish it would stop. Two scoops?"

"Sure, why not?" She took a seat at the table while her mother scooped several generous helpings into the bowls, then put the ice cream away and got them each a spoon. She sat down and examined the baby with elaborate interest.

"His hands remind me of starfish," she said. "All pink and curled."

"Mom?"

"Yes?"

"I can't take this baby."

Lily nodded. "I know."

"I've got to go back to work soon," Daisy said. "But

see, what I'm asking is . . . do you think you can handle it?"

"Me?" Lily smiled at the sleeping baby. "I'll manage somehow. I managed all those years with you two girls, didn't I?"

Daisy said nothing. The world felt strangely empty. "Mom?"

"Yes?" she said.

"I know about Dr. Slinglander."

Lily stared at her ice cream, spoon lifted midway to her mouth.

"Dr. Slinglander is Louis's father. Right?"

She dropped her spoon and stood up in one long rush of movement.

Looking into that stricken face, Daisy thought she saw her own grieving eyes. "I don't get it. Why is it such a deep, dark secret?"

"Don't you have secrets?" Lily asked in a raw voice.

The silence stretched. Daisy had to be careful. Her mother seemed as delicate as a ghost; one puff and she'd blow away. "Mom? Sit down and talk to me."

Lily slumped into her seat. "After Gregory died, I was so heartsick," she said. "I just knew I needed help. I knew I couldn't cope with this alone, so I went to see a therapist. Arnold was a kind man. Very patient and gentle. I would cry and cry, and then one day he got up and held me. It felt so natural, being held by him. At the end of each session, he would get up and hold me, and it was wonderfully comforting. Just what I needed. Then one day the hug turned into a kiss."

The baby was sound asleep in his carrier.

"One thing led to another," Lily continued, "and I

suddenly found myself pregnant. I thought about having
an abortion, but for the first time since Gregory's death, I
felt . . . I don't know. Whole again. Anyway, Arnold offered to pay for an abortion, but in the end, he respected
my decision. We agreed nobody should ever know who
the father was. Arnold was a happily married man. Besides, it was nobody's business. He agreed to pay child
support. He was very generous. He paid in cash so his
wife would never find out. Edgewater's a small town."

Daisy frowned. "What did you tell your friends?"

"That I'd met a man on vacation and that we talked
about getting married. Later I said he'd jilted me and I
never wanted to speak of him again. In the meantime,
Arnold was as good as his word. He paid for all the
baby's medical expenses, whatever the insurance didn't
cover. I felt ashamed of what we'd done. We both knew
it was wrong.

"He called it transference, what had happened between us. He said that I'd fallen in love with him because
I missed Gregory so much. Something like that. Anyway,
after I became pregnant, he told me it should never happen again. We stopped seeing each other. It was hard at
first, but I got over it. He blamed himself. He was very
embarrassed, actually." Lily chucked the baby under the
chin.

"Mom, don't. Let him sleep."

She drew her hand away. "Anyway, later on . . . after
Anna got sick, Arnold agreed to treat her for free. He
never asked for a dime, and psychotherapy can be quite
expensive, believe you me. But he treated Anna like she
was his daughter. Louis had been his only child, and I
guess he missed being a father . . ."

"It's despicable, Mom," Daisy spat. "You were vulnerable. He took advantage of you, then lied to Anna for years."

"This was about protecting his wife, protecting his position in the community, protecting me . . . protecting us, Daisy. We couldn't tell anyone the truth. Not about that."

She glanced at the baby. He was sleeping soundly now, lulled by the cadence of their voices.

"Life is a series of paradoxes, I think," Lily said. "A combination of mistakes and missteps and lucky accidents. I would never ask you about your innermost secrets, Daisy. You shouldn't ever ask me about mine."

"I don't have any innermost secrets, Mom."

"It was a mistake, okay? I made a mistake. Orson Barsum was a mistake, too. I've made a lot of mistakes in my life, Daisy. You will, too."

Daisy lowered her spoon. She wasn't hungry anymore. "Not that kind," she said sullenly.

"Don't you dare judge me." Lily stood up.

Daisy looked at her. "You knew about Mr. Barsum, didn't you?"

Lily moved toward the doorway so abruptly she knocked her chair over, and it landed with a crash.

"Mom," Daisy said furiously, "do not walk away from me!"

Lily stood in the doorway.

The baby stirred in his carrier and began to whimper.

"You know what Mr. Barsum did to us, right?" Daisy repeated.

Her mother's face turned crimson. She gripped the

door frame. "I don't have to explain my actions to anyone."

"Yes, you do! You owe us an explanation. Me and Anna."

Her body tensed, and she cried out, "You don't know how terrible I felt that I couldn't see what was going on right under my nose! Mothers are supposed to help their children, not hurt them." She clung to the door frame. "The only reason I asked Orson to come live with us was because I didn't want you girls growing up without a father. He used to play games with you for hours. Maybe that should've clued me in. Don't look at me that way!" she shrieked. "Don't you think I carry the guilt around with me constantly? When I found out what was happening, I thought my heart would break! It was such a black day for me. Am I a mind reader? No. He was deceptive. He was clever. I hate him every day of my life for what he did to us."

"He said that if we told you about it," Daisy said quietly, "you'd leave us."

"Oh, that makes me so sad. Where was I when this was going on? How could I have let it happen?" Looking at Daisy, she said, "Was I a bad mother?"

"Oh, Mom."

"You think I'm a bad mother, don't you?"

"He did these monstrous things to us," Daisy said, "and all you did was kick him out of the house. You never called the police. How come he wasn't arrested? On top of that, the three of us never mentioned it again. It was as if it hadn't happened. Anna and I had to live with it every day of our lives . . . just sitting there inside of us. I really wish you'd had him arrested or something,

Mom. Then maybe we could've told somebody about it. We could've gotten rid of some of the guilt and the ickiness . . ."

"I screamed at him and threatened to call the police if he didn't leave immediately," Lily said with tears streaming down her cheeks. "I watched him collect his things, put them in the car and drive away. I never heard from him again, thank God. Yes, maybe I should've called the police. Maybe I should have. But I thought I'd solved the problem. I figured he'd never bother us again."

"That was a chickenshit way of dealing with it."

"You have to understand! I was so confused! I honestly couldn't react any other way. Don't torment me, Daisy. Why didn't I call the police? I don't know. Maybe because I didn't want to think about it ever again. If I could just push it out of my mind, then it wouldn't be so terrible for you girls. Besides, he promised me . . . he swore to me you were virgins."

"Virgins?" Daisy laughed. "He made us suck his cock."

"Stop it!" Lily screamed, clamping her hands over her ears. The baby started to wail, a full-throated howl. "I don't want to talk about this anymore. Why did you have to bring it up?"

Daisy picked up the baby and bounced him in her arms, then cradled him until the screaming shrank to little gasps, fretful intakes of air.

"I tried to be the best mother I could, given the circumstances." Lily's eyes blazed. Her nose ran freely. "I don't know if you remember, but I was taking accounting classes at the time . . . and between raising you girls and the cooking and cleaning . . . between going to work and helping you out with your homework and taking care of Louis and doing all of this without your father . . . I was exhausted every day. Every single day. But I wanted you girls to grow up happy. I sincerely wanted my girls to become successful adults."

Daisy watched her mother's anguished face and tried to forgive her.

"I prayed you'd forget about the terrible things he did to you," she said harshly. "I knew it wouldn't be easy, but you were both so young. I just thought that maybe you'd forget, that the damage wouldn't be so bad. I was so angry. I wanted him to suffer, but I was afraid. What if I called the police, and he lied to them? What if they thought I was a bad mother? What if he came after us? Would the police protect us?"

"Mom," Daisy said, rocking the sleeping child in her arms, "we need to talk about this some other time."

"But we're talking now, aren't we?"

"No," she said. "You're talking. I'm listening."

She looked away. She seemed inordinately sad.

"We'll talk about it again," Daisy said, "when we aren't so tired. We'll talk about it later."

"I'll listen next time, sweetheart. I promise."

"Good night, Mom." She took the baby upstairs and tucked him snug in his crib.

6.

Daisy crossed the yard toward Jack's rental car, which was parked in front of the house. The rain had stopped, and the night sky had cleared. She could see stars scattered across the heavens and hugged herself inside her bulky sweater. In the spring, the days started cold, then warmed up nicely, but they always ended cold again. She could hear John Coltrane's "A Love Supreme" wafting from the tinny speakers as she approached the little foreign import. "Hi," she said.

"Hey." Jack turned the volume down.

"Brought you something." She handed him a thermos of hot coffee through the rolled-down window.

"Thanks. Nice of you."

"Yeah, well. New England hospitality and all." She glanced around at the moonlit hills and shuddered. Their house was surrounded by wildly overgrown stone walls that kept the property separate from the slowly encroaching forest. "Are you going to be out here all night?" she asked, and he nodded. "What about tomorrow night?"

"I'll stay as long as you need protecting."

"That could take a while."

He blew the steam off his coffee. "Fine with me."

She gave him a soft smile. "Then what?"

He put down his coffee and rested his hands on the steering wheel. He wore a clean black T-shirt, a pair of old jeans and beat-up basketball shoes, and for some reason, this made her feel sad. "I'll stay until the locks are changed and the alarm system is installed. As for what comes next?" His eyes were a little too vulnerable. "That's up to you, Daisy."

"The only thing I'm sure of is that I have to go back to work." She glanced at the full moon and drew her sweater closer. The cat had stopped crying. It was too quiet now, too isolated, the woods crowding in on them like an unwanted hug. "I'm sorry about what happened earlier."

"You mean Herr Professor?"

She smiled. "Perfect timing, huh?"

"He wants you."

"At the lab."

"Uh-huh."

"You're jealous. Are you jealous?"

"I'm concerned."

"About what?"

"That you'll make the right decision."

"Don't worry about me, Jack. I've got my head screwed on right."

"Do you?"

"What d'you think?"

"Okay, here it is. My inner self. I haven't had a date

in three years. I scare all my dates away, apparently.
Look at me, for God's sake. I didn't want to be anything
like my father. I swore that my life was going to be more
meaningful than that, so I became a cop, and now here I
am. On suspension. I'll probably lose my job. I've got
three ex-wives and no future with the LAPD, and I want
to be more than just a footnote in your life, Daisy. I don't
know what you plan on doing with that beautiful baby
boy upstairs, but whatever you do, I'm all for it. You're
funny, you're smart as a whip, you're beautiful, you're
emotional, you're vulnerable . . . and I just really want to
hang out with you for a while."

She laughed. "Hang out with me, huh?"

"For as long as you're willing to put up with me."

"Yeah, okay," she teased. "Let me sleep on it."

He clutched his heart. "Ouch."

She walked over to the car, leaned in the window and
said, "You'll never be a footnote, Jack."

They kissed for a while, slow, gentle kisses. Then the
baby started to cry again, his baleful wails like arrows
whistling through her heart. She straightened with a
shiver.

"Lock the door behind you," he told her. "And keep
your gun handy."

A nauseating fear gripped her. "He's here, isn't he?"

"I got a call earlier. I didn't want to alarm you."

She looked at the surrounding forest.

"They spotted him in West Virginia two days ago."

"I'll never use it," she said. "The gun."

"Don't worry. I'm gonna be out here all night long."

"Good night," she said.

"See you in the morning."

DAWN

1.

At some point during the night, Jack must've fallen asleep, because now here he was, waking up with a startled jolt. The car smelled funny. He blinked his crusty eyes. His cell phone was making a feeble sound, its battery slowly dying. He clawed through the paperwork and fast-food wrappers scattered over the front seat, then found his phone and held it to his ear. "Hello?"

"Detective Makowski? This is Sheriff Lafferty. We just apprehended your fugitive . . ."

Jack jerked forward in his seat, and the horn erupted. "Oops. Sorry. When did this go down?"

"About ten minutes ago. One of our patrol officers spotted him at a gas station. I need you to come down to the station house and identify him for me."

"Yeah, of course. Be right there." He hung up. He could hear the cascading sound of the meltwater all around him, that tickle-in-the-throat sound as the earth absorbed the rest of last winter's excesses. The early-morning light was faded pink, every blade of grass, every sparkling new leaf stunning his eyes.

He got out of the car, his balls shrinking in the cold morning air, and took a staggering step forward. It was as if there were heavy weights on his feet. His bones ached from sitting in an upright position all night long. Every tooth in his head wanted to crack. What time was it? No newspaper on the front stoop yet. He checked his watch— 6:15.

Jack crossed the soggy lawn toward the front door. Every window shade in the Hubbard house was drawn. Should he knock? Ring the doorbell? He didn't want to wake Daisy and her mother if he didn't have to. He didn't want to wake the baby. He stood examining the door's painted fir panels, its brass knocker and the small window made of rippled glass. A sticker on the window warned of armed guards and alarms, but that was just a bluff. He'd put it there yesterday as a temporary measure until they could get the real system installed. Now he cupped his hands over the glass and looked into the tidy kitchen, an L-shaped room with a self-venting cooktop, miniature white roses in a blue vase, a quaint wood-handled basket on an antique sideboard.

His scalp itched, and he scratched it violently, then took out the extra house key Daisy had given him the night before, unlocked the door and went inside. He could hear a clock ticking somewhere among the Colonial pieces. He tiptoed past the living room, his brain spinning. It would make his command officers back in L.A. very happy to hear that they'd caught the fugitive. It might even help his case with the department. More important, Roy Hildreth was behind bars. For good this time.

Jack found Daisy in an upstairs bedroom at the end of the hallway. The room had a painted hardwood floor and those old-fashioned wide windows, gauzy white curtains tapping into the room like nervous fingers. Scattered across the modest surfaces of the room were the girls' childhood toys—a Magic 8 Ball, Barbie's Dreamhouse, a microscope and butterfly collection that were evidence of Daisy's early infatuation with science. She was sound asleep in one of the twin beds, and he tiptoed across the room and knelt down before her, then rested his hand on her shoulder. "Daisy?"

She opened one eye.

"It's me."

"Jack?" She sounded groggy. "What's it mean when you dream you've killed an angel?"

"Look at me."

Her eyes gradually focused on his unshaven face. There was a prescription bottle of sleeping pills next to a glass of water on her nightstand. He wondered how many pills she had taken to knock herself out last night.

"Good news," he said. "They found him."

She opened both eyes. "Really?"

"I'm going down to the sheriff's station to start the extradition process. I wanted you to know so you wouldn't worry if you woke up and noticed my car was gone."

"Thanks." She smiled. "That is good news."

"Go back to sleep. I'll call you later."

"Okay," she said, her eyelids drooping shut. "You're my hero, Jack."

He kissed her forehead and left.

2.

Daisy lay in bed—not yet asleep but not fully awake—thinking she must have dreamed Jack's presence in her room. She vaguely recalled hearing his car go roaring out of the cul-de-sac, accompanied by that funny rattling in the rear suspension. Sunrises in Vermont began with cautious optimism, a pale pink hue illuminating each room before thin lines of crimson sunlight streamed across the walls and floor, invading the house wherever the roller shades didn't close all the way. What was that smell? She sniffed her armpit. Oof. She needed a shower. She should get up and take a shower and wash off all the baby drool and sour milk, but instead, she just lay there, stretching and yawning like a cat on a windowsill.

Yesterday's rain had left the streambeds running full. She could hear the meltwater gurgling downhill, trickling through the gullies into ditches and ponds. The last of the winter snowpack would evaporate in today's sun.

This murmuring cacophony reminded her of the time when a migrating flock of blackbirds rose up from the woods one autumn day and swooped through the air, dipping their wings at the exact same instant together. It was an exhilarating experience, those drumming black wings blocking out the sun and jarring her sense of equilibrium. She remembered staring in awe at the circling, swirling birds as they moved like a single organism. The memory soared, reminding her of the incestuous relationship between safety and danger, order and chaos, soft and loud, light and dark.

She could hear the baby whimpering in his makeshift nursery, and her body straightened as she prepared to get out of bed and go to him. No, wait. That wasn't the baby. It was just the wind sifting down the chimney. She re laxed again and listened to the soft symphony of sounds inside the house—the toilet's leaky flush valve stopping and starting; the water meter ticking through the copper pipes; the familiar clank of the faulty toilet ball cock, what Mr. Barsum used to call the water hammer. Daisy's eyes were drawn to a far corner of the room. A draft had caught on the Pennsylvania rocker, setting it in motion. Perhaps it was Anna's ghost watching over her. The movement of the chair was hypnotic, and Daisy closed her eyes and listened to the soft orchestra of the house slowly falling into ruin.

Daisy woke up moments later to the sound of a door clicking shut and whirled upright with a sharp intake of breath. No, it was nothing. Just the water hammer. She lay back down against her pillow with her eyes open. Something wasn't right inside the house.

She glanced at her clock—6:30 A.M. Jack was probably at the sheriff's office by now. The atmosphere had lightened perceptibly. Thin beams of light came through cracks in the roller shades, and she extended her hand so that her fingers glowed magically, signaling the warm birth of the day. She cataloged each new sound—a branch clawing at a window, the rattle of the baseboard heater, a floorboard creaking.

Floorboard?

She sat up in bed. "Mom?"

There was no reply.

A small worry took root and began to grow. Fright got her out of bed. She stood in the center of the room, listening to her own ragged breathing, convinced that there was somebody else inside the house with them. Now she heard footsteps—*creak, creak, creak*—definitely footsteps this time.

"Mom?" she said.

The footsteps stopped.

Her brain seized: *Go get the baby.*

She pivoted around, the painted hardwood floor chirping under the balls of her feet. She knew that sound—human weight had created that sound. She ran down the hallway into the nursery and was stunned to find that the crib was empty. Noah was gone. His pale blue blanket was gone. He wasn't on the floor or snug in his stroller; she didn't see his face among the cheery monkeys on the walls or the stuffed teddy bears grouped together on the seat of the rocker. He wasn't folded up inside the top drawer with his bright little outfits or tucked inside the diaper pail.

"Mom?" she cried. "Do you have the baby?"

A door clunked shut beneath her.

She heard a snap like twigs and the scrape of a heel on flagstone and ran to the window, where she spotted a figure walking away from the house. A tall man was carrying a small bundle in his arms. As he moved out of the shadows and into the light, she could see his frowning face as he looked up. Roy Hildreth's eyes were hard, his stride purposeful.

"No!" Daisy screamed.

He took off with the baby in his arms.

Daisy raced back to her room, where she opened the top drawer of her nightstand and grabbed the gun. The old-style revolver with its rotating cylinder held ten rounds. Jack had given her a box of bullets, fifty rounds of .38-caliber ammunition. She tried to steady her hands as she plugged ten bullets into the cylinder, dropping some on the floor. They rolled across the painted boards and underneath the bed. She scooped out another handful, shoved them in her pocket, stepped into a pair of Anna's slippers and flew down the stairs and out the back door.

She darted across the backyard and could see Roy through a line of trees. He was hurrying toward a car parked on the abandoned dirt road that nobody used anymore. Spring was in full riot. Wildflowers saturated the hillsides, the kind of colors that dilated your pupils— fuchsia, crimson, marigold. It almost hurt to look. Her heart drummed furiously in her chest as she clambered over the old stone wall and tromped through last year's low-bush cranberries popping through the melted snow. Roy was only a few yards ahead of her now.

"Stop!" She gripped the gun in both hands, aimed it at the parked car and fired wildly. The noise was explosive.

She gave out a small cry as she cocked the hammer and pulled the trigger again and again, firing four more shots in rapid succession. Vibrations rolled throughout the car as volley bursts of gunshots pierced the windshield and shattered the headlights. The gun kept bucking in her hands. Five more rapid-fire shots and the cylinder was empty. It all happened in a split second.

The bullet-riddled vehicle stood rocking on its shocks, its Firestone tires leaking air. Daisy turned toward Roy, her teeth set.

He gave her an ashen look before he disappeared into the woods, taking the baby with him.

3.

Jack blasted his horn at the slowpoke pickup truck driver crawling along the road ahead of him. "Move it!" He tailgated the truck and flashed his high beams, then got on his cell phone and dialed the Sheriff's Department. "Lemme talk to Sheriff Lafferty," he said. "It's Jack Makowski."

"He hasn't come in yet," the deputy said.

Jack rubbed his broad forehead with the flat of his hand. "I don't understand. He just called me."

"He might've called you from home," the man said. "But I wouldn't know about that."

Something clenched in Jack's gut. "Lemme talk to whoever's in charge."

"One moment, please."

Easing into a right-hand turn, Jack lost the slowpoke driver and started gaining speed again. There was a click at the end of the line, and a nasal voice said, "This is Deputy Hamilton. How can I help you, sir?"

"Lafferty just called me about my fugitive, Roy Hildreth."

"No, sir," he said.

"What?"

"I don't know anything about it. The sheriff is at home, probably asleep in bed. He doesn't get in until nine."

"Fuck!"

"Excuse me?"

Jack dropped the phone in his lap and made a hard left turn, the car fishtailing all over the road. He tapped his brakes to slow down, but that only caused him to slide sideways into a ditch, where he hit a wooden post. *Thunk.*

"Shit!" There was a sudden ache between his eyes as if a bullet had just exited his forehead. He couldn't believe he'd fallen for it. *We found your fugitive.* He shifted into reverse, hit the gas and doubled back, his right front tire squealing. Great. He'd gouged up the wheel well. How much was that going to cost?

He could feel the rough road bumping up the steering column while the persistent sunlight struck the last patches of melting snow in the fields all around him. He grabbed his cell phone and dialed Daisy's number one-handed.

It rang three times before her mother picked up. "Hello?"

"It's Jack. Is Daisy there?"

"I heard gunshots!"

"What? Put her on."

"She's gone." Lily Hubbard's voice was a snarl. "I saw her run out of the house, then I heard gunshots . . . and the baby isn't in his crib . . ."

A quaking anger swept through him. The sun shone directly into his eyes as he stomped on the gas and took the winding route back to Daisy's house, past a checker-board of farmland and forest. He rose over a small knoll, flooring the gas pedal.

4.

Daisy kept shoving bullets into the cylinder as she ran, the steel revolver almost slipping from her grip several times. Roy was a dozen yards ahead of her now, and she fell to one knee, slid her index finger behind the trigger guard and took a deep breath. *Don't shoot the baby.* She aimed high and fired a warning shot into the air. The bullet punctured a shiny green leaf, making a perfect smoking circle.

He didn't stop.

She fired another round and hit a silver maple, chunks of bark exploding into the forest canopy. Birds sprayed into the air, crying out for order, while Roy veered off the path and cut through the trees, their rust-colored buds just emerging.

Daisy hurtled after him, bounding up and down the wooded hills and leaping over a toppled stone wall. She scrambled up an incline where the land sloped sharply, using the branches of a massive elm to help propel her over the rise. *Please don't hurt the baby.* She followed him down into a ravine, where the rusted-out hulk of a John Deere tractor was slowly disintegrating in the morning sun, its orange hood eaten away in places like a lace tablecloth. She waded through a sea of brambles, her face and arms swelling from small cuts and scratches, while flies droned in the early-morning sun and a bird cawed high in the canopy—*caw! caw!*—sounding more like a poor imitation of a bird than the real thing. She paused to catch her breath, then realized she had lost them.

Oh no.

She twisted around, heart thumping like a rabbit's hind legs. The path she'd been on had disappeared, and she was standing alone in the freckled shadows amid the crocuses and coltsfoot. "Noah?" she screamed, scalp bristling as she searched the woods. A warm wind dispersed the shimmering seedlings and shook the new leaves on their tender stems.

Daisy gripped her gun and listened. She thought she heard something and cocked her head. No, that was just the gray squirrels quarreling. Flies droned in the sun. Her breath caught in her throat. Sap flowed from broken twigs as spring forgave winter. She caught the faint sound of a baby crying and turned toward it. Was that a baby? Or a bird singing? The sound was coming from somewhere to her east. Yes, Noah was crying, each sob designed to get his mother's attention.

Please don't hurt him, please don't hurt my baby . . .

She followed the cries deeper into the woods—legs pumping, elbows pistoning. She went bounding up and down hills, then burst through a thicket of blackberry bushes, and a shock of swallowtail butterflies geysered into the air. The earth had absorbed as much water as it could, and now dozens of snow trilliums and marsh marigolds swelled up from the soggy ground. Her slippers were a muddy mess—Anna's fuzzy tiger slippers. What had she been thinking? Why hadn't she put on her running shoes instead? These soggy gunboats were slowing her progress through the woods.

The land dipped sharply downhill, and she found herself tunneling through a wall of undergrowth, fiddlehead ferns brushing against her face like prehistoric fingers. She leaped over a meltwater ditch and nearly tripped, then paused again to listen. *Where are they? Where are they now?* She tried to pinpoint the baby's location by honing in on his birdlike cries. *There.* She tracked the sound with her eyes, each new scream hitting her in the solar plexus. The air was warm and clear, the birds were singing, and Noah was somewhere over there, beyond the tall red pine trees and Canadian hemlocks. She cut northward through the woods.

5.

Twenty minutes later, Daisy got a thick, curdled feeling in her gut as she held the gun in front of her, her hands closing around cold steel. She couldn't hear the baby anymore. All she heard were the birds, hundreds of them, singing in the canopy. A thick mist rose up from the old lake bed, cool air pooling into the valley. Now she heard a faint sob. *There.* She turned and headed west, the muscles of her legs cramping as she ran. Shadows broke across the trail as the forest began to thin out, and the land grew flatter and more tame as she closed in on the park.

She could hear children shouting. "Mommy, watch me! Push me higher!" She froze with the gun aimed in front of her, and it suddenly dawned on her that she may have been following the sound of their voices all along. Not Noah's newborn screams, but the sound of children playing in the park. *Squeak, squeak, squeak.* Her heart grew caked with fear. What if the swing-set chains creaking on their steel tube frame had lured her to this place?

Drenched with sweat, she followed an impenetrable wall-of-China hedge toward the sturdy wrought-iron gate, pushed it open and entered a sunny clearing where the structured chaos of the playground came into view. She knew this place intimately, since she and Anna used to come here as little girls. She recognized the seesaws and the trapeze bars inside their fenced-in perimeter, but the activity gym with its crawl-through holes was new. Over a dozen mommies sat on the park benches, coveting their unobstructed views of the playground. Some were nursing and comparing notes, while others plucked toys from the sandbox or pushed toddlers on red resin swings with yellow safety bars.

Daisy lowered the gun and held it close to her side. This was all wrong. She'd been chasing phantoms. Inside the white fenced-in perimeter, dozens of stringy-haired little boys and girls ran around in a blur. "Zap! Gotcha!" Some were having imaginary ray-gun fights while others tunneled their way through the redwood fantasy fort or rolled around on the wood chips and rubber mulch designed to cushion their fall. Rolling and giggling, toes pointing skyward.

A grove of shade trees shielded the play area from the strong sunlight. Some of the mommies stood around in groups, slathering suntan lotion on their arms or munching protein bars. One of the mommies was taking pictures with a Polaroid camera. "Smile!" she said.

Daisy's heart almost forgot to beat. Across from the trapeze bars was Roy Hildreth, seated on a park bench.

He was smiling at the camera, and in his arms was the squirming baby. Anna's baby. Daisy's baby.

"Say cheers!" the mommy said, and the baby reached for his father's face with tiny grasping fingers.

Daisy could feel the sweat evaporating from her body as she watched this nightmare unfold before her horrified eyes. The air grew electric, brilliantly illuminated, as she circled the trapeze bars and crossed the blacktop. Pointing her gun at Roy, she said, "Give me the baby."

The mommy lowered her Polaroid and gasped.

"Please, lady," Roy Hildreth said in a trembling voice. "Put the gun down . . ."

"Give me the baby!"

There was silence all around. Terrified faces.

"Lady, you don't want to hurt anyone . . ."

The play activity had ground to a halt behind her. Daisy glanced back at the mommies and realized that every single one of them was reaching for her cell phone.

"He took my baby!" she screamed.

"I don't know what she's talking about," Roy said, sounding vastly more reliable. He was sitting in a beam of sunlight, holding the baby close, and Noah was no longer crying. "Please, lady. You don't want to hurt anyone."

Her adrenaline spiked. Her eyes fixed unwaveringly on him. "You're the one who wants to hurt the baby!" She aimed the gun between his eyes, wanting him to understand exactly how serious she was. "Now put him down!"

"Please . . . point that thing away from me . . ."

Mommies gasped and snatched their babies off the

glide slide. A dozen cell phones were out now, fingers dialing frantically. A toddler on a tether got reeled in.

Roy shifted the baby into a football hold. "Nobody wants to hurt you, okay? Just put the gun down, lady."

The mommies were all watching them, and Daisy suddenly understood what it was they saw. How strange she must look in yesterday's rancid T-shirt, her dirty gray jogging pants and pink terry-cloth socks with the holes in them. She had a serious case of bed-head, and her arms were scratched and bleeding from running through the brambles. Worst of all were Anna's fuzzy tiger slippers—the footwear of a crazy person.

"He's lying," she told them. Her head whipped back and forth hysterically as she realized that none of them believed her. "He escaped from prison! He's wanted by the police. That isn't his baby. It's my sister's baby!"

Roy held Noah close, as if to protect him from her. "Whatever you do, lady . . . please don't hurt my son."

Your son? The gun felt warm and alive in her hand. "Don't listen to him!" she screamed. "He's lying!"

She could hear the women whispering among themselves. ". . . Anna Hubbard's sister . . . schizophrenia . . . runs in the family . . ."

Something skirted her field of vision, and Daisy was suddenly hit in the face with a toxic mist. She couldn't see. Her eyes burned. Her lungs were on fire. Several people descended on her and wrestled the gun from her hands.

"Quick! Grab it!"

Daisy dropped to her knees and screamed in pain. She couldn't see. She couldn't breathe. She released the gun and cupped her stinging face in both hands.

"Got it! I've got it!"

The gun went off by accident. The shot went high and wide. Mommies jerked back, their kids in a contest to see who could scream the loudest. There was no clear winner.

"Oh my God!" Daisy wailed. Her eyes were on fire. She stretched out her T-shirt and wiped her face. She couldn't stop coughing. Somebody handed her a bottled water, and she rinsed out her eyes, then drank greedily. When she finally parted her swollen lids, a thin clear light poured in through the trees. She blinked away the tears and saw that Roy was gone. The baby was gone. The park bench was empty.

She turned to the mommies in abject disbelief. "He's got my baby!" she screamed. "What is wrong with you people? Why'd you let him get away?"

The mommies just stared at her and clutched their children to them protectively. A woman in UV-resistant glasses was holding a canister of pepper spray in her hand, and a skinny dark-haired woman with a baby strapped to her chest had the gun.

"Give it to me," Daisy pleaded, reaching for the revolver.

"Calm down. The police are on their way."

"Do you have any idea what you just did?" Daisy shrieked.

One of the mommies pointed. "He went that way."

"Shut up," another one hissed.

Daisy staggered to her feet and, without the gun, ran off into the woods.

6.

Roy jogged through the woods with the baby in his arms. Whenever it opened its mouth to scream, big round sounds came from its lungs. "Quiet, baby." He touched the soft pink cheek, and it gazed up at him, unafraid.

Roy remembered the day his daughter died. Her casket was just this big. It rained the whole time. He found the rain comforting. Now he broke through a spiderweb spanning the trail and brushed bits of web and leaf debris off his face. He crashed through a thick wall of vines and came upon a clearing, where the glittering trees spread their awkward limbs. The field was littered with automobile carcasses—a Volkswagen Beetle listing in the weeds like an art installation, dozens of airless tractor tires, a bubble-fender pickup truck, its candy-apple shine gone. He sprinted across the field and strode up another hard-muscled hill, then came upon a river twisting like a silver ribbon through the forest.

He took a deep breath. The air here was sweet. The sound of rushing water was thunderous. The downhill climb was slippery with moss. He steadied his hand on a yellow birch tree that had lost its grip on the earth. The rotting roots reached down into wet rock, where the crashing current masked the sound of his footsteps. Roy hopped from boulder to boulder, then landed on a marshy bank where deer tracks peppered the soft dirt. He tossed a stick into the stream and watched the current take it. It was swift.

The baby was gazing up at him now. It almost hurt to look into those eyes. Roy tapped his fingers on the gorillas and bananas all over the little shirt and could barely comprehend this tiny life-form in his arms. It had come from Anna's body—from the blood in her veins, the food in her stomach, the hope in her heart. Roy knew this baby was a carrier because *he* was a carrier. Anna's brother had died of Stier-Zellar's disease, and that meant that she carried the mutant gene, as well. Carriers passed on the disease to their children. Roy couldn't let that happen. No. "Sorry, baby," he whispered, and the baby cooed back. "Sorry."

He hurried along the marshy bank, crushing stalks of skunk cabbage underfoot, his athletic shoes sinking into the muck while he looked for a good place to ford. The fetid aroma of skunk cabbage competed with the earthy smells of the wood fungus. Roy's left hand supported the baby's head, and this tiny motion sent him reeling back into the past. Suzy had been such a healthy baby, you never would've suspected there was anything wrong with her. But then on her first birthday, she couldn't roll over anymore. When she turned two, she couldn't grasp objects with her fingers. Suzy never learned to crawl or talk, but she knew how to laugh. She liked butterflies and sitting in the sun. When she was three, the doctors drilled holes in her head and introduced foreign substances into her brain in an effort to slow the progress of the disease. When Roy saw his three-year-old girl with her head completely shaved, it reminded him of the day she was born.

To his left, the river crashed and gurgled; to his right, the forest teemed with life. Ravens raided the berry bushes, swallows dive-bombed for insects, caterpillars rippled along plant stems, tiny black bugs slowly drowned in tree sap. He stopped to adjust the child's blanket, and its little feet popped out.

"Oops." He tickled the baby's soles. "Yes, yes."

Its toes spread wide apart, and it followed him with its dark blue eyes. Anna's blue eyes.

"You know me, don't you? You know who I am?"

The baby made a cooing sound.

Roy's brain hurt. He woke up doing ninety miles per hour into a concrete wall. He hadn't meant to kill Anna. Anna and Roy were supposed to be together forever. He hated this baby. This baby had stolen Anna away from him. He folded the blanket over the child's legs and lowered his tired arms until the baby was just inches from the roiling water. *Drown him. Get rid of him.* A green leaf fell out of the sky and landed directly in front of them. He read the leaf before it floated away; he read the child's future. This child would not live past the age of three. He would get the defective gene. He would have Suzy's floppy head and those rheumy, suffocated eyes. He would die prematurely. His coffin would be only so

big. It would rain at the funeral. Roy would find the rain
comforting. The bottom would fall out all over again. He
couldn't let that happen.

Drown him now. Drown the soft, soft baby.

Roy jiggled the child from side to side. "You understand what has to be done."

This powerful creature crumpled its tiny face. It
howled with indignation. It waved its tiny arms.

"Be quiet, baby. Don't cry." Roy heard a voice.

"Noah!"

It was distant but distinct.

"Noah!"

Anna's sister was coming. She was coming after
them, and she had a gun. Roy needed to cross the river
now. He raised the baby high overhead and waded into
the swift-moving current. After a few steps, he began to
shiver. The water was freezing cold. He leaned forward
and forced his legs to take short, deliberate steps. Soon
he was waist-deep in the strong current, the child riding
high in the saddle of his hands. He moved sideways like
a crab, fighting for stability, but the stubborn force of the
water nearly buckled his knees.

The baby responded to the mysterious change in
brightness by swinging its arms wide, then crashing its
hands together like cymbals. It gurgled and cooed while
Roy probed the bottom of the riverbed with his foot,
hunting for submerged objects and loose rocks. He
moved through the water like a slow, difficult dream,
sliding his feet along the bottom until he was almost up
to his chest in the thundering river.

Then something happened. He couldn't move forward. He couldn't go back. His feet were numb. He

could no longer feel his legs. His testicles had shrunk way up inside his body, and his clothes had absorbed about twenty pounds of water. The current held him fast. He was stuck in the middle of the raging river. He girded himself against it. It took every ounce of strength he had just to keep from floating away.

7.

Jack parked crookedly in the driveway, then ran inside the house, where he found Lily Hubbard in her bathrobe, looking like hell. She pressed a rumpled tissue to her mouth and said, "I saw her go into the woods!"

"Which way?"

"I think he took the baby with him." She pointed out the kitchen window. "That way! Daisy ran after him. I heard gunshots!"

Jack shot out the door and crossed the backyard, then clambered over the old stone wall into the woods. "Daisy?" he yelled, his voice echoing back at him. He ran through the woods, slapping away branches, and birds flew up. He dug into his shoulder holster for his gun, then aimed it down one gently sloping hillside after another. He called Daisy's name again and again, but there was no response.

The sunlight was dappled beneath the new leaves of

the slippery elms and yellow birches. His heart rate soared as he kicked through vines creeping across the trail—big leafy vines that swallowed up the ground and slowed his progress through the woods. After a while, he realized he was lost. He turned and headed into the tall weeds, where he accidentally knocked over a pyramid of rusty cans, triggering a noisy avalanche. He stood gasping for breath. Directly in front of him was an ancient rowboat with an anchor tied to it, the ropy threads unraveling like the hair of a corpse. A pair of rotten oars sagged in the stern like stalks of asparagus.

Jack heard a sudden cry—high-pitched and desperate—and trained his eyes on the small, round hill erupting from the forest floor. Crowning this hill, about twenty-five yards from where he stood, were the ruins of an old house. "Daisy?" His tight voice betrayed his fear. "Are you in there?"

Another piercing cry.

With his jaw set and his heart racing, he ran toward the hill and scrambled up the steep incline, hands clawing at the dirt. He surmounted it with some difficulty, then waded through a maze of thickets and tangled branches. Beyond the trees stood a house, its front door hanging open on its hinges. Without any hesitation, Jack went inside.

The front hallway was dark and musty-smelling, and he could see something moving around in the shadows. A dog barked and ran out the door. Once Jack's eyes had adjusted to the darkness, he could see several paper plates stacked with ancient corncobs, four or five per plate. He moved through the rest of the downstairs, aiming his gun at shadows. "Daisy? You in here?"

The seasons had warped the walls. The forest was slowly swallowing the house. Vines tumbled in through the broken windows, and wildflowers carpeted the floor. Decades of postgraduation parties had been held here, but the house was too delicate now to carry the weight of one more celebration. It was sagging and infested and would soon fall.

Jack steadied his hand on the blackened banister, then paused for a moment to listen. The lesions were still healing around his throat, and they throbbed a little with each beat of his heart. More vines pushed up the narrow staircase. He could hear a rustling sound in the walls as he mounted the stairs slowly and deliberately, making sure that every tread supported his weight. He paused again as he reached the top of the landing. Somebody was crying. He turned down the hallway, where the floor was unstable and the walls were beginning to buckle like a fallen cake. His thoughts grew fast and tangled as he followed the sound to its source, carefully testing each new step until he came to a bedroom door.

Something stirred behind it.

"Hello?"

The crying stopped.

Jack pushed open the door and peered into a room so sunken and rotting it would surely cave beneath his weight. Part of the ceiling had collapsed against a far wall, revealing hundreds of bats roosting in the attic. Some of the roof beams had rotted through, letting in brilliant patches of sunlight.

Jack took a step inside, and the whole structure shifted slightly. He stopped where he was and tried not to breathe. He saw something unfurl from a darkened corner and scurry away through a hole in the floor, and the hairs on the back of his neck rose. Some sort of pathetic creature had been sitting there, crying. He looked at the moldy mattress covered with beer bottles and fossilized condoms. He saw syringes on the floor next to encrusted gym socks and old textbooks gnawed by mice. On the wall above the mattress, he could see etched in pencil, "Promise not to erase this." A shudder ran through him. The place was evil.

He turned to leave, and that was when he saw the message spray-painted on the ceiling in large Day-Glo letters.

The iridescent-green paint was stuck to the ancient cobwebs, proving that it had been a recent addition. But who had put it there? And what did it mean?

END 70

Something in the house shifted. Convinced that Daisy was nowhere in the vicinity, Jack hurried down the stairs.

8.

Daisy dodged the elegant limbs of a dogwood tree as she ran through the woods, then stopped short. The river was too wild to ford. She scrambled through the undergrowth, moving parallel to the muddy bank, until she spotted a figure in the fast-running channel and froze. Roy Hildreth was standing chest-deep in the raging river with the baby held high above his head. She clawed her way through the bushes, prickers digging into her skin until her arms were streaked with blood. Her footing grew unsteady as she stepped down onto the rock stratification and dipped her toe in the water. It was shockingly cold. She withdrew her foot quickly and stood shivering on the bank, struggling to come up with a plan.

About twenty paces ahead, she saw a dead hickory tree that had fallen over some time ago, its soggy trunk and elegant branches partially submerged. Her slippers grew waterlogged as she crossed the native granite braiding along the waterway, then climbed down onto the hickory tree and waded out into the icy water. Her heart stopped. Goose bumps sprouted everywhere on her skin. Her teeth chattered convulsively. It was so cold she lost all feeling below the knees. The shock was too much. She dragged herself back out of the water and stood hugging herself on the marshy shore. She looked around for something to get his attention with, then picked up a rock and threw it at him.

The rock plopped in the water directly in front of him, and Roy Hildreth turned and aimed his unfriendly face at her. He was up to his chest in the current, all his muscles trembling with tension as he held the bundled baby high in the air. His lips were blue. Water splashed across his face as he said with a sputtering gasp, "He's got his mother's eyes."

She released a terrified sob and waded back into the frigid water. She grabbed hold of the wet hickory branches and moved purposefully into the river, walking as far as she could without letting go. "Give me the baby!" she shouted.

His eyes were grim.

"He's not a carrier!" she lied. "I had him tested!"

He looked at her and frowned.

"I took him to a lab that does genetic screening for newborns," she continued, trying to convince him. "They took a blood sample and searched for the faulty gene, but it's not there. He isn't a carrier! Give him to me!"

Roy didn't respond. He appeared to be in a trance.

"Please," she begged, reaching with numb fingers.

"The current has me," he told her. "I'm stuck."

A paralyzing sense of disbelief came over her. She

clung to the slender branches with one hand and stretched her other arm out over the water as far as it would go. She could almost reach the baby's dangling legs. She adjusted her grip, grasping a handful of twigs and inching her way further into the water, where the current was so strong and so swift she had to gird herself against it. It took every ounce of strength she had left just to withstand its pull. "Hand me the baby," she yelled over the onrush of water. "Hand him over!"

A tree swallow swooped territorially above their heads, and the baby batted his arms playfully. She was slowly losing her grip. The water was so cold she could barely feel her fingers anymore. She grasped the skinniest branches of the tree, then inched her way out into deeper water, her feet slipping over rocks. She clung to the twisted ends of the hickory tree as she leaned into the current. It felt like an arctic blast pushing her dangerously forward. "Give him to me!"

Roy's face was very pale. His lips were purple. She had a strange feeling of empathy for him. It was an entirely new sensation, something she did not welcome. She stretched out her arm as far as it would go, and a clogged weeping rose in her throat.

"Take him," he said, transferring the baby to one hand.

Her wet fingers slid down the branch, her knees buckled and suddenly she was plunged underwater. Everything went black. She swallowed half the river, then quickly found her footing again and came up sputtering. The rotten branches she'd been clinging to swayed dangerously, as if the whole tree might give way. She got to her feet and fought the current. She fought her fear. She fought the cold. She stood up and reached for the baby again.

"Take him," he said. His eyes were stern. He was holding the baby out to her now. "Go on. Take him!"

Her limbs pulled like taffy as she pawed at the air.

Roy cupped the baby in one hand, his muscled arm straining to hold Noah out to her. The blue blanket fell off and got swept away instantly.

Panic seized her. She strained to snatch Noah's foot. She could almost touch his toe with her index finger.

"Take him!" he commanded.

She looked deep into those hooded eyes and wondered if this was a trick. Would he grab her at the last second? Let go of the baby? Save himself by climbing over her?

"Take him. Hurry. I can't hold on much longer."

The water made a pounding drumbeat up her tailbone. A tightness gripped her throat as she reached for Noah one more time—ligaments pulling, tendons stretching. Something in her arm snapped, and she looked up at the immensity of the pine forest, shadows falling down around them like huge glacial stones. Everything was too brilliant. Too smooth. Too cold. She could hear the baby orioles peeping high in their nests in the treetops. She ignored the pain in her arm and overextended her reach.

Noah clasped his wobbly hands to his wet mouth, oblivious to the dangers around him. Daisy dug at the air, her fingers finally touching skin, and this brief contact electrified her. She didn't know that she could reach that far. Every muscle in her strained as she gave it one last shot, and now her hand closed around the baby's leg. It shocked her how insubstantial he felt. There was hardly any meat to him. She gave a sharp tug, and the baby slipped from Roy's grip and dangled upside down over the water.

She drew the baby quickly to her, pressing him against her chest where he'd be safe, but Roy moved aggressively now and grabbed her by the wrist. He used his strongest stroke to reach for her head, then dunked her underwater and climbed on top of her.

Daisy and the baby went plunging into a cold black place, where the fast-moving current pinned them against the tangled branches of the fallen tree. She held her breath while Roy's feet dug into her chest and neck. He was climbing right over them, trampling them, while the cold current pushed them against the tree like a strainer. She was stunned. He had tricked her.

Roy climbed over them and was gone, and she and Noah came bobbing back up, sputtering. The baby's next scream was like a cool pang of shock. He coughed and sneezed against her chest, and Daisy gently pressed his stomach in order to get all the water out. Even a small amount of water in the lungs could be fatal for an infant. "You're okay. You're okay," she whispered.

Noah wailed pitifully in her arms while she snorted and blew water. Then she turned and watched Roy reel himself in, hand over hand. She watched him pull himself out of the water.

"Help me!" she said.

He stood dripping on the mossy bank, his pale face washed in sunlight.

"This is your son!" she screamed. "He's just a little boy. You can't let him die!"

"He's a carrier."

"No, he isn't! I just told you—"

"Don't lie to me."

Daisy tried to gain traction on the slippery rocks. She found better footing on a slanting slab of granite and adjusted her grip on the tree, clinging to it one-handed. In her other arm, she clutched the baby. Noah was shivering all over. She would have to get them out of there soon, or they'd both become hypothermic.

Roy put his foot on the waterlogged tree trunk and rocked it hard, and the whole thing inched forward into the water.

"Don't!" she screamed.

He paused to study her face.

"Why are you doing this?"

He gave her an ashen look. "My daughter died when she was three years old. By the time I was three, I was climbing all over the house. I could reach the top of the refrigerator. I drove my mother nuts."

She could feel herself going numb from the neck down. She looked into his stone-cold eyes. "I'm starting clinical trials soon. You could be part of that," she said desperately. "Clinical trials will lead to a cure—"

"I've studied the data. There is no cure, no treatment, nothing."

"You're wrong! Gene replacement therapy works. It's already been proven to work. This is your son!"

He shook the waterlogged stump hard.

"You can't do this! You're not God!"

"Neither are you."

"Don't," she screamed.

"Sorry, Daisy."

She could feel the hickory tree coming loose from the

bank and clung exhaustedly to its waterlogged branches. Her face felt hot against the baby's cool forehead. She kissed him and said, "Hush, don't cry."

Roy worked the dead tree back and forth with his foot, easing it along the bank, sliding it further down into the water. She knew they would float away soon. She couldn't feel her hands anymore as she hugged the baby and whispered in his ear, "Your mother loved you very much . . . so much she lost her life protecting you."

The baby responded to the sound of her voice. His head was erect. He seemed to smile. The truth slammed into her. She was holding the full measure of Anna's life in her arms.

She clung to the soggy tree and looked up at Roy. His eyes seemed already set apart from this world. She took a deep breath, white spots floating in her peripheral vision, and reached for his ankle. She gave a sharp tug, and he landed in a semicrouched position on the log, then grabbed her wrist. He looked into her eyes and pushed her head underwater.

She clutched the baby while the swift-moving current held them fast against the dead tree. Daisy fought to push herself back to the surface, and they both came up sputtering.

Roy was standing on the bank, rocking the tree with his foot.

Daisy could hear the meltwater cascading downhill after yesterday's rain. She was very far away now, hovering somewhere on the edge of the universe. "I'm sorry, Noah . . . I'm so sorry." Weak with exhaustion, she closed her eyes.

Roy continued to work the dead tree back and forth

with his foot, easing it down the bank, sliding it further into the water, when all of a sudden, a shot rang out.

Daisy opened her eyes.

Roy slumped forward, a river of blood flowing from the wound in his leg. In pain and shock, he tried to crawl away.

Jack was standing on the rise above them, looking down. He aimed his gun and fired another round into Roy's back. Blood gushed from a pulpy chest wound the size of a fist.

Daisy screamed as Roy crawled out onto the trunk of the fallen hickory tree. He looked down at her for a moment, blood fountaining from his two terrifying wounds. Then he fell headfirst into the fast-moving current and was gone in an instant.

SIX MONTHS LATER

1.

By late October, Jack's wounds had mostly healed. His eyebrows had grown back, and the scars around his throat had faded. He still had nightmares, but he was getting better every day. He wanted to be healthy for the baby's sake. He wanted to provide Noah with a good role model.

Jack had tendered his resignation six months ago. He was no longer a cop, no longer a proud member of the LAPD. He called Tully occasionally, and his ex-partner would update him on old friends in the department, the cases he was working on, the politics, the bullshit. The weather in L.A. was always beautiful. Tully's wife and kids were doing great. He spoke nostalgically about the Stier-Zellar's Strangler case. "You're a hero, Jack. Everybody in the unit regards you as a goddamn hero."

It played to the secret reason that most cops became cops in the first place. Every once in a while, you came across a genuine monster, and you just wanted to put him away forever. Every cop harbored this fantasy in his heart. *The dream case.* But life wasn't a TV show. Sometimes bad guys did good things and good guys did surprisingly stupid things. Real life was a lot murkier than Freddie the Fuzz could've ever imagined.

Jack started a pot of water boiling on the stove, then checked his watch. Half past five. He was running late. He plunked the baby's bottle into the pan of water, then took the big frying pan out of the cupboard, put it on the front burner, got out the cutting board and started chopping onions. The baby was in his Johnny Jump Up, playing with his numbers board. He dropped the plastic board on the kitchen floor and began to whimper.

"Noah, Noah," Jack crooned, his voice oscillating between sympathy and comfort. He picked up the board and said, "Your mom's a whiz with numbers. The only time I use math is for tipping waitresses."

The baby howled. He'd had his immunization shots today, and his arm was still sore. At six months, Noah had a lot of restless energy. He wriggled and rolled around a lot. He was constantly moving his head back and forth, following the sound of their voices. He'd discovered his feet and liked to chew on his toes. He knew who his mother and father were, and he'd often burst into tears when either one of them left the room.

Now Jack got the baby his favorite stuffed animal from the bedroom—a fuzzy white duck with an enormous yellow bill that made a sick moo-cow sound when you hugged it. He knelt down to take off the baby's hat. The funky soft knit hat had bells attached, and Noah liked to wear it indoors.

The baby screamed, his voice rising in an operatic crescendo of despair. *"Ahh . . . ahh-ahhh . . . ahh-wahhhhh!"*

"Okay, big guy. Keep it on. But don't tell Mommy, okay? She thinks I spoil you."

Noah stopped crying and squeezed his toy duck. *Moo.*

"That's the big news of the day. *Moo.*"

Noah laughed. He liked the funny faces Jack made. He could sit up without assistance and was beginning to vocalize. Those former cooing sounds were starting to distinguish themselves to Jack's ears.

"What's your opinion, huh?"

The baby pooped his pants.

"Phew. Your opinion smells pretty ripe."

Noah eagerly reached out to be picked up.

Jack lifted him out of his Johnny Jump Up and changed his diaper. He took his metal badge out of its hiding place in the diaper drawer—it felt surprisingly heavy—and gave it to the baby, who gummed the leather holder.

"You like that, huh?"

The baby smiled, the tips of his new teeth like glistening white barnacles trying to break through the pink and healthy gums.

"Okay, big guy. Listen up. I believe in fair play," Jack told his son. "I believe in honesty and justice. I know that sounds corny, but it's true. That's why I became a cop in the first place. To protect and serve. To be noble. Do you think that's arrogant? It's pretty arrogant."

The baby's dark blue eyes hooked Jack with their eagerness. He had a head of silky red hair, and Jack liked to think he had the Makowski nose and the Makowski jawline, but fortunately for everyone, Noah had Daisy's lovely eyes and pretty ears.

"Hey, Noah," he said in a voice as light as dust motes. "Let's call Mommy."

The baby gazed up at his father, captivated by his tone, by the pleasant cadence of this suggestion.

Jack held the bottle, which the baby accepted greedily, his soft pink cheeks mushrooming. "Whoa, slow down, tiger. It'll last longer." Jack smiled at his son, then took out his cell phone and dialed Daisy's number at work.

2.

"Clinical Trials," Daisy answered.

"Hello, wife."

She smiled. "Hello, husband."

"Guess who got his shots today?"

"Ow. Poor guy. Did he cry much?"

"Only when he saw the needle coming."

She was in love with Jack Makowski. She loved his blind spots, his annoying little habits, his emotional rawness and availability. She loved the brown moles on his back, the ones she sometimes played connect-the-dots with. Often he'd be so exhausted by the end of the day that he would leave Noah's toys scattered all over the house, and her evenings would be spent picking up after them while Jack slept with the baby in front of the TV. But that was okay. She wouldn't have it any other way.

"So guess what? We're in perfect health," he told her. "We weigh nineteen and a half pounds. We're twenty-nine inches long. We can start eating solid foods, if by solid you mean strained beets. You coming home soon?"

"Six o'clock."

"Good. Because I'm making something special for dinner tonight."

"Spaghetti again?"

"How'd you guess?"

Daisy laughed. "You need a new cookbook, guy. Did you pick up those baby wipes?"

"Yes, as a matter of fact. I had the most embarrassing shopping cart today. I suddenly needed all this humiliating stuff at once. Odor destroyers for my feet, arthritis cream for my shoulder, wart removal for the plantar wart on my big toe, hair coloring for me touch o' gray. I made sure there weren't any pretty girls standing in line when I went to pay for it."

"Well, I like you, Jack Makowski. Plantar warts and all."

"And you're a very pretty girl. So I must be doing something right."

"See you at six." She hung up, a warmth radiating from her breastbone. The days were growing fitfully colder. She loved this time of year. They were going to buy a pumpkin next weekend and carve a jack-o'-lantern for the baby's first Halloween.

She turned off her computer and frowned, a shadow moving across her good mood. Six months ago, the police had fished Roy Hildreth's body out of the river. They'd found him two miles downstream from where he'd fallen in, and Jack had made sure that the fingerprints and dental records matched so there could be no question as to his identity. It was over. The bogeyman was dead.

Still, there was one unanswered question that remained to be resolved. Daisy had seen the spray-painted *END 70* that Jack discovered in the old house on the island. They'd both assumed that Anna had put it there. Not years ago, but recently. And the question remained, why? What was she trying to tell them? *END 70.* Something had ended. The molestation had ended after Mr. Barsum had gone away. After Lily had kicked him out of the house on that gloomy January day, nineteen years ago.

Daisy wrote the date on a legal pad. Anna had dabbled in numerology once. Did the numbers add up? She did a quick calculation, but they didn't add up to seventy. Another dead end.

She sighed and capped her pen. Taped to the wall above her workbench were drawings from some of the young participants of the first clinical trial for Stier-Zellar's disease. Daisy's clinical trial. She smiled at the crayoned rainbows and roses and bumblebees. The news couldn't have been better. Half the patients had shown dramatic improvements over the past six months. Daisy's team had been able to measure substantial gains in head control, alertness, muscle tone and cessation of seizures. Her one regret was that her brother hadn't been around for gene therapy. Now she put her paperwork away and fetched her backpack from the bottom desk drawer.

"Congratulations, Daisy."

She turned.

Truett stood in the doorway with a bottle of champagne in his hands. *Cuvée Williams Duetz 1990.* "Forty-seven percent of the candidates have shown remarkable improvement," he said. "It's a blazing success."

She smiled, enjoying his praise. "Almost a miracle."

"No miracle. Science." He held out two long-stemmed glasses and waggled his eyebrows at her. Marlon Truett could be a dangerous man to contradict. He wasn't called *enfant terrible* for nothing. "I thought we'd start with a toast," he said, but she shook her head and smiled. They had worked through their awkwardness together, and he'd stepped aside gamely in the name of science. Now she viewed him with great tenderness and respect.

"I'm going home, Truett," she said.

"Already?" He checked his watch. "Whatever happened to burning the midnight oil, Daisy?"

"We can celebrate tomorrow. Over lunch. Okay?"

He frowned. "So how's the baby?"

"Fine." She drew on her coat. "Save me some champagne."

His face was damp near his hairline. He stepped aside to let her pass, then said, "Do you want to know what I dislike the most about you?" He paused before answering his own question. "You have a life, Daisy."

She kissed him on the cheek and headed out the door.

On the ride home, traffic slowed to a crawl near Kendall Square, and Daisy turned on her radio. Mozart's Requiem in D Minor was playing. The storefronts were decorated with cardboard witches and Halloween masks. The car's heater was broken. It was getting darker much earlier lately, and she had Popsicle toes. The bumper-to-

bumper traffic inched along, and the sweet smell of
ozone wafted into the car. Just then she noticed a big orange road sign up ahead. Her stomach dropped. It hit her
all at once.

END CONSTRUCTION

She could feel Anna's psyche touching hers. Anna had
loved anagrams and wordplay. Suddenly, everything became clear.

3.

The moonlit road unraveled before them, the autumn corn on either side so tall and leafy that Daisy couldn't see the tops of the trees beyond their tassels. She felt swallowed up by these amazing Idaho cornfields. Jack was driving. The baby was back in Vermont, spending the weekend with his grandmother, and they were somewhere south of American Falls, taking this neglected farm road past endless golden rows of corn. They'd been driving since early that morning, when they'd watched the meadow mists turn pink in the rising sun. They'd driven for hours in the hot sun, listening to one another complain. They'd watched the day fade and the sun melt into a puddle of gold along the horizon. Now Daisy was sweaty and tired and just wanted it to be over with. She turned to Jack with a fluttering heart. "Are we there yet?"

"Almost."

She hunched into herself, concerns about the baby

lingering in her mind. Tormenting her. But she refused to
dwell on what might be. Genetic predisposition hadn't
been proved yet. She would not torment herself for years
to come, watching for the telltale signs of mental illness—inability to think clearly, personality changes,
aural hallucinations, visual hallucinations. Instead, she
would do everything within her power to make sure that
her son was a healthy, happy, active child. She would not
live in fear of the future. She would celebrate Noah for
who he was.

Daisy listened to the hum of the pavement beneath
their wheels. The moon had a yellow ring around it. The
radio promised rain tomorrow. She glanced around nervously. The corn had swallowed up most of the town of
Punkin Wells, Idaho. It had gobbled up farmhouses and
barns and pretty much everything else in its path, and there
was just the two of them tonight, and the road and the corn
and the moon.

Jack braked. "We're here," he said.

The old county highway ended at the cornfield's edge.
In the headlights' glare, she could make out two road
signs posted in a field. The county signs were dwarfed
by the towering cornstalks. One said *END,* the other said
70.

END 70.

Daisy caught her breath.

"Where the old county highway 70 ends." Jack parked
by the side of the road and said, "You ready?"

She nodded.

He handed her a flashlight. "Let's go."

"The question is, what are we looking for?"

"I guess we'll know it when we find it."

They got out and walked over to the signpost, then aimed their dueling flashlight beams into the cornfield. She closed her eyes, the lids scalding hot, and recalled Anna's words: *It's a gift for you. You'll find out when you get there.* Taking shallow, anxious breaths, she swung her flashlight in an all-encompassing arc and waded fearlessly into the corn, moon shadows stretching across the hard-packed soil, dry stalks rustling in the breeze. She walked along the dirt path, shining her light between thick rows of corn. Farmers in these parts liked to turn their fields into Halloween corn mazes. She'd seen signs posted along the highway, advertising FLASHLIGHT NIGHT CORN MAZE, $6 FOR ADULTS, $3 FOR KIDS.

Hairs rising on the nape of her neck, she doubled back, then made a wrong turn. Soon she was lost. "Jack?" She looked at the moon beyond the paper-dry tassels and pulled her sweater tighter. All these rows seemed identical to her. She stumbled over a rise in the ground, then took a step back, her nerve endings tingling. "Jack?"

"What is it?" he said, coming toward her.

They aimed their beams at the mound of overgrown earth, like an old grave. Half buried in the soft dirt was a deflated synthetic-leather football with *Wilson NFL* written on one side. She cupped her hand to her mouth.

"What is it?" he whispered.

She kicked at the dirt, and the old football rolled out, a phosphorescent red *X* spray-painted on the imitation pebbled cowhide. *X means no. X means stop.* She hadn't seen that decaying football in over twenty years. "Mr. Barsum," she whispered.

He nodded. "A gift to you."

"Oh my God. She did it."

"With Hildreth's help."

Daisy turned her moist face toward the wind, the unreality of it shimmering in her bones like gamma particles. She burst into tears, and Jack held her close.

"Shh," he whispered. "It's okay. It's over."

She looked at him significantly, recalling her sister's words. *I thought it would bring me peace, but it didn't.* The moment crystallized. Her eyes closed like windows.

"Are you okay?" Jack said.

"It feels like death just blew me a kiss."

SNOWFALL

1.

Daisy woke up, shivering and cold. Jack had hogged all the blankets again. He was snoring beside her, and she lay awake in bed, watching his rib cage rise and fall, rise and fall. She wondered what he was dreaming about. Chasing bad guys, probably. Jack still chased bad guys in his sleep. She slipped out of bed and went to check on the baby.

It was warm inside Noah's room, cold outside. She touched the butterfly mobile above his crib, and it spun around effortlessly. The baby stirred. He stretched his little arms and opened his sleepy eyes, and she picked him up. "What a big boy," she whispered, cradling him in her arms. Outside, it was snowing. The first snowfall of the year.

"Promise me you'll do your own laundry when you grow up."

Noah yawned. He knew his mother's face and reached

for it. He knew the smell of her skin. He was interested in the sound of her voice, and whenever she made cooing sounds, he cooed back.

"Promise me you'll do your own laundry," Daisy whispered. "Don't make your girlfriends or your poor wife do it, okay? Promise me you'll marry an intelligent, independent woman, Noah . . . and that you'll be considerate of other people's feelings. And that you'll vote. It's very important that you vote in each presidential election. And the Senate races. And that you'll always be happy. Promise me."

Noah wrapped his strong little fingers around her thumb. He could eat solid food from a spoon. He "talked" to his toys. He could sit up without falling over. She wasn't afraid of his genes. She didn't believe that life was predictable. She had read the Minnesota Study of Twins Reared Apart. Two adopted twins, reared separately until the age of thirty-nine, had discovered that they had many things in common—they liked the same brand of cigarette, drove the same kind of car, had both married women named Linda and remarried women named Betty, had both named their sons James and their dogs Toy. But the "Jim twins" were the exception rather than the rule. The world was much more wondrous, much more complex, than the study indicated. There were no genes that could make you a good person, for instance. There was no gene that could determine how empathetic you would be toward others. Daisy didn't believe in fate, she believed in love. And there was no specific gene for love.

She carried Noah into their bedroom and rolled the window shades up. She stood in front of the bedroom windows for a moment, watching the snow swirl down from the sky. The luminous orb of the moon had a soft white ring around it. This ring was formed of many ice crystals very high up in the clouds, and tonight the whole world was in a trance. Each snowflake started as a tiny ice crystal. As the updraft pumped more water vapor into the clouds, thousands of ice crystals began to clump together, forming snowflakes that grew heavier and heavier, until they began to fall. There were an infinite number of ways in which the molecules could arrange themselves in three-dimensional hexagonal patterns—stellars, needles, columns, diamond dust. Every snowflake had six sides, but no two were alike.

Daisy crawled into bed and made a nest for Noah between herself and Jack. Just for tonight. Just for the first snowfall. She shivered as she pulled the blankets up around them. "Shh, Daddy's sleeping."

There was a change in Jack's breathing. He opened his eyes. "Look who's up."

"We're watching it snow," she whispered.

"You're in love with me, aren't you?" he said.

"I catch myself liking you."

He smiled. "We have a lot in common."

"Are you asking me out, Jack?"

"No. I'm asking you to marry me."

She smiled. "Again?"

"Why not? I'm a big fan of marriage."

They watched the snow, cold and white, as it eddied down from the sky. A gust of wind lifted a swarm of flakes and held it aloft for just a second, before blowing a sweeping glaze of white powder across the window. Daisy inhaled the perfume of their bodies and pulled her family close while frozen threads of ice formed on the glass.

ACKNOWLEDGMENTS

Many thanks to Caryn Karmatz Rudy, Jamie Raab and Emily Griffin for their collective insight; thanks to Wendy Weil for her support; thanks also to Susan Richman, Harvey-Jane Kowal and Bill Betts; thank you again, Helen; thanks to Jennifer Rudolph Walsh for her confidence in me; and thank you, Doug, always. Heartfelt thanks to my brother, Carter, my sisters, Sandra and Eliza, my mother, Lucile, and my father, Al.

ABOUT THE AUTHOR

ALICE BLANCHARD won the Katherine Anne Porter Prize for Fiction for her book of stories, *The Stuntman's Daughter*. She has also received a PEN Syndicated Fiction Award, a New Letters Library Award, and a Centrum Artists in Residence Fellowship. Alice Blanchard lives in Los Angeles with her husband.